continued . . .

Other Novels
by Diana Pharaoh Francis

Novels of Crosspointe

The Cipher
The Black Ship
The Turning Tide

The Path Novels

Path of Blood
Path of Honor
Path of Fate

THE
HOLLOW
CROWN

A NOVEL OF CROSSPOINTE

Diana Pharaoh Francis

A ROC BOOK

ROC
Published by New American Library, a division of
Penguin Group (USA) Inc., 375 Hudson Street,
New York, New York 10014, USA
Penguin Group (Canada), 90 Eglinton Avenue East, Suite 700, Toronto,
Ontario M4P 2Y3, Canada (a division of Pearson Penguin Canada Inc.)
Penguin Books Ltd., 80 Strand, London WC2R 0RL, England
Penguin Ireland, 25 St. Stephen's Green, Dublin 2,
Ireland (a division of Penguin Books Ltd.)
Penguin Group (Australia), 250 Camberwell Road, Camberwell, Victoria 3124,
Australia (a division of Pearson Australia Group Pty. Ltd.)
Penguin Books India Pvt. Ltd., 11 Community Centre, Panchsheel Park,
New Delhi - 110 017, India
Penguin Group (NZ), 67 Apollo Drive, Rosedale, North Shore 0632,
New Zealand (a division of Pearson New Zealand Ltd.)
Penguin Books (South Africa) (Pty.) Ltd., 24 Sturdee Avenue,
Rosebank, Johannesburg 2196, South Africa

Penguin Books Ltd., Registered Offices:
80 Strand, London WC2R 0RL, England

First published by Roc, an imprint of New American Library,
a division of Penguin Group (USA) Inc.

First printing, June 2010
10   9   8   7   6   5   4   3   2   1

For Tony, Syd, and Q-ball

Acknowledgments

As always, I have a lot of people to thank for their support and input into this book. First, I want to thank Tony, Quentin, and Sydney for their patience and willingness to ignore my more insane moments while writing. Next I want to thank Lucienne Diver and Jessica Wade, without whom this book would never have made it into print, and who, as always, gave me valuable feedback and advice to improve it. I also want to thank my beta readers, Megan Schaeffer, Christy Keyes, Melissa Sawmiller, and Kenna. They gave me invaluable feedback and made this a much better book. They also kept me from sticking my head in the toilet when I thought the book was broken.

I want also to thank all of you wonderful readers who have chosen to read my words. Thank you for picking up my books and for giving them your money, time, and attention. Without you, I could not do this job that I love so very much. For more on my books, to read my blog, or check out some stories I've written, come to my Web site: www.dianapfrancis.com.

White Sea

swamps & rain forest

Saithe River

Esengaile

Glacerie

Kalibri

forest

Pradith-na River

Reshnival

forest

Pradith-na River

Huantar

Tiro
Pilan

low plains

Harmattan

Orsage

The Gallows

The Leg

Pelkisad

desert

Sirica River

Sirica River

Chaturak

high plains

Berilak

Normengas

Benacai Bay

N

Beynto dal Corus

the great desert

Map by Cortney Skinner ©2008 Diana Pharaoh Francis

THE WORLD OF CROSSPOINTE

* Countries now ruled by the Jutras

White Sea

White Sea

Avreshar

swamps & rain forest

Calenfor

Broken
Lands

Jutras
Territory

Shipa-Ren River

Lelant Uly

Azaire

Saithe River

Gwatney
Mountains

Relsea*

Bokal-
Dur
Jutras
Territory

Kutranil
Bay

Roche
Bay

Goa
Maru

The Root

Upper
Jaw

The Bramble

Cipher's
Point

The
Bites

Tongue

Taptsriya*

Lower
Jaw

Ankerton
Strait

Naz Peninsula

Ibarra River

Crosspointe

Inland
Sea

Hatrine
Bay

Revahait

Opiloron

Guel River

Shavil River

Lanivet

Penrean

Dow River

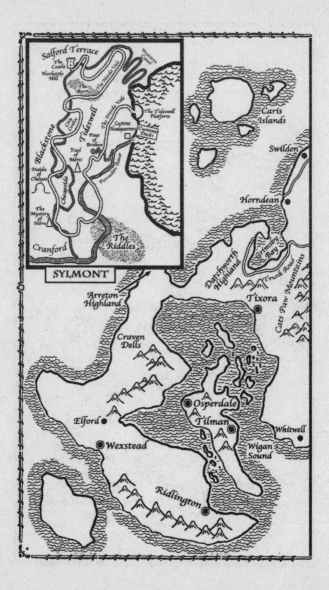

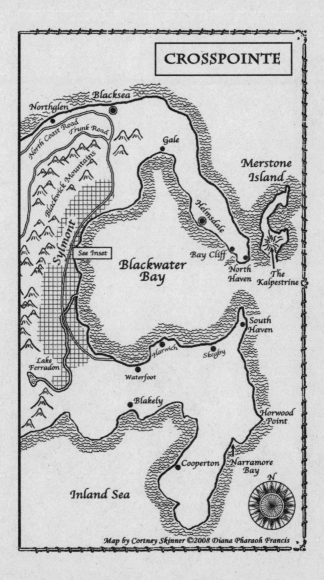

CROSSPOINTE

Blacksea

Northglen

North Coast Road

Trunk Road

Blackwick Mountains

Gale

Merstone Island

Heimsdale

Sylmont

See Inset

Blackwater Bay

Bay Cliff

North Haven

The Kalpestrine

Lake Ferradon

Harwich

Skegby

South Haven

Waterfoot

Blakely

Horwood Point

Cooperton

Narramore Bay

N

Inland Sea

Map by Cortney Skinner ©2008 Diana Pharaoh Francis

Chapter 1

Margaret had no intention of dying today, though her pursuers had other ideas on the subject and, just at the moment, the odds were in their favor.

She ran down a flight of steps, taking three at a time. Her skirts tangled her legs and she snarled silently as she lost her footing and twisted her ankle. She fell against the wall and pain spun around her leg in rings of fire. She bit down on her cry, tasting blood, then plunged onward, clutching her satchel tightly to her stomach. She could hear the voices of the Crown Shields too close behind. Their armor clanked and their booted feet echoed.

At the bottom of the stairway she paused, trying to quiet her gasping pants. She peered around the corner. The long gallery was empty but for a scattering of pedestals holding bronze and marble statuary, a line of plushly cushioned benches along the left wall, and a series of doors recessed inside pointed archways marching along opposite. Margaret rubbed her knuckles across her tense lips as she glanced over her shoulder. Her mind raced.

She couldn't afford to hide and wait for the Crown Shields to give up the chase. Not that they would. The mother-cracking regent would tear the castle down stone by stone to find her. And to add insult to stupidity, she'd let them herd her into the sovereign wing, which left her precious few escape routes.

But while she was out of time, she wasn't helpless. In an instant she settled on her plan. She fled purposefully, threading her way through the gallery as fast as she could manage on her throbbing ankle. Her back itched as she listened for the guards to thunder down the stairs and find her.

She reached the other side before they spilled into the gallery. The noise of their arrival echoed. There was a crashing sound as a statue shattered on the parquet floor. Margaret ducked into a narrow cleft artfully concealed behind a display of lacquered Chaturakian armor. She went quickly to the door at the end and slid through, pulling it firmly closed behind her.

She paused in the shadowed corridor, listening. While the gallery outside had been deserted, the servant hallways were much more likely to be busy, no matter what time it was. She breathed a sight of relief. No one was lurking, thank Chayos. Licking her dry lips, Margaret turned right. Her plan was insanely risky, but she had little choice. She was trapped.

This passageway had plain wood walls and a rough slate floor worn smooth by hundreds of years of scuffling feet and trundled carts. *Sylveth* sconces lit by majick cast a dim yellow glow every thirty feet or so. Several tall cupboards lined the narrow space, with three plain doors interspersed between. Margaret tried the handles. The doors were barred from within, and a tingle in her fingers revealed they were also protected with powerful wards. Each led into the opulent quarters of the regent—formerly the lord chancellor—and his wick-sucking wife. Just months ago these rooms had belonged to the king and queen. But both had been murdered.

Margaret slammed the shutters on the memories before they could surge up and overwhelm her. She couldn't afford the distraction, especially with the Crown Shields breathing down her neck. But one day, she promised herself again, she would find out who was responsible for killing her parents and cut them into tiny little pieces. Starting with the regent.

She tensed, hearing the murmur of voices and the soft metallic clink of armor and weapons. She edged to the corner of the cross-corridor and peered around it. A full squad of twelve Blackwatch stood in a cluster on the right side, talking avidly together in low voices. Margaret drew back out of sight, biting hard on the insides of her cheeks. She'd expected—no, she'd hoped—there would only be a pair. Even with a bad ankle, she could have handled two without undue trouble. No one ever thought anyone so small and fragile-looking could possibly be a threat. They would let her approach, and then she'd scratch them with one of the poisoned rings she wore. They'd died within grains.

Margaret drew a deep breath. She had counted on the regent sending his personal guard running after her instead of the Crown Shields. He trusted the Blackwatch more and as much as he wanted what she carried, it should have been a safe assumption. But apparently he was feeling too nervous to risk trusting his safety to the men and women who'd served the man he murdered. She turned and started back the way she'd come. But it was too late. Light wedged into the passage through the door she'd shut so firmly behind her.

She slid into the shadows beside a tall cabinet, pulling her skirts close. Her chest tightened and her hands clenched on the leather strap of her satchel. There was nowhere left to run. She was going to be caught. Quietly she lifted it over her head, and stretched up on tiptoe. The cabinet was too tall. She dropped her arms, tucking the strap beneath the top flap, and then lifted it high again. She rested it against the wood, and then gave a leap, thrusting hard with her fingers at the same time. The satchel jolted and dropped out of sight behind the tall molding.

Margaret froze. But the soft thud went unnoticed over the sounds of the Crown Shields and Blackwatch. Sooner or later they would find it, but it would mean a little delay and she wasn't going to make anything easier for the cracking regent to get his hands on it if she could help it.

She drew a breath. She'd known in sneaking into the castle this time that there was a better than good chance she'd get caught. Her brother had forbidden her to try. But she was determined to see what was in the regent's personal papers. The secrets she could glean outweighed the risks, whatever Ryland thought.

Margaret smothered a cynical snort. Ryland was younger by five seasons and still wet behind the ears when it came to the dirty work of politics. Never mind that he was the crown-appointed prelate and supposedly the regent's equal in the regency of Crosspointe. Just like every other member of the royal family, he was in hiding with a price on his head. The regent had always been a greedy, ambitious bastard and he planned to keep the throne for himself, even if it meant destroying Crosspointe. Besides, she knew what had to be done and she wasn't going to sit around and wait for her baby brother to give her permission, especially on anything so crucial.

She twisted her rings around her fingers. Each one held at least one poisoned needle. A flick of her thumb or a pressed gem was all that was required to pop them free. They were the best first defense against a superior force. Margaret could take out two or three attackers before they knew what was happening. She touched the six short throwing blades tucked into her hair. Her entire body bristled with weapons. She would not be taken easily. Her teeth clenched. These were the same men and women who should have been protecting her and her family. She felt no guilt about killing them. In fact—she smiled with predatory anticipation—it was good to finally make a stand.

The Blackwatch squad must have heard the Crown Shields entering the corridor, but they were too well trained to desert their post. That, and the two forces despised each other. The Blackwatch would never deign to acknowledge their rivals, thereby crediting the Crown Shields with being any sort of threat. But it still left Margaret trapped between the two, and the Blackwatch *would* come running at the sound of a scuffle. She'd be chewed between their jaws.

Boots scuffled as the Crown Shields organized themselves. At the same time, Margaret came aware of the rumble of a trundle cart coming from the north side of the cross-passage. The voices of the Crown Shields and the Blackwatch broke off suddenly. The jolting grumble of the cart drew closer. Margaret pressed herself into the triangle of shadow between the wall and the cabinet, knowing it was futile. Whoever was pushing the cart could not help but see her.

"Halt! Name yourself," a Blackwatch soldier demanded.

From up the corridor, the sound of the wheels stopped and a husky feminine voice answered the Blackwatch's challenge. "I'm Ellyn. Mistress Alanna sent me to fetch refreshments."

There was a note of annoyance in her voice, as if she thought her interrogator should have known that. Margaret's mouth twitched.

"Get on with it, then," answered the brusque voice.

Ellyn didn't answer, but the cart began to rumble forward into the intersection of the passages. Her blond head turned curiously, her gaze settling almost instantly on Margaret. There was a slight widening of her eyes and then her attention flicked away to the Crown Shields.

Margaret tensed, waiting for the lady's maid to scream an alarm. But unbelievably, Ellyn continued on without a word. She disappeared and the Crown Shields rustled to life again, shifting instantly into a businesslike march.

They started past her, none looking to the left or right. Swords swung on their hips as they marched two by two. Some were armed with crossbows, others with pikes. Each wore chain shirts, helmets, plate gauntlets, and greaves. The first three pairs passed before a sudden wave of force rippled through the cross-corridor where the Blackwatch were stationed.

Margaret's ears popped painfully as wild brambles of majick lashed her skin from head to toe. She gasped and tears burned her eyes at the sudden pain of the majickal attack. Her head knocked against the cupboard loudly as she jerked backward. But there was no escaping it. The Crown Shields shouted and thrust apart as thorny majick whipped across them. Purple welts rose on their skin. One dropped to her knees, screaming and grabbing her eyes. Another clutched his cods and moaned as he collapsed unconscious. Margaret sucked in a sharp breath. She wasn't the target—or at least, not the only one. Who was the majicar and what did he want?

But she had no time to consider the question. There were ten Crown Shields left, and three had already seen their prey. Ignoring the flailing majick, they closed on her. She pressed back with artful fear, letting her mouth fall open and raising trembling hands. She let tears roll down her cheeks and made a little whimpering sound. More majick struck and she flinched dramatically. They lowered their weapons and moved closer.

She didn't lunge. She waited for them like a spider in a web. The *sylveth* lights flickered and dimmed, then flared brilliantly and faded to sparks, casting the corridor into murky darkness. She released the needles on three rings. When the first Crown Shield grabbed her wrist, Margaret shook and staggered, letting her knees buckle as if overwhelmed by pain. Her twisted ankle made her performance all too real. An arm came around her and she grasped it as if to balance herself, then pressed her hand to the shoulder of one and gripped the hand of the other. The poison was quick and ugly. The two Shields spasmed and dropped to the floor in convulsions. They were dead within grains.

The chaos and the dying lights kept anyone from noticing. More majick snapped, and now she smelled burning flesh and hair. She didn't waste time. As more Crown Shields moved into range, she poisoned them. Each movement was calculated and methodical. When there were only two left, she snatched a dropped crossbow and snapped away a bolt. It burrowed through the throat of the taller man. That left one.

He turned, searching for her. Blood ran from wounds in his scalp and face, and even in the gloom he looked shaken and angry. He leveled his pike and strode toward her over the bodies of his fallen comrades. Margaret pulled a throwing knife from her hair. The light sputtered and brightened for a moment. She saw the curved gleam along the edge of the pike's blade and a flickering shine on the Crown Shield's breastplate. His eyes were black holes in a rectangle of shadow. Her fingers flicked with practiced ease as she flung her blade. It bit deep into his right eye. He dropped with a clatter.

She scanned the carnage, rubbing her hand absently at a tickle on her cheek. Her palm came away sticky and wet. Blood. It trickled freely from a wound that ran from her eyebrow almost to her chin. Suddenly it burned like fire. Her mouth tightened and she wiped her hand on her skirt.

A husky female voice from the cross-corridor startled her. "You'd better come quick if you plan to get away."

Margaret spun to face the maid who stood in the opening. "Who are you?"

"I'm a lady's maid for Mistress Alanna. Are you coming?"

"What did you do to the squad of Blackwatch? Hit them with pillows?" Margaret asked. Ellyn might be a lady's maid, but that wasn't all she was. The explosion of majick had come from somewhere and there was no other likely culprit.

"Yes. That is exactly what I've done," Ellyn said with breezy insincerity. "But we're wasting time. If you want help to get away, now is the time. Otherwise I should be about my business. M'lady Alanna will want her feet rubbed." She made a face.

"Why would you help me?"

"Perhaps because I would do anything to avoid touching M'lady's revolting feet. Who knows? I may be hoping to earn a splendid reward, Princess Margaret."

That Ellyn knew who she was should have startled Margaret, but it didn't. Something about the other woman told Margaret that she knew a whole lot more than she ought to. "I wouldn't count on it. The regent has made paupers of the entire royal family."

That was met with a disbelieving snort, but Ellyn didn't argue. "Then I must want to help you out of loyalty to the crown, don't you think?"

No, Margaret thought. *I definitely do not think.* But she was running out of time. Whether or not she accepted Ellyn's assistance, she had to get moving. Did she dare grab the satchel? But the real question was whether she dared leave it behind. The answer was unequivocally no. There would be no chance to ever come back and get it, and those documents were needed *now*.

She glanced again at Ellyn. Taller than Margaret by

several inches, the woman had a gamin face with a narrow chin, dark sunken eyes, and long blond hair she wore wrapped in a tail down her back. She held herself balanced and taut in the way of a predator. She wore an air of untiring patience and contained ferocity. A wolf in lady's maid clothing. She said nothing, a faint smile curving her lips as if she knew Margaret's dilemma and was both entertained by it and indifferent to the outcome.

"Crack it," Margaret muttered and turned to face the cabinet. She leaped up, ignoring the shooting pain in her ankle. Gripping the top edge, she pulled herself high enough to reach behind and grab the satchel. She smothered a yelp of pain when she landed; then, lifting the strap over her head, she started picking her way toward Ellyn over the bodies of the Crown Shields.

The Blackwatch squad lay crumpled in front of Ellyn's cart. Their bodies were mangled and torn as if they'd been through a butcher's grinder. Blood splattered the walls and seeped and puddled on the floor. It matched the splashes on Ellyn's apron and the red rim around the bottom of her shoes.

"Messy," Margaret said. Unnecessarily so. She flipped a needle open on one of her rings. Ellyn was clearly a majicar, and she just as clearly enjoyed killing. That made her more dangerous than Margaret could live with.

The other woman scowled at the bodies. "It shouldn't have happened like that. Something's wrong with the majick in Crosspointe. Has been since the Kalpestrine fell."

Margaret hesitated. The day after her father was assassinated, Merstone Island had simply collapsed. The craggy mountain that had contained the majicar stronghold—the Kalpestrine—had fallen in on itself without warning. Seawater had drowned the crater it left behind. Most of the majicars had been on the mainland, but rumor had it that majick had not been working right since. Some reports said it was driving the majicars insane. So maybe Ellyn's spell *had* gone wild and killed the Blackwatch squad.

Or maybe she just liked carving people to shreds.

"Trust me or not, you've got to go if you want to escape," Ellyn murmured. "If I don't come with you, I'll have to raise the alarm."

"Is that a threat?"

"It is reality. I must rub M'lady's feet, or I must go with you and be generously rewarded. If I go to her, I will have to mention the bodies in the corridor, or else they will think me a conspirator in the murders."

"What are you up to? What do you want from me? What is a majicar doing serving as lady's maid to the lord chancellor's wife?" Margaret demanded.

Ellyn cocked her head. "Do you really want to waste time on that now?"

"How do I know you aren't just leading me into another trap?"

"I saved you."

"And I'm grateful for it. But that neither makes you friend nor ally. I am not a stupid woman. You want something. What is it?"

"I want to help you get out of the castle safely."

"And then?"

"Then we'll have more time to talk without worrying about getting killed."

Margaret glanced again at the bloody Blackwatch squad. "With you at my side, how can I not worry?"

Ellyn's lips curved. Her smile was bitter and her eyes ancient. Margaret knew that look—she'd seen it in her mirror a thousand times. It was the expression of someone who lived by the blade—an assassin and a spy.

"Would you rather be caught by the regent? He's all too eager to put a chain around the neck of every member of the royal family. He would no doubt offer me a rich reward for you."

Bile rose on Margaret's tongue. The regent had set about enslaving her family and anyone he thought might be a Rampling ally. She would never have thought her people would stand for it, but many had dragged the new slaves away in chains. For these people she risked her life. She pushed the thought away. "Regent True-helm would. More than I can give."

"But I do not think he can give me what I want."

"And you think I can?"

"Yes."

"Then you don't want money." It wasn't a question. A majicar lady's maid in the regent's service was certainly looking for something far more valuable than dralions. But Margaret had no idea what, except that it was likely a price she couldn't afford to pay. Neither could she afford not to find out exactly who Ellyn was. It was the sort of mystery that could only come back to bite Cross-pointe in the ass. "I make you no promises," she said at last. "Except that I will hear what you have to say."

"Good enough," Ellyn said. "Let's go."

True to her word, Ellyn helped Margaret get out of the castle. Margaret hid in the belly of the trundle cart and Ellyn wheeled her into a storage closet. Margaret exited the cart and donned a mob cap and an unbloodied apron, hiding hers behind a stack of sheets. She hoped the spatters of blood on her sleeves would pass as food stains. She next pulled up her skirts and belted the satchel to her waist. She took up two baskets from a shelf, then hunched her shoulders and limped after Ellyn, clutching the stained handkerchief she found on the floor and sniffing loudly behind it at regular intervals.

Maids in the service to lady's maids were by definition, beneath notice. Margaret muttered and snuffled so that she could not escape attention and, as a result, was summarily dismissed as being exactly what she appeared to be—an arthritic, querulous servant. As Ellyn strode imperiously down the serving passages ahead of her, other staff dodged out of her way. Ellyn's status as a lady's maid to Alanna Truehelm put her among the elite in the hierarchy of castle servants.

Twice they were stopped by patrols of Crown Shields, but the guards asked only desultory questions of Ellyn and ignored Margaret altogether. She watched them sharply. Were they simply incompetent? Or had they decided that chasing a Rampling princess was against their oath of loyalty to the crown? Hoped sparked in her breast that perhaps she wasn't risking her life for people who cared nothing about her family after all.

Each time they were halted, Ellyn explained their middle-of-the-night venture into the city as a whim of her mistress, rolling her eyes and heaving an exasperated sigh as she spoke. "She's got a sick headache and a bitter stomach, and wants a tisane blessed at the Maida of Chayos. I've been up all night, rubbing her feet and putting cold cloths on her forehead." She grimaced and bent toward them conspiratorially. "Her feet are scaly and they smell like spoiled cheese." The entire squad snickered. Ellyn straightened, making a sudden fearful look and glanced around like they were being watched. "I had better hurry."

After each performance, the guards gestured for the two women to move along. The second time, one of the men groped Ellyn's ass as she passed by. She started and giggled flirtatiously at him, then hurried away.

They made the city center just as the sky was beginning to lighten. There Margaret had turned to her. Her ankle had been so sore and swollen that she could hardly stand on it, and their progress had been slower than she liked. At least majick still worked well enough to heal. She'd see about that very soon.

"This is where we part ways," she told the majicar firmly.

Ellyn frowned, her gaze turbulent and dark. "You said that you would listen to me."

"I have no time now," Margaret said. Exhaustion was dragging at her. She'd been awake for nearly two whole days. Her body shook with the leftover pain of Ellyn's majickal attack and she needed to get the satchel somewhere safe.

"Then when?"

Margaret eyed her narrowly. "You're awfully eager."

"I am," Ellyn said sincerely.

Truth be told, Margaret wanted to hear whatever it was that Ellyn had to say, and to know what she was doing working as a lady's maid to Alanna Truehelm. She couldn't afford to walk away without some answers. She thought rapidly. "Meet me in three days at the Spotted Lace Teahouse. I'll be there at the ninth glass."

"Three days?" Ellyn repeated dubiously.

"I cannot promise sooner. I have obligations." In fact, she didn't know if she'd be able to get away in three days. Everything depended on what was in the satchel. She'd opened the vault in her father's—or rather, the regent's ill-gotten—office. It was hidden beneath the rug under the regent's desk chair. To everyone it appeared to be nothing more than a solid parquet floor. Unlocking it required the proper words, chanted with the right intonation and cadence, as well as wearing the right bit of jewelry.

Every Rampling born on the right side of the blankets was given a cipher at birth. The pendant was hung on an unbreakable necklace that could not be removed and it offered some protection against majickal attacks. The

white *sylveth* drop in the center of the its compass rose
had turned black upon the death of the Margaret's father and would not turn back until a new king or queen
sat on the throne. Without the cipher necklace, it would
be impossible to unseal her father's vault. But with majick acting so erratically, she feared that those protections would not last much longer and she was afraid of
what the regent might discover inside.

She'd not taken the time to examine what she took,
merely snatching up everything and stuffing it all into
her satchel. She'd resealed the vault and had begun to
leave when she'd noticed the papers littering the desk.
Geoffrey Truehelm's personal correspondence. She'd
cleared the desk and rifled through the drawers, taking
everything that looked important.

She glanced at Ellyn, waiting for her reply.

The other woman pursed her lips and then gave a
short, ungracious nod. "I have no choice. I will be there.
Do not be late."

Margaret arched one brow. "Or else what?"

"I'll find you."

"Will you, now. And what then?"

The majicar's smile was slow and predatory. "I'll do
what's necessary."

Ellyn turned and walked away, disappearing with an
uncanny swiftness. She didn't use majick; she faded into
the shadows like a thief. Margaret stared after her. Who
was she? *What* was she?

Suddenly making that meeting seemed of paramount
importance.

Margaret's first stop after splitting with Ellyn was to
find a safe place for the satchel and get some sleep.
She would find a healer in the evening before she took
the contents of the satchel to her brother Ryland. Her
mouth thinned. He was going to be very unhappy with

her. Like most people, he believed in her helpless, simpering, public princess persona far too much to bring
himself to acknowledge her as an assassin, a spy, a thief,
and sometimes whore. He didn't want to think his sister
capable of such things, really, nor did he want to think
of how the king—their father—turned her into such a
weapon.

She sighed, limping along the street to the corner. She
wanted to flag down a footspider and have him pull her
in his cart, but it would only call attention to her. Better
to walk.

By midmorning she made her way to a ramshackle
room down near Blackwater Bay on the north side of
the customs docks. The place was located in the back of
a tavern and looked like nothing more than a lean-to
storage shed. As she unlocked the door wards, the first
drops of a chill rain pattered against her cheeks. She
made a face. Halfway through summer and it felt like
late fall.

She slammed the door and sneezed as dust swirled up
from the floor in a thick cloud. The place was cold and
damp and smelled of brine and moldy bread. From the
undisturbed dust in the rest of the room, it was clear no
one had trespassed here since her last visit six months
ago. Margaret's stomach growled in the silence of the
room. She hadn't eaten since she'd stolen a half-eaten
sandwich that had been hidden in a maid's workbasket.
That was more than a day ago.

She yawned, her jaw cracking. She lifted her skirts
and unbuckled the satchel. She stepped forward and
turned back to the door and knelt. She placed a splayed
hand on the middle of the warped wood floor. White
light ran around the edges of her palm and fingers
and a feeling like a mass of sticky squirming worms
engulfed her hand. After a moment, the sensation dis-
solved and the light spread across a rectangle of the

wood-slat floor. The boards shimmered and then melted downward.

Inside the space below was an iron box with no visible lid. Margaret traced a sigil on the top. It flared orange and the top of the box turned into a layer of oily, thick smoke. She pushed the satchel down into the box. The touch of the smoke was greasy and cold. She pulled her hand back out and traced a different sigil across its slow-swirling surface. Immediately it firmed back into solid iron. Next she closed the wood floor and stood, scuffing the dust to make it less obvious she'd disturbed it. Then she slid her hand over the door to reactivate the locking wards.

She turned around and longingly eyed the potbellied stove in the corner. There was a full bin of coal beside it. But if she lighted a fire, Markham, her landlord, might come to find out if someone had broken in. He was discreet enough and loyal to the crown, but now was not the time to take needless chances. The satchel was too important.

She crossed to the bed in the corner and carefully peeled the sheet off the top, folding it back along itself to keep the thick layer of dust covering it from erupting into the air. Beneath, the straw mattress was swathed in a thick layer of blankets. Margaret took off her boots and apron and crawled under, falling almost instantly asleep as she ignored the loud protestations of her stomach.

She woke after dusk. The room was pitch-dark, and outside the wind whined and the rain pelted the slate roof like pebbles. Margaret sat up and stretched. Her ankle throbbed, and when she examined it with the tips of her fingers, she found that it was swollen twice as large as it should be and was hot to the touch. She sighed and swung her feet over the edge of the bed. Her breath caught hard in her chest as the pain throbbed through her ankle like a deep-rung bell.

She fumbled for a striker in her bed table drawer. She found it and scraped alight the thick candle on her bed table. Flickering light melted the darkness away. She breathed slowly in and out, then reached for her boots. Lacing them on her hurt foot was an exercise in self-torture, but eventually she succeeded. She pulled the bed right and slid the dust sheet over it again. A few minutes later she had retrieved the satchel. She started to buckle it on beneath her skirts, then hesitated.

Her father had made Ryland prelate until their brother Vaughn could be crowned king, following a proper election, of course. Margaret was to serve as their weapon and spy, the same as she had done for her father. But her father had confided in her—trusted her. Ryland thought she needed protecting and kept far too many things from her.

With a decisive movement, she unlatched the satchel and dumped its contents onto the bed. Quickly she sorted and scanned the letters,, flipping through a journal and a ledger. There was so much information that Margaret had not known—secret allies, hidden caches of money, ongoing plots and intrigues in foreign countries, locations and names of spies, and a series of papers detailing specific plans her father had set in motion. It was all as if he expected to be murdered and so had made sure that his heirs could follow in his footsteps. Even if Ryland did complain that she'd disobeyed him, he'd be very glad to have this information.

The last set of papers were those she'd swept from the regent's desk. Most were letters confirming shipments of slaves. Her mouth twisted in a snarl. She should have hunted him down and killed him while she was in the castle.

Her attention snagged on one last parchment. She picked it up and read it through three times, torn between gloating triumph and horrified fury. The letter reported that the regent had kidnapped the son of Nicholas Weverton, a powerful merchant and crony of the regent's. The fact that Weverton had a son was stunning in and of itself—he had so many spies watching him, it hardly seemed possible he could cut his toenails without generating fifty reports. Yet even she had not discovered the boy's existence. Margaret had to admire him for keeping something so important a secret for so long. She smiled, sharp as a dagger. In her hand she held the revenge she craved for her father's murder. For she had no doubts he'd had a hand in her father's assassination, if he wasn't solely responsible. It served the mother-cracking bastard right that his puppet, the regent, had turned on him. She folded the missive up and started to tuck it into the satchel with the rest. But something stopped her. She hesitated, chewing her thumbnail as she considered the letter.

Could she do it? Could she just let the regent kidnap an innocent boy as a pawn in this game of political intrigue? The child was innocent. Her hand clenched on the crisp parchment. Emotion swelled inside her and her teeth ground audibly together. Why should she care? Because of the regent and Weverton hundreds of her family and friends had been rounded up and sold into slavery. A traitorous thought chased hard on the heels of that question: Why should she care about Crosspointe at all? The same people who had bought those slaves were the people she was trying to save from Weverton's machinations and the regent's brutal rule. Even Weverton was getting a taste of the monster he'd created. Let the wick-sucking bastard reap what he sowed.

She started to push the letter into the satchel again, and again she stopped. She felt like she was caught in the battering waves of a Chance storm. Her chest was tight with unfamiliar indecision. Her job was to protect the innocents of Crosspointe and it was in her power to help the boy. All she had to do was give the letter to Weverton. She could help so few. Ryland was afraid of exposing the growing group of resistance fighters by moving too soon. That meant ignoring too many of the people chained up and marched onto ships to be sold in villages along the coast or even in other countries. In fact, Ryland forbade Margaret to do much of anything but run messages and spy from afar. It grated on her.

He would strangle her for certain if he found out she'd helped Weverton in any way.

Unless—

Margaret chewed her thumbnail again, her mind racing. Weverton was the wealthiest man in Crosspointe, with a wide network of allies. If she helped him, he might not only withdraw his support from the regent, but join forces with Ryland and Vaughn in destroying the usurping bastard.

Weverton prided himself on loyalty. He would most definitely turn against the regent once he learned of his son's kidnapping. As much as he despised the Crown, he would want to annihilate the regent for daring to touch his son. Margaret·nodded. It could work.

She folded the letter up and tucked it inside a weatherproofed pouch that was strapped around her waist. Ryland would never approve such a risk. But if her plan worked, she would not only help an innocent child; she'd help save Crosspointe. Weverton's help could be all the difference. She was sick to death of doing nothing while Ryland and Vaughn planned without her. At last she had something to do, and she wasn't going to let either of them tell her no.

She rose off the bed and fastened the satchel beneath her skirts before wrapping herself in the warm wool cloak she took from a trunk at the foot of the bed. She hobbled out into the driving wind and pelting rain, resetting the wards as she shut the door. She made her way up into Tideswell just south of the Burn. Rivers of water ran in waterfalls off the roofs and Margaret was soaked before she'd gone a few blocks.

The weight of the sodden cloak only increased the pain in her injured ankle. It felt like her entire leg was on fire. She made herself keep moving through the gloom, careful to watch for anyone following her. At last she came to an alley behind a row of tall buildings. On the first floors of each were businesses, and above were the living quarters of the proprietors' families.

The water here was ankle deep. The darkness was like walking into a coal mine. Margaret stepped on something and her ankle twisted to the side. She splashed to her knees, biting back hard on the string of epithets that rose to her lips. Instead she pushed herself erect and kept slogging to the end of the alley. It dead-ended at the back of a tavern. She could hear music and laughter within. She ignored the pair of doors leading inside and turned to the left, her nose wrinkling at the stench of wet, rotting garbage. Things floated and bobbed around her legs and she made a sound of disgust deep in her throat.

A rusty iron stairway led upward. Margaret mounted two stone steps inside a shadowy doorway opposite to wait. Grains dribbled past. and she felt the shivers starting deep inside her as cold eeled through her body. She bit her lips to quiet the chattering of her teeth and forced herself to remain still. Up the iron stairs was one of the meeting houses for Ryland and the resistance. The meetings moved constantly and randomly from place to place, with Ryland posting times and locations in coded handbills. No guards loitered outside where they might be noticed. They weren't really needed. Each alleyway door was protected by strong turn-away wards that had been activated before sunset. Any soul considering passing through would soon think again. But just in case the meeting house was discovered, a small army of armed men and women as well as majicars waited within. Anyone attacking would need a substantial force.

Grains turned to minutes and then a glass. Nearly another slipped by before the first visitor arrived. Margaret watched him, unmoving. He wasn't the one she'd come for. More guests arrived one at a time, twelve in all. Keros was the last to arrive, as usual.

The majicar slouched through the rain, pausing at the base of the rusty steps as if he wasn't particularly eager to go up, which he wasn't. He hated these gatherings. In all truth, Keros was a renegade and a loner with a strong sense of disrespect for all things regal. Yet somehow her father and Ryland had roped him into serving the Crown anyhow.

Margaret emerged from her hiding place just as a loud clatter arose behind the double doors of the tavern. Both she and Keros started and then he twisted to face her, his hands tense, ready to hit her with a killing spell.

Margaret pushed her hood back. "It's me," she said in a low voice.

He relaxed and stepped forward, pushing his own hood back. In the gloom, all she could make out was the shape of his long shaggy hair and the soft edge of his bearded jaws. "I thought you'd be upstairs by now, not skulking out here in the rain."

"I was waiting for you. I need you to take something to Ryland for me."

She bent, pulled up her sodden skirts, and unfastened the satchel from her waist. She handed it to him.

"What's this?"

"I went into the castle," she said obliquely.

Keros gave a low whistle. "Ryland will be irritated. He did tell you specifically not to go."

She snorted. "He'll have a litter of kittens. But I raided father's secret vault as well as the regent's desk.

He'll want the information, even if he doesn't like how he gets it."

"You want me to deliver it for you?" He shook his head. "That's not your style. You like poking pins in him."

She grinned. "I do, but I've got something to take care of. It shouldn't take long, but it's best if Ryland doesn't slap any decrees on me before then. I wouldn't want to disappoint him twice and so close together."

Keros chuckled quietly. "One day when he figures out just how formidable you are, he's going to be kicking himself for not making better use of you sooner."

"If he doesn't send me to the Bramble for treason first," she said as she turned away. Her ankle gave way again and she fell against Keros, who caught her in a firm grip.

"What's wrong?"

"I hurt my ankle a little. I plan to see a healer tonight."

She could hear the frown in Keros's voice. "Be careful. Majick hasn't been acting right and most majicars have been on edge since the Kalpestrine fell. I think some might have become unbalanced. Maybe you should wait for me at my place. I'll heal you when this is over."

"Thanks, but Ryland's bound to tell you to order me back here if you run into me. Plus, I don't have time to wait."

Something in her voice must have alerted him. His voice sharpened. "What are you up to?" Before she could answer, he said, "Whatever it is, you know I'll help you. All you have to do is ask."

She smiled. She'd not known Keros more than a few months, but in that time, she'd discovered in him a true friend. He understood who she was—her rebellious spirit, her violence, and her desire for revenge and justice. Her brothers, on the other hand, couldn't see her at all. She'd lived her life performing tasks that would have horrified them—not just that she had done them, but that her father had forged her to be such a weapon. Assassination was her art; spying was her trade; stealing was her entertainment; seduction was her sport. Keros understood all of that, and did not flinch from the knowledge.

"I know," she told him, squeezing his arm. "Thanks. Tell Ryland I'll be back in a few days to let him castigate me in person."

With that, she went back up the alley to find a healer and to prepare to break into Nicholas Weverton's well-protected manor. She'd go in tomorrow night. That didn't leave her a lot time.

Chapter 2

The wind howled, tearing at Keros's sodden cloak as he picked his way along the headland. His boots squelched in the mud and his clothes clung to his skin. Rain pelted him with hard, wet drops. It was a wild storm, the sort that happened only in the month of Chance. But it was midsummer and Chance was far off yet. It worried him. Every day the papers stirred up fear with headlines claiming bad omens—that the gods were angry, that the Jutras had somehow stirred the weather against Crosspointe, that the Black Sea was about to swallow the island nation whole. And for once, Keros wasn't sure the papers were wrong. Worse, he wondered if the storms were this bad now, what would happen in four months when the Chance storms rose again? Would the Pale hold?

He glanced out across the black waves of the Inland Sea to the shimmering green and yellow wards that looped around Crosspointe like a double string of pearls. Above were the storm wards, below were the tide wards. Between them, they kept out *sylveth*—a majickal substance that ran through the Inland Sea in silvery streams. A single drop would transform whatever it touched. Usually *sylveth* created horrific spawn, mindless creatures from the nightmares of the insane. Those spawn would eat and destroy everything in their paths unless stopped by knacker gangs dressed in majicked clothing. But unbeknownst to most of Crosspointe's population, *sylveth* created other spawn, too—Pilots, who alone could navigate a ship through the chaotic and dangerous Inland Sea, and majicars, like Keros. He shook his head. He'd recently been shocked to discover that some of the horrific and frightening spawn had turned out not to be mindless at all. As terrifying as their outward appearance was, they were sentient and desired much the same things that ordinary people did. When it was revealed to the population that majicars and Pilots were spawn—there would be panic. People would not only fear them, but it would destroy what little faith they had left in Rampling rule. They would wonder what other secrets the Crown was keeping from them. And the time was coming when the secret would be exposed. Keros could feel it like a looming storm. Combined with the worries of famine and the fall of the Kalpestrine—

Crosspointe would tear itself apart.

His stomach twisted and his gaze shifted farther out, beyond the Pale. A shudder rippled down his spine, and it was all he could do not to close his eyes and look away. With firm resolve, he scanned the too-empty water. Four months ago the Kalpestrine had fallen. It had been the island stronghold of the Majicar Guild. Then one day, the entire mountain fortress had collapsed into itself. All that was left was a small tree-covered hump called the Thumb that had sat on the western edge of Merstone Island.

It's not that Keros regretted the destruction of the Kalpestrine. He'd never even set foot on Merstone Island. As an unregistered majicar, the Guild was his enemy. If they'd discovered him, they'd have forced him to serve inside the rigid bounds of their rule, or else they'd have imprisoned him. But it had taken an enormous force of majick to destroy the Kalpestrine, and that was a reason to fear. Because he was one of just a handful of people who knew that the destruction had been caused not by the gods or invading Jutras, or the story that the Crown and the surviving majicars were spreading—that a bore had opened in the bottom of the sea and had weakened the mountain so much that it collapsed. Most believed this. After all, the Inland Sea was a place of chaos and change—what was shallow a moment ago was now deep. Bores were enormous holes that opened up randomly, sucking in vast amounts of water before shutting again. Where they might open was unpredictable, and the phenomenon made for a reasonable explanation. But it was a lie. The truth was that the Kalpestrine had been destroyed by two renegade majicars that the Guild had been holding captive. And if that wasn't frightening enough, just at the moment, those two enormously powerful majicars were not friends to Crosspointe.

Keros rubbed a hand over his jaw and shook his head, turning to hurry along the headland path. The Jutras were vicious and greedy and they coveted Crosspointe like starving wolves after a meaty carcass. He'd witnessed firsthand their horrifying blood majick. They'd carved the flesh off two living people right in front of him and he'd been helpless to stop them. He shied away from the horror of the memory. Even now he could not sleep through the night without waking in a cold sweat.

The worst part was that even without Pilots and majickal compasses to guide them, the Jutras had managed to cross the Inland Sea once, and it was only a matter of time until they did it again. Without an army and without a king, Crosspointe was nearly defenseless. Even with so many surviving majicars, it wouldn't be enough. The Jutras had majicars of their own, and they had an army, and both were well practiced in war. Crosspointe was going to need Fairlie and Shaye Weverton—the two majicars who'd destroyed the Kalpestrine. But Fairlie was one of the terrible spawn, and neither she nor Shaye had any love for the Ramplings, especially Prince Ryland, who'd been the one to transform Fairlie against her will.

Keros sighed heavily. It was a mother-cracking mess and he was right in the middle of it. How had he let that happen?

He reached a stair cut into the side of the vertical cliff. It zigzagged recklessly down to the boulder-strewn strand. The steps were slick, and the wind and rain smashed into him. He skidded and held tight to the rocky wall. From time to time he glanced at the frothing surf far below. He saw no sign of anyone, but didn't really expect to.

Taking three-quarters of a glass to get to the bottom, by that time he was limping. His soaked boots had rubbed his heels and toes raw. He grimaced. As an unregistered majicar, he made it a point to not use his power ostentatiously, which meant not majicking his clothing against the weather. He sobered and a shaft of cold that had nothing to do with the storm ran through his lungs. Majick wasn't working the way it should anymore. It was increasingly volatile and unpredictable, and, as often as not, a well-cast spell went badly awry. Even old spells that had been reliable for years went suddenly haywire. Having majick around was not safe for anyone.

The problem was so pervasive that Keros had taken to using his majick as little as possible and praying that the problem soon settled. He hoped that it was nothing more than the aftermath of the Kalpestrine's fall. But the failing majick wasn't the worst of it. Keros had begun to notice odd behavior among his fellow majicars, and nothing good. They were becoming strange—paranoid, fearful, full of rage . . . The list went on. He didn't know if it was because they used majick or because they had been in some way tied to the Kalpestrine, so that when it fell, it damaged their minds. But more and more of them were acting peculiar. Keros pulled his sodden cloak around himself, the cold inside him growing sharper. If it could happen to them, it could happen to him.

He pushed the thought away violently, but it clung to him like pine pitch.

He walked along the shingle above the outgoing tide, heading for the small wooded cove just west of the steps. He slipped and stumbled over the wet, rounded rocks that made up his path, groaning a little with relief when he reached the shelter of the tall firs. They smelled pungent and green.

The footing was better here with a thick bed of brown needles, and he broke into a limping jog. He slowed when he reached the tree line curving around the small inlet.

She was waiting.

Lucy sat on a rock wearing hardly anything. Just a chemise and a pair of thin trousers. Her bright red hair was caught up in a thick braid down her back, wet tendrils clinging to her cheeks and neck. Her eyes were telltale majicar silver, ringed with crimson—the same color as his own, when he wasn't disguising them with illusion. She sat with her arms around her knees. As he stepped out onto the rocky beach, she leaped to the ground and ran to him, flinging her arms around him.

"Keros! It is good to see you!"

He returned the hug. She was warm, like she'd been sitting beside a fire. He pushed her away and frowned. "You've lost weight. A lot of it." Lucy had always had a rounded face and a plump body, but now her cheeks were almost hollow and he could feel her ribs beneath his hands.

She made a face. "I'm fine. I haven't been eating all that well."

Something in her voice made Keros stiffen. Lucy was one of the most powerful majicars in the world. Before Fairlie and Shaye had pulled down the Kalpestrine, he would have said she was *the* most powerful majicar. Little frightened her. But she was scared; he could hear it. "What's going on?"

She took his hand and led him over to the relative protection made by a tall rock and a cluster of wind-tossed pines. She pulled him under, close to the trunk of one, where the wind and the rain could not easily reach.

"I don't like the beard," she said, reaching up and pushing his unkempt curls out of his face. "You look like a stray dog."

She was stalling. He caught her hand and held it, his thumb rubbing lightly over the back of it, like he had a right. Reluctantly he let go. "Where's Marten?" he asked.

Marten had been Keros's best friend, before Lucy came along. He was a sea captain and had hired Keros to sail with his crew. He'd known Keros was a majicar and had protected his secret. He'd also been a gambler, and when his debts had become too much, he'd been paid to trick Lucy into breaking the law. The result had got them both sent to the Bramble with all the other convicted criminals of the year. They were to be exposed to the Chance storms. But the *sylveth* had turned Lucy into a powerful majicar and Marten into—

Keros still wasn't sure what Marten was. A son of the sea god Bracken, perhaps. He could manipulate the waves and the storms, and every creature in the sea seemed to answer his call. He was also Lucy's husband.

Keros smothered the hot spike of jealousy that stabbed through his chest. Lucy had never known how he'd felt about her, and she loved Marten deeply. If the truth was told, Keros was jealous of their bond as much as anything else. They were his best friends—his only friends, except for Margaret, but he rarely saw them or heard from them anymore.

At the mention of Marten's name, Lucy's mouth hardened. "He's exploring the Kalpestrine, again."

"Why?"

"Something's wrong. Majick isn't working the way it's supposed to."

He nodded. "I know."

"No, you don't. Keros. There's less *sylveth* in the sea than there used to be. And"—her mouth pulled tight and her voice dropped—"the Pale could fail."

He rocked back as if struck, his mouth falling open. "Fail?"

She nodded somberly. "I've done all I can to strengthen it, but I can't find what's draining it." She shrugged. "I'm going back to the Bramble. Errol Cipher hid his library there and maybe I can find something in his books."

Errol Cipher had been one of the founders of Crosspointe. He was the most powerful majicar in Crosspointe's history. Lucy had discovered his library when she and Marten had been exiled on the Bramble. They were the only records he'd left behind. Majicars had been searching for them for years, hoping to discover the key to so many lost spells—like the one that created the Pale.

She drew a breath and blew it out sharply. "You need to warn my cousins that the Pale could fall. And that I will not answer their calls until I sort this thing out."

Lucy was a Rampling—a member of the royal family. The cousins she was referring to were the princes Ryland and Vaughn and Princess Margaret. The other two, Prince Perry and Princess Ivy, were somewhere in Glacerie making a royal visit to shore up relations. Ryland, whom Keros had agreed to serve as a private majicar—was serving as prelate. He was, ostensibly, supposed to have equal power to the regent until a new king or queen could be elected from the ranks of the royal family. Vaughn, who had the support of the Merchants' Commission and the Majicar Guild, was expected to win that election. But Regent Truehelm wasn't willing to let go of his newfound power, and had been hunting down every Rampling and Rampling ally he could find and selling them into slavery.

Keros's mouth twisted. Slavery enraged and disgusted him. Ryland tied his hands most of the time refusing to do much about it, or to let Keros do anything. Ryland provided safety for those who could find him, and at first there had been quite a few, but he wasn't ready yet to free those bound in chains. It was too risky for the fledgling resistance. They needed time to build strength first. Keros understood the argument, but he burned in the caldron of his helplessness.

Part of the problem was that, for years, an angry sentiment had been growing against the Rampling family—fostered by a powerful coterie of merchants like the powerful Nicholas Weverton. Many people now believed that it was time to be done with royalty, and so chose to toss in their lot behind the regent. Keros shook his head. At least the Ramplings cared about what happened to Crosspointe and her people. Geoffrey Truehelm only cared about money and power. He had an unquenchable thirst for both—and as regent, he was in a position to get them.

"Vaughn has gone to Brampton, a village south of Wexstead along the coast. They have begun staging their army there. Ryland continues to try to stir up support against the regent among merchants and majicars, and Margaret—" He broke off with a shake of his head and wry smile. "Margaret does what she does."

Lucy's brows rose. "What is that?"

"Needles her brothers relentlessly, for one. She disagrees with much of what they do."

"And they don't listen to her."

"No."

"Is she right?"

"Probably." He shrugged. "But neither prince listens. They don't really understand what she is."

"And you do?" Her head tilted and brows arched.

The corner of his mouth twitched. "She and I recognize each other. She's no more the pampered princess than you are, despite the fact that she grew up in the castle. She's a weapon and a spy, and she's brilliant."

Lucy looked surprised and Keros knew why. Margaret was a small, delicate thing. She looked fragile—the kind of woman you might keep locked away from the world for fear she'd break. But she had nerves of iron and a will of ice. She could fit in among both the worst criminals and most elite rulers. She was, in a word, dangerous. She also had a tongue like a razor, and Keros liked her very much.

"I always thought she was . . ." Lucy waved a hand. "Soft, maybe. Frail."

"You were meant to, I think."

She shook her head. "So much happened in the castle that I never began to understand. And with cousin William dead, I wonder how much has been lost that we desperately need to know? He played his cards so close to his chest. He had to, of course. What he was doing was too dangerous not to."

Keros nodded. Like Lucy, he'd been appointed to the king's Chosen Circle of advisors, much to his own chagrin. That meant he knew as much as anyone did about the king's plots, and it wasn't much. "Margaret is intent on discovering his secrets. She's been sneaking about inside the castle, much to Ryland's horror. He's ordered her not to, but . . ."

Keros shrugged. Ordering Margaret was like ordering a cat. If she wanted to obey she would; if not, she would do as she pleased, and to the depths with the consequences.

"Tell her to be careful."

"I will."

Suddenly Lucy twisted and pushed out from their shelter. Keros followed hard on her heels. Rising out of the surf was a naked man. His skin was pale white, his long hair dark brown. Silver scales spangled his cheeks and trailed down his neck, chest, and thighs, finally condensing into a silver net around his feet. But more unsettling were his eyes. They were midnight black from corner to corner, making him look inhuman. *Spawn.* But then, all three of them were.

Marten paced up over the rocky shingle without a hint of embarrassment at his nudity, nor did he seem to feel the sharpness of the ground beneath his feet. He put an arm around Lucy as if he couldn't resist touching her, and stretched out the other to Keros.

"It's been too long, my friend," he said.

"And whose fault is that? You have need of neither ship nor Pilot to travel across the sea. One would think you'd visit more often."

Marten grinned, looking almost like his old, pre-spawn self. "Lucy has been very busy on the Root. I could not get her to leave."

And he would never leave her alone. That went without saying and Keros understood. Marten had betrayed her terribly once, and he now lived his life entirely devoted to her. The Root was a massive complex of mountain ridges twisting into the sea like the roots of an old tree. It was north of Crosspointe and believed to be a haven for spawn. King William had asked Lucy to establish another Pale there so he could build his own fleet of armed ships to battle the Jutras when they invaded. He was also cultivating alliances with the wild spawn who lived there.

"What about the Kalpestrine?" she asked Marten.

He brushed wet hair from his face. "There is *sylveth* there."

"Still? I thought it would be gone by now," she said.

Worked *sylveth* was a hardened form of the majickal substance that ran throughout the Inland Sea. It was used to both amplify and anchor spells and only master-level majicars had the power to harden it. Once worked, it was safe for anyone to touch. But when it fell into the sea, it seemed to summon raw *sylveth* to it, and the encounter always returned the worked *sylveth* to its original form. Once that happened, it drifted back out into the sea on the tides. The sea always took back what it gave.

Marten frowned. "There is a *sylveth* ball there. It's the size of a ship and it simply hangs there, deep down— nearly forty fathoms below the surface of the sea. It is not quite liquid and not quite hardened."

"But that is impossible," Lucy said. "*Sylveth* flows— it moves through the water. It doesn't pool or make a ball."

"This is."

She nodded, her face turning harsh. "We need to get to the Bramble. Do you need to rest?"

Keros's eyes narrowed. Marten never needed to rest, not after swimming in the sea. "What's going on?"

"Nothing," Marten said, his chin jutting like an ax blade.

"Crack that. I'm not stupid, whatever you may think."

Lucy looked down at the ground, saying nothing for so long Keros gave up on an answer. Anger heated his gut and he clenched his hands on his cloak.

"The sea is sick. It's hurting Marten," she said softly.

He looked at Marten, scanning him up and down. "You don't look sick," he said, but fear prickled across his skin.

"Lucy exaggerates," Marten said with a dismissive shrug. "I simply get more tired than I used to. But it very well may be my nature now. I have not been spawn long—less than half a season." An edged smile curved his lips. "Perhaps I am with child."

Keros stared, uncertain if it was a joke or a real possibility.

"Don't be an ass," Lucy said, trying to pull away. Marten only snugged her closer. "It's more than tired." She looked at Keros, grooves cutting sharply into the skin around her mouth and nose. "The waves don't answer to him the way they used to—they are sluggish. And he hasn't been coming to Crosspointe because the journey is almost more than he can manage. Whatever is wrong with the majick, is also wrong with the sea and with Marten. If we don't fix it—" She broke off, swallowing hard and clutching Marten's hand tightly.

"What can I do?" Keros asked, cold wriggling deep inside him. He wasn't sure he'd ever be warm again.

She bit her lips and shivered. "Just— Make sure my family is safe. My mother is in hiding and should be all right, but my brother Jack and my other brothers' wives—Sissy and Caroline . . . They are all I have left. Don't let the regent find them. Please."

"Of course," he said, tasting ash. When Marten and Lucy had been sent to the Bramble, her father, two older brothers, and a number of her friends and servants had been convicted of treason and sent with her. Only her mother, Jack, Sissy, and Caroline had escaped. But the ship had dropped Marten and Lucy on the Bramble; the others had been taken to Bokal-dur in Jutras territory to be sold. Keros didn't dare think of what might have become of them. Making matters more painful, King William had forbidden Lucy or Marten to seek them out, saying she was needed in Crosspointe. With her mother pleading for her to obey the king, Lucy had acquiesced. Duty to Crosspointe always came before anything else—a loyalty carved into the soul of every Rampling. She could not refuse it.

"What else?" Keros asked. "How can I help you?"

Lucy shook her head, then gave a little nod. "If you can, feed the Wall tree. It needs blood for strength. The tree anchors the Pale. The stronger it is, the better." She swallowed hard. "If anything happens to the grove on the Bramble, that one will be the only one left. Don't let anyone see you. If the regent or the Majicar Guild should find out there's a blood oak tree right here on Crosspointe, they'd cut it down for sure. It's worth too much money and its magic is too powerful—but that would snap the Pale. Be very careful," she urged. "I would do it, but I must get to the Bramble as soon as possible."

The Wall tree was hidden inside a black granite triangular tower on the castle grounds. The Rampling family tree was inscribed on the outer walls of the tower and included every living legitimate heir. From that diagram, a new king or queen should be chosen to rule. For that alone, Keros was surprised that the regent hadn't had the tower knocked down. Lucy had discovered the existence of the blood oak hidden within less than a year ago, and only a handful of people knew of its existence. Luckily the regent was not among those privileged few. King William had never trusted Truehelm, and had been maneuvered into making him regent.

How Keros was going to feed the damned thing, he had no idea. First he'd have to get inside the castle walls, and then get to the tree itself. There was no entrance in its protective tower. The only way to feed it was to dig down to a root and pour blood on the wood—it was not called blood oak for its color alone. All that while Crown Shields marched around the battlements.

It was a nearly impossible task. "I'll do it," he said.

"Then we must go. I'll get word to you when I can. But be careful. I am not certain how safe it is to use majick." She pulled away from Marten and hugged Keros fiercely. "Take care of yourself."

He hugged her back. "I always do."

She stepped back and Marten reached out a hand. Keros clasped his forearm hard.

"One other thing," Lucy said slowly. "If the Pale on the Root fails, they'll have to come here. Everybody— including our spawn allies. You should warn Ryland and Vaughn. An immigration of spawn could be more damaging than if the Pale snaps."

Keros repressed a shudder and shook his head. "Any more good news you want to share? Maybe the sky will fall and the sun stop shining?"

Neither of his companions smiled and he felt fear dragging skeletal fingers through his entrails. He was just an unregistered majicar; he wasn't meant for politics. He looked at Lucy. "Good luck."

He wanted to hug her again, wanted to pull them both close and not let them go. Instead he stood and watched as they walked to the shore and into the water. A small skiff appeared in the water, conjured by Lucy. It looked faintly wrong somehow, though Keros couldn't place why. She and Marten clambered inside. After a long moment, a thick wave rose behind and it started to move away, slowly speeding up until Lucy and Marten disappeared around the promontory.

Keros turned to retrace his steps, dread weighting him like an anchor. He stiffened his spine and defiantly thrust out his chest. Lucy would prevail, and he would make sure that when she wanted to come home, Crosspointe would be waiting, safe and sound. But even as he promised himself, he knew it was empty. He was a master majicar, but Lucy was practically a god. If she could not stop whatever was tainting the sea and majick, then no one could.

Bile filled his mouth and he spat. But that didn't mean he couldn't try.

Chapter 3

Nicholas Weverton was at his wit's end. Impotent fury wrapped him in iron bands.

"Damn him and damn me," he muttered as he paced before the tall windows in his spacious office. His secluded manor house was situated above Sylmont, north of the castle. On a clear day he could see all of Blackwater Bay, and from his south tower, he had an unobstructed view of the castle. He liked to think that it allowed him to simultaneously keep an eye on both his business empire and the idiot Crown—or these days, the regent, formerly lord chancellor, who was proving to be far worse than any Rampling had ever been.

He dragged his fingers through his shaggy brown hair. He'd always been well aware that Geoffrey Truehelm could not be trusted. The bastard was a necessary evil, however. If not for his taking the regency, the election for a new queen or king would have already taken place. The interregnum offered a small window to change Crosspointe's charter and be rid of the Crown forever.

The trouble was that getting rid of Geoffrey might prove equally difficult. Nicholas had expected him to assassinate the king once the new Edict of Regency had been added to the Charter, and Geoffrey had promptly done so. He had been biding his time for many years, waiting for the opportunity to snatch up real power. This was his opportunity and he wasn't going let it go without a fight.

Nicholas had underestimated the man's lust for power and the viciousness he was willing to employ to gain his ends. Within sennights of ordering the king's assassination, the lord chancellor had firmly ensconced himself in the castle as regent and denounced all Ramplings as traitors and criminals. In another month he'd managed to put hundreds of Ramplings and their most influential supporters into iron collars, seizing everything they owned. Astonishingly, the people of Crosspointe seemed to accept his actions with little protest. Or rather, Geoffrey used the vast wealth he snatched to reward his supporters for their unflinching loyalty. He lavished them with houses, land, jewels, art, ships, and slaves—in return they quashed any objections, hunted down Ramplings, and loudly proclaimed that Regent Geoffrey Truehelm was the only salvation of Crosspointe in this time of terrible crisis.

It was terrifying. Nicholas had to do something about it. But the only legitimate way to get him out was by electing a new king or queen, and Nicholas would not do that. It had taken too long to get to the point of ousting the Crown. But killing Geoffrey was not going to be easy. He'd surrounded himself with an army of Blackwatch guards, he used a poison taster even among friends, and he had walled himself up behind dozens of majickal protections.

In time Nicholas knew he would succeed, but then what? No new lord chancellor had been appointed, so there would be no new regent. If that happened, Prince Ryland and Prince Vaughn would crawl out of the holes in which they'd been hiding and stir up an election. Better to wait until the spine of Rampling power was shattered. What he really needed to do was find Ryland and

Vaughn and turn them over to Geoffrey. Then he could have Geoffrey retired.

Nicholas rubbed a hand across his mouth. By doing nothing, he was helping to kill and enslave an entire family. It was repugnant and made his stomach churn. But what else could he do? Rampling rule had brought the nation to its knees. If the Crown had listened to the needs of the people, of the merchants and the guilds, this would not be happening.

A knock sounded at the door.

"Come in," he called as he moved to stand behind his desk.

His butler stepped inside, a tall broad-shouldered man with a lantern jaw and a barrel chest. "Sir, a messenger has arrived. She claims it is urgent."

"Send her in."

A few moments later, Grimes escorted the woman in. She had a weathered face and a nose that had been broken once or twice. She was angular and thin and plastered with mud. She carried a messenger pouch over her shoulder and a cutlass on her left hip. Two daggers protruded from her belt. She sidled from side to side, aware that she was dripping on a very expensive rug.

"Sorry t' bother ye, sir," she said, bobbing her head. "But he said 't was urgent."

"Who said? What have you brought?"

She dug in her pouch. She didn't use the majickal lock. He frowned. Bonded messengers always used majickal protections on their messages. It was part of their bonding.

"Where's the lock?" he asked.

"Don't work no more," she said with a grimace. "Paid a majicar t' fix it, but didn't work. I come from Oaksmere five days ago," she said with a quick shift in subject.

"Oaksmere?" Nicholas stiffened, his eyes narrowing. His hand curled tight.

"Aye, sir." She pulled a parchment rectangle out of her bag. It was heavily creased and there was a wide brown smear on it that looked like dried blood.

Nicholas fairly snatched it. It was sealed with a glob of blue wax. Something had been pressed into it, but he couldn't tell what it was. He slid the tip of his belt knife under the wax and pried it free. More blood smeared the inside. His entire body clenched as he scanned the hurried writing. It was a scant two lines:

House under attack. We have escaped, but they hunt us. Send help.

It was unsigned, but Nicholas knew the writing well enough. He drew a sharp breath, hardly aware that he'd forgotten to breathe. "Who gave this to you? Where?"

"Didn't give his name," she said, quailing beneath the hot rage in his gaze. "Found me in a tavern in Oaksmere. Was stoppin' off on my run t' Wexstead. Paid me five eyes t' turn around and bring this t' you. Said you'd pay me th' same."

"How was he? Was he alone?"

"Didn't see nobody w' him." She shrugged. "That don't mean nothin'. He came in lookin' for me. Said he saw my mule in th' stable." She gave him a hesitant look. "Was breathin' rough—wet-like. When he coughed, there was blood. And he was listing t' the side, like he was hurtin' hard. Face was swollen and beat up too."

Nicholas bit his tongue to keep from swearing. "Anything else?" he said at last.

She shook her head, looking down. "No, sir."

He opened a desk drawer and fished out a dralion. It was worth ten Hurn's eyes. He tossed it to her, watching her eyes widen. "Don't speak of this to anyone else," he said.

She nodded. "No, sir, I won't."

He went to the wall and pulled the bell. A moment later Grimes opened the door. "Send Rawson to me immediately," Nicholas ordered. "Take her to the kitchen and give her a hot meal."

The door closed behind the messenger and Nicholas read the missive again, fear tying knots in his gut. Few knew how important the house at Oaksmere was to him—or why. Most thought it was just one of his summerhouses. But living at Oaksmere was his son, Carston. Nicholas had fanatically protected Carston's very existence from almost everyone. Every servant at Oaksmere wore a cipher to prevent them from revealing who Carston was. As part of the settlement he'd made when taking custody of the boy, Nicholas had also required Dorinda—the boy's mother—to wear one. He'd also had the minds of her family and servants majickally altered. He'd learned young that being a Weverton made him a target. As he grew older and had inherited the leadership of the Weverton empire and begun his campaign against the crown, the attacks had come more frequently. Carston was not going to be a pawn on the battlefield.

But something had happened at Oaksmere.

Cold fury thickened in Nicholas's chest. If Carston had been captured, then there would be a ransom demand. If not, there was still time to help. *It had been five days already*. He thrust the thought away. Falke, Carston's tutor, companion, and bodyguard, was clever and he would do anything for his charge. But either way, Nicholas was certain that Carston was alive. He did no one any good dead. Nicholas clung to the thought with all the desperation of a drowning man.

It was a half a glass before Rawson banged a hard fist against the door. He strode in. He was Nicholas's arms master. Just over six feet tall, his frame was lanky, his bones wrapped in thick corded muscle. His face was leathery above his beard, and his eyes were a pale blue and hard. Around his neck hung a chain with a collection of what appeared to be charms—all were ciphers. He wore a sword on his right hip and a variety of other weapons secreted about his person. He'd no doubt left his crossbow in the vestibule. He was, in a word, dangerous. He gave a minuscule bow and waited for Nicholas to speak.

"There's been trouble at Oaksmere," he said grimly, passing the parchment to Rawson.

The other man examined it. "They're after Carston, then," he said in a soft, low voice.

"I can't imagine it's anything else."

"I can take a full squad of twenty men. We can be on the road in half a glass."

"Take the horses." In Crosspointe, few could afford to own even a single horse. The feed was horrendously expensive on such a small island nation. Nicholas bred them.

Rawson's cheek twitched and he shook his head. "The mules will hold up better. The roads are mud bogs. We'll take dogs too."

"Whatever you think best. Take this"—Nicholas pulled a pouch of coins out of a drawer and tossed it to the other man—"and buy provisions, bribes, and anything else you need. Do whatever you have to to get there quickly. Get Carston back and find out who's done this—" He hesitated. Then said, "You should take a majicar with you. Klepeysian or Forzidel perhaps."

Rawson chewed his bottom lip. "Can't trust 'em— can't trust their majick to work. Like carrying a cracked sword. It's not whether it's going to break, it's when."

"Still, the enemy may have majick and you'll need to counter it with something. Take them both."

"Yessir. Anything else?"

"Hurry. Bring him back to me alive." Nicholas's voice

cracked on the last word and hot tears burned his eyes. He didn't let them fall.

Rawson touched his forehead with his fingers in a salute and left without another word. Nicholas slumped in his chair, staring at the door. It would take days to get to Oaksmere and by then the raiders could have gone anywhere. It might be weeks before he discovered what had happened, if not longer. He closed his eyes, his throat tightening. Carston was his life. From the moment he was born, Nicholas had loved him. The boy was now six seasons old and full of curiosity, independence, and courage. Nicholas missed him terribly and found every excuse he could to visit Oaksmere.

He'd kill the bastards who did this.

Slowly he rose to stand before the windows again. The storm continued to rage outside, matching the violent turmoil inside him. Who had done this? The obvious choices were the Ramplings and the regent. But Geoffrey was his ally. Nicholas had practically given him the regency. But Geoffrey would eat his own young if it would give him more power. The man was insatiable. The question was, what did he gain by kidnapping Carston?

As for the Ramplings—he didn't know if Ryland or Vaughn were ruthless enough to steal children. But if not Geoffrey or the princes, who? He had plenty of enemies, and he would pay anything to get Carston back. But who would have the means to discover Carston's existence?

It was dark before he retreated from his study to his private quarters. He was in no mood to attend the dinner he'd been invited to and sent his regrets. He poured himself a glass of dark Kalibrian whiskey, and tossed it back, the smoky burn of it searing his gut. He poured another and drank it just as quickly. With a curse he turned and threw the glass, shattering it against the wall. His attention was suddenly caught by the small parchment in the middle of the bed.

He stared at it, hardly comprehending it. It wasn't possible. His security was impenetrable. And yet . . . there it was.

Slowly he moved to the side of the bed. He didn't pick up the page. It could be poisoned or majicked. The writing was feminine. His heart leaped into his throat as he scanned the words.

I know where Carston is. Do you?

He made a choking sound, gripping the bedclothes and wrenching them aside with a shout of rage. He knocked over the bed stand and threw a chair against the windows. They were majicked and did not break.

"My, my, my. Such a temper."

He spun around, pulling the dagger from his belt. He held it ready. "Where are you?"

The woman laughed softly and slid from a narrow crease of shadow on the near wall. She wore close-fitting black clothing. A hood covered her hair and most of her face, leaving only a narrow band for her eyes. They were blue. She had two knives strapped to her thighs and another tucked into the top of her right boot.

"Who are you?" he demanded. "What do you know of Carston?"

"I told you," she said in a cold, cutting voice, "I know where your son is."

Shock rippled through him. "How do you know he's my son?"

"Does it matter?"

"Do you have him?" he said in a demanding tone.

The expression in her eyes was contemptuous. "I do not steal children."

"What do you want? What is your price? Tell me where my son is." He strode forward, standing over her. He wasn't a tall man, but she was much smaller. Her head barely came to his chin. She looked up at him, not backing away. She was not frightened.

"Price? For the life of a child? Oh, no. That is your game, not mine."

She reached up and pulled off her hood. Nicholas could only stare. Princess Margaret stood before him, but instead of the soft, porcelain doll he was used to seeing at fashionable functions, this Princess Margaret was made of ice and iron. Her body was tensed and fluid, like she was prepared to fight and knew how to kill. Her mouth was a flat line and her face was a mask of hate. He jerked back as if he'd been struck. He had spies everywhere—how did he not know what she was?

She snarled at him, the rage rolling off her in tangible waves, but her voice was quiet and controlled. "How many Rampling children has the regent stolen and sold into slavery? How many have been beaten and starved? How many have been chained to beds in brothels? You have done this. You made him regent—what he does is your fault as much as his." Her face contorted and then smoothed into blandness. "Part of me says that your son deserves everything he gets—*you* deserve it. But I won't leave even a child of yours in the regent's hands if I can do something about it."

"Geoffrey is behind this? But he doesn't know I have a son," Nicholas rasped.

"Doesn't he?"

"You could be behind this; it could be a trap—a way to turn me against Geoffrey and win back the throne."

She nodded and smiled with bright fierceness. "It could. But you'll have to play the game to the end to find out. I know where Carston is. Come with me now and I'll show you."

Nicholas hesitated. It would take hours for a rider to overtake Rawson and bring him back. He didn't think Margaret would wait.

"Just you," she said and took a step back as if preparing to leave. "We go now." Her brows rose in a question. Her eyes taunted him.

Nicholas swallowed and made up his mind. "Let me dress and leave a note for my staff. I don't want them to raise an alarm. Geoffrey will learn of it and be wary, if he is the culprit."

She nodded and gestured with her hand. "Be quick."

He retreated to his dressing room and quickly changed his clothes, donning wool trousers, a heavy cotton shirt, tall boots, and a long wool vest. Over it he pulled a caped greatcoat and buckled on his rapier. The belt was made of two layers of leather, with three dozen dralions stitched between. He added a stiletto to each boot and hung another around his neck, turning it so it hung between his shoulder blades.

He opened his jewelry box and took out a necklace with several ciphers. As erratic as majick was acting these days, he didn't know how useful these would be, but they couldn't hurt. He slid the charms over his neck. One was for healing, another was a shield against majickal attack, and the third would give a boost of strength. He touched the shield amulet thoughtfully. But, no. Not yet. With majick so uncertain, he should wait to activate it.

Lastly he donned a hat, pulling the brim low, and tucked a pair of gloves into his belt. With that he returned to his bedchamber.

Margaret stood just to the side of the window, looking out. It was difficult to pick her out of the shadows, as if she'd faded and was no more substantial than a ghost. She turned to look at him as he went to the desk and took out a purse, tucking it into a pocket inside his vest. He then took out a parchment and pen and scribbled a quick note to Fawke.

I'll be gone for a short while. Do not let anyone know.

He signed it with a flourish and took the time to heat

wax and press his signet into it so that Fawke would know it was official.

"Ready?" she asked.

He nodded. "Where are we going?"

"First to get a little help."

"Help?" His surprise was sharp.

She stared at him and her blue eyes weren't as condemning and cold as they had been. "The two of us might be able to rescue the boy. But our chances would be better with a bit of support."

"The two of us—," he repeatedly stupidly, then shook himself. "You're going to help me? Why?"

She smiled. It was as bitter as arsenic. "Because I am a Rampling and that is what we do—we protect the people of Crosspointe. Even cracking bastards like you. Besides, you will owe me, and I already have a price in mind."

She strode toward him, graceful and deadly—like a wolf. She swept past and out into the passage. She smelled of wind and pine. He followed.

Margaret led him to an opulent set of rooms not far from his own. They would be his wife's one day. The room was dusted and clean, the linens fresh on the bed. He had it kept as if someone might use it at a moment's notice. Margaret didn't call the lights, but went through the room as if she was a frequent visitor. Nicholas's stomach tightened. Perhaps she was.

In the boudoir she opened the east windows that opened onto a narrow balcony. Wind buffeted through the opening and tossed the heavy drapes. Rain pelted the glass and drenched Margaret as she went out. Nicholas followed, letting the windows close behind him. She climbed up onto the balustrade, holding the downspout with one hand and glancing at him over her shoulder. "This part could be tricky. Try not to fall."

With that she stepped out onto the ledge that ran

along the side of the house. A hundred feet below, the wet cobblestone courtyard gleamed sleekly in the light cast out from the first floor windows. She eased along the ledge without hesitation, body pressed against the house. She found handholds in protruding bits of masonry and on window ledges. Forty feet away, she dropped down onto another balcony and turned, waiting for Nicholas.

He grimaced. Majick kept the rain from soaking his greatcoat and weighting him down, but he was bigger and heavier than Margaret, and clearly she had a great deal of practice. But she just as clearly wanted to take no chances that they would be seen leaving, and then, too, she no doubt enjoyed seeing him suffer.

Drawing a hard breath, he climbed up onto the balustrade and followed her path. The wind pounded him, pulling at the voluminous sweep of his coat like a sail. He clung to his precarious perch, sliding his feet over the slick stone. Inch by inch he crossed until he reached the balcony where Margaret waited. His arms and legs shook with the effort and cold turned his hands to claws.

"Come on," she said and went to the other side. A tossing hemlock crowded close. From her waist she unwound a rope. It was hardly bigger around than his pinky finger and looked like it wouldn't hold a child, much less a grown man. She tied it off and slung it over the edge.

"Go," she ordered, pointing downward.

He looked at the rope and then back at her. It was a matter of trust. She could cut the rope and he'd fall to the pavement and kill himself. But, then, she could have killed him many times already. He'd thought his house well warded against intruders, but she'd broken through easily.

He reached for the rope, climbing over the rail. He braced himself, wrapping the rope through his legs and then he let go, easing himself down hand over hand.

Nicholas was no soft dandy. He prided himself on keeping himself fit. He spent hours every sennight fencing, boxing, climbing, and running. Majick could only keep him so safe—and clearly not safe enough. He wanted to be able to defend himself in any situation.

The branches of the hemlock battered him as the wind swung him like a pendulum. His cold hands slipped on the wet rope and he clenched them, feeling the burn on his palms. He kept going, his arms aching with the strain, his head spinning with hunger and the Kalibrian whiskey he'd drunk. *Fool.*

He reached the ground at last and stepped back out of the way to allow Margaret room. But the rope suddenly pulled up and away. He waited, gazing upward to find her. Suddenly a hand gripped his shoulder. He spun around. She stood behind him. There was a tear in the shoulder of her shirt and a red scrape made a seam across her pale skin. Hemlock needles tangled in her hair.

"Let's go."

"How far?" he asked quietly, not moving. She just looked at him, not answering. "I have horses," he explained. She didn't, he knew. The Crown kept only a few, and Geoffrey had taken possession of them.

She hesitated. "They'll call attention to us."

"But we'll make better time, wherever we are going."

She licked her lips and brushed the rain from her eyes, then nodded. "Can we get them out without notice?"

He lifted his shoulder in a half-shrug. "I think so." The horses would be bedded down for the night and the staff would be dining in the kitchens.

"All right."

He didn't ask her if she could ride, as he would have done even an hour before. He had a feeling she could do a great many things he never would have expected of her.

They slipped into the barn through a small door at the west end, farthest from the house. It was dry and warm, heated with woodstoves on either end of the barn. The musky smells of horses, grain, and hay filled the air. There were soft nickers, the sounds of chewing, and the scrape of hooves. Nicholas eased out into the main corridor that ran the length of the barn. There was no sign of anyone. He motioned Margaret to follow him and hurried down to the tack room, holding the hilt of his rapier to keep it from jingling or scraping against the wall.

The door of the tack room opened with barely a creak. He slipped inside, touching the *sylveth* lamp inside. A gold glow illuminated the room. It flickered and was weaker than it ought to have been. He went quickly to the bridles and selected what he wanted, then did the same with the saddles. He lifted one down and handed it to Margaret, then retrieved his own.

"We'll need another," she said when he started to leave.

Ah, yes. Their "help." He wondered who it was.

"Can he ride?" Nicholas asked as he sorted through which horse to use.

"It's going to be fun to find out," she said with wicked humor dancing in her eyes.

That caught Nicholas up short and he stared. "All these years," he said, shaking his head slowly. "I never even suspected what you were. I thought of you as soft, insipid—even stupid."

One brow rose in a roguish look. "And what is your impression of me now?"

"I think you won't fool me again."

She smiled and it was cold and dangerous. "Think again."

Chapter 4

The horse that Nicholas gave Margaret was a leggy gray gelding with a smooth gait. He was a quiet animal, but responded quickly to her legs and heels. She had heard many times that his horses were the highest quality and best trained—he sold them across the Inland Sea for a tidy sum.

She glanced at her companion as they jogged along. She hadn't intended to help Nicholas retrieve his son, but his reaction to his son's kidnapping had changed her mind. It was clear that he not only loved the boy, but that Nicholas would sacrifice himself for his son. Her father had loved her, but he would never have allowed that love to interfere with his kingly responsibilities. Margaret had never questioned that. But faced with Nicholas's agonizing fear for his son, she'd known she had to help. Besides, it could win his support to the Rampling side. It was worth the risk. She hoped Keros agreed. She grinned. If only he'd known what he was getting himself into when he promised to help her.

The rain had let up and was now a slow drizzle. They'd left his manor through a rear gate. Nicholas promised that only he knew of it and only he had the key to the wards, though he eyed her narrowly as he spoke, clearly wondering how she'd obtained entrance. Margaret only watched him smugly. Let him eat himself up with curiosity and worry.

"How do you know about Carston?" he demanded suddenly.

She debated her answer a moment, then gave a little shrug. It didn't matter if he knew. "Two days ago I stole some information from the regent's office." *Father's* office, she corrected herself with silent bitterness.

Nicholas was scowling at her. "You were in the castle? Are you Pale-blasted? He's desperate to capture you and your brothers. He won't sell you. He'll carve you apart until you tell him all your father's secrets."

She shrugged. "It's what I was made to do," she said. "I am harder to catch than you might think." Though it had been close. If not for Ellyn—

Margaret frowned. She had intended to make their meeting at the teahouse tomorrow, but now it seemed she was going to miss it.

"Where is my son? How is he?" Nicholas growled.

She shook her head. "I don't know. I know where they took him and that he was alive when the kidnappers sent the message to the regent."

"What did they say?"

"They said they killed everyone at Oaksmere and then hunted the boy and his guardian down. They killed the man and took Carston."

When he said nothing, Margaret glanced at him. She felt herself recoil. Before he'd been angry and scared, but now he had become something else—angry still, but more than that. It was a rage so deep and cold that it curled her toes. His eyes had turned vicious and brutal and he held his body like a knife ready to throw. His horse pranced beneath him and he mechanically patted its shoulder soothingly. When he spoke again, his voice was soft and modulated, as if he was speaking to guests over a dinner table. The lack of emotion sent shivers running through Margaret.

"Where did they take him?"

She could have prevaricated. If she told him straight out, she risked him running off in the night to rescue the boy himself. But why should it matter? His choice. "He's in the village of Molford, just south of Lake Ferradon. He's being kept at Molford Manor. The regent confiscated it and is using it to house part of the private army he's been building."

"Why are you doing this?"

"I told you: I'm a Rampling. And you'll owe me. I know you pay your debts."

"I have worked to destroy your family."

Her mouth twisted. "I am well aware of that."

"Your brothers would not help me in this, I think."

She shrugged. "They are trying to clean up the mess that you made by installing Geoffrey Truehelm as regent." Her teeth gritted and her chest tightened. "If I find out you were responsible for my father's death, I will kill you," she whispered tautly.

"I did not order his death." His words were short, staccato.

She twisted her head to glare at him. "Why should I believe you?"

"Because it suited my purposes better for him to remain on the throne."

"That I do not believe."

"It is true. Your father no longer had the faith of the people. He allowed the Burn to happen, the Jutras invaded and the Pale snapped, and the majicars had only become more recalcitrant. In time, Crosspointe would have revolted and thrown off Rampling rule. It is what I was hoping for."

Hot anger burned in Margaret's throat. She curled

her lip, wanting to spit at him. She controlled herself with hard effort. "You have no idea what's really been happening," she said. "If you did—" She broke off.

"I know more than you think," he said.

She only shook her head. What he didn't know would tear Crosspointe to bits. The truth was that her father had committed treason. He'd sold ships' compasses to Crosspointe's allies in an effort to put more ships onto the sea to defend against the Jutras. He believed that in time the Jutras would invade again and he wanted to have armed allies to help repel them. He'd planned to use the earnings from the compasses to quietly build fortresses around Crosspointe and fill them with an army of Crown Shields. He'd been murdered before he could do that.

But selling ships' compasses was high treason, even for the king; if the people of Crosspointe learned of what he'd done, they'd panic. They'd fear that the Jutras would obtain the compasses. More than that, they would do exactly what Nicholas wanted—they'd overthrow the crown permanently and likely cement Geoffrey Truehelm in power.

That wasn't even the worst of it. The making of compasses was an unusual ability. Most majicars could not do it. The last of the compass majicars except one had been killed in the fall of the Kalpestrine, and Fairlie, the one who'd escaped, hated Crosspointe and the Ramplings, especially Ryland. Compass majicars were spawn—not like ordinary majicars and Pilots—but the terrifying kind. They were misshapen, malformed monsters, and only they could make compasses that allowed Pilots to guide ships across the chaotic Inland Sea. If anyone learned that Crosspointe had lost all its compass majicars, there would be rioting.

Margaret rubbed her forehead with cold fingers. If Nicholas knew any of that, he'd have the weapons he needed to destroy Rampling rule forever. And that still wasn't the worst of it. Not as far as he was concerned. His nephew was Shaye Weverton, the majicar who had become so powerful he had helped bring down the Kalpestrine with Fairlie's aid. The two had fled to the Root to be safe from those who would hunt and imprison them, and learn their secrets. But Nicholas knew none of that. All he knew was that Shaye and Fairlie had disappeared and no doubt believed that her father had had them murdered. Even Margaret wasn't supposed to know the truth. She'd been reduced to spying on her brothers for information. It was a secret she had no intention of ever telling Nicholas. Shaye hated the Ramplings and Ryland in particular for deliberately transforming Fairlie with *sylveth*. The two had been best friends, which made the betrayal even worse. Add in the fact that Shaye loved his uncle, if Nicholas ever discovered Shaye's whereabouts, he'd have the services of one of the most powerful majicars in the world, if not *the* most powerful. Luckily, Shaye had decided he wanted to live in seclusion for the moment, helping Fairlie adjust to her transformation. In time—

Margaret shook off the thought and urged her gelding faster. One worry at a time.

They were following a cart track that wound through the foothills above the city. It was faster and less conspicuous than riding through Sylmont. It took a little more than an hour to travel down past the city center and Cheapside, past the Maida of Chayos and the Mystery of Hurn, until they reached Cranford and the Ferradon River.

"You should leave the extra mare," she told him. "We'll come back for her. It will be safer." She waited as he tied the chestnut beneath a traveler pine where she was protected from the rain and prying eyes.

When Nicholas rejoined her, Margaret turned east and crossed the Westenra Canal. She'd retrieved her cloak from where she'd left it outside Nicholas's manor house and now pulled the hood up to hide her face. Her companion did the same.

"We are going to the Riddles?" he asked dubiously.

"We are."

He pulled his horse to a halt, eyeing Margaret suspiciously as she followed suit. "With horses? I thought you did not want to call attention to us. We'll be a beacon for every thief around. Add in the fact that you have a spectacular bounty on your head, and we'll be swarmed in minutes."

"We'll have to chance it."

He scowled, his face pinching in desperation and anger. "Are you mad?"

"Let me consider. . . . I'm about to expose to you, my enemy, one of our safe houses, which will render it useless. After that, I'm planning on revealing the identity of an unregistered majicar who has been critical in the resistance against the regent. All this to save the son of a man who hates my family and likely murdered my father, just in the hopes of cultivating an alliance. Am I mad? You tell me."

With that she wheeled her horse and trotted away. Much as she wanted to spur the gelding into a dead run, the racket of his hooves on the cobbles would wake everyone within hearing and bring them running. Instead she pulled him down to a quiet, springy walk, gritting her teeth as Nicholas settled in beside her.

"My apologies," he said stiffly. "I will repay you for your sacrifices."

"You can't," she spat without thinking, then more quietly, "Your help to put a Rampling back on the throne is all I want."

He didn't answer. Margaret gave a silent sigh. This was all futile and stupid if she didn't win his support. And yet— She wanted to help him. Or rather, she wanted to help the boy. She was so tired of sitting on her hands and doing nothing while innocent people suffered right in front of her. And this boy *was* innocent. No matter who his father was, Carston had done nothing to deserve this kidnapping. She grimaced. It was exactly that sort of thinking that made her unfit to rule. Given the choice, she let her emotions rule her actions more often than not.

They reached the edge of the Riddles and plunged in without pausing. The place was a sprawling, nonsensical maze. It had originally been built by the founders of Crosspointe before they realized that no one could follow them across the Inland Sea. What they'd been running from, Margaret didn't know; the history books didn't say. But they were terrified of being found.

The Riddles was full of roads that dead-ended into buildings, or corkscrewed and wound about in mad tangles, leading back on themselves. There were stairways that led nowhere, buildings without doors, doors that opened onto the river—it was a place designed to confuse armies, separating them so that soldiers could be picked off one by one. Now it confused tax collectors and Crown Shields. It was a haven for thieves and murderers and people who did not want to be found. Ryland had located several safe houses here for family members who managed to escape the regent's hunters, and Keros had long made his home here.

The roads were buckled and many of the cobblestones had been pried up to make other things, like makeshift hovels, walls, or baking ovens. It made for treacherous footing and more than once their horses stumbled. Nicholas cursed steadily in a low voice. Margaret smiled, liking him the better for it. It made him seem more human. She had always thought of him as the spider in the web, cold and calculating as he ruled his business empire. But he surprised her. He'd managed himself on the

ledge and clambering down the rope, and his willingness
to go after his son himself spoke well for him.

They were forced to go single file between two buildings that seemed to sway dangerously together as if
they were about to tumble down. Margaret drew a knife
from her boot and held it ready, the hair on her scalp
prickling. Her glance swept the ground before them like
a scythe, then moved upward. She saw the first bully-
boy crouched in the cross braces beneath a balcony. He
sat waiting like a vulture inside a cloak of shadow. He
couldn't be alone.

Margaret tipped her head subtly, scanning the roof-
line. More shadows clung to the downspouts and window ledges. They intended to drop down as she and
Nicholas exited. She didn't doubt that more roughs had
moved in behind to block their escape.

"Company," she whispered. Damn them to the black
depths! But she'd known that even as late as it was—
or early—there was a risk to bringing horses into the
Riddles.

"So I see," came the quiet answer from behind her.

"Be ready to run."

The trouble was, if she timed it right, she could probably win free, but the brigands would fall on Nicholas
like an avalanche. As entertaining as it might be to see
him get a mouthful of knuckles or someone's boot to his
gut, it wasn't the right time. Maybe one day ...

She held her knife ready and surreptitiously short-
ened her reins. Her gelding bowed his head and pawed
the air, sensing her tension. *Good.* She passed the man
perching above on the cross braces and was nearly to
the end of the alley when she suddenly clamped her
legs tight around the barrel of her horse and gave a
loud cry. The sound echoed shockingly and her mount
sprang forward as if launched from a catapult. Behind
her she heard shouts. She cleared the alley and whipped

her horse around. He reared and landed, standing more steadily than she had expected. He was a horse trained for trouble.

Nicholas had his sword in one hand and his knife in another. He swung at the figures dropping down around him. His horse was snapping and kicking at them— trained for trouble indeed.

Margaret didn't wait. She clamped her legs tight and her gray bounded forward again. She didn't have a sword and the reach that Nicholas did, but she had her knife and rings. She spun them on her fingers and flicked open the needles.

Three men and a woman were trapped between the enraged horses. They screamed and ducked as the horses snapped and lunged. Someone leaped onto the rump of Margaret's mount and grasped her around her neck. She gripped his arm, digging needles into his flesh. He stiffened and gave a soft moan before dropping to the side, dragging her with him. She braced herself in the stirrup, bending and twisting as he fell away.

She heard the sounds of Nicholas's rapier cutting the air, smelled the coppery sweet scent of blood and the fetid smell of the alley. A hand grabbed her ankle. She kicked and swiped at it with her knife. The hand released her.

"Go!" shouted Nicholas.

She sat back hard and pulled the reins and her gelding obediently scuttled backward, thank Chayos. She swung out of the alley opening with Nicholas lunging after her. She urged her horse into a choppy canter, zigzagging between buildings and around to the south. She didn't slow down as they turned into a dead end. She reached out, trailing her fingers down the wall. Ahead, the brick wall melted away as the majick thankfully answered, and they plunged through. She swung about, slapping her hand down on top of the *sylveth* knob topping a post set just within the small courtyard. Instantly the wall behind them faded back into being and the knob burst into radiant light.

Margaret let out a heavy breath as she reached down to pat her sweating mount. "Good boy," she murmured.

"Are you all right?" Nicholas asked sharply.

She turned to look at him. He carried his sword high. Blood dripped from it like thick red ink. There was a large rent in his caped coat, one eye was swollen and blood ran down his face from a cut across his cheek.

Margaret took stock of herself. Her throat would be bruised from where the bastard had grabbed her, and there were three deeply grooved scratches across the back of her left hand. Other than that, she was unhurt.

"Fine," she said and slid down to the ground. She set her bloody knife on the ground and ran her hands over her mount, looking for wounds. He had a cut in his left shoulder and another on his fetlock, but was otherwise sound. When she turned back to Nicholas, she found him doing the same, though he had not let go of his rapier.

"What now?" he asked when he saw her looking at him.

"We wait."

"For what?"

"A friend." She nodded at the *sylveth* knob on top of the post. "That signaled him. In the meantime, we can water the horses." She went to the pump that stood beside a deep stone basin in the center of the courtyard. She cleaned out the leaf debris at the bottom and pumped the handle vigorously. After a minute, water began to flow into the basin. Her gray gelding nosed her in the back and then rubbed his head up and down against her. She stumbled to the side with a laugh and pushed him away.

"Patience, sweetheart," she told him, rubbing behind his ear.

Nicholas came to stand on the other side of the gray.

He rested his sword against the basin, point down, giving Margaret a frowning look, as if she confused him. Next he unbuckled the horse's bridle and slid it over his ears. The gelding gave a moaning rumble of satisfaction and buried his nose in the water. Behind them a rumbling whinny reminded them of the bay. Nicholas gave a lopsided grin and retreated to remove the animal's bridle to allow him to drink.

The grin disturbed Margaret. There was no doubt that Nicholas Weverton was a charming man. Like her, he wore his affability and charismatic roguishness like a mask. It set people at ease and deflected their suspicion from what they each really were—treacherous.

She did not know how long it would be before Keros could answer the signal, so she unbuckled the cinches on the saddle and pulled it off, tipping it up against the wall. Nicholas had already begun to do the same and swiftly settled his tack beside hers. He grabbed the corner of his greatcoat and began rubbing the animal down. Margaret did the same, first dipping her cloak into the water to dab at the gelding's wounds. Keros would heal them when he got there.

"They are remarkably steady in a fight," she said.

"It seemed advisable," he replied. "One never knows, after all."

Margaret nodded sober agreement.

Silence fell then as they worked. When they were done, Margaret felt warm. She glanced again at Nicholas. The blood on his face had dried. She looked up in vague surprise. When had the rain stopped?

"Come here," she said and pointed to the water basin. She dug in her pockets and found her black hood. Before she could tear it apart, he pulled out his handkerchief and wetted it in the water. He squeezed it and dabbed at his cheek and winced.

"Let me," she said, taking the handkerchief. She

dampened it again and deftly cleaned the wound. He
flinched away and she reached up to hold him firmly. He
stiffened, staring down at her with narrowed eyes. It was
uncomfortably intimate.

"There," she said when she was through. She stepped
back and rinsed the square of linen in the basin, then
handed it back. Before she could turn away, he gripped
her hand.

"Your turn," he said.

He dipped her scratched hand in the water and then
scrubbed it gently with his handkerchief. His skin was
warm, his hands calloused. Margaret's cheeks flushed
and she barely resisted the urge to yank away. At last he
let go and reached for his rapier. Using his handkerchief,
he cleaned the length of it. Margaret retrieved her knife
and rinsed it in the water. She dried it on her cloak and
returned it to its sheath, then strode away to a square
corner on the opposite side of the courtyard where she
pushed open a narrow door.

"There's no room for the horses inside, but they
should be safe enough out here," she told him.

Inside was a small room with a woodstove in the corner, a long table with twenty chairs, and a set of shelves
loaded with food, weapons, clothing, candles, and a vast
number of other supplies. A door on the opposite wall
led into a dormitory containing two dozen bunk beds
lining either side of the walls. They were made of wood
and rope and topped with straw-filled mattresses. The
place had been prepared not only as a safe house for
Ramplings escaping the regent's hunt, but also as a staging area as they gathered for the resistance. It was one
of several in the Riddles. There were a dozen scattered
throughout Sylmont.

She went to a shelf, pulled down a wax-sealed jar and
handed it to Nicholas, then reached for several more.
She pushed aside the sacks of rice and beans and found

a plump dried sausage. Nicholas had set the jars on the table and had found two metal trenchers. He dug away the wax on the first jar with the point of his knife. It contained preserved peaches in thick syrup. He speared one on his knife and slurped it down, even as his stomach growled loudly in the silence.

Margaret sawed off a hunk of the sausage and peeled away the casing. She hadn't eaten since breakfast—almost a full day ago. She was famished. She pulled out a chair and sat down. Nicholas pulled out the chair beside her.

They polished off another jar of peaches and one of cherries and the rest of the sausage. Exhaustion weighed on Margaret. She yawned and shook her head to wake herself up and wished for a pot of strong tea. She looked up and found Nicholas watching her. He looked worried and tense. All of his wealth and he still couldn't keep his son safe. It had to be tearing him apart.

"You astonish me," he said quietly.

"Do I, now?" Margaret drawled, the corner of her mouth quirking up.

He flushed slightly and gave a little shrug. "My sources of information are generally thorough. Still, I had no idea of what you are."

She rubbed her finger on the table, tracing the grain of the wood. "And what am I?" she murmured. Just at the moment she wasn't sure. Neither Ryland nor Vaughn would forgive her for going to Nicholas; they would never trust her again. Still, she couldn't regret it. She was doing something at last, and it could even turn the tide in the battle for Crosspointe. Nicholas reached out and captured her hand in his. She looked at him, startled. He bent forward, his gaze locked with hers. "Thank you. I owe you."

She felt her cheeks heating and her stomach curled as his touch sent sparks tumbling through her veins. *No, no, no!* She *would not* be attracted to Nicholas Weverton of all people.

She pulled away, balling her hand into a fist. "Then when we get Carston back, you can help pry Truehelm out of the castle and put a Rampling back on the throne," she said sharply, then stood. "I'm going to rest. Wake me when someone comes."

She strode away into the dormitory, but the heat from his touch did not fade. She swore.

Chapter 5

Keros didn't return to the Riddles until well after dawn. He had walked from the headland back to Helmsdale through the raging storm and finally located a hack to carry him into Sylmont. It had taken him as far as the edge of the Riddles, but no hack was willing to cross inside without hefty monetary motivation, something Keros was ill prepared to provide. He paid the woman and got out and started for his home. The rain had subsided and the wind had died sometime in the early morning hours. Lucy's warnings tumbled in his mind, cutting and gouging like shards of glass.

He stumbled over a pile of broken bricks and tangled weeds, biting back his annoyance. Close by, a girl laughed and a chip of stone bounced off his chest. He growled and stalked away.

His house looked like it was about to collapse. Trash and debris were piled up all around it, and a fetid mix of water and human waste trickled in a steady runnel in front of his front door. The shutters hung drunkenly or were gone altogether, and several of the top-story windows gaped like empty mouths. The door was a collection of planks tacked together by odd-sized strips of wood hammered crosswise. It looked like a gust of wind would knock it down.

Keros crossed to it and brushed his hand over the

locking ward. It felt rubbery and weak, but opened for him.

He pulled the door just wide enough to squeeze inside and shut it tightly behind him. He leaned back, his head resting on the polished oak. The exterior of his home was a reality supported by illusion. Inside was cozy and well-cared for, with warm colors and the scent of herbs and spices. He drew a deep breath and let it out, then stripped off his wet clothes. Goose pimples rose on his flesh and his teeth chattered as he shivered. He left the wet things on the tile floor and dashed through the kitchen and up the stairs.

In his room he ran a bath, hoping the majick that kept his boiler piping hot had not failed. It hadn't. He climbed in the tub gratefully, letting the heat seep through his cold muscles. It was only then that he noticed the slow pulse of light throbbing in his *illidre*. He sat up sharply and water sloshed over the rim of the tub.

His *illidre* was not like those of most master majicars. It served as a focus for majick, and while most majicars carefully crafted theirs into artistic shapes and colors, Keros's was a misshapen blob, looking very much like a shattered rainbow that he'd squeezed with his fist. He'd been angry when he formed it and had left it that way as a reminder to himself that he was an outsider to majick. He'd not asked for the gift and it had cost him far more than anyone should ever have to pay.

The pulse inside it told him that someone was waiting for him at one of the safe houses. Only Margaret, Ryland, and Vaughn could activate the summons and Vaughn was on the other side of Crosspointe. That meant that one of the others was in trouble, or they'd never have risked activating the summoning ward. He thrust himself out of the tub, toweling off vigorously. The fluctuations in majick made the safe houses a lot more vulnerable than their name implied. Not only that, but with so many majicars in the city, someone might have sensed the spike of majick from the signal and followed it back to its source.

He dressed and was out the door in less than five minutes, taking the time to make a sandwich from stale bread and sharp cheese, biting into it as he ran out the door.

The signal pulled at him, drawing him toward the southwest and he realized that the Lily house had been activated—each safe house was named for a flower. He strode through the gray morning and soon a drizzle began again, the breeze picking up. Keros pulled his hood up and snarled up at the pewter clouds. Damnable weather.

He wove through the nonsensical sprawl of buildings that made up the Riddles. He came to Ashford Avenue and halted in the shadows, glancing up and down. The avenue was the one place in the Riddles where law and order reigned. Here ornate expensive gaming houses crowded each other. Though illegal in Crosspointe, gambling was permitted in the Riddles. Or rather, the Crown elected to ignore it. Too many influential and wealthy men and women—including Ramplings—frequented these establishments. Raiding them would only embarrass important friends and strain alliances.

The street was full of workers raking away leaf debris, mule manure left behind by hacks, and whatever other random bits of flotsam and jetsam had accumulated during the day. Most were wearing only ragged trousers and shirts and no shoes; iron collars circled every neck. Their hands were red and chapped, their faces splotched with bruises. Most were thin nearly to the point of emaciation. The heavy rains had damaged crops and imported food was too expensive to waste on slaves. The various crews were made up of mostly men and boys and guarded by footmen and women carrying cudgels and short, stiff leather whips. Girls were kept for the scullery and the brothels.

Keros's lip curled in a snarl and his fingers hooked into claws. Damn the regent! Damn every soul who bought slaves or stood by while others did! He swallowed, hot fury burning through his chest and turning his stomach. Bile flooded his tongue. He was one of the latter, his hands tied by Ryland and Vaughn's orders. He'd promised to support them, never realizing that he'd have to stand by and watch people be dragged from their homes and sold like livestock. He gave a negative shake of his head. No—livestock was worth taking care of; these people were rags, to be used up and then tossed away.

Three loud cracks sounded in quick succession. A man crumpled to his hands and knees. Above him, a woman in pale orange and blue livery shouted at him, her whip cocked back over her head. She swung again and then two other servants joined her, one in matching livery, the other wearing cream and tan, and together they began to shout and kick the now-prone man. Keros sucked in a ragged breath and jolted forward. The rest of the slaves had cowed away, while more liveried overseers joined the attack. In front of the ornate building facades, men and women of the Blackwatch, Eyes, and Howlers watched the fracas impassively. They were paid to keep the peace for the owners, nothing more.

Keros stopped short, helplessness swallowing him. What could he really do? Even if he killed every mother-cracking bully bastard, he'd probably also kill their victim and likely a good number of the other slaves. But he couldn't do nothing; he was tired to death of just watching helpless people being tortured. Looking down at the magic snapping and flashing around his hands like blue fire, he clenched them into fists, his body shaking with indecision. But then the decision was taken from him.

"Hey! Get on with you!" A hand struck him sharply in the middle of the back and sent him sprawling. "Move along. Your kind don't belong here."

Keros rolled to his feet, his jaw jutting. Majick sizzled through him. He spun and found himself facing the points of four halberds. On the other end were four determined Howlers in dark blue uniforms with high collars, shining black boots, and caped greatcoats. They glowered at him and, as one, they stepped forward, prodding the air before him with their weapons. He was suddenly aware of the scruffiness of his appearance—his long hair, tangled by the wind and weather; his untrimmed beard; his muddy cloak and battered boots. He was not the sort of man who frequented the businesses on Ashford Avenue, nor was he the sort who worked in them.

With instinct born of a life of wariness, he yanked back hard on his majick and pulled his hands up inside the sleeve of his cloak. He ducked his head. "Yessir. Just watchin' th' show."

Someone spat and it hit Keros's boot. "It's not a show, wick-licker. It's a cracking nightmare. Now get outta here before I shorten you by about a head."

Keros bobbed a swift bow and jogged away in the other direction, his chest tight, still hearing the thumping of boots on flesh. His mouth twisted. He'd done nothing. Again. He was a coward. He turned a corner and stopped, leaning against a wall and breathing slowly, pulling his emotions and majick under control. Next time. He would not let it pass next time, and to the depths with the consequences.

As his breathing steadied, he suddenly became aware that majick hung thick in the air. It swirled about in sticky, spiny swirls and sank beneath Keros's clothing, stroking painfully across his skin and making him shudder. It felt *wrong* in a way he couldn't describe. But its touch sent his heart racing like a hunted animal. He

swallowed and felt the majick pulsing from the buildings
lining the avenue. They were smothered in majick—
wards of protection against weather, fire, and attacks;
wards of strengthening and comfort; and more to keep
out bugs and dust. But their majick was . . . if not quite
fraying, then softening. It felt to Keros like thick honey
that had been warmed and had begun to run. Soon the
wards would start to break apart and that could be di-
sastrous. For they wouldn't just dissolve and disappear.
No, their majickal fragments would combine and transform into something else. Or they would smash against
each other and explode wildly. This part of the Riddles
could be leveled.

Keros swallowed, his mouth dry. So far things were
holding, but that could change at any moment. How
long could this wrongness last? He thought of the Pale
and Lucy's warnings. Too long.

He was about to set off across the avenue when
something stopped him. It's wasn't precisely a sound; it
was more the impression that there ought to have been
sound. He turned his head, trying to hear.

A fine molten threading spiderwebbed across the inside of his skull. It burned like venom and made him reel.
He staggered back against a tree and clutched the rough
bark with clawed fingers. It was a spell—or rather, the
side effect of one. Using majick always caused a ripple
effect that disrupted other spells, unless contained within
a smother room. It was like a ghost of the original spell,
but unpredictable both in the form it would take and
what it could do, especially if it insinuated bits away from
other spells or collided with other ghost spells. Careful
majicars planned for the ripple effect and found ways to
harness or contain it. Sometimes it wasn't possible.

This one was strong—violent even. His knees sagged
as pain ripped through him. He clenched his teeth, heat
enveloping him in a smothering fist. What *was* this?

He yanked at the laces of his shirt and freed his *illidre*, grasping it tightly and invoking its powerful shield spell. Instantly the pain faded, the majick curling away like burnt hair. He sucked in a harsh breath and straightened, his legs trembling. His skin was feverish and his entire body felt desiccated.

The majick continued to bombard him. It came in steady waves and there was no dodging it—there was simply too much and it expanded as it gnawed away bits of majick from every spell it passed. Each time a wave rolled over him, Keros's *illidre* pushed it away. But he could feel the ghost majick eroding the shield, nibbling away at the structure of it. He reached in and strengthened it, then began to trail the majick back to its source. He had no other choice.

It led him northwest on an angle leading away from the Lily house. He strode quickly, repairing the shield spell every twenty steps. He stumbled over the uneven ground, climbing over a stile spanning a stone wall. Beyond, the ground dropped away sharply. A set of crumbling steps provided the route downward. At the bottom, several paths spoked away and quickly wriggled out of sight between hovels. Keros stood a moment to take his bearings, then followed the middle one.

Fear crept up his spine on beetle feet. He swallowed and repaired the shield spell again. Since the Kalpestrine had fallen, even properly constructed spells twisted strangely. It was like the rules of majick had changed. But that wasn't the worst of it. Using majick now seemed to do something inside the majicar's mind. It was a numb feeling, like part of himself didn't belong to him anymore. He'd avoided using his own majick as much as possible, hoping that the strangeness would pass. But now he had no choice, and couldn't help but wonder what it was doing to him. His stomach tightened and he continued on.

At this time of the morning, there should have been a bustle in the Riddles, but it was deserted. There wasn't even a stray cat or rat. A clatter behind him made him start. He spun around. A handful of roof tiles had fallen. Now he noticed that the weeds thrusting up between the buckled cobblestones were vibrating. As he watched, the house beside him shifted with a grating groan. Keros turned and bolted. Just in time. A moment later, the house collapsed with a thunderous roar. A cloud of dust billowed in the air. Keros coughed and continued on, hoping that no one had been inside. It was a frail hope.

The majick trail took him over the Ferradon River to the edge of the Riddles. He paused at the stone bridge. It arched over the swift-running river in a graceful span and was wide enough for two carriages to pass without touching. At some point the original stone rails had been replaced with wrought iron, which now was rusting and flaking away. The road across was in good repair, however, because the businesses on Ashford Avenue used this bridge for their supply wagons.

As he watched, the bridge twitched. But the trail led to the other side. Keros started over in a quick jog. The wind gusted and rain slapped his face as his hood slipped off his head. He crested the span and stopped dead.

The bridge ended in a broad roundabout on the other bank. A half-dozen streets fed into it. Normally this was a bustling market. On the fringe of the Riddles, it attracted the denizens of Sylmont. Here was where you could buy a vast array of smuggled and illegal things. Except now the carts and tents were flattened and debris littered the area as if a tornado had struck but moments ago.

As he watched, a streak of majick erupted from the mouth of one of the streets. It disappeared up an opposite street. Keros waited for the sound of an impact, but there was only eerie silence. Then suddenly a ball of ma-

jick floated out of the second street opening and floated
gently toward the first. Before it got there, the sickly
green bubble burst. Droplets of majick sprayed outward
and dripped down on the ground. Where it landed, stone
bubbled and ran in thick, viscous trickles. The side of a
bakery sweated away and the wall crumpled with a wet,
grating sound. A bed tumbled from the third floor and
screams from within echoed and then cut off sharply.

Ghost majick swirled away from the two spells. They
tangled together and found a weaving, then drifted away,
this time toward Sylmont's city center. Keros bit the
tip of his tongue, tasting blood. What in the holy black
depths was happening?

He scuttled forward, feeling too exposed on the
bridge. He reached the other side and dropped to a
crouch beside the pier anchoring the bridge to the bank
of the river. More majick erupted from the two streets.
Different colors this time—gray and orange. The gray
flung itself out in sticky strands. The orange meandered
over the ground like a blind animal, nosing its way across
the roundabout. The two majicks collided and flames
erupted. Black greasy smoke billowed and tumbled
down close to the ground, spreading outward in a thick,
menacing cloud. Keros gripped his *illidre*, feeding the
shield spell as he drew a deep breath and held it, closing his eyes tight. The smoke enveloped him. It was cold
and it groped his exposed skin with a corrosive touch.
Blisters spread over face and ears, traveling down his
neck and over his hands. The grains dribbled past and
the smoke settled slowly, flowing away like water draining out of a tub. It slid down his chest and thighs and lay
across the ground like a sulfurous mist.

Keros let out the breath he was holding with a gasp.
His face was on fire. The blisters on his eyelids split
open and seeped as he blinked. He pushed to his feet
and staggered forward. It didn't take guild-schooling to

realize that what was happening was a majicar battle. It was unheard of—it was insane. Yet it could be nothing else. He had to stop this—somehow—before they leveled Sylmont and killed everyone inside the city.

He crossed to the middle of the roundabout, standing between the two streets where the battling majicars hid from one another. From the left, a thin scarlet skein of majick rolled out, spinning through the air like a corkscrew. Fury swelled in Keros. He reached for his majick, drawing deep. He didn't try for finesse. His cardinal affinities were Stone and Water. He wove them together with Bone, Stillness, and Ice, forming a massive club. It glimmered blue and white. With it, he battered the twisting scarlet spell, smashing it to pieces with brutal determination, knowing that the recoil on the casting majicar would be painful, if not fatal. He did the same to the streamer of green majick that unrolled like a ribbon of silk on his right. The attacking majicars were either getting tired, or they were not masters; Keros shattered their spells easily.

"If you don't want to die today, come out of your holes now!" he shouted hoarsely.

A peculiar *something* licked his mind. It was not painful, but not entirely comfortable either. He shook his head, watching the two street entrances balefully.

At last there was a rattle of stones and flicker of movement from the left. Two figures slowly emerged, one half carrying the second. A moment later a single woman emerged from the other street. She limped and wove back and forth as if drunk. She stopped a dozen paces away from Keros, staring belligerently. She was filthy, her clothes torn and muddy, her face covered with scratches and bruises. Her pale hair was singed and her lips were pulpy, like she'd been chewing them hard. Her eyes gleamed with majickal fire and her body shook with coruscating tremors. Her *illidre*, shaped like a moon moth, hung from her neck on a silver chain.

"Who are you?" she rasped. "What right have you to interfere?"

Keros snarled. "I am a master majicar and I will not let you destroy the city." He glanced at the other two majicars who slumped to the ground. Both were men. One had passed out, blood seeping from his ears and nose. The other swayed back and forth, his eyes wide as he stared at his filthy opponent. He was equally dirty. His hands were swollen and bloody like he'd been smashing them against stone walls. Like the woman majicar, his eyes glowed with majickal fire. None of the three wore coats or cloaks.

Keros licked his lips, not letting go of his majick. He didn't like this at all. Majick *didn't* make eyes glow. Except that clearly it did. What was happening?

"Who are you? What is your fight about?" he asked.

The female majicar's right hand curved into a claw and she yanked it back and up as if about to throw something.

"Stop it now," Keros ordered. "I'll kill you if I have to."

She glared at him and her eyes flared orange. She shifted and even as she flung her hand forward, he smashed her with his majick. She slammed to the ground with a crackling sound as her bones snapped. Keros swallowed the bile that rose in his throat and spun to face the other majicar who continued to sway. He'd begun to sing—no, he was chanting, Keros realized. Gray majick coiled like vines around the kneeling majicar's hands. Keros didn't wait. He struck with his majick and the other man smashed to the ground, his body twisting, his bones snapping like the female majicar.

Keros stared at his handiwork, panting raggedly. Slowly he pulled his majick back in. He went to where

the third majicar lay still breathing. Keros squatted beside him, gripping his chin and turning his head. The
other man blinked. Majick fire swirled red in his eyes.
He was insane. They all were. Biting his lower lip, Keros
pulled the dagger from his belt and found the artery at
the majicar's neck. He didn't give himself time to consider, but jabbed his blade into the man's throat and
jerked. Blood fountained and spattered Keros's hand
and face. His mouth twisted and he wiped at the warm
liquid with the back of his arm, and was glad of the cold
rain.

He stood up, turning in a slow circle. Faces peered
out from windows. Slowly, his body feeling like he was
a hundred seasons old, Keros bent and wiped his knife
clean on the man's shirt. He straightened and headed
back for the bridge. He was shaking. Cold condensed
into ice inside him. He'd killed men twice before. But
never like this. What had happened to them? What was
the majick doing to them?

Again he felt the phantom brush of *something* inside
his mind and felt his prick swell in instant response. Keros recoiled from the reaction. His stomach clenched
into a hard ball and he tightened his hand on the hilt of
his dagger. But he couldn't stab the thing in his mind,
and he had a bad feeling that using his majick would
only feed it.

"Sweet Meris," he swore softly. Had that intimate
touch in his mind driven those other majicars to madness? *Please the gods, no*.

It took most of a glass to reach the Lily safe house.
Keros found himself having to rest, which only made
him an inviting target for thieves and brigands. Once he
was forced to use his majick to drive them off, and then
he forced himself to keep moving, despite his weakness.
Outside the safe house, he keyed open the wards. The
bricks at the dead end of the alley vanished. He hesi-

tated, seeing two horses, then went inside and resealed the entrance.

He gave the two big animals a wide berth and slipped quietly inside the house, only to find the point of a rapier pressing against his throat. His eyes widened as he realized that the rapier was held by none other than Nicholas Weverton.

"How did you get in here?" he asked in sharp surprise.

"I was invited," came the cool reply. He didn't take his eyes or his sword off Keros as he called over his shoulder, "Margaret! I think your friend has arrived." He looked Keros up and down. "Though I think you may need more help than we do," he muttered.

The majicar slumped back against the door as Margaret appeared in the doorway of the dormitory. She was dressed in close-fitting black clothing that was nothing like her usual ornate dresses, and the side of her face was red and creased as if she'd been sleeping.

"Keros!" She ran forward, pushing Nicholas's arm away. "What happened to you?" She lifted his arm over her shoulder and helped him to a chair by the table, then pulled off his wet cloak. She stood back, frowning at him, one hand brushing the air near his cheek. "What happened to your face?"

He reached up and touched his fingers to his cheeks, wincing at the flare of pain. He'd forgotten the blisters caused by the black smoke. Now his skin throbbed as if on fire. He felt weak as a kitten.

"Build a fire," Margaret said to Weverton before snatching up a basin and pushing out of the door to fetch water.

Keros was stunned to see Crosspointe's most wealthy man and one of the Rampling family's greatest enemies obey her command. He went to kneel by the potbellied stove and rolled up his sleeves. He shoveled in coal

and then lit it with a match from a basket on the shelf
just above. He was blowing on the growing flames when
Margaret bustled back inside.

She set the basin on the table and found a rag. She
dipped it into the water and began dabbing at Keros's
face. He flinched away and she grabbed his chin firmly.

"Sit still."

He obeyed, closing his eyes and leaning back.

"See if you can find some tea," she told Weverton. "I
know I want a cup."

Once again Keros heard the other man obey. "What's
he doing here?" he asked Margaret.

"The regent has kidnapped his son. I was hoping you
could help us rescue him," she said bluntly.

"That's what you had to do?" he asked. He whistled
softly. "Ryland's head is going to explode when you tell
him this." Then, "Weverton has a son?" He jerked as she
brushed over a particularly painful spot.

"I do," came the husky baritone response. "Though
I've kept him a secret."

"Wise," Keros said.

"It would have been, if I had been successful." Weverton's voice was taut with worry and anger.

Margaret finished her ministrations then and Keros opened his eyes. She frowned at him. "You need a
healer."

He gave a short, adamant shake of his head. "No."

That surprised her. "Why not? What happened?"

Keros hesitated, glancing first at Weverton and then
Margaret. He'd spent his life hiding what he was. It was
difficult to baldly reveal himself in front of a stranger.
To his surprise, Margaret nodded for him to continue his
story. When he had finished recounting his adventure,
his two listeners stared soberly.

"What was wrong with them?" Nicholas asked finally.

Keros shook his head. "Since the Kalpestrine fell,

majick has been acting strangely. I have wondered . . ." He trailed away. He had never been in the Kalpestrine and knew almost nothing about what was inside it. Nor was he a registered majicar. He had no grounds to offer opinions.

"What?" Margaret demanded.

Keros gave a reticent shrug. "It is nothing."

"Crack that. Tell me."

He started to rub his hand over his forehead and stopped when he touched his bubbled, seeping skin. Pain and then a rabid itching rolled over his face. He grimaced. Nicholas rose and took the kettle off the stove. He poured three cups of strong black tea and handed them around before sitting down again. He watched Keros from beneath lowered brows.

"When a spell is cast, it creates a kind of a ripple effect—a ghost spell. That majick is formed into a kind of spell, but it is usually twisted. It disrupts other spells nearby, tearing down their structures or sticking to them and turning them into something new.

"Inside a smother room, that majick is absorbed and nullified. Outside, majicars usually create a way of capturing it, otherwise spells would fail or change and become something else—as the problem grows, there would be increasing mayhem as loose ghost spells triggered more spell failures."

He sipped his tea. "I believe that the fall of the Kalpestrine did two things. First, I believe that layered into it were spells that collected that ghost majick for all registered majicars—those who had ties to the Kalpestrine itself. Obviously, it is no longer doing so and I'm not certain that any majicars think to gather it up themselves; they've never had to. If I am correct," he added.

"And the second thing?" Nicholas prodded.

Keros rubbed a finger around the top of his mug. "The Kalpestrine was full of majick. When it fell, all of

that was torn apart and released. What if that created a
mass of ghost spells that are attacking all the other spells
in Crosspointe? With every one that breaks or combines
to make something else, new ghost spells are created. If
that is the case, then those spells are feeding on the majick in Sylmont and multiplying. The pressure will build,
like steam in a kettle, until it bursts."

"By the gods," Margaret murmured, then thrust to
her feet and paced back and forth along the length of
the table. She turned, bracing her hands on the back of
a chair. "What is happening to the majicars? Why were
they battling? Why did they try to attack you?"

He shook his head. "I don't know. I've never seen majick burn in the eyes like that. It might be that something
happened just to those four and it's not going to happen
to anyone else."

But he knew better. Something was in his head. It had
come in a door made using majick. He didn't know what
it was, but doubted he or the majicars he'd killed were
unique. He simply had to use his majick less.

"What do we do about this ghost majick?" Margaret
looked at Weverton first, then to Keros.

"It may not be ghost majick," he pointed out. "I am
an unregistered majicar. I know almost nothing about
the Kalpestrine.

She just gave him a long steady look. He flushed and
averted his eyes. She did not tolerate fools, and she demanded truth.

"Well? There has to be something that can be done."

She caught her breath audibly, then stopped before
she spoke, her eyes heavy on Keros. He knew what she
was thinking. Lucy. He gave a faint shake of his head.
Weverton couldn't know about her. And Lucy wasn't
going to be able to help. He thought of what she had
said—that there was something wrong with majick.

Maybe there was more going on; maybe the Kalpestrine's fall had done more than he knew.

"You said his son has been kidnapped?" Keros asked, gesturing toward Weverton.

Margaret nodded, letting him change the subject. "When I was in the castle, I found correspondence indicating that the regent had the boy kidnapped. He plans to keep him as a hostage against your good behavior," she said to Weverton.

"My good what? No. He trusts me. You are lying." Then more quietly, "Or perhaps mistaken."

She hesitated, then reached into a pocket, and withdrew a folded piece of parchment. She stared at it a moment and tossed it across the table to Weverton. He snatched it up and flattened it out, scanning it quickly.

"The cracking bastard," he muttered with quiet violence, his face turning white.

"No disagreements here," Margaret said, her voice accusing.

Weverton's head snapped up and he glowered at her a moment, then returned to reading the page. He read it twice before slapping his hand down on it. "We must go."

"He's not going to kill Carston. He needs the boy alive. We have time."

"Then I'll go without you."

"Fine. Go. Good luck." She went to the door and thrust it open. "You know if the regent sees an army coming at him, he'll kill Carston. You need to sneak in and steal him. I'm very good at that sort of thing, but of course, you have more trustworthy people at your disposal who are no doubt skilled enough for this sort of thing."

He didn't move. His face was a mask of fury, fear, and indecision. Keros sympathized. Margaret pulled the door shut and marched back to the table. She didn't gloat; it wasn't her nature.

"I know another majicar. She might be willing to help us. It may cost you."

"Anything," Nicholas said heavily.

Margaret smiled unpleasantly. "Careful. I don't know what she'll ask. She is no friend of mine."

Keros frowned, wondering who the majicar was. Margaret looked at him. "Would you come with us to meet her? Just in case."

"In case of what?" Weverton demanded.

"In case we have to kill her," Margaret said without even a hint of a smile.

Chapter 6

Nicholas was reeling from Keros's revelations and Margaret's last announcement. He still had difficulty imagining her killing anyone, though he'd seen her fighting off the brigands in the alley. He followed her out to the courtyard with Keros trailing behind. The majicar was unsteady on his feet and he glowered at the horses.

"You can't ride those into Sylmont," he said.

"I know," Margaret replied. "We'll take a hack and return for them later."

She glanced at Nicholas and he nodded. Soon the three of them were walking back up toward the Ferradon River. They went slowly, Margaret taking Keros's arm to steady him. Nicholas kept his hand on the hilt of his rapier, scanning ahead for trouble and turning frequently to watch their trail. The closest bridge over the river was outside the Riddles in Cranford—more than half a league away. They'd be able to find a hack there.

The rain fell steadily, the wind gusting now and again. Nicholas's mind tumbled madly over the events of the night and all that he'd learned. Primary in his mind was Carston. The fact that Geoffrey had taken him to guarantee Nicholas's cooperation meant that he was up to something—something he knew Nicholas would fight him on. But what? He had no idea and that bothered him. How could Geoffrey hide anything big enough to warrant this action so well from Nicholas's spies? And then this business of the majicars—if they were being driven insane, then Crosspointe was in real danger from them. And even if they weren't a concern, the ghost spells were—if Keros was right. But the majicar's logic seemed sound. He made a compelling case. What could possibly be done about it? Nicholas would have to consult his own majicars.

His thoughts spun to Margaret. Her tactics were straightforward enough—she'd help him get his son back and he'd owe her, enough to go against all he'd worked for by putting her family back on the throne. Would he do it? He grimaced. What wouldn't he do for his son? He glanced at her, still marveling at her transformation. How often had she been inside his house and he'd never known? What secrets of his had she ferreted out over the years? And all this time he'd only seen the simpering young miss, as dull as dishwater and clever as mud. He was a fool. And not just about her, but about Geoffrey as well. He felt like everything he thought he'd been certain of was crumbling to ash, and he'd been too stupid to know it.

That thought brought him back to his son and Geoffrey. Once they retrieved Carston, Geoffrey would have no reason to hide his plotting from Nicholas anymore. Which meant he would no doubt come after the Weverton empire, confiscating whatever he could get his hands on and putting every Weverton he could find in an iron collar. His mouth twisted. If Geoffrey wanted a war, Nicholas would give him one. No one went after his family, his only son, with impunity. He might not help put a Rampling back on the throne, but as sure as the black depths, he'd make Geoffrey pay.

He glanced again at Margaret and found her looking at him. Her expression was knowing and there was no triumph in it. For that he was grateful.

They found a hack near the corner of Chalky Street and Trisfield Lane. They bundled Keros quickly inside so that no one would see his ruined face and Margaret called out the address: the Spotted Lace Teahouse in Blackstone.

Margaret and Keros sat opposite to Nicholas. Keros leaned into the corner and fell almost instantly asleep as the hack rattled over the cobblestones.

"Where did you find him?" he asked Margaret, nodding at the majicar.

She shook her head, swiping the rain from her face with her sleeve. Not a question she was willing to answer. He tried a different tack. "Do you think he's right about these ghost spells?"

She shrugged. "It sounds plausible. If it's true ..." She trailed away with a helpless twist of her hand. "I hope he's wrong," she said. "And what will you do about your friend the regent? He'll come after you the way he's come after us Ramplings." She folded her arms. "Some would say that you are a fool to tip your hand. Some would say you should let him keep the boy while you make arrangements to eliminate Truehelm."

She was right. His lip curled. "I will not leave my son in that bastard's hands longer than I have to."

"That's stupid."

"Perhaps."

She tipped her head back, watching him from beneath lowered lids. He couldn't read her expression.

"My father would not have come for any of us," she said. "Any more than Ryland or Vaughn will stop the slave auctions of our family. Not until they are ready to attack the regent and defeat him. Crosspointe always comes first."

Nicholas didn't answer. He didn't know what to say to that. He'd worked to discredit and undermine her father for years. He'd thought the man lacked foresight

and was too bent on clinging to outdated policies instead
of embracing the future. He had also ignored the Jutras
threat, and had been too complacent about believing
the Inland Sea would forever provide a barrier against
invasion. He'd been criminally wrong and nine months
ago Queen Naren had paid the price with her life when
the Jutras had managed to send a ship into Blackwater
Bay. The captured Jutras had all been majicars and had
escaped their prison, infiltrating the castle and attacking
the throne room. The official story that was told later
was that the Crown Shields had fought back, side by
side, with several Rampling family majicars who happened to be in the castle that day.

But it was a lie. Nicholas had paid well for the stories
of those who had been in the throne room and witnessed
the attack. The Jutras majicars had begun casting a spell
that involved dreadful human sacrifice. They killed two
people, carving them up alive before they were stopped
by a single powerful majicar, a woman everyone had
thought was dead.

Lucy Trenton, a niece of the king, had been convicted
of treason and murder and sentenced to be exposed
on the Bramble during Chance. She'd been sent on the
Bramble ship, but even before the first Chance storms
struck, she returned with powerful majickal abilities.
She stopped the Jutras spell, allowing the Crown Shields
to destroy the invaders.

She'd not been seen since. Margaret's father had no
doubt been keeping her in his pocket—his own private
majicar to use at will, and by all accounts, a very powerful one.

Nicholas rubbed his thumb along his lower lip, forcing himself to consider Margaret's words. In truth, King
William had had a much stronger backbone than he did
when it came to family. But there were sacrifices Nicholas was unwilling to make—sacrifices that perhaps a

king must make. But that was only another argument for why there should be no monarchy in Crosspointe. There should be a council made up of representatives from the guilds and merchants—the people themselves.

He became aware that she was looking at him as if awaiting an answer. There was something about her that demanded honesty and he found it hard to resist.

"I put no one above my family," he said at last.

A smile flickered across her lips and was gone. "I know."

That piqued his curiosity. "What else do you know about me?"

"Enough."

He sat forward. "And yet I am disconcerted to discover how little I know about you. Not nearly enough, I find. Tell me about yourself."

The request surprised her. Her mouth pursed as she thought. She shook her head. "I have revealed far too much to you already."

The sharp spear of disappointment at her words startled him. He *wanted* to know her. She intrigued him. He sat back again, his expression shuttering as he considered his reaction. He enjoyed women. He liked their company and he liked them in his bed. But he wanted no attachments and his relationships lasted no more than a month or two at best before he found another companion. Carston's mother had been the exception. She was both lovely and smart—an artisan who worked with glass. But both she and he had known it was a relationship of companionship and the bedroom—nothing more. Carston had been an unpleasant surprise for her and a joyful one for him. After the boy's birth, Nicholas had given her a generous settlement and they'd gone their separate ways, though they remained on friendly terms.

But Margaret stirred him in a way he'd not experienced before. She made him curious and angry and confused. He was drawn to her brashness—a side of her he had never suspected. He admired her cool nerve and her loyalty. She was brave—reckless even. He wanted to know how she'd become her father's spy and perhaps assassin and thief. What was it like to hide behind the demure mask of beauty she habitually wore? He wondered what books she liked to read and whether she could use a sword as well as she could use her knife. He wondered if she had a lover.

He found his jaw tightening at the notion, and for a brief moment wondered what it would like to be in her bed. *Don't be ridiculous*, he told himself firmly. *She is a Rampling and bedding her would be sheer idiocy.* All the same, he felt himself hardening as he considered what her skin would feel like . . .

They said nothing more as the hack clattered through Cranford and Cheapside and up into Blackstone. By the time they pulled up, the rain was pounding on the roof and the wind had begun to blow harder.

"You and Keros should wait for me here," Margaret said as she prepared to get out.

"I don't like it," Nicholas said. "You said this majicar was not your friend. I'm coming with you." His tone brooked no arguments. He donned his hat and reached for the door handle.

"If you like." She nudged Keros awake. He sat up groggily, his hood falling back to reveal his scabrous face. "We'll be back," she told him. "Try not to get into any trouble while we're gone."

He smiled wearily. "I don't promise anything."

She hesitated. "Thanks. You know my brothers will have kittens about this. They'll probably send me to the Bramble."

The majicar covered her hand with his. "Then we'll run away together. Somewhere warm."

She grinned at him and kissed his cheek. "Just you and me."

"We are wasting time," Nicholas said sharply, unaccountably annoyed. She frowned and followed him out of the door. He held out a hand to help her out. She looked at it and ignored it, jumping lightly down. He shut the door and told the driver to wait while Margaret dashed inside the shop.

It was a cozy place and large. It was past the tenth glass and most of the tables were full. The smell of baking pastries and fragrant tea made Nicholas's mouth water. Their makeshift meal in the safe house had been at least five glasses ago. Margaret scanned the tables, settling on one near the window. A woman sat there. She was only slightly taller than Margaret, with blond hair that was pulled back from her face in a braid. Her eyes were brown, her face triangular and sharp featured. She met Margaret's glance with raised brows and pointed to the chair opposite.

Margaret wound between the tables without removing her cloak. Nicholas followed, keeping his hat pulled low. There were murmurs of annoyance as they dripped water on the other patrons and the floor. They stopped at the woman majicar's table. There was a pot of tea in front of her, a pitcher of cream, and a half-drunk cup. A plate covered with crumbs was pushed to the side.

"I had begun to think you were not coming," she said to Margaret.

"I almost didn't."

"And who is your gentleman friend?"

Margaret glanced at him, then back. "I'll introduce him later. Are you ready to go?"

The majicar's brows winged downward. "Go where?"

"Outside in a hack for now."

"And after that?"

"Better we discuss it outside."

Margaret didn't wait for an answer. She turned and pushed past Nicholas, going to the counter. She ordered a basket of muffins and rolls, fishing a small purse out of her clothing. She gathered the paper-wrapped parcels and went to the door. The majicar waited. She was dressed in sturdy clothing, tall boots, and a gray oilskin cloak lined with wool. Margaret swept past without a word.

"Ashford Avenue," she told the driver and then climbed into the hack to sit beside Keros.

Nicholas gestured at the woman majicar to precede him, settled himself on the seat beside her, and removed his hat.

"What's this about?" she demanded as Margaret tore open the package of pastries and offered them first to Keros and then to Nicholas before taking one for herself.

"It's about a job," Margaret said before biting into a poppy-seed cake

"A job?"

"That's right."

"What kind?"

"Stealing."

The majicar woman folded her arms. "And what are we going to steal?"

"My son," Nicholas said. "He's been kidnapped. We're going to get him back."

The majicar looked at him. "I didn't think you had a son."

That took him aback. "You know who I am?"

"Doesn't everyone?" Her attention shifted to Margaret. "And you are helping him? That is unexpected."

"Who are you?" Margaret demanded suddenly. "Before this goes any further, I want to know who you are and why you were in the castle working as a lady's maid for Alanna Truehelm. Why did you help me?"

The majicar shook her head. "That is for your ears alone. At least for now."

There was a vague threat in that "for now," as if she had information that she might share with Margaret's enemies—Rampling enemies, like Nicholas. His mouth twisted. Just at the moment, he didn't care to be lumped in with them, especially Geoffrey Truehelm.

"Fine," Margaret snapped. Before she could say any more, Keros convulsed in the seat beside her. His hands flailed and his feet kicked. His fist connected with Margaret's cheek and she lurched sideways. Nicholas caught her and she jerked away just as Keros slumped over.

"What's wrong with him?" the woman majicar asked.

Margaret pushed him back. Nicholas reached out his hand to help steady him. Keros's head lolled back and his hood fell away. His skin appeared about the same. Many of the blisters had broken and wept; his face looked as if someone had taken a vegetable grater to it. His hands were the same.

"He's feverish," Margaret said, her fingers brushing the air above his forehead. "I can feel it from here."

"What happened to him?" the majicar woman asked and her tone was crisp and businesslike.

"It was a majick attack," Margaret said. "He was shielded, but—" She shrugged. "Can you help him?"

The woman lifted her brows. "You trust me?"

"If you hurt him I will kill you," was Margaret's flat response.

"I can try. I may fail. I am not a master and majick does not work as it should."

"Do it."

"Open his shirt. I need bare skin," she said.

Margaret unfastened Keros's coat and unlaced his shirt, pulling it wide. His skin was pale and muscled. He was not a soft man.

The majicar reached inside her tunic and pulled out her *illidre*. It was a slender rod about five inches long. The ends were slanted and smooth, the sides faceted. It was a cloudy mix of purple and dark blue with specks of dark pink. She held it cupped between her palms, looking deep inside it. A moment passed, then she gripped it in one hand and pressed the other flat end against Keros's chest.

A thread of green grew from her fingers, curling like vines across dirt, then they spread out and burrowed into his skin. The unconscious man jerked and went rigid. The majicar woman drew a gasping breath, her jaw knotting. Margaret's fingers knitted together, her knuckles white. Nicholas had no comfort to offer. He could only watch.

The majicar's fingers stiffened and gouged into Keros's chest. Sweat gleamed on her forehead. A minute dribbled past. Another. Finally the skin on Keros's face began to smooth, the blisters closing and shrinking until his skin was unblemished. When she was through, the majicar gave a gasping sob and slumped back against the seat, panting, her eyes closed.

Margaret rested her hand on Keros's head. "The fever is gone."

"He was dying. It wasn't majick. He was poisoned."

"Thank you, Ellyn."

The majicar's eyes opened and her mouth curved. It was like watching a snake smile. "That's twice you owe me." Then her gaze fell on Keros. The smile slid away. She sat up slowly, shock making her look very young. "What is this?" she asked. She looked at Margaret, her gaze as cold and bleak as the bottom of the sea. "How did you do this? Why? What is your game?"

"What do you mean? I have no game with you; I don't know you."

Ellyn's gaze slipped back to Keros as if pulled. "It

is not possible," she whispered, her *illidre* still clutched tight in her hand.

"What isn't?"

Just then Keros's eyes flickered and opened. He stared at Ellyn. He frowned and slowly sat up straight. He reached out a hand, his fingers stopping a breath from her face. They trembled, then jerked away like he was burned. His hands curled into fists. His mouth snapped closed, his face contorting.

"You can't be here," he said, his voice guttural, the words violent. "They didn't pull you out. I saw. I *saw*."

She jerked her head from side to side. "No. I came out. You were gone." There was pain in that last word.

Keros's jaw knotted and he scowled. He looked as if he wanted to break something. "They threw me in and I swam. I was never going back." He paused, his lip curling. "You serve them, don't you?"

She nodded. "I had nothing else."

Margaret interrupted. "Who are you? What's going on? Keros?"

He flinched, glancing first at Margaret then at Nicholas. He leaned back, staring up at the roof of the hack, his mouth drawn tight.

"I was born in Azaire. I lived in a village on the edge of the Verge—as close to the sea as we could be without having to worry about the Chance storms. When I was thirteen seasons old, the Gerent sent soldiers. He had learned the nature of majicars and he intended to make some. He took the entire village—every last one of us— down to the sea. We waited for a *sylveth* tide. When it came, they threw us in one after another. Most of us turned to spawn—my mother, my sisters, my brothers, my cousins . . . No one was spared."

He looked at Ellyn. "I had a friend—the daughter of a neighboring farmer. Her name was Sperray. We were inseparable. I meant to marry her one day. We had already—" He broke off. He reached out for Ellyn again and again pulled away. "I saw them throw her into the *sylveth*. She never came out—at least not in any shape I could recognize. There was spawn everywhere in the waves. They slaughtered them all as they came out." Tears rolled down his face and dampened his beard. "I had lost everything. I had nothing to lose. I tore away from them and ran into the water. I dove under and swam. I felt my transformation and I kept going. Whatever I was to be, they could not have me."

He looked at Margaret, jerking his thumb at Ellyn. "She wears Sperray's face. But it is not possible. It is *not*."

The agony in his voice was wrenching. Nicholas swallowed, thinking of Carston.

Margaret took Keros's hand and looked at Ellyn, asking the question that her friend could not. "*Are* you Sperray?"

Silence. And then slowly, in a voice of iron, "I was once. Now I am only Ellyn."

Keros twisted back around. "You can't be."

"Can't I? Do you remember that day in the tall grass? It was only a month before. We'd finished our chores and we went to swim at the river. Remember our spot? The bank was hollowed out and the bottom was sandy. We stopped on the way to check your rabbit snares. Do you remember what happened next? Do you want me to tell you?"

Keros swallowed hard, holding up a hand as if to stop her words. "I remember," he choked. "Why are you here?" he asked.

"For Azaire," she replied. "That is all."

For a moment he didn't move. Then his expression closed, emotion flattening out into nothing. Nicholas watched the transformation with a deep sense of pity. It was a tragic moment, one that didn't deserve to be witnessed by strangers. He looked down at his boots and then at Margaret. One hand was caught in a fist at her throat, the other was on Keros's shoulder. Her eyes glittered with tears. She blinked them away and the chill, hard mask slipped over her face.

"Then perhaps it's time we got to business," she said to Ellyn. "We want to hire you to help us retrieve Nicholas's son."

"Hire me? Why?"

"Keros is unable and we need a majicar."

"Unable?" Ellyn flicked a look at Keros.

"I will come with you. She is not required," he said.

"No," Margaret said. "It's too risky for you."

She meant the ghost spells and the risk of madness. Clearly the two of them were close and she was unwilling to endanger him further.

"I am fine."

"You're still as weak as a newborn lamb," Nicholas said brusquely. "And we are going by horseback. Can you ride?"

Keros snarled. "No."

"Can you?" he asked Ellyn.

She frowned at Keros a moment, then nodded. "Of course."

"Then it is settled."

"I am not sending Margaret off alone with an Azairian majicar," Keros said emphatically. "I am coming."

Nicholas looked at Margaret. It was her choice. "Very well," she said. "But we'll need another horse."

"You and I will double up," Nicholas said. She eyed him suspiciously. "Together we are lighter than you and Keros. I doubt he'll permit you to ride with Ellyn. There is no time to go back to my manor, and we would have a difficult time sneaking out another mount without being seen. At any rate, we've wasted too much time. We must be on our way as soon as possible. My son cannot wait."

Margaret gave a short nod. "We will need supplies." She knocked on the roof of the hack. A moment later it slowed and stopped. "I'll meet you all at the safe house."

She opened the door and stepped out. Before she could close it, Nicholas slipped out behind her, shutting the door firmly, tossing the driver a coin and waving him on. The hack trundled away.

"What are you doing?" she demanded.

"We'll need more than you can carry alone," he said, taking her arm and pulling it through his as if they were out taking a leisurely stroll. He pulled her beneath the awning of a milliner's. She drew away, turning to face him.

"You left them alone together? After that? They'll kill each other."

He shook his head, sobering. "No, they won't. They need time together without any witnesses." Her eyes widened and he gave her a wry smile. "I am not made out of stone. Contrary to your low opinion of me, I do have a heart."

"Really? Where do you keep it? In a box in a vault somewhere all covered with dust and cobwebs?"

He put a hand on his chest. "You wound me."

"Not possible. Come on. Let's get back before one of them kills the other."

She started to walk away. Once again he grabbed her hand and slid it through the crook of his arm. She tipped her head, giving him a distrustful look.

"Never let it be said that I was not a gentleman," he said.

She rolled her eyes and shook her head, then settled her hand more firmly on his arm. He smiled to himself. It was a beginning.

Chapter 7

Margaret and Weverton slipped out of the hack so abruptly that Keros had no time to call them back. The carriage wheels began rolling again and he was left sitting opposite Sperray— No, Ellyn. She was no more the girl she had been then than he was the boy.

As if reading his mind, she asked, "Keros? Is there some meaning to that name?"

He shrugged stiffly. "After my transformation, I washed up somewhere in Relsea—long before the Jutras conquered it. I had some trouble—I didn't know to glamour my eyes to hide what I was. I had no money, no clothing, nothing. For a while I lived on the headland, snaring rabbits for food. I learned to make fire with my majick and eventually figured out that I had to disguise my eyes, but had to kill two men who thought I was spawn before I did." The memory was an old hurt, savage still. He didn't let the pain color his voice. He wasn't going to give her that. He didn't know who she was anymore; she was here on behalf of the Gerent, who'd done this to the both of them. She was not to be trusted.

"Eventually an old hermit found me. He gave me clothes and I helped him gather salt to sell in Berell. He took me there and I found work at an inn. In time I realized there was no one like me in Relsea. At least, if there was, they were disguising themselves so that no one would know. I needed to go to Crosspointe. I found passage on a tramper—I worked the season before they anchored in Blackwater Bay."

"And the name?" she prompted when he didn't speak again.

"It belonged to the hermit." He chewed the inside of his lip. He didn't want to ask. He knew the answer, but hearing it was a different thing. The words came anyway. "My family? Did any survive?"

She averted her face and shook her head. "No. Nor mine."

"How many majicars did they harvest from Etelvayn?" he asked, bitterness sharpening every word to knives. Their village had been small, just under two hundred people.

"Six. Plus you."

"Who?"

She raised her head, her lip curling. "Does it matter?"

"No. I suppose not."

"And now you are one of Crosspointe's majicars," she said. "Lucky you weren't in the Kalpestrine when it fell."

"I was never a member of the Majicar Guild."

Her eyes narrowed. "But you serve the Crown."

"I do," he said, more firmly than he expected. It was a harness that didn't fit and he frequently struggled against it, but he didn't want her knowing that. He didn't know why. "Why are you here?"

"I told you—for Azaire. You lied to them. Why? You were never an ordinary villager."

"I was that day."

She snorted. "You were the middle son of the thane of Etelvayn."

"And it meant nothing," he said.

"If your father had been there . . ." She trailed away.

"He would have shoved us in himself. Even his family was not more important than serving the Gerent." The words were bitter and hot. He'd seen his father little in those thirteen seasons before being sacrificed to the *sylveth* tide. The burly thane of Etelvayn was always needed, whether to push back raids from Kalibri, Glacerie, and Ayvreshar, or to subdue ambitious thanes who thought to overthrow the Gerent. Ryerdal mi Etelvayn had been one of the Gerent's most trusted thanes. He was both loyal and ruthless. Enough to allow his family and villagers to be thrown into the *sylveth*. "He married again, didn't he? He has new heirs. He lost nothing that day."

Her eyes widened. "You believe that?"

"I know it."

She shook her head. "You're wrong. I've seen him. It hurt him dreadfully. I don't think he's forgiven the Gerent."

Keros's face hardened. "I doubt that. He still jumps when the fat bastard crooks his finger."

"How would you know? You ran away," she said disdainfully.

He smiled, tight and thin. "I am not unaware of what happens in Azaire. I will make the Gerent pay one day."

She shook her head. "Better hurry, then, if you want to get there before the Jutras do. They are already pushing into the Gwatney Mountains. It will not be long before they reach the Saithe. The river will not hold them, and we don't have enough majicars to hold them back." The last was accusing.

For a moment his face went slack. "You think I should have stayed and helped Azaire?"

She flushed, but didn't look away. "It's your home," she said. "Even if you hate the Gerent, you love the people and they needed you. They still do."

He laughed, a harsh sound. That didn't even bear answering. "Why are you here? What do you want in Crosspointe?"

"I've come to gather information."

"You want more compasses," Keros said shrewdly.

Her mouth fell open. "You know of the compasses?"

He knew far more than that. Unintentionally and wholly against his will, he'd been dragged into the center of Crosspointe politics. "There are no more," he said quietly.

She recoiled. "You're lying."

"Am I?"

"Azaire needs compasses. We know what Pilots are. But without compasses, we cannot put our ships to sea. King William wanted this alliance. Surely Prince Vaughn and Prelate Ryland will as well."

It was widely assumed that Vaughn would be elected to the throne, if there was ever an election. "Perhaps you should be talking to the regent," he said.

She scoffed. "He will not survive long. This business with Weverton will get him killed all the more quickly. It is better to go to the Ramplings, especially now it appears Weverton is no longer against them."

Keros smiled with real humor. "Margaret is breaking with her family to help Weverton. Her brothers will likely drown her when they discover what she's done."

She shrugged. "It costs me little to help him and I do not mind making trouble for the regent. He and his wife are gutterscum."

"On that, at least, you and I agree," Keros said.

Prickly silence fell between them. He was spinning from seeing her alive, and *here*. His mind drifted unwillingly to that brilliant day when they went off to swim at the river. The insects had been buzzing, and her hand had been warm in his. They were young, and so ready for each other. They had kissed and he had run his fingers over her skin, so hot it was almost feverish. They made love for the first time, there in the grass—swift and desperate at first; the second time slower and more gentle. He still remembered the soft sweep of her tongue on his, the sweet and salty taste of her skin, and the soft, urgent cries they'd both made.

The memory was a knife in his chest. He savagely thrust it from his mind. And not just that one, but all the memories of his life in Etelvayn, from the sound of his mother's voice to the laughter around the dinner table. He wanted none of it.

He intended to stay awake, but found himself dozing despite himself. His battle in the Riddles had taken far more out of him than he liked. He felt the *presence* in his mind. It was coiled and quiet now, but he felt it watching, waiting. For what? For him to use his majick? That would be soon enough.

He woke again when the hack stopped. He blinked groggily. Ellyn was watching him, her face expressionless. He sat up and reached for the handle and stumbled down the steps. The rain was falling heavily. A stream ran down the middle of the street and puddles abounded. Keros didn't bother to offer Ellyn his hand. He turned to pay the driver and then wordlessly started away. He wound a circuitous route to the safe house. They were followed a short way by two women with sagging, withered bodies sporting bruises on their faces. Keros turned and glared at them and then walked on. They didn't follow farther.

The two majicars slipped inside the safe house without any more adventures. As he keyed the wards, Keros half expected that the thing in his mind would rouse, but it remained quiescent. The entrance opened sluggishly and closed more so. He shook his head. What was happening to the majick?

He circled the horses, who nickered and scraped

their hooves on the courtyard pavement. It wasn't that he didn't know how to ride. In fact he'd started riding when he was but three seasons old, sitting in front of his father, brother, or mother; later he had his own pony, followed by a spirited horse. But horses belonged to his old life and the boy he used to be. Now he wanted nothing to do with them.

"You told them you couldn't ride," Ellyn observed as she followed him inside.

"I haven't since—" He resisted the urge to spit. "I don't anymore. I doubt I remember."

"It isn't something you forget."

"I can try," he said and stirred the fire before putting more tea on. He rifled through the shelves for something to eat. He wasn't that hungry, but he needed to be busy. He put on some rice and stirred in dried apricots, raisins, cinnamon, salt, pepper, and a pinch of shifta grown in Beynto dal Corus for a little heat. He stirred it as it began to boil, aware of Ellyn wandering aimlessly about.

"How strong are you?" she asked suddenly. "Are you a master?"

"How can I be? I'm not in the guild," he said. "Only the Majicar Guild can name you a master in Crosspointe."

She snorted at his prevarication. "If you were?"

He blew out a breath. What did it matter? "Then I'd be a master." He looked at her, brows raised "You?"

She shook her head, chin raised, eyes snapping. "I'm a journeyman. There are few master majicars in Azaire." It was an accusation.

"That's because you are too far from the sea," he said. "*Sylveth* is what gave you your majick and it's what feeds it. Why do you think the Kalpestrine was outside the Pale?"

"I am no stronger here than I was in Azaire."

"Then maybe you were a meant to be a journeyman."

"You should come home. Azaire needs you."

He gave a sharp shake of his head. "No. It is not my home. I never lived there. I was born in the *sylveth* and Azaire means nothing to me."

When the rice was done, he spooned it into two bowls. Ellyn took hers and sat as far as she could get from him.

"This is good."

"Don't sound so surprised," he said dryly.

"I never thought I would ever see you cook anything," she said.

"I enjoy it and I don't have servants. Either I feed myself or I starve. It seemed wise to learn to cook something edible." He smiled, happy enough to talk about something harmless. "It has come in handy. For many seasons I served aboard ship. I healed those who needed it and in return, they kept my secret. During the second season, the ship's cook went overboard in a storm. I volunteered to man the galley and they were pleasantly surprised to find me capable. I remained their cook until—"

"Until?" she prompted.

"Until recently. When I got involved with the Ramplings."

"How did that happen?"

He shook his head. "Not a story for Azaire, I think. But you may ask Margaret if you like."

His words shut the door on any more conversation. They each finished eating and drank their tea. Margaret and Weverton had still not returned and Keros went to lie on one of the bunks in the other room. He had a feeling there would be little enough opportunity to sleep in the next few days and felt heavy with exhaustion.

A hand on his shoulder woke him. He sat up groggily.

"Time to go," Margaret said. Her voice dropped and
she sat beside him. Her hair was wet and her cheeks
were flushed. She reached up and brushed his unruly
hair away from his eyes. "Are you all right?"

He wanted to dismiss the question with a casual af-
firmative, but it was pointless. As little time as they'd
known each other, she understood him. They were very
much alike. "I'll survive," he said finally.

The corner of her mouth rose in a wry smile. "There's
something to be said for celibacy. No nasty surprises
turning up later."

He chuckled. "There's something to be said for a willing woman and a warm bed, also."

"True. But it's risky."

He sobered and glanced through the doorway. Weverton was watching them. He was scowling.

"I don't think your friend likes you sitting on my bed
with me," he murmured.

"My friend?" She glanced behind and then back at
Keros, disbelief coloring her voice. "You are maggot-
brained."

"I don't think so."

"I do. Come on. We've a long way to go."

She stood and Keros followed her out, aware of
Weverton's brooding gaze. Keros suppressed the urge
to laugh. Nicholas Weverton had his prick in a knot over
Margaret Rampling. The gods were laughing.

Outside the horses were already saddled and loaded
with fat packs and rolled blankets inside oilskin sheets.
Weverton went to his bay and mounted, reaching out an
imperious hand to Margaret. She eyed it a moment, then
took his hand and leaped up behind him.

"I guess that leaves us," Keros said without looking at
Ellyn. "Front or back."

"I'm the one who knows how to ride," she said sardonically, and swung up on the gray. She dropped her foot out of the stirrup and Keros put his toe in and pulled himself up behind. He settled his hands on the cantle. He was reluctant to touch her. He didn't let himself think about why.

Weverton wheeled the bay and Margaret opened the ward. This time the gate didn't open fully, though there was room enough to squeeze through. As he closed the ward, Keros boosted it with his own majick. It shut quickly and the thing in his mind twitched and settled.

They trotted out into the alley and broke into a canter. The rain was still falling heavily, enough to cover the noise of their passing. They left the Riddles and passed through Cranford. Before long Keros felt his legs start to ache as he clamped his thighs tightly. Ellyn was right—his body remembered how to ride. He felt tears burn in his eyes as he squeezed them shut. The memories didn't want to stop with riding, but fled to the stables and racing out along the flats and from there moved to faces and sounds. He choked on a sob, his fingers clawing into the leather.

The next turns of the glass were an agonizing journey through the memories of his childhood. Every one was drenched in the horror of that day when the Gerent's soldiers had come, of watching them march the villagers into the sea in groups of ten, and the carnage as the spawn came wriggling and crawling out of the waves, only to be hacked to pieces. But the soldiers did not stop their dreadful project and slowly the villagers were decimated.

How many more villages had vanished the same way? How many majicars had the Gerent required before he stopped? The thoughts made Keros want to puke. But, no. He caught himself in a hard grip. No. It was an old story and old pain. It no longer belonged to him. It belonged to the middle son of Ryerdal of Etelvayn who had died some fourteen seasons ago. Keros was a different man—not really a man at all. He was spawn.

He released the memories and the unbearable pain, letting them wash away with the sheeting rain, and relaxed into the rhythm of the horse.

The spare mare was tied beneath a traveler pine. She was a red chestnut with white socks. She whinnied ringingly as they approached. They all dismounted and Weverton set about saddling her. He spoke softly and rubbed her down with a rag before unrolling her saddle from its oilskin sheet. Within a few minutes she was tacked up and ready to go. Weverton handed the reins to Keros.

"I can put a lead line on her if you need it," he said coolly.

"I'll manage," Keros said.

"Where are we going?" Ellyn asked.

"South of Lake Ferradon. We'll follow the river to the lake."

There was nothing else to say. They mounted, Margaret behind Weverton again and Keros and Ellyn riding separately. They turned south, tracing their way around the outside of Cranford at a trot. The rain lightened and turned back into a drizzle. Weverton looked over his shoulder at Keros.

"You learned to ride quickly," he observed. "It's quite impressive for a man who's never sat a horse before."

"Perhaps I underestimated my abilities."

"Or maybe you lied."

Keros smiled. "That's a possibility too."

Margaret looked at him, her face hidden from Weverton. She grinned and winked. Keros felt himself grin back and his chest swelled. He did have a place here in Crosspointe—a home.

They rode until darkness fell. The rain quit at the

same time. They found a clearing near the river and set up camp. They collected a pile of wet wood and built a fire pit. Keros lit it with a spark of majick and soon the flames were roaring merrily. They tended the horses, rubbing them down and cleaning their hooves before giving them each a bait of grain. Margaret and Keros dug in the packs, bringing out vegetables, cheese, bread, and potatoes. Keros put the vegetables and potatoes into a pot of water and set them to boil. In the meantime, Weverton and Ellyn strung a thin line between two trees and hung the coats and cloaks to dry.

They spoke little. Keros was too tired and his body ached. Ellyn watched everyone with a sharp gaze, and Weverton brooded, staring down at his linked hands as he sat by the fire. Margaret paced circles around the clearing. After a few minutes, she wandered away into the trees, heading for the river. Keros followed her.

"Am I insane?" she asked as he came abreast of her. "To think that helping Weverton could make him a Rampling ally?"

"He is at least the enemy of your enemy," Keros said. "That makes him your friend."

"Still, I've risked a lot that isn't mine to risk. Ellyn is a majicar and a spy from Azaire. Nicholas is—" She shook her head. "Ryland is going to slit my throat. I walked Nicholas into a safe house and I told him what you are. I told him what *I* am. He will not hesitate to use any of this against me—against the Crown. I am a fool."

"Surely not. He will owe you for your help, and he does not take such debts lightly."

"He is a pragmatic man and will not hesitate to do whatever he thinks necessary to further his goals."

"And if I promise I will keep your secrets?"

Margaret and Keros both started, turning around. Weverton stood behind them, leaning a shoulder against a willow tree.

"I wouldn't believe you, even if I wanted to. I may be helping you rescue your son, but I have not forgotten who you are and what you've done." She shook her head. "This is pointless."

She stalked forward, heading back to the camp. Nicholas straightened and his hand flashed out as he gripped her arm. She stopped, glaring at him.

"This isn't settled," he said softly.

She tipped her head. "Is that a threat?"

He shook his head. "It's a promise. You have risked a lot—sacrificed a lot—for me and my son. I will not let it hurt you."

She smiled and it was as bitter as lye. "That's what sacrifice is: you suffer so someone else doesn't have to. You can't stop the consequences. No one can. Even if my brothers forgive me, they will never trust me again. Keros will never be a secret from you again. And you—" She grimaced and yanked away, disappearing into the trees without another word.

Keros met Weverton's gaze. "You want her." It wasn't quite a question. The other man tipped his head slightly as if in agreement. "Why?"

For a moment he thought Weverton would not answer. Then, "She's . . . remarkable." There was a lot of meaning in that word.

"You have hundreds of women begging to climb in your bed. Pick one of them—pick all of them—just leave her alone. She's not for you."

Weverton laughed, a harsh bark. "You sound like a jealous lover."

"I am her friend. Leave her alone. You'll hurt her."

The other man gave a slow shake of his head. "I don't think I can; I don't want to."

"You're a selfish bastard."

"I am. I know what I want and I get it." He offered no apology.

"Even knowing what it will cost her?"

"It won't cost her anything."

"Don't be an ass. It already has." Keros ran his tongue around the sharp edge of his teeth. "I don't have any family anymore, at least not of blood. But I count Margaret as my sister. I don't believe she'll ever accept your advances. Your crimes against the Ramplings are too many. But if, by some bizarre circumstance, you manage to sway her, then be warned. If you use her ill, I will destroy you." He lifted his hand and spun majick around his fingers in a lacy blue-green ball. "I'll fry you where you stand."

He lifted his fingers to his mouth and blew the majick from his fingers. It spun away and stuck to Weverton's chest. For a moment nothing happened. Then tiny filaments of majick unfurled from the ball, snaking around Weverton's body, containing him in a loose cocoon. It flared with brilliant light and he let out a sharp scream as he crumpled to the ground. The majick faded as quickly as it had flared.

Keros knelt down, grasping Weverton's chin and ignoring the oily *shift* of the thing in his mind. The other man was shaking as if with a palsy. The pain of that spell was excruciating. "Think hard. This is just a taste of what I will do to you."

He rose and walked away, leaving Weverton lying on the ground. He met Ellyn and Margaret on the trail.

"What happened? What was that scream?"

Keros smiled, a cold, vicious smile. "Turns out Weverton is afraid of snakes. He'll be along soon. Let's leave him to recover his dignity in peace."

Chapter 8

Two days later they skirted Lake Ferradon and dropped down along the foothills of the Grimstone Mountains, stopping a league outside the village of Molford. They were dragging with exhaustion and wet to the skin. The rain had continued on and off and the previous night had been miserable. Margaret had slept little, sitting up all night against a tree. Her hands were pruny with the unceasing damp and her mood was black. She was miserably sore. Though Nicholas and she had switched back and forth, each having the opportunity to sit in the saddle, she was woefully out of shape for riding and her lower half was a fiery mass of aches.

Something had happened between Keros and Nicholas, she was certain of it. When Nicholas returned to camp two nights before, he had been dusted with leaves and twigs as if he'd been lying on the ground. His face appeared sickly pale and his hands had been shaking. He'd hardly been able to hold his food. He'd said little since then, and he and Keros did not speak. Even now it made her smile with spiteful satisfaction. He deserved so much for what he'd done to her family over the years, and there was little enough she could do to pay him back. But Keros had made the effort.

She eyed the majicar. He looked more tired than she did. His shoulders slumped and he was having a hard time keeping his eyes open as he sat on a log, his arms propped on his knees, his head sagging low.

"What now?" Ellyn came and sat beside Margaret.

They'd built a small fire and ate stale bread and cheese. Margaret shivered and pulled her cloak more tightly around herself. Its majickal protections were unraveling, allowing the wool to absorb the wet. Her boots were the same. She glanced at her companion.

"Carston was being held at Molford Manor, just east of Molford village. First we need to discover whether he's still being held there. After that—" She shrugged. "We'll figure it out once we see what we are up against."

"How do you expect to find out whether he's there?" Nicholas asked. He stood in the shadows outside the light of the fire. "They will be suspicious of us—four strangers on horseback."

Margaret touched her forefingers together and pressed them to her lips. She'd been piecing together a plan for the past two days. "We have two choices. We can try to sneak into the village and learn what we need to know, but this is one of the regent's strongholds. They will be expecting spies to come sniffing in the shadows and will be wary."

"And the second choice?" Keros asked from across the fire.

"Nicholas and I pretend to be a wealthy couple on our way from Blakely to Tixora for a wedding. I, of course refuse to do the sensible thing and sail around through Wigan Sound because I want my horses there so everyone can know how rich I am, and I love them like children. My long-suffering husband, who is also weak-willed, gives into all my whims no matter how silly. So when there was a flood in our village and all able bodies were called out to help, I refused to wait and chance being late for the wedding. Thus we've set off on this adventure without a proper escort. Unfortunately, in a mudslide, we lost everything but ourselves, a precious packhorse, and our two servants. We are now in need of an inn to recuperate while we send for clothing and necessities from home. We'll have to stay for several days at least, but we'll pay very well. After all, we didn't lose all our money."

"You aren't dressed properly," Nicholas said. "You look like a thief, not a wealthy woman."

"We'll arrive after dark. I'll be overcome by the emotions of the events and you'll hurry me directly to our rooms. No one will see anything but my cloak. My maid, Ellyn, will purchase things for me in Molford."

"Evelyn," Ellyn corrected. "I've only been here once for a short time, but there is no sense using a name someone might recognize."

Margaret nodded. "Good enough. It sounds enough like your real name that if one of us slipped up, we wouldn't be in trouble."

"It's dangerous. If they suspect us, they'll be able to sweep us up without much effort," Keros said. "Truehelm is likely to have at least one or two master majicars here. I'm not sure how well Ellyn and I would do against them. Not only that, but you and Weverton could be recognized. You aren't exactly unknown in Crosspointe."

"No one will expect to see us here in these circumstances. It is simply unfathomable that the prim and proper Princess Margaret would be in Molford in such straits—and sneaking about with a man. It is inconceivable. As for Nicholas Weverton—I doubt anyone would believe that he would be here. But we'll have to hope for the best. We'll have to risk it if we want to rescue Carston before the regent becomes suspicious. Nicholas has been gone for three days now and I'm certain the regent has sent his ultimatum. He is no doubt waiting for a response. Who knows what he'll do if he doesn't get it? This is the quickest way to find out what we need to. We'll simply have to be convincing so that no one suspects we could be who we are," Margaret said. "I can do my part. Can you?" she asked Nicholas.

He gave a low bow. "Anything you wish, sweet wife," he said in a nasally, obsequious voice.

She smiled, despite herself. "We should go now, tonight," she said. "No time to waste."

"Ah, my love, anything your heart desires," he said. "There's nothing I wouldn't do for you. Tell me to fetch the moon and I will get it for you!"

"Laying it on a bit thick, aren't you?" Ellyn said.

"I am but a humble man and this fine woman is my dearest treasure. I would do anything for her," Nicholas said in that ridiculous voice.

Ellyn shook her head and rolled her eyes. Keros only stood up. The two men exchanged a long, dark look, and then Keros put the fire out. Margaret took possession of the gray gelding, while Keros and Ellyn rode double on the chestnut mare. As his companion settled behind him, Keros's expression pulled tight. Margaret wondered what he was thinking.

She rode beside Nicholas. They'd neared the outskirts of the town when he spoke again.

"Are you well, my sweetest darling?" he asked. "You are so quiet. You've not taken a chill, have you? Oh, my dear, I will never forgive myself if you are ill."

She grinned. This was going to be fun. "Avery, I have told you over and over. I am desperately ill and unhappy. How could you have let this happen? My brother will be distraught with worry. We must send him word. And my things! All my beautiful things gone with the wagon and the mules. We cannot go on this way. We must send to Shevring. I will not move another inch until I have proper clothing. I will not appear at my brother's house as a pauper!" Her voice rose shrilly.

"Now, now, my dear," Nicholas said. "Anything you

want. I'm sure Molford will have an inn. We will stay there as long as you want."

"Molford?" She sniffed. "It will be a hovel. Oh, my nerves. It is too much. How will I survive?"

The village was a solid, well-crafted place. It was larger than Margaret expected. Many of the buildings were recently built and there were more people on the cobblestone main street than she had anticipated at this hour. They found the inn near the center of the town. It was an imposing three-story structure. The first floor was made of rock and the upper stories were half-timbered with oriel windows and a roof of cedar shakes. Yellow lights gleamed warmly from the windows and the smell of warm bread and stewed lamb drifted tantalizingly through the night. Margaret's mouth watered and her stomach rumbled.

They pulled up in the inn yard. "Keros! Fetch the innkeeper," Nicholas ordered and then leaped to the ground. He tied his gelding to a bush and came around to help Margaret down.

"Easy now, my precious, dearest love," he said as she slid down into his arms and collapsed weakly against his chest. His arms held her tightly. "We shall soon be warm."

"Do you have a secret yearning to be an actor?" she whispered.

"Just keeping us safe," was his murmured reply.

The innkeeper came bustling out after Keros. He was a small man with a belly that sagged over his apron. His head was bald and he wore a thick beard and mustache. He goggled at the horses, hardly looking at his new guests.

"Sir, how may I help you?"

"My wife and I have had a terrible trial," Nicholas said in his nasal voice. "We must have rooms—your best, mind you. I don't care about the cost. We need hot baths and food and wine. Quickly, man. My wife is about to faint!" He swung Margaret up into his arms.

The innkeeper gaped a moment longer, finally tearing his gaze from the horses to stare first at Nicholas and then Margaret, then back at the horses. "W-who are you?" he stuttered at last.

Nicholas swept himself up imperiously, an impressive feat, given he was sopping wet and holding an equally wet and ungainly Margaret. "I am Avery Dedlok of Shevring and this is my wife, Sophia. We've lost our carriage in a mudslide. We need your best rooms, a meal, and hot baths. Money is no object, but I insist you show us the way now." His voice rose, managing to sound both querulous and demanding.

"Avery, I'm going to catch my death. I can feel my life slipping away. I'm so cold. Just lay me down here and I will die, surely I will," Margaret whimpered woefully. "I don't want to be trouble for anyone. Truly I don't. I'll die here and you can find yourself a younger wife. Julia Slitterpod would make a good mother. Oh, our poor, poor motherless son," she wailed. "Poor little Dicky. He's young, yet. He will forget me, his poor, neglected mother. Oh, my baby, my sweet baby!" Her voice rose in a shriek and then her head fell back and dangled as if she'd fainted or died.

It was enough to jolt the innkeeper into action. He motioned desperately for Nicholas to follow. He guided them through the taproom. Margaret scanned it from between slitted eyelids. It was crowded and far too many were well armed. None of them seemed drunk. Everyone fell silent as they watched the small parade of the innkeeper, Nicholas and Margaret, with Ellyn bringing up the rear. Keros had remained outside to care for the horses.

They were led into a large suite of rooms in the rear of the house. It had a large bedroom with an attached

dressing room, a spacious sitting room, a broad tiled garderobe, and a smaller attached bedroom with two beds
for the servants. The suite was well appointed, with floral upholstery and bedclothes, and ornate furniture in
fashion some fifty seasons before. Nicholas carried Margaret into the bedroom. He was about to put her down
when she opened her eyes.

"I am filthy. Do not get this bed all wet and muddy or
I will cut your throat," she whispered fiercely.

He grinned and turned to set her in the chair. "Oh,
thank Chayos, my sweetest love. You are alive! I was so
worried." He bent and kissed her hands and then turned
to look at the innkeeper, who had followed them in.
"Food, man! And brandy and hot tea. Quickly! Evelyn,
come help your mistress." He stood and waited until Ellyn pushed around the stout innkeeper, then guided the
man out and shut the bedchamber door firmly.

Margaret stood with a small groan and unbuttoned
her coat. She hung it in the closet and pulled off her
boots, first removing the knives hidden in the tall shafts.
She dropped them to the floor and then her socks. She
wriggled her toes. They were wrinkled and cold.

"I'm going to take a bath," she told Ellyn and didn't
wait for a reply. She went into the garderobe and shut
the door.

There was, thankfully, a hot-water spigot. There was
no cold. She turned the handle and steaming water fountained into the tub. It was straight out of a spring, and
was slightly milky and smelled of minerals. There were
baskets on a nearby shelf containing soap, washrags,
brushes, and towels. She opened a jar of flowery soap,
scooped out a thick dollop, and held it under the water. Next she began stripping away her clothing, leaving
it in a pile at the foot of the tub. She stepped into the
tub, gasping at the heat on her cold flesh. She gritted
her teeth and set her other foot inside, then sank down

to sit. Her fists clenched as the hot water rose up. Steam filled the room and her skin turned bright red. When the tub was full, she turned the spigot off and began scrubbing herself. When she was through, she ducked under the water to rinse her hair and then pulled the plug and let the water drain. When it was done, she opened the spigot again and filled the tub to her chin.

It was tempting to stay soaking in the water until it turned cold. She felt her sore muscles beginning to ease. But Nicholas would want a turn as would Ellyn and Keros. She was about to stand and reach for a towel when there was a knock at the door. It opened before she could answer and Nicholas stepped inside. She pulled the towel over herself.

"Good evening, wife," he said as he leaned back against the door. He was still dressed in the filthy clothing he'd been wearing for the last three days. "Care for some company?" he asked with a meaningful look at the tub.

"I'd prefer dinner," she said, glad that heat hid her flush of embarrassment. She didn't understand it. She'd had many lovers, most as part of the jobs her father had given her. But something about Nicholas set her on edge.

"Then you are in luck. It is served. You should come eat while it's still hot."

He made no effort to move, his arms folded over his chest as he watched her. Dared her. Margaret was no coward and she was not about to back down from Nicholas Weverton. She pulled the plug on the tub and stood, letting the sopping towel fall to the floor with a plop. She didn't hurry as she stepped out onto the floor and reached for a dry towel. She pulled it around herself and tucked the corner between her breasts.

She looked at Nicholas. "I'm afraid I have nothing to wear to dinner," she said.

He looked like his ears had been boxed. He stared at her, then gave a slow shake of his head. "You continue to surprise me."

"I killed my first man when I was seven seasons old. I have trained my entire life to be the Crown's weapon—spy, assassin, thief, whore, and whatever else might be required of me. That is what I am. Not that prim, insipid, sugary girl I pretend to be." She pushed her hair back behind her ear. "Do not presume that you know me."

He straightened, coming to stand before her. He touched his fingers to her neck and rubbed them lightly down her shoulder and then back up. She couldn't hide the shiver that trembled through her, chasing a streak of heat. She didn't push his hand away. She wouldn't show weakness.

"I want to know you. I plan to."

She moved so quickly that he didn't realize she had his belt dagger before she was pressing it to his throat. "Consider this your first lesson, Weverton," she said, making his name an insult. She pushed until blood trickled freely down his neck. "You've confused this game of wife and husband with something real. But it most definitely is not. Don't make Carston an orphan before you even get him back."

He reached up, covering her hand with his. He made no attempt to pull the knife away. "You wouldn't," he said, his thumb rubbing against the inside of her wrist. "You need an alliance with me."

His touch sent curls of heat through Margaret's chest and settled low in her belly. *No.* She would *not be* attracted to this mother-dibbling bastard. Margaret yanked away. She flipped the dagger in her hand and threw it. The blade bit deep into the wood of the door and the hilt quivered.

She started to push past him, then stopped. "Touch

me again and I'll cut your hand off." She was turning the door handle when he spoke.

"I'll make you change your mind." It sounded like a vow.

She spun around, her mouth twisting in a snarl. "What game are you playing? I came to you because I wanted to help your son—an innocent boy. And you repay me with this feeble seduction? You have persecuted my family. You put that bastard Geoffrey Truehelm in the regency. It is likely that you had my father killed."

He frowned. "I told you that I did not."

"I don't trust you. I don't believe you." Anger made her shake. She should have killed him long ago. Her father had refused to order it and was dead instead. Now Ryland was demanding the same thing—to leave Weverton be. But she'd broken the rules to tell Nicholas about his son—why shouldn't she break them to cut out his heart?

But the truth was that as angry as he made her, she didn't really want to. She'd only just lost her father, and though they had never been truly close, his death had left a hollow inside her that was ringed with puls-ing hurt, the kind that could never go away. There had been unfinished business between them and she'd never have a chance to get the answers she needed. Now she never would. The boy deserved better than that. Besides, Nicholas clearly loved his son and she didn't doubt that the feeling was returned. After all, she'd loved her father desperately, despite what he'd made out of her. If she killed Nicholas, she'd be responsible for causing Carston an indescribable agony. She couldn't do it.

She stared at the door, her spine stiff, jaw hard. "I am here to help you get your son back. After that, we are done. I don't want anything else to do with you, unless it means I can slit your throat. Don't give me a reason to do it; you don't want your son to grow up without his father."

"I thought you wanted an alliance."

"Ryland or Vaughn can handle it."

"I don't want them. I want you. Think about it."

She pushed out of the door, leaving him inside. In the bedchamber, she found two dressing gowns lying across the bed. She slipped the smaller one on, buttoning it up to her chin. It was made of green wool and lined with flannel. It was also far too big. It dragged on the ground and she felt like a child inside it. She rolled up the sleeves. Behind her, she felt Nicholas watching her. She ignored him, picking up the skirts of the dressing gown and going into the sitting room.

The meal was on the table. There was a spicy pork roast with early carrots, brown rice and white beans, an apple tart, a plate of cheeses, and a loaf of crusty bread as well as wine and hot tea. Ellyn and Keros were nowhere to be seen.

"They are dining in the kitchen," Nicholas said as he pulled out a chair for her. "It may be that they can glean some information from the servants."

She sat down without answering, grateful for the crackling fire that heated the room. He sat opposite. Soon they were both too caught up in eating to bother with conversation. But all too soon the meal was over. She looked at him over her glass of wine. "You should go bathe." Her voice was expressionless.

The corner of his mouth twitched as he looked down at his empty plate. "Should I now?"

"If you don't want to chance having the maid haul you out with the chamber pot."

He stood. "I'm afraid I've made your meal less palatable. You'll excuse me, I hope." With that he retreated back into the bedchamber.

Margaret swigged down the rest of her wine as she

watched him go, her meal sitting heavy in her stomach. He'd withdrawn into chill formality and for that she was grateful.

She'd drunk another glass of wine and was halfway through another when there was a soft knock at the door. It swung open just wide enough for Keros and Ellyn to slide inside. Instantly Margaret was on her feet. Keros was twisted so tight he was about to snap. His face was pale and graven. He paced across the room and back, his hands clenched at his sides. Ellyn shut the door and leaned against it, watching him with a slight frown.

"What is it? What's happened?" Margaret demanded.

Keros rubbed a hand across his mouth as he swung around to look at her. "Slaves," he said in a guttural voice. "The entire inn is run with slaves. They've been beaten and half starved. Down the street is a brothel. Every woman inside is a slave. There are apparently two more just like it, servicing the private army the regent has been building here."

Margaret didn't move—she couldn't. It felt like she'd been struck in the stomach. They were likely family, friends, or supporters of her family. She swallowed the rocks that filled her throat. "There's nothing we can do. Ryland says we wait until we're ready to take Crosspointe back."

"He didn't tell you to help Weverton," Keros retorted.

Margaret ignored that, focusing on the real issue. "What do you propose? What should we do? You said it yourself—the regent is building a private army here. Majick isn't reliable. Anything we do will likely get us killed and do nothing to help."

"We can go kill the damned regent," Keros growled. "And Weverton. Then your brothers can take Crosspointe back."

Margaret agreed wholeheartedly. But she couldn't say so. "Getting to the regent may be more difficult than you think. Both he and Weverton have powerful allies. Don't think that we won't have a civil war. Not only that, the people love them, both. They don't trust Ramplings anymore. They've gleefully supported Rampling slavery. If you stir in the weather making food scarce, the worries for the winter, not to mention majick failing and majicars battling in the streets, you've got a recipe for riots."

His head jerked from side to side. "I've sat by long enough. It has to stop." He reached for the door and stalked out, slamming it behind him.

Margaret looked at Ellyn. "Go after him. Stop him, whatever he is going to do."

"How? He's essentially a master majicar and I am just a journeyman."

"He will not attack you. I can't go after him without making people suspicious. I'm supposed to be teetering on the edge of Chayos's altar, after all. I can't very well be running about after a common servant."

"Perhaps I agree with him," Ellyn said after a moment.

"You don't have the luxury," Margaret snapped. "Any more than I do. You work for Azaire and your country doesn't benefit from Keros stirring up trouble on his own. Now go or I'm done with you."

The other woman's lips tightened and she left without a word.

Margaret sagged down into a chair, pulling her fingers through her hair. She made a face as they caught painfully in the snarls. She hadn't bothered to look for a comb. She stood and went into the bedchamber. The door to the garderobe was closed. In the middle of the bed was the dagger she'd thrown at the door. She eyed it. *A cracking brilliant marriage bed*, she thought acidly.

She went to the bureau and found a wooden comb. She sat, looking at herself in the wavery mirror and beginning untangle her hair, picking out some pine needles that hadn't got washed out.

Of course there would be slaves here. The regent would want to demonstrate his wealth and power. She swallowed. It meant that there was a better chance that someone might recognize her. Her hand clenched in the comb. How long would Ryland and Vaughn wait? How many of her family and friends would suffer unspeakable things or be murdered? She thought of the brothels and her stomach lurched. She lunged to her feet, reaching for the chamber pot beneath the bed. But the violence of her reaction was too strong and her dinner splattered the rug and the edge of the counterpane.

"Dammit," she muttered, wiping her lips with the back of her hand.

She found the towel still wet from her bath and did her best to clean up. She was still on her knees wiping up when the garderobe door opened and a cloud of fragrant steam billowed into the room. She sat back on her heels. Nicholas was flushed with the heat and his hair was slicked back against his head. He looked at her and then at the floor.

"Are you unwell?"

She made no effort to get to her feet. The weight of exhaustion and frustration hung heavy on her. "Keros may be out burning down the town. I sent Ellyn to try and stop him."

His brows rose. "What brought that on?"

"He's not fond of slavery or sitting around helpless watching people suffer for no better reason than the regent's greed," she said, levering herself up. She looked down at the dirty towel. "Neither am I." She went into the garderobe and dropped the towel into the basket, drawing a hard breath. Time to let it go. She could do nothing. There was no point wallowing in her hatred and rage. Later—when she could do something about it— she'd open the door on the violence that burned in her spirit.

A moment later she returned to the bedroom. Nicholas wasn't there. She found him in the sitting room. He had poured another cup of tea and held it out for her. She took it silently, gulping it down. She grimaced. It was tepid. She held the cup out for more.

Instead of the pot, he reached for a bottle of brandy. He held it up and she nodded. He filled her cup and then poured an equal measure for himself. She eyed the full cup and then took a healthy drink. It heated her belly and steadied her shaking nerves. She just didn't know what Keros would do. She had not known him long, though they were kindred spirits in many ways. He was more like a brother than the three she had. Maybe that's what worried her. In his place, with his freedom to act, she'd burn Molford to the ground and every slave-master bastard with it.

She sat on a chaise, pulling her legs up beneath her, holding the cup between her palms. Nicholas sat facing her at the other end, setting the bottle of brandy on the low table beside him. They did not speak and after about ten minutes, Margaret held her cup out for more. He filled it again.

"What will he do if Ellyn doesn't stop him?" Nicholas asked her.

She shrugged. "I don't know. He *is* a master majicar and he's angry. I know what I'd like to do," she added darkly.

He bent forward, his expression intent. "For what it's worth, I never imagined Geoffrey would do this—that he would sell his enemies into slavery. It's appalling— unconscionable. I never meant for any of that to happen."

"Yet you let him continue on without lifting a finger to stop him. But tell me this—have you ever wondered what else he might do that you would never have expected?"

He had no answer.

Chapter 9

Keros left the inn and strode down the street. He pulled majick to him, feeling it crackle over his skin. Blue sparks danced across the backs of his hands and snapped in his hair. Inside his mind, he felt the thing there waking. He stopped, jerking around to face an alley. A man held a woman against the wall and thrust his hips into hers with a grunting sound. The noises she made were anxious and eager—it wasn't a rape. Keros clenched his hands, almost wishing it was.

Months ago when the lord chancellor—now regent—had convicted Lucy of murder and sentenced her to be exposed on the Bramble, he'd also taken her father, two of her brothers, her best friend and many other friends and sentenced them as accessories to her treason. It had all been mere legal maneuvering—there had been no real evidence. They had manufactured what they needed. Then they had left Lucy and Marten on the Bramble and the rest they'd sold in Bokal-dur—the Jutras capital city.

Then, no one had connected any of the conspiracy to the lord chancellor; he'd covered his tracks all too well. But it was clear he'd started something that he meant to continue. The king had forbidden Lucy, Marten, and Keros to try to rescue those who'd been sold because Crosspointe needed Lucy in case the Jutras invaded or the majicars rebelled. He had refused to risk any of them.

It had eaten at Keros, leaving those people—Lucy's friends and family—to the bloodthirsty Jutras. After what had happened to his village, it was almost more than he could bear. Seeing it here in Molford—he was done. He wasn't going to stand around anymore, doing nothing while innocent people suffered.

He strode down the middle of the street. He felt weak and tired. The fatigue that followed his battle in the Riddles and his illness still dragged at him, and the added journey to Molford had not allowed him to recuperate as he should have. He should be in bed. Majick and exhaustion were a bad mix, especially with majick not working properly.

The first brothel wasn't far. He ignored the knot of men on one corner as they laughed and began shoving one another. They all were all well armed and sporting a ribbon of orange and dark green around each of their upper arms, the same colors as the regent's livery. It marked them as members of the bastard's growing mercenary army.

He rounded a corner and found the brothel. It was a new building. The paint was still a bright white. It was a two-story affair with a small muddy courtyard. Iron bars covered the windows, most of which glowed with light despite the lateness of the hour. Keros stopped, his legs braced wide as he faced the despicable building.

"What are you planning to do?"

Ellyn's voice made him start. He jerked around to look at her, saying nothing.

"You can't burn it. You'll kill the women inside."

"Children," he grated. "Children too."

Her expression went flat. "The princess sent me to stop you. I have to, or she won't listen to me about Azaire."

He turned away. He still hadn't come to terms with her—with the knowledge that she'd survived that awful day. Every time he looked at her he remembered his childhood and the day it had ended in screams and blood. He'd mourned Sperray; he'd buried the memories of her where he wouldn't have to think about them. Now he looked at her and it felt like someone had ripped open his chest. Worse, instead of hating the man who'd done this to them, she served him. His jaw knotted and he swallowed hard.

"But instead I'm going to help you," she said.

"What? Why would you want to?"

"This is wrong."

"What about Margaret and Azaire?" he rasped.

She hesitated. "Because," she began slowly, "I wish someone would have stopped the soldiers that day they tossed us into the *sylveth*."

His brows rose. "Yet you serve the bastard who was behind it all."

"I serve Azaire. I disagree with what the Gerent did; I wish it hadn't happened. But I still love my country and I will protect the rest of her people the best I can. If that means serving him, then that's what I will do."

"Then you should go back. Margaret won't like you helping me."

"Can I stop you?"

He smiled, his eyes cold. "If you can kill me. Or knock me unconscious. Your majick isn't strong enough to take me down. Not if I'm on guard."

She nodded as if expecting his answer. "Then I will help you. Because going back is no option. Margaret will like me leaving you to do this alone even less than not stopping you."

He shrugged. "You know best."

"What's your plan?"

"Come with me. Somewhere private. We need to prepare."

He led her past the brothel and out through the cluster of houses and shops that sprouted like warts on the edge of the town. Beyond was a field of what appeared to be grain, though it was stunted and the incessant rain had smashed it flat. Keros walked out along the hedgerow until they came to a small copse of trees. Within, he found a tree with a horizontal low-hanging branch. He sat, gesturing for Ellyn to join him.

"What are your affinities?" he asked.

She frowned at him. "Affinities?"

He blinked. "The majickal compass rose. The cardinal directions are Wind, Water, Stone, and Fire. There are thirty-two lesser elements. From these you can build complex spells. You are not familiar with this?"

She shook her head. "I learned focus and purpose in honing a spell to my will."

He rubbed a hand across his mouth, then shook his head, biting his lower lip. What was he doing letting her take part in this? He knew majick wasn't working and she didn't know enough about what she was doing to keep herself safe even if conditions were normal.

"I'll do this on my own," he said abruptly. "There's no time to sort out what you know or teach you what you don't."

"I'm not helpless," she snapped, lunging to her feet.

"I know that."

"I am a skilled journeyman majicar," she said, hands on her hips.

"But you don't know what the majickal compass is."

"That doesn't mean I can't do majick and do it well."

"May I see your *illidre*?" he asked.

She drew it out of her tunic and pulled it over her head. He held out his hand. She hesitated, then set the

slender rod across his palm. He closed his fingers around
it. Carefully he used majick to scan the surface. Most *illidres* carried protective spells to keep other majicars from
using them. He didn't want to accidentally trigger one.
There seemed to be no guard on hers, however. He pen-
etrated deeper. Most *illidres* held the building blocks of
spells—bits and pieces the majicar could assemble and
combine with newly built majicks. It saved time so that
he could put together a quick spell. The more powerful
a majicar and the longer he'd been practicing, the more
building blocks he stored inside the *illidre*. A journeyman majicar depended on a master to create his *illidre*
for him, then inserted a few of his most important spell
foundations.

He wasn't sure what to expect from Ellyn's *illidre*.
He was surprised to find it held only one single complex spell. He could not follow all of its making. It contained elements from all over the compass, combined
in unexpected ways. Many were oppositional—*Dream*
mated with *Flesh*, *Shadow* mated with *Blood*. Oppositional pairing was very difficult and this was done with
astounding elegance and control. To have done so in the
illidre of a mere journeyman was startling.

Keros withdrew and handed it back for her. "Who
made it for you?" he asked.

"Her name is Dechuan. There are six master majicars
in Azaire and she is one."

"What does the spell do?" He nudged his chin at her
illidre, now hanging back around her neck.

Ellyn frowned. "It focuses me. I concentrate and
pull majick into the focus and can do almost anything
I want."

"What about the ghost effect?"

At her look of confusion, he waved his hand. "The
phantom spell that is released when you cast. It's usually
twisted and sticks to other spells, pulling them apart and

re-forming into new spells. You have to capture it or it will disrupt whatever it touches—surely you know this?"

She nodded. "But my *illidre* collects it back automatically."

Which meant the spell inside had a shield on it, otherwise the collected majick would chew it apart in time. This Dechuan was clearly a very skilled master majicar.

"So are you going to let me help you?" Ellyn demanded.

He hesitated. "It's risky for you."

Her hands folded over her chest and she glared at him. "I can handle myself. Besides, I get to choose the chances I take, not you."

"That is true, but you don't understand. There's something . . . ." He trailed off and began again. "The injuries to my face that you healed, and the poison—they came from a battle between four majicars. I got caught in the middle. None of them were sane. Majick did something to their minds."

"And you think that will happen to me?" she asked, still doubting.

He nodded. "It could. I think the more majick you use, the more you invite it in."

"But you're safe from this insanity," she said, her brows arching.

He shook his head. "No. I'm not. But if I'm going to be Pale-blasted, I'd just as soon do it helping these people. But you deserve the chance to choose for yourself." A choice neither had gotten when they'd been made majicars. He could see the understanding in her eyes.

"What will you do?"

His face hardened. "I'll make a spell web so that anyone who enters or leaves that house will get ill. First it will attack their genitals, and then it will move through their bodies, rotting them alive. It will be a slow, ugly death."

"What about the slaves? They must come and go."

"The spell I cast will know the difference."

That took her aback. "You can do that?"

He could. But it would take a lot out of him. He wasn't all that sure he'd be sane when he was done. But he didn't care. Here, now, he could make a difference. He wasn't going to walk away. He was done walking away. "I can do it," he said firmly. "Stand watch. This will take a little time to prepare."

The minutes flew past. Keros pulled out his *illidre* and sat back against the trunk of the tree. He sank down into it and began pulling majick to him recklessly. It came sluggishly and in his mind, the *presence* began to throb with what felt like eagerness. He began weaving his intent. He wasn't sure how much time had passed when he was near to finishing. But he needed help.

"Ellyn," he rasped, his mouth and throat dry as dust, his hands tightly fisted around his *illidre*. His chest felt tight and he felt the edges of his vision wavering as the thing in his mind wriggled and swelled. A sharp shaft of pain ran down his back and into his left leg, then vanished. He jerked, his muscles spasming.

A pause. "I'm here. Your eyes—they are beginning to glow." She sounded more curious than frightened.

He ignored that. He was reaching the limits of his sanity. He felt the presence sliding down deeper into his mind, sending sucking tentacles into the center of his being. He had to hurry. "I need you to focus. I need you to make a web—like a spiderweb. I'll weave my spell into it and then we'll attach it to the doors of the brothels." He hoped.

Ellyn sat down beside him and gripped her *illidre*. She cupped it between her palms, drew a breath and blew across it. She closed her eyes. Keros sagged back against the trunk of the tree. He'd pushed his spell inside his *illidre* and now all he could do was wait for Ellyn to be ready. Her lips moved as she murmured silently. Her hands folded over the slender rod.

As with his healing, vines spilled from her hands. These were fine—like strands of a morning glory as it clung to a trellis. They knitted together in a lacey pattern, the loosely woven net rippling gently over hands like fine silk. It took less than half a glass for her to complete it. His guess was that one of her cardinal abilities was Water.

"What now?" she asked, holding her fists up.

"Give it to me."

She held out her hands and he put his over hers. Taking someone else's spells, even willingly given, took some work. He'd hardly eaten anything during their late dinner, once presented with a slave serving as staff. They had not been as beaten and bruised as the street cleaners on Ashford Avenue, but still his stomach had revolted. The making of his part of the spell had depleted all his shallow reserves. What he did now was on sheer stubborn fury alone.

He traced its lines, understanding its weaving. It was elegant and deceptively simple. He recognized that the strands were a twisting of multiple affinities—minor and major—but he could not separate them. They melded together in a unified thread. The junctions were knotted together loosely to allow the spell to expand to fill a doorway. It invited touch. It was sensual and eager.

He looked at Ellyn. "You made it to lure?"

"It is only an invitation. Only those coming from the outside and within a few feet will feel it," she said defensively.

He smiled, hard and angry. "Well done."

Now he lifted it, hooking it with his majick and pulling it into his hands before letting go of Ellyn. It was like lifting two hundred pounds. He strained. Slowly it pulled free. He sat a moment, collecting himself. Then he reached inside his *illidre*, pulling out his spell. It was thorny and sharp and full of poison—the venom of his hatred and helplessness. It was the same venom he imagined that the slaves felt.

He pushed it into the Ellyn's net, spreading it out like clay. The spells resisted each other. Melding them was a matter of strength of will and majick. He reached deep, pulling hard from the ground beneath them. Stone. He reached for *Pain*, *Blood*, and *Tears*, minor affinities close to *Stone* and *Water*. These he spun into hot glass, layering it over the clay and the net. He dusted it over with *Blossom* and *Gold*—adding to the enticement of Ellyn's web. Last of all, he pulled it inside his *illidre*, ready to be placed.

Doing it let the presence inside him spread. It squeezed him, spreading roots through his mind and down into his flesh. He felt like someone was pulling at him, like he was a marionette. He resisted with the strength he had left. But he knew it would not be long before he lost himself entirely. He had to get away from Ellyn and Molford before that. He didn't want to kill innocents along with the guilty.

"Come on," he said, standing up. "It'll be dawn soon. Now is the best time. Most everyone should be asleep." His knees sagged and Ellyn caught him around the waist. He leaned against her until his legs firmed and then he drew away. There were memories in that touch that felt like rusty spikes through his chest.

They returned to town the way they'd come. The sky had begun to clear and the moon was a sliver hanging between the shreds of clouds. As he expected, the town had quieted down. As he might have expected from the military domination of the town, there were no beggars huddled in doorways or alleys and no drunkards lying facedown in their own puke.

They stepped inside the courtyard of the brothel.

Fighting his shaking hands and the black vise squeezing his body, Keros pulled out his *illidre*. He looked at Ellyn. "Stand back, over there." He pointed across the street.

She stared into his eyes a long moment and he could see his reflection in hers. His glowed bright green. He thought there might have been a yellow shine to hers, but he wasn't certain. She shook her head. "You're about to fall down. I'm staying right here."

His jaw clenched with the struggle to stay focused. He was beginning to feel fuzzy and confused. The one solid thing in his mind was the need to place the spells. "If this goes badly, I'll kill you and I won't be able to stop myself. Stand back and you'll have a cracking chance." When she still hesitated, he shoved her. "You've got a duty to Azaire, don't you? Don't risk yourself."

Finally she nodded and backed away. He waited until he thought she was far enough, then turned to face the door. This was the easy part. Except he didn't know how much more majick he could use until the thing in his head chewed through his sanity. It was strong—his arms and legs twitched with strange urges to go somewhere, to do something. He didn't know where or what. His vision blurred in and out with flashes of blindness. Not much time.

He dipped inside his *illidre*. The spell waited. Reaching down again into the earth, he siphoned majick up inside him. The thing in his head quivered and it felt like teeth bit sharply into the side of his head. His right arm and half his chest went numb. He quickly poured majick into the spell, lending it life. Slowly he pulled it from his *illidre*, leaving behind a duplicate. Now that the spell was made, he could copy it infinitely; it had become one of his stored building blocks. It sat in his fingers like a ball. Lifting it to his lips, he blew it, just as he had with his attack on Weverton. He put all his intent into that sharp breath. It floated away, growing and spreading in the air until it caught on the doorjamb, covering it like a spiderweb. It clung there and faded, disappearing from sight.

Keros drew a heavy breath. One down, two to go. An arm wrapped his waist again. He look into Ellyn's scowling face. "I could be insane," he reprimanded her. "You have to stay away."

"Crack that," she said. "I'm hear to help."

She pulled him out of the courtyard and down the street, pushing him down on the edge of a wooden sidewalk in front of a chandler. She squatted down before him, reaching for her *illidre*. He shook his head.

"No. You mustn't waste majick on me. The thing—" He waved the fingers of his left hand near his ear. His right was still numb. "It feeds on it. The more you use, the more it grows."

"The thing?" she asked.

He shook his head. "Something is inside of me. It . . . I don't know what it is. But it's there and it's getting bigger. I can't quite see you," he said, squinting through the blur. "My right arm is numb. I can't move it."

She shook her head. "You should have stopped."

"I've got two more brothels to go."

"They'll just get healers. It won't make a difference," she said.

"They won't heal from this," he said with malevolent satisfaction.

"Why not?"

"It is not poison and it is not disease. It is revenge and it is tied to their souls. They'll be dead before a healer understands the spell."

He became aware of her hand on his chest where it was numb. Green vines curled around him and he tried to wrench away. He only fell over on his side, his face pressed against the wet wood of the sidewalk. "Don't," he said, but Ellyn only moved up kneel beside him, her face set.

"I'll do whatever I damned well please," she said. "I'm not letting you leave me again."

He stared. "I didn't leave you."

"I saw you," she said, her lips stiff as wood. "I saw you."

"I thought you were gone. I couldn't stand it. I couldn't stand any of it."

She shook her head. "It doesn't matter now. It's ancient history."

"Then stop trying to heal me. There's no good purpose for it. You can't help me and it will only make you insane."

"Margaret will skin me alive if anything happens to you. I need her. She's my key to meeting with Prelate Ryland and Prince Vaughn. It's what I'm here to do."

"It'll do you no good if you go mad. Stop." He wrenched himself backward, rolling away from her. The green vines snapped and slithered away. He sat up. His arm was no longer numb and he felt stronger. "Don't be stupid," he told her, clambering onto his hands and knees and then to his feet. "Let's finish this."

They found the second brothel near where they'd entered Molford. Keros repeated the placing of the spell, and though the healing Ellyn had given him had lent strength to his body, the thing inside him continued to swell and delve deeper. He could see out of only one eye now and could hardly feel his body. Only the drive of his rage kept him moving as he wanted. When he finished . . . he doubted he would be himself any longer.

The last brothel was halfway to Molford manor. It was a larger affair, and just as new as the first one. No doubt it served the regent when he was here as well as his guests and senior officers. The low iron gates were closed and latched. It didn't matter. Keros leaned against the brick gatepost and blew the spell to the doors, watching it settle with satisfaction. If he was right, then the regent would find himself stricken. "The sooner the better," he muttered before turning away.

They started back toward the inn. The eastern sky was turning pink and orange as the sun started to rise. Keros didn't fight the arm that Ellyn thrust around him. His thoughts shifted and swirled like sand stirred up in water. He faintly heard a noise, but couldn't sort out what it might be. Ellyn shoved against him, pushing him off the side of the road into the ditch. They fell, splashing into the foot-deep water. Keros lay on top of the woman—*who was she?*—unable to understand her words. At last she slugged him in the shoulder and squirmed out from beneath him, lying on the bank as the rumbling approached closer.

He crawled up beside her, his head reeling, his muscles twitching and jerking. "What?" he said stupidly. Sounds rang in his ears, and everywhere he looked, the world melted together. Something was wrong. He reached for majick and it came to him, filling him with crackling, hot energy. His vision twisted and shadows leaped up malevolently around him. His heart pounded and he swung whips of crackling energy at them.

The woman banged his head with her fist and the majick fled away as he— Where was he? Who was she? What was happening? A hand pressed against his mouth and she lay across his back, pressing him down. "Quiet."

A carriage rolled into view. It was large and pulled by four horses slathered in mud. A squad of ten Blackwatch rode on horses before and after. The company clattered by, heading toward the manor. He saw them clearly for a single moment, then felt something stab through his head.

"The regent," the woman muttered nonsensically, then climbed quickly to her feet. "Hurry. We have to tell the others."

He staggered up, his gaze fixed on the retreating coach. He hated that coach. He couldn't remember why. He lifted a hand as if to cast a spell. She caught his arm, yanking him around. Majick crackled around and he tried to pull away. He didn't want to hurt her. He knew that.

"Keros! Come with me. Come with me now," she ordered sharply.

She grabbed his hand and dragged him back toward Molford. He followed, turning to look over his shoulder one last time. Pinpricks wrapped his skull and his mouth tasted like brine. He wondered who he was.

Chapter 10

It was several turns of the glass before Nicholas could convince Margaret to go to bed. "You're exhausted and you can do nothing until they get back. Better to get your rest while you can."

She'd risen and withdrawn into the bedchamber, shutting the door firmly behind herself. Nicholas had lain on the chaise and dozed. Every time he started to sleep, he was tormented with visions of Carston. His son was a sweet child, trusting and innocent. Nicholas dragged his fingers through his hair. He was going to make Geoffrey pay for this. Painfully.

He was on his feet the moment he heard the light knock at the door. He turned the lock and swung it open. Ellyn led in Keros. He was gray. He shuffled inside, his body awkward and clumsy. Nicholas drew back as he met the majicar's eyes. There was a bright green shine in them that reminded Nicholas of the reflection of firelight in a mad dog's eyes.

Ellyn led Keros to a chair and pushed him down into it. Just then, Margaret opened the door of the bedchamber. Her hair was tousled and eyes were sunken and hollow. She saw Keros and hurried to his side.

"What happened? Where have you been?"

"I couldn't stop him," Ellyn said and then coughed.

Nicholas handed her a cup of water and noticed a yellow shine softly glossing her eyes. Fear prickled down his neck as he recalled the story of the insane majicars Keros had fought in Sylmont. She gulped the water down and then dropped down on a chair. "I couldn't stop him, so I helped him. We made a spell and set it at each of the brothels." She shook her head as if to clear it. "The regent is here."

"What?" Margaret exclaimed, whirling to look at Ellyn. "Are you sure?"

Ellyn only nodded and drank more water. Margaret looked at Nicholas as if asking for help. He started to reach out to comfort her but stopped himself. There was nothing he could say. He looked at the wasted majicar.

"Let's see about him first. Then we'll come up with a plan for Geoffrey."

Margaret hesitated, then nodded. She turned back to Keros and grasped his face between her palms. "What have you done?" she whispered.

He blinked at her slowly. "Who are you?" he asked. "I don't want to hurt you." Then a spasm rippled down his body and he convulsed. His feet thumped against the floor and his body twisted and wrenched from side to side. He bit his lips and blood ran down his chin and flecked his cheeks. Nicholas snatched a wooden spoon from the table and shoved it between Keros's teeth to keep him from biting his tongue in half.

Majick streaked beneath Keros's skin like forked lightning. Nicholas yanked Margaret away, holding her by her arms as she fought him. "No. It's too dangerous," he told her grimly.

Ellyn stood, holding her *illidre* in one hand and setting her hand on Keros's shoulder. She rocked back on her heels and majick raced up her arm. Green vines sprouted from her hand and nosed across Keros. The majick sizzling through him reacted violently. It rose in a whirling cloud of metal thorns. They spiraled in the air, expanding like a cloud of angry wasps. Nicholas shoved Margaret down behind a chair, covering her with his body.

She struggled. "Let me up!"

She was strong and knew how to fight. She elbowed him in the ribs and thrust herself sideways. He fell on top of her and she put her hands flat against his chest, shoving as she twisted. Both of them were hampered by their long dressing gowns, Margaret more so because hers was so big. Nicholas clamped his legs around hers and gripped her hands. His greater strength and weight kept her still.

"Stop. You can't help him now. You'll only get hurt."

"Get off me, you cracking bastard," she said, arching her back and bucking her hips, trying to get enough leverage to free herself.

"No. It serves neither of us." She went still, her body rigid in his arms. He became aware how intimate their position was and that only their dressing gowns separated their naked bodies. He pulled back, easing his hold. "You aren't going to do anything stupid, are you?"

"I'm fairly certain I already have," she said, glowering at him. "Let me up."

He rolled off her, keeping one hand on her shoulder. He didn't trust that she wouldn't rush out from behind the protection of the chair. He didn't have to worry. Shock held them both frozen in place.

The spinning majick from Keros had coalesced around both majicars. Blood ran from a hashing of slices on Ellyn. Her clothing was tattered and wet with more blood. Her eyes gleamed bright yellow now. But she hadn't moved. Her hand was still pressed to Keros's chest. Green vines writhed about the majicar's body so that Nicholas could hardly see him.

Margaret sucked in a sharp breath. "They'll kill each other."

"She's trying to heal him."

"The battle that Keros stopped in the Riddles—it could have started as a healing."

His hand tightened reassuringly. "Don't borrow trouble."

"You saw his eyes. And he didn't know who I was." Her expression tightened and for the first time since their journey began, Nicholas could read fear on her face.

"He knew enough to know he didn't want to hurt you. He'll be all right," he said without any conviction at all.

They both watched, helpless to do anything else. Then suddenly something changed. Margaret clutched Nicholas's arm. "Do you see that?"

"It's stopping," he said. The silvery white ball of Keros's majick had indeed begun to slow. As it did, its sharp, protruding spines began to soften and melt. Soon it turned into a shapeless blob and settled down to lay like a mantle over the mass of Ellyn's healing vines.

Ellyn was panting, her ribs pumping like bellows. She was so covered in blood that it was nearly impossible to find a clean patch of skin. She sagged against Keros's chair, half lying across his chest. As she did, Keros's majick rose and wrapped her in a silvery sheath. The green vines of her majick tickled the air and then dropped lifeless before fading to nothingness.

"Sweet mother Chayos," Nicholas murmured.

Margaret shook off his hand and went to stand beside the two of them. Keros was unconscious and his eyelids twitched as if he had bad dreams. His breathing was shallow and quick. She put out a hand to touch him, then curled her hand into a fist and dropped it back to her side. "What do we do with them?"

"There's nothing we can do except wait."

"I hate it," she said, starting to pace.

Nicholas watched her, rubbing his hand against his ribs where she'd elbowed him. "I am shocked."

A smile flickered across her mouth. "You must be tearing yourself apart wanting to rescue your son."

He looked down, his stomach hardening around the lead ball that had formed when he'd learned of Carston's kidnapping. "I have whatever patience is required," he said.

"I know," she said. "I've studied you for years now. You are quiet and steady and never let your temper get the best of you. You lay plans like a farmer plants seeds. You are ruthless and rarely show mercy to your ene-mies. You tend your plots and wait with infinite patience until they come to fruition. You'll do a quick prune or weeding if need be, but you don't let emotion rule your actions"—she paused—"unless it comes to family. Then there's no limit to what you will do—even master pa-tience when you want to be smashing down doors."

He stared at her. It was strange hearing her assess-ment. He would not disagree with any of it, though there was more to him than that. More that he wanted to show her, though he was unlikely to ever have the opportu-nity. Because she was right. In a way, he was responsible for her father's death. He had waged a war against her family and he had encouraged others to do so—others like Geoffrey who were more willing than he was to kill and do worse. Nicholas had trained the dogs, then let them loose. He hadn't killed William Rampling, but he'd forged the weapons.

"Would it surprise you to learn that I admire you?" she asked.

He gaped. "Very much."

"You are driven. I understand that. And you believe in what you're doing; it is not mere greed and ambition like the regent. I sometimes wish I could be as ruthless as you, as patient. It would make things easier. I certainly would not be here now. I would have let Ryland and Vaughn handle things as they saw fit. I would not have revealed the safe house to you and I would not have betrayed my brothers. But most of all, I would not be standing here watching my friend die. It was all right to risk myself, not Keros."

"I'm sorry," Nicholas said.

She blinked and then snorted. "For what?" Because he had so much to apologize for and both of them knew he'd do most of it again.

"I wish this had not cost you so much."

"It was my choice. And in the end, maybe it will be worth it. Maybe you will ally with the Ramplings and we'll take Crosspointe back." She didn't sound as if she thought any of it was worth losing Keros.

Nicholas eyed the unconscious majicar, feeling an unfamiliar wriggle of jealousy in his gut.

It was almost a full glass later when the majick cocooning Ellyn began to shrink and fade away. It rippled like silk in the wind, then turned ghostly pale and disappeared altogether. Nicholas came to his feet.

Both majicars lay as if asleep. Margaret reached out and shook Ellyn. The other woman did not respond.

"Help me carry them to the bed," she said.

Nicholas grabbed Ellyn's arm and lifted her over his shoulder, her head dangling down his back. He flopped her down onto the bed and returned to get Keros. Margaret had pulled Keros's arm over her shoulder. Nicholas did the same and together they dragged him across the floor.

They pulled the boots and coats off the two unconscious majicars. Margaret sucked in a breath as she examined Ellyn. The majicar's wounds were scabbed over, and as he watched, Nicholas saw them starting to fade into healthy skin.

"How is that possible?" he asked.

"I don't know. Perhaps it's a miracle." But he saw her shiver. She fetched a washbasin of warm water and a washrag. She cleaned the blood from Ellyn as best she could and then covered both of them with the counterpane before retreating to the sitting room. She snatched up her clothing from where she'd hung it near the fire after washing it in the bathtub.

"What are you doing?"

"We need clothing appropriate for Sophia and Avery Shevring, and we need information. I'm going to get both."

"Is that wise?"

"Do you have another suggestion? You want Carston back, don't you?"

"Of course I do," he said, stung.

"Well, then—we're running out of time. When they wake up, we'll need to be ready."

When, not if. "Then I'll go with you."

She tossed an angry glance at him, her cheeks flushed. "No. Someone has to stay here and watch them."

He crossed the room, grabbing her arm and twisting her to face him. She'd channeled her worry and fear into anger and purpose. But it made her reckless. "Someone has to watch your back. I'm not letting you wander around this nest of vipers alone."

"Nest of vipers?"

"This is the regent's stronghold, and let us not forget how hungry he is to capture Ramplings. And you are not just a Rampling, but you are Princess Margaret. He is very hungry for you; he'll treat you with extra-special care." The idea was beyond repugnant. "You need me."

"If anyone recognizes you, we'll be in a lot of trouble. I'm almost invisible. No one ever associates me with the putridly stupid Princess Margaret."

"They won't," he promised. "There's nothing I can do for Keros or Ellyn. Staying here is pointless."

"Fine," she said, giving in suddenly. She'd been drawn too tight and was ready to snap.

She went back through the bedchamber to the garderobe to dress. Nicholas pulled on his clothes. They were still damp and clammy. He grimaced and pulled on his socks, stamped into his boots and slid his knives down into the shafts. The one around his neck he'd never removed. His rapier he left hanging over a chair. No serving man wore a sword like that.

He heard Margaret come out of the garderobe. When she didn't immediately return to the sitting room, he went to look in. She had stopped beside Keros's head and was smoothing the counterpane with gentle hands. She stroked his hair away from his face, then bent down and whispered something Nicholas could not hear.

Nicholas felt a surge of something that bore a horrifying resemblance to jealousy and retreated to the sitting room. He choked back a harsh laugh at his stupidity. Margaret Rampling? He was a fool.

"We should go," Margaret said as she joined him. She donned her cloak with businesslike determination. "If Ellyn did see the regent, then we must move very quickly. The longer we are here, the more likely he is to want to meet the Shevrings and find out their business." She frowned at him. "You can't wear your greatcoat. It's too expensive." Her gaze ran from his head to his foot. "Everything you're wearing is too expensive. Wait here. I'll fetch something less conspicuous."

She slipped out into the hallway and shut the door before he could take more than two steps to interfere. He found himself facing the door. He reached for the latch and then drew back his hand. She knew what she was doing.

Still, by the time she returned more than a quarter of a glass later, he was seething. She knocked at the door softly and he yanked her inside. "We go together next time, or not at all," he rasped.

She handed him the clothing—brown wool trousers and vest, a canvas shirt and a moth-eaten cloak. He ignored the garments, still scowling at her. Her expression turned haughty. "I am not yours to command," she said. "You may bluster and order me about all you want, but I know the business of the shadows far better than you. It is what I was made to do. Now, put those on before I go without you."

He hesitated, then turned and stripped with no regard for her presence. He was afraid if he went into the dressing room to change, she'd be gone before he returned. His movements were jerky with anger—mostly at himself. His attraction to her was foolish and unwarranted. She was merely the best means he had for rescuing Carston—he would not let himself mistake gratitude for real feelings. He told himself this firmly and made himself believe it.

The inn was bustling and the taproom filled with men in search of breakfast. Margaret and Nicholas slipped out through a storage area and hurried down the main street. The smells of fresh bread and smoked meat filled the air. The sun gleamed from between the tatters of storm clouds, and there was a jauntiness to the villagers. The news of the regent's arrival ran through Molford like a wildfire. His name was on everyone's lips.

Nicholas was astonished at the way Margaret faded from sight. He almost didn't recognize her. She carried herself in the tentative way of servants, her voice alternately sharp and wheedling. She bought a variety of things for her supposed mistress—a dress, underskirts, a shawl, stockings, a lace cap, and more. They were basic, as readymade items tended to be, but Margaret twittered on about how she'd tailor them to suit her mistress who was so very ill after the terrible events of their travel.

With each conversation, she picked up more and more of the information they needed.

" 'Tis a fine old manor," she said when stopping to purchase lavender oil. "How many rooms? And where does the family sleep, then? And how many servants does the regent keep—and such a fine figure of a man he is, too, don't you think? And such a vigorous town—how many people live here? You must all be so proud. And does the regent have guests? It must take a lot of food and wine to entertain such fine folk. How many visitors did he have, then? How big are the grounds? How to get in and out? An old manor like that—it must have its secrets, no? Hidden passages and all that. I had a cousin once who got lost inside the walls of one of the great houses in Sylmont and nearly starved to death before they could find her!"

She kept up a running patter, gossipy and homey, going to nearly every business in town. Nicholas marveled at her as he trailed silently behind with the parcels.

"Now, that's what I call a good man," a stout woman with a hairy upper lip said to Margaret in a loud whisper as she cast a lascivious look at Nicholas. "Nary a word spoken and strong as an ox, carrying all your trifles. That's a man worth keeping."

"Don't I know it. You know he wants to marry me," Margaret said breezily. "But I told him no. John, I said, not until you have a bit put by for a home of our own will I marry you." She looked from side to side as if searching for anyone trying to overhear. Her voice dropped conspiratorially. "Did the regent's wife come with him? I hear she's quite a handsome woman. I'd like to catch a glimpse of her myself."

"As handsome as they come," the baker's wife said. "Though she's sharpish. I wouldn't want to be working in her house." She bent forward. "I heard she's beaten her maids so they can hardly walk afterward, just for nonsense like spilling tea on her glove or making an uneven hem in her skirt." She added an extra sugar bun to the dozen she'd already counted out. "They say she's the real power behind the man. A lady-Koreion—she'll eat you whole. But good for the purse." She patted her apron pockets as if they contained money. "Just this morning she sent an order. I'll be up all night." She smiled, her jowls shaking. "I'll borrow some of those collared servants to help me. I tell you, that regent is good for Molford and Crosspointe too."

At the cobbler, Margaret gleaned another piece of information, this one disturbing.

"Ain't got no time right now," the harried man said, hobnails sticking out of the corners of his mouth. "Regent wants his men ready to march within a sennight. I'm burning the candles at both ends and still won't finish with all this in time." He waved at the piles of boots in need of mending that littered his shop. "Come back in a sennight." He bustled away without waiting for an answer.

Margaret stepped back out onto the wooden sidewalk, her brow furrowed. She glanced at Nicholas. "Where do you suppose they are marching to?" she asked. "And why?"

"Do you have a stronghold? Somewhere you are assembling your own army?" he asked as they began to walk.

She slid a suspicious look at him and said nothing. Annoyance stirred in him. More, he realized, because it was becoming clear that Geoffrey was more dangerous than Nicholas had anticipated. How had he been so blind to the other man's plotting?

They returned to the inn and went inside the way they'd departed. Margaret unlocked the door and pushed it wide. Nicholas dropped his many packages on a chair and slipped off his borrowed cloak. Margaret went to the bedchamber and then returned.

"They are still asleep," she said shortly. "We should dress and ring for lunch."

She rifled through the parcels, finding the clothing she'd bought for Sophia Dedlok of Shevring. It was more serviceable than fashionable, but beggars couldn't be choosers, and in a village the size of Molford, one couldn't expect much of a selection of readymade clothing.

She retreated to the dressing room.

In the meantime, Nicholas changed into the clothing she'd purchased for him. There were gray wool trousers, a silk shirt, a vest stitched with simple embroidery, and cravat. He had just pulled the bell to summon the servants when Margaret returned.

She was wearing a soft green wool dress over a layer of underskirts. "Would you button me?" she asked as she approached him and turned, the full fabric of her dress sweeping across his feet.

He obliged, glad for the thin chemise that kept his fingers from touching her skin as he fastened the long row of buttons. It was an intimate act, the kind shared by lovers and married couples. He let out a silent sigh.

"Thank you," she said and began tightening the laces along her sides. Just as she finished, a knock sounded at the door. She went to answer.

He was warned only by the sudden stiffness in her back, and then the servant appeared. She was only seventeen or eighteen seasons old. Her hair was caught behind her head in a severe bun and her clothing hung loose as if she'd lost a great deal of weight. Her arms were covered with bruises and there were patches where she'd been burned. Around her neck was the thick iron collar that had once meant indentured servitude, and now meant slavery. She shuffled inside, her gaze fixed on the floor.

"Good morning, ma'am," she said with a curtsy. "How may I serve you?"

Margaret shut the door with a loud thump. She stared

at the wood, her arms crossed tightly over her stomach.
Nicholas fought the urge to go to her. He could offer no
comfort that she would want. The maid had jumped at
the noise and now cowered into herself, waiting for an
expected blow, no doubt. Nicholas snarled and went to
the sideboard to pour a brandy. The bottle was nearly
empty. He slugged it down in one gulp. He could blame
Geoffrey for the slavery, but in the end, he was responsible. He'd made Geoffrey regent and had never tried
to stop him.

"I'm sorry if I've offended you, ma'am," the girl said
into the silence.

"Offended me?" Margaret said, her voice rising. "By
Chayos, you *do* offend me. You and that damned collar and—" She broke off like she'd been strangled. "I
must apologize," she said more softly. "I'm—" She drew
a harsh breath and her gaze flickered to Nicholas. It was
a helpless, desperate look and he moved quickly to her
side. He put his arm around her, and though she held
herself stiffly did not push him away.

"What is your name?" he asked the girl gently.

She started and her gaze flicked to his boots. She
would not look him in the face. "Cora, sir."

"And your family name?" he prodded. Margaret
clutched his arm.

"Blickley," she said even more softly.

Nicholas frowned. He couldn't place the name. "How
did you end up here?"

The girl gave a little shrug. "They say my uncle's wife
committed treason. She's a Rampling." She sniffed. "I
should get to work, sir. Missus Drumpolt doesn't like it
when I dawdle." She rubbed a hand over her arm.

"I can't do this," Margaret said in a strangled voice,
turning away from Nicholas.

His own chest was tight. The girl had been made a
slave by virtue of a distant connection to the Ramplings.

She wasn't even blood. Not that it would have made it any more excusable.

"Clear the table if you would, please," he said and Cora hurried to remove the remains of last night's meal. There was a trundle cart in the hall and she loaded everything onto it. "May I bring you lunch?" she asked when she finished. "Cook has cold ham or lamb and hot potato salad with greens, a fruit tart, some roasted tomatoes with dill sauce and fresh rosemary bread." She repeated it as if by rote.

"Yes," he said. "That will do."

The girl bobbed another curtsy and then quietly shut the door.

"It's monstrous," Margaret said, her voice strangled. "That poor girl. By the gods, what have we done?"

"We?" Nicholas asked, startled.

"Yes. You, the regent, me—my family. What have we done that that child can have a collar put around her neck and be sold to whoever wants her? That she can be beaten and burned and even raped? This must be stopped. It cannot be allowed to go on."

"I agree."

She turned. "Do you promise? No matter what happens, no matter what it takes, you'll stop this?"

He reached out and took her hands. They were cold and they trembled, with anger or hatred or horror, he didn't know. "I will. We will."

She tightened her fingers on his a moment, then let go, her gaze suddenly remote, like she was looking at him from across a vast chasm. "I won't let the regent put me in one of those collars," she said.

The thought made Nicholas's stomach turn. Geoffrey liked to feel his power. If he had Margaret in a collar, he'd use her in the most degrading ways he could think of. And he had a fertile imagination. Not that Margaret would ever let him have the satisfaction. She'd kill herself first. "If it happens, I'll come for you. I promise you that. Don't do anything stupid. I *will* come."

She shook her head. "Don't," she said. "Don't make promises to me. I'll take care of myself. I always have."

He knew she didn't believe him. Why should she? But he meant every word.

She licked her lips and her expression turned stoic—a mask to hide everything she might be feeling. "We have to make a plan. It's time to do what we came here to do." She glanced at the doorway of the bedchamber, her brow furrowing. "It looks like it will be just you and me."

Nicholas wanted to tell her no. It was too dangerous. But an image rose in his mind of a terrified Carston, an iron collar on his neck, his body bloody and bruised. He closed his eyes, letting out a shaky breath. "Thank you," he said, knowing it was not enough. It would never be enough, not for the history that lay between them and not for Cora and the women in the brothels and every other innocent who'd been chained up and enslaved; and not for Keros, who might not wake up and know her, and not for her dead father and her angry brothers who might never forgive or trust her again.

She smiled, sad and bitter, as if reading his mind. "I wasn't born to walk an easy path."

"You deserve better," he said, wanting to give it to her and knowing she wouldn't take it, not from him.

"What is better? Tonight we will rescue your boy and if nothing else, you will turn your hand to stopping slavery. If my entire life is measured by that much, then it is all worth it."

Chapter 11

He awoke slowly. It was like swimming up from the depths of the Inland Sea. He opened his eyes and blinked. Everything was limned with a shifting rainbow of light. He watched it, fascinated. Pinks chased blues and greens as they ran down edges, bubbling together on corners and then sliding away again.

A pain cramped his stomach. He was hungry. He sat up slowly. He was on a bed. Beside him lay someone. A woman. She was sleeping. He reached out and set a hand on her shoulder. He pushed out and his awareness flashed through her. Something inside her woke and swept through him—tasting, testing. It retreated, harmless.

He let go of her and swung his legs over the side of the bed. He sat there, staring at the kaleidoscope of colors and shapes. He tried to understand it. He reached out his hand and set it on the bed stand. It was solid, the wood—*Yes, wood*. He knew what that was—flat and satiny with a lace doily spreading across the top. He knew these words, too, and what they represented.

Something moved inside him. It was physical—a sliding touch against bone and brain. He heard something. Almost a voice. More a feeling. Wonder. Uncertainty. Fear. Anger. Melded together in a choir. He cocked his head as if it could help him listen.

He heard voices. There were people in the next room. They sounded familiar—a low male voice and a quick woman's voice. He stood and padded to the door and paused within the jamb. The colors continued to run and yet everything was sharp edged and clear. He saw the woman—Margaret. She was sitting at the dining table, her food hardly touched. Her colors were the liquid green of new leaves mixed with a dark velvet blue. Bright specks of orange, pink, yellow, and crimson chased through the green and the blue. She was arguing with . . . Weverton. Weverton was made of black and silver with striations of butter yellow and twilight purple. His colors were misty and not as sharply-edged as Margaret's. Keros—*I am Keros*—wondered why.

And then suddenly memory flooded back. He rocked back on his heels as it washed over him in a torrent. Margaret and Weverton. The majicar battle in the Riddles. Ellyn. The journey to Molford. The slaves. The spell crafting with Ellyn. The casting at the brothels. There was a long gray blank and then—

He squeezed his eyes shut. Melting. He could only describe it as melting. He'd felt himself dissolving as the thing in his mind expanded. He'd fought but it was like he had been tearing chunks out of his own mind. He'd not been able to stop. He ripped at himself, shredding himself apart, chasing the illusive thing that darted through his mind like a phantasm. Then something happened.

Healing. Ellyn had tried to heal him. But it was impossible to heal what wasn't sick. He was *invaded*. But her spell had distracted the thing inside him. It had given him a moment to think, to stop fighting. He'd surrendered, knowing that fighting was killing him.

After that he did not remember anything until he'd woken. The thing was still there—it was part of him and yet separate. It was waiting for something; he didn't know what. He glanced behind at Ellyn. His chest knotted as he remembered the majicars in the Riddles. They had gone insane and he knew, without knowing how, that there had been an invader in each of their minds as well, and they had driven themselves mad fighting it. Would she survive?

There was little enough he could do. It was Ellyn's battle. And yet, watching her lying so still, he remembered that blue morning on the beaches of Azaire when the *sylveth* tide rolled in and, one after another, all his friends, family, and neighbors were thrown into the sea. He'd watched then, too, helpless. And less than a season ago, when Lucy was taken and the Jutras had come, he'd been bound in majick, unable to lift a finger. He was so very tired of being helpless. The echoing emotion in his mind was resounding—the thing most wholeheartedly agreed, supposing it had a heart.

"Keros!"

Margaret leaped to her feet and ran to him, grappling him in a hug. He hugged her back, smelling the floral scent of her hair. It was stronger now, more intense, like he'd developed a new capacity for the spectrum of scent. He sniffed. Smells opened like a fascinating bouquet— sharp and sour, sweet and musky, dank and foul. Margaret stepped back, examining him. Her brow furrowed.

"What is it?" he asked.

"Your eyes."

He touched beneath them, concentrating on re-forming the illusion that covered the telltale silver and red eyes of a majicar. He felt it snap into place. "Is that better?"

She shook her head and the fluid light of her being swirled and shifted. "No. I mean, yes—the illusion is covering them, but no, your eyes have *changed*. They were white—all white. Like a bowl of milk."

He blinked. "That's new," he said dryly.

"Indeed," she said. "Any idea why?"

"A guess," he said. "I'll explain over food. How's Ellyn?"

She looked past him at the prone woman. "She's been like that since you both collapsed. Can you help her?"

He shook his head slowly. "I don't think so. This is a battle she fights on her own."

"Battle?"

"I'll explain. But first"—the food called tantalizingly, but every bit of his body itched—"I'd very much like a bath."

She wrinkled her nose. "You *are* a little past ripe. I bought clothes for you. I'll get them."

She retrieved the parcel and he went to wash. He remained in the tub longer than he planned, captivated by the shifting lights of the steam. They were mesmerizing. At last Margaret knocked at the door.

"Did you drown?" she asked through the wood.

"Not quite yet," he said, standing and reaching for his towel. He quickly dried himself and dressed. On the way through the bedchamber, he stopped to check Ellyn. She had not moved. She was made of mossy green light with scarlet twirling through it like windblown ribbons chasing sparks of white. But her lights were sluggish. He put a hand on her chest and again that awareness within her swept him. He tried to catch at it, but it slipped too quickly away. He followed, but he could not get past the barrier of her lights. He lifted his hand. He hesitated a moment, then bent so that his lips were close to her ear.

"Sperray—do not fight yourself. Surrender as you did that day in the *sylveth* tide. Be what you will be." He turned his head and kissed her cheek, inhaling her scent. He straightened and backed away, joining Weverton and Margaret in the sitting room.

His stomach felt like it was chewing its way out of his ribs. He stabbed some ham from the platter and wrapped it in a slice of chewy bread. He ate it quickly, then reached for the potato salad and roasted tomatoes. The flavors of food exploded on his tongue. He wanted to eat slower and savor, but he was too hungry and his companions were impatient. Neither Weverton nor Margaret spoke as he ate. They sipped wine and waited. Keros could feel the anger that simmered between them.

Their lights were quick and brilliant—jewellike. He eyed Weverton more closely. The man's lights remained misty—like they were reflected through water.

"Is something wrong?" the other man asked when Keros had stared too long.

"I'm not certain," Keros said without a hint of humor.

When he said nothing else, Nicholas leaned forward, resting his forearms on the table. "I would very much like you to explain that."

Keros swallowed and took a drink of tepid tea before answering. He sat back and steepled his fingers together. "When I look at you, I don't see you as I once did," he said. How could he possibly make them understand?

"How *do* you see us?" Margaret asked, her attention sharpening.

"In colored light—it moves, tracing the lines of you." Keros waved his hands. "I cannot explain. But it isn't just you—everything appears so."

"Why? Is this permanent?" Margaret asked, almost at the same time that Weverton asked, "Why do you think something might be wrong with me?"

"I don't know if it's permanent or not." He gave a short explanation of what had happened to him.

"This *thing* is still in your mind?" Margaret asked, drawing back slightly.

"It is."

"And you've no idea what it is. How do we get it out of you?"

He shook his head slowly. "I don't know." It felt

deeply anchored, as if it had infiltrated every muscle, every drop of his blood, every beat of his heart. "I don't know if I can be rid of it." There was a confirming wash of agreement inside him followed by a not entirely comfortable caress across his mind. He twitched uneasily, the touch deeply intimate.

"Will it—" Margaret broke off. She looked down at her hands. "Are you still you?"

He smiled. "Would I know if I wasn't? You should tell me."

"You sound like yourself."

"Maybe you were hoping that some of the rough edges got ground off."

"I like you fine the way you are."

"That's because you have no taste," he said.

"What do you mean there might be something wrong with me?" Weverton broke in impatiently.

Keros looked at him, watching the soft, watery shift of his brilliant colors. Thin gauzy strands floated free like the tatters of a sail. "Your lights aren't crisp and sharp the way everything else is. They—" He shrugged. "I have no experience to say whether this is normal or not."

Nicholas stretched out a hand, laying it flat on the table. "Look with majick."

Keros hesitated, then covered the other man's hand with his own. He looked down at his own lights. They were a pale blue and lilac with twists of black and yellow rolling around them. He reached for his majick. It came with sluggish unwillingness and his lights flared as it filled him. He stared a moment, fascinated. He should have still been exhausted after creating the spell for the brothels, but he felt fresh and invigorated.

He pushed out with his majick. At this point he needed to concentrate on Nicholas's body, not the intriguing play of his own lights. He closed his eyes, feeling his majick spreading out along the other man's arm and up over his shoulders, then down his back and chest to his feet. He pushed harder and his majick sank inside. He reached for his *illidre* with his other hand. For a moment his attention was riveted on the ugly squash of hardened *sylveth*. Its lights were spectacular. There were too many colors to count and they rolled and flared and pulsed separately and together in an enthralling slide of color. He could have stared for days.

With an effort, Keros tore himself free and concentrated on the spell he kept for diagnosis. It was a complex weaving that was designed to search for *wrongness* of body or spirit. It was one of his early spells. A miracle really. He'd had no more business creating that spell than he had the *illidre*. He'd come to Crosspointe with no idea how to be a majicar and a desperate need to learn to harness his power. He'd taken to stalking the guild-trained majicars and eavesdropping on them. He'd picked up bits and pieces of information, but in the end, it was a puzzle that did not fit together. He was going to have to figure out how to be a majicar himself. And to start, he needed an *illidre*.

It wasn't something he could buy, so he knew he had to make it himself. Unaware it was a master's level skill and entirely beyond his abilities, he'd taken a skiff outside the Pale and landed on one of the Caris Islands clustering along the north shore of Crosspointe. There, where *sylveth* ran freely in the tides, he was certain he could learn what he needed.

He'd stayed there for sennights that turned into months while he experimented. It had been maddening how little he understood. Every time he thought he learned something, he found out he was wrong. Toward the end, he'd begun taking wild risks, coming close to death more than once. Looking back, he doubted he was entirely sane at that point. Hunger, lack of sleep, exposure, and isolation had driven him to the edge of reason.

They boiled together with desperate rage and frustration and unexpectedly, that maelstrom of emotion and deprivation honed the focus he needed.

There had come a *sylveth* tide. He'd waded out into it, scooping some into his hands. He'd struck it with every bit of majick he could muster. He didn't remember what had happened then, but when he returned to awareness, he found himself lying facedown on the rocky shingle, a crushed hardened blob of *sylveth* clenched in his fist. Over the seasons, he'd never tried to refine it or make it more pleasing to the eye, though he'd learned far more about majick since then. It was a testament to that boy and his strength and determination.

Since that day, he had impressed many spells inside it. The one he reached for now had been born one night after an illness had attacked his ship. It had been only two seasons since he had crafted his *illidre* and he had only managed simple spell castings. Then the plague had struck. It was an insidious illness, quietly killing the men one after another. The first three went in their sleep with no symptoms. The fourth simply dropped on the deck. They were days out of Crosspointe and Keros was all that stood between the ship and certain death.

By the time anyone realized a shipmate was sick, he was already falling down dead. Keros had needed to create a spell that would quickly seek out those who were ill. He had to be quick or there wouldn't be enough crewmembers left to bring the ship to port and everyone would die. If the captain—Marten—and Pilot were killed, the ship would be lost at sea.

Keros had never understood his limitations—that what he was doing would have taken a master healer sennights, if not months, to fashion. Instead he set to work with that finely honed desperation and intensity that he'd used when he'd made his *illidre*.

He'd saved his ship and he'd used the spell over and

over again through the seasons since. Now he turned it on Weverton. He felt the majick unfold in a lattice. It swept through Weverton like a fine sieve. The other man stiffened, his hand balling into a fist beneath Keros's.

"There's nothing wrong that I can see," Keros said, withdrawing his hand at last. "Beyond the fact that you are a cracking bastard, of course," he said.

"Of course," Weverton said with an edged smile. "Maybe one day you'll find a cure for that."

"I can think of at least one," Keros said and he spun blue-green majick around his fingers. It was unformed and hardly dangerous, but Weverton drew back sharply. Keros smiled.

"We should get back to planning Carston's rescue," Margaret said suddenly. "We must move quickly before we are discovered or the regent tries to take the boy somewhere else."

"Are we certain the boy is still here?" Keros asked.

She shrugged. "No. We've learned some information about the grounds and the house, but I will simply have to go inside and search. I had hoped Ellyn could give me some information but—" She shrugged meaningfully. "After that, we can build a plan for rescuing him. We have to hurry. The regent will hear about the horses and then he'll want to be introduced to us. We have little time."

"No," Weverton said stolidly and Keros realized that this was the argument he'd interrupted when he'd woken up. "You will not go in alone. It is too risky. Now that Keros is awake, we can go in together."

Margaret shook her head tiredly. "I go in and scout. I find out what we're up against. Then I come back out and we figure out the best way to get Carston out without getting caught. Why is that so hard for you to understand?"

Weverton looked up at the ceiling covered in artful

plaster leaves. "Because you risk too much and I risk nothing," he said and his gaze dropped heavily back to Margaret. "I'm his father and you— You've already done more than anyone could possibly expect of you."

She shrugged. "I'm willing. Besides, I'm hoping you'll repay me with an alliance. So you might consider this my duty."

"That's a load of horse shit," he said.

"Nevertheless, this is what I do and I am very good at it." She paused. "I do not need your permission, though this will go better if we work together."

He stared, then thrust to his feet. His chair skidded backward and bounced off the wall. His mouth opened and then snapped shut. He looked at Keros. "Have you anything to say?"

The majicar looked at Margaret. "What do you need from me?" he asked.

Weverton swung around and stomped to the window, shoving his hands in his pockets.

"Nothing until I get back."

"And if you don't?" Weverton jerked, half turning around.

"Then I would consider it a favor if you'd send word to my brothers."

Weverton spun around with sharp violence. "And tell them what?"

Her look was cool. "That I'm dead. I won't allow the regent to use me. I'll rob him of his fun first."

He stared, his expression lethal. "If you go in alone and you get caught, then you wait for us. Do you understand? You wait. We will come; *I* will come. I don't cracking care what he does to you or how bad it gets— *you wait for me.*"

She looked askance, blinking surprise. She didn't answer. But the silence said enough. She didn't trust him. But Keros was beginning to wonder. He knew Weverton wanted Margaret. He'd thought before that it was because she was a challenge—someone the other man couldn't have, which therefore made her all the more desirable. While Weverton had no doubt been bored to tears by the Margaret that the rest of Crosspointe knew—the pretty doll who laughed correctly and said just the right thing and was concerned with fashion and gossip—he clearly found the rogue Margaret intriguing. More than that—his attachment seemed real, like he had truly come to care for her. Though whether emotion could or would win out over personal interest was the perennial question.

Suddenly Weverton came around the table and dropped to a crouch in front of her, startling Keros no less than Margaret. Nicholas grasped her hands, waiting until she met his gaze. "*You wait,*" he ordered. "I will not fail you. Promise me."

Keros stared as the soft flowing tendrils of his lights curled around her wrists, clinging gently.

"He won't catch me. And anyway, why would you believe me any more than I believe you?" she asked. She didn't pull away. "Ramplings and Wevertons don't make promises to each other."

"I promise you," he said with quiet fervor.

She shook her head slowly. She wanted to believe, Keros realized. But she couldn't. There was too much history that argued against it.

"At least take these." Weverton pulled a chain from around his neck. On it were a collection of powerful ciphers. "This one has a shield spell, this one is for rapid healing, this one will let you hear at a longer distance—" He broke off as she shook her head.

"No. But thank you," she added when he glowered ferociously. "Except for this cracking family pendant that I can't take off, I wear no other ciphers. I don't like relying on crutches. They make me careless and I can't afford it. Anyway, I don't know how much help they'd be the way majick is working lately."

Weverton stood with a jerking movement and backed away, his hands hanging loose at his sides. The silence was molten. Finally Keros broke it.

"Well, if you won't believe him, believe me. If you get caught by the regent, I'll be coming for you. If you won't wait for him, then wait for me."

She just shrugged without agreeing and glanced at the window. "No time like the present. I'll get my uniform on." She stood and gathered her travel-stained clothing. Before she retreated into the bedchamber to change, she turned, her gaze taking in both of them. "I won't get caught. But if I do"—the corner of her mouth turned up in a self-derogatory smile—"If I do, don't be late." She looked at both men. "Either of you."

Chapter 12

The wind was warm and humid. Mud clung to Margaret's boots. She ran through the woods that ran alongside the Molford Manor. The house was more like a castle. There were rows of new barracks along the west side and new barns to the south. The former were teeming with recruits and the latter were stuffed with supplies, including cattle, pigs, sheep, and goats. The regent was preparing to go to war and he was going to make sure his battalions were fed, even if the rest of the country starved. With the weather as wet and cold as it had been, Crosspointe's crops were going to be meager at best, and there was little enough coming in through the shipping channels. Every day there were reports of more ships lost. Just as majick wasn't quite right in Crosspointe, it was most definitely not right at sea. The danger of food riots in the winter season was all too real.

Not her problem, Margaret thought. Not now. She had to get inside the manor and find Carston.

She slipped through the twilight shadows like a wraith. She was angling for the east side of the manor where the kitchen gardens were. They would get her closer to the house than any other cover. From there she'd have to cross open lawns. There were no bushes or trees near the house, which meant she'd be all too visible to watching eyes.

The manor was old and ornate. The front was triangular with a blocky tower on each corner—each a different size. Attached behind were two square wings, with rounded towers on three of their four corners. The walls of the building jutted and lumped with windows, balconies, cupolas, finials, and ornate decorative veneers. The roof bristled with chimney pots and pointed spires.

She'd spent the afternoon getting her bearings and now it was sundown. Most everyone would be inside eating or settling in for the night. Clouds had begun to roll in late in the afternoon, hiding the moon and the stars. Rain would start again soon. It was a good night to prowl.

The gardens were bounded by four-foot walls topped by four more feet of wood lattice to keep out deer and other hungry animals. Margaret took off her cloak and cached it in the crook of a maple tree, and once more scanned her surroundings. No one was about. Quickly she touched each of her knives and poison rings, then her garrote necklace and the throwing knives in her hair. She'd lost two of them on their journey and only four remained. Her fingers paused over the woven strip of leather circling her wrist. Keros had majicked it with a spell to allow them to locate whoever wore it. When she found Carston, if she could, she'd fasten it to him so that if anything went wrong and he was moved before they could rescue him, they'd be able to track him easily.

She thought of Nicholas, her brow furrowing. He truly seemed to fear for her safety. It was inexplicable. What could he benefit from such a pretense?

Unless it wasn't pretense.

Margaret swallowed a groan at the skip of hope her heart made. No. Absolutely not. She could not be attracted to him; she could not let herself be so stupid. But still . . . he *was* strangely solicitous and the expression in his eyes when he looked at her was hungry.

But then again, he was a master liar. Just like she was.

She pushed all thoughts of Nicholas out of her mind. She couldn't afford to maunder. She needed all her attention to find Carston.

Crouching down, she scuttled through the limp, scrubby grass to the wall of the outer garden. Without stopping, she leaped smoothly up onto the top of the stone wall. The lattice was lodged firmly in place and did not wobble. She shimmied over it and dropped down into the garden, crouching low in the shadows. She eased out of the bed, the smell of rosemary and tarragon rising around her. She followed the path through the herb garden to the gate on the other side. It was open a few inches. She nudged it wider and peered through. She faced a crushed-rock walkway. Ahead was another garden and to the left was a path leading out into the grounds.

She opted to go through to the next garden enclosure. It was lush, green, and vibrant. The beds were raised up off the ground, and though the path was squelchy, the drenching rains had been able to drain out of the beds instead of drowning the plants. Pumpkin vines spilled across the path, intertwined with cucumbers and melons. She picked through them, careful not to step on any leaves.

The gate on the other side opened up onto a small circular lawn bordered by a two-foot hedge and hemming a bronze Chayos, her long hair lifting in a rising wind. Her bottom half melded into the trunk of a tree, its roots knobby and thick as they snaked in a circle through a menagerie of animals. Tall stems of flowering plants spilled water into the copper basin below. Benches ringed the tiled circle surrounding the fountain.

Margaret eased out of the gate and froze in place as voices floated through the air. There was a giggle and a quick female patter followed by a slower male voice. Margaret couldn't make out the words, but the couple was moving farther away. She slipped across the lawn, hunching down beside the statue before moving across to crouch in the shadows of the hedge. Now all that lay between her and the house was a tide of yellowing lawn. The lights of the manor were brilliantly lit and there was music playing somewhere.

She ran across the grass to press herself into a crease where a tower jutted from the main wall. She didn't wait to see if anyone had seen her, but jogged left around the tower and into a notch between wings. It was dark here and no windows looked out on this wall. The stone was roughly hewn and gave enough finger- and footholds to climb. She started up just as fat drops of rain began to pop against the wall. She rolled her eyes. Just what she needed.

She went slowly and carefully, firming her grip before risking her weight on the hold. Halfway up she slipped. She had her feet braced wide on the corner lip of the wall and for a moment she swayed, thirty feet above the ground. She threw her weight forward and scrabbled for handholds, legs shaking with the strain of holding herself up. She found a new grip and breathed a sigh of relief between gritted teeth and started up again.

She clambered onto the slate roof, her heart thudding as she rolled onto her back. She flexed her cramped fingers and breathed deeply. But there was no time for rest. She rolled up onto her feet. The servants' quarters were at the top of the house and most of them would be downstairs working. Many had left their windows open for the fresh air.

Margaret walked across the roof. The rain was coming down harder, making the slate slippery. She skidded and slid, landing on her side and grabbing a chimney pot to keep from sliding off the edge of the roof. She pulled herself back up and finished her journey with no more incidents.

She crouched beside a dormer window. The shutters were open wide. Margaret peered inside. There were four beds spaced around the walls. Three were neatly made and the last one was beneath the window and was unmade. Margaret slid inside. She rubbed her feet clean on the sheets and then dropped to the floor. She folded the coverlet up and tucked in the bed, hiding her mess. With any luck, its owner would think it was a practical joke by one of her fellow maids.

Margaret went to the door and eased it open. Now was the hard part. She had to find a place to hide for a few glasses until the house went to bed for the night. Then she would try to locate Carston. She planned to return to Nicholas and Keros before the house stirred to life again.

She went out into the corridor and made her way to a narrow stair. These passages were austere, designed only for servants. There was nowhere to hide except inside the rooms behind the plain doors. Margaret hurried as fast as she dared. She wanted to get down to the first floor, and below, into the kitchen level. Carston would be hidden there somewhere, she was sure. The upper levels were too public. The regent would keep him underground where there were no windows to allow an easy escape or rescue. It would also keep too many servants from becoming aware of the boy.

She passed two floors of guest rooms and reached the family floor with only two encounters. The first time she was able to run back up the stairs until the two maids passed. The second time she was trapped. She started through one of the doors, twisting the knob, then heard voices on the other side. A pair of footmen were coming up the stairs and another opened a door farther ahead. Margaret didn't hesitate. She ran down the corridor and slid in behind the opening door, sliding a stiletto free as she did. The footman stepped out and shut the door with his foot. He held a tray of dishes, which he set on a sideboard. He stopped to adjust his cuffs and dab at his vest with a napkin, muttering a curse as he did.

Margaret chewed her lip. So far he hadn't seen her, but in less than a minute, the footmen on the stairs would appear and she'd be caught. That left her no time.

She stepped up behind the griping footman. He was tall with broad shoulders. Perfect. She slipped around in front of him, grasping his waistband and digging her knife sharply into his cods.

"If you ever want to enjoy another woman again, you will do what I say," she whispered. "Understand?"

His face was pale and he nodded.

"Come with me." She pulled on him, stepping back until they fetched up against the wall. She pressed herself into the corner and pulled him after her. "Now kiss me."

His eyes widened and lips dropped open.

"Now," she said, pushing her knife harder into his groin. The other footmen had stepped out onto the landing. "Be convincing or I'll cut your prick off."

He hesitated only a moment, then obeyed. He bent, his mouth pressing against hers, his arms coming up to circle her stiffly. She couldn't have that. She needed this to look natural. She opened her mouth and licked her tongue against his lips. He started, and then pressed closer, his tongue tangling with hers. Men were so easy. He moaned as she sucked gently and slanted his head, deepening the kiss. Margaret rolled her eyes. He seemed to have totally forgotten her knife against his prick. He ran a hand down over her breast and squeezed. She made a loud sound of pleasure and he responded with a low growl.

Behind him she heard silence and then a chuckling. "Look at Davey. Who's he got there?"

"He's about to roast her on his stick. Maybe he'll give us a taste."

Davey's back stiffened and he started to pull away. Margaret held him and wriggled, pressing her breasts against his chest. He forgot their audience as his lust ignited again. He kissed her, harder this time.

Under other circumstances, Margaret would have enjoyed his attentions. He knew what he was doing and a tumble in bed with him would have been more than enjoyable. And it would help put all distracting thoughts of Nicholas from her mind. But she was on business. She heard the other men tromp up the stairs, leaving her alone with her companion. Gently she pushed Davey back. He stared down at her. He was handsome, with a cleft chin and lovely green eyes. He brushed a hair from her forehead.

"You don't belong here," he said, then glanced down at the knife still prodding his cods, then back up at her. "I'd have kissed you without such encouragement," he said with a grin.

"I can't let you give the alarm," she said. She should kill him.

"I wouldn't be able to if I was busy, say, with you." He lifted his brows and bent, kissing her again.

Margaret smiled beneath his lips. He was brash and arrogant. She liked that. And his suggestion held certain charm. She could pass the time with him until the house was quiet enough to explore. He might be just what she needed to cure herself of her attraction for Nicholas Weverton.

"Where do you suggest we spend our evening together?" she asked seductively.

"There are empty guest rooms. We wouldn't be disturbed."

"Someone would miss you."

He shrugged. "I'll think of an excuse." He kissed her again and pulled away. "I would very much like it if you eased up on that knife. I've got a bit of swelling down there."

She hesitated. It was a risk. But an empty guest room was a good place to hide. She could tie him up and leave him there, and he wouldn't soon be found. Then she wouldn't have to kill him. She slid the knife into her waistband. "Lead the way."

He grinned more broadly and grasped her hand. They went up a flight and then wound through the crisscrossing corridors. At last they ended up on the south side of the house. He stopped two doors from the end, turned the knob, and eased the door open, peering inside. He pulled her within and shut the door. Instantly he drew her close and began kissing her, his hands fisting in the back of her shirt. He rubbed his hips into hers. His eagerness was catching. Margaret pushed off his coat and pulled at the buttons of his vest. In moments his chest was bare. She rubbed her fingers over his skin, delighting in its smooth warmth. He groaned and tugged at her clothing, then swung her up impatiently and carried her to the tall four-poster bed.

They passed the next few hours in delightful activity. Davey was both enthusiastic and energetic. Margaret did not think about Ellyn, Keros, her brothers, or her mission inside the house. Nicholas crept into her thoughts a time or two, and each time she banished his image with firm determination.

Davey had fallen into a deeply contented sleep and Margaret lay curled beside him. By her estimate, it was close to midnight. She should begin her search. She eased out of the bed and cut strips of cloth from the sheets. She braided them together into sturdy ropes, then tied Davey hand and foot without waking him. It wouldn't hold him forever, but long enough. It took her but a few minutes more to dress. She eyed his livery, then shook her head. If she needed a disguise, she'd steal one later.

She was on the first guest floor. Below was the family rooms and on the first two floors were the entertaining rooms. *Sylveth* lamps lit the corridor with a soft glow, brightening as she moved past them, their majick working as if nothing was wrong. She went quickly, careful not to make any noise. There was no one in the halls. She passed a billiard room where a man stood over a woman who lay seductively on the table, her skirts bunched around her waist.

She slid past the arched door opening and went through a long gallery. It overlooked a large ballroom. The scent of the night's dinner permeated the air and made Margaret's stomach grumble. She paused at the top of the sweeping stairway. It was the fastest way down, but footmen stood inside the front doors. She couldn't get past them unnoticed.

She retreated, going back through the gallery and threading her way round to the rear of the ballroom. It ran the length of the manor, dividing the great house in half. Below it were the kitchens and various food cellars, and on the sides were offices, salons, sitting rooms, and small intimate dining rooms. Margaret chanced entering the servants' passages again and dropped down to the first floor.

She came down onto the landing at the same moment a yawning scullery maid rounded the corner. The curly-headed girl stopped short, her eyes springing wide. Her mouth opened and Margaret leaped to clamp a hand over the emerging scream. She spun the girl and held her tight against her chest. She flipped free a poison needle in a ring and started to drag it across the maid's neck. She stopped suddenly, feeling the girl's chest rising and falling rapidly. The girl was innocent—a maid. One of the people she was supposed to protect. *She's working for the wick-sucking regent!* But a maid still must feed her family and buy her clothes, and that meant working for whoever would pay her.

Margaret flipped the needle back into the ring and then pulled her dagger and cracked the girl across the back of the head. The maid slumped to the ground.

Margaret hooked the maid's body beneath her arms and dragged her to the closet beneath the stair. She pushed aside the buckets, brooms, and mops and pulled the body inside. She found a pile of rags and used them to bind and gag the girl. She stood, considering the closet critically. It was clearly used frequently. She did not want the girl to be found too soon. Margaret grabbed three mops and pushed their butt ends against the bottom of the shelving on the far wall. Pulling the door around, she squatted and reached through the opening to settle the damp heads against the back of the door. She pulled her arm out and snicked the latch closed. The mops dropped down to the floor with a thump. She turned the handle and pushed. They didn't budge. That would buy a little time. Eventually the girl would wake up and find a way to make a racket that would bring rescuers. Hopefully not too soon.

She shook her head. She was going soft. She should have left neither Davey nor the girl. Both were expendable. The future of Crosspointe was at stake. For a moment she hesitated, then shook her head. It was too late now.

She began a systematic exploration of the first floor. She found the regent's office empty. She went inside, her fingers itching to pick the locks and rifle through the drawers. But she had no time. She continued her search, finding nothing of interest. At last she slunk down into the kitchens. She had to be more careful here. The cook slept in an attached room and her helpers were scattered about on thin straw mattresses. The room was hot from the day's cooking and the oven fires were banked. *Sylveth* didn't work for cooking—somehow food didn't cook evenly with majick.

She stepped carefully around the exhausted bodies and stroked a cat who purred loudly into her hand. She took a small cake from the basket on the counter before going through to the buttery and out into the cold cellar. Beyond that was a cold storage for vegetables and herbs and another for wine and liquor. Margaret wandered through, looking for a door into the rest of the basement area but found nothing. There had to be more. The kitchen and cellar took up no more than half of the manor's main floor area. That meant there was another half where Carston might be imprisoned.

She was retreating back to search for another passage out of the kitchen when she found what she was looking for. It was a door hidden behind a rack of whiskey casks. It was well disguised, and if she hadn't been looking for it, she wouldn't have seen it. There was only about a six-inch gap between the rack and the hidden door. Margaret pushed against the heavy wood frame but it didn't budge. She ran her fingers over the wood, pressing and digging into crevices and knotholes. She went around and reached as far as she could down the gap, then began on the casks. She brushed past a rough spot on the bottom of the third cask. She felt the tingle of a ward and then a click. The rack shifted slightly and she pushed against it. It swiveled away from the wall and Margaret smiled.

The door wasn't warded. She picked the lock with ease and turned the handle. The hallway on the other side was paneled with polished wood. The floor was black and white marble and the walls were decorated with paintings, sculptures, and a variety of other bric-a-brac. Margaret peered both directions and saw no one. But the corridor was brightly lit, which likely meant that people had passed by recently.

Margaret slid out into the passage. She turned left for no better reason than it went deeper into the space and she figured the regent would bury Carston as far back in this warren as he could.

She found a number of empty rooms and kept going, pushing deeper. Ahead she heard the rumble of voices and dodged into a room on the right. She glanced around, shutting the door behind her. An odd chill ran up her spine. This was a sitting room of a princely variety. Everything was ostentatiously sumptuous. The carpets were deeply piled, the furniture layered with gold leaf, the decorations rare treasures from around the world. Beyond were equally luxurious bedchambers. The place was fit for any king, but what was it doing hidden in the basement?

Margaret tensed. Instinct told her something was very wrong about this.

Another rumble, this time of laughter. Margaret eased back out into the hallway. She moved silently, her heart pounding. She slid a knife into her hand. At the corner she pressed close to the wall and peered around the edge, only to yank herself back.

Holy Mother of All!

She licked her lips and looked again. The hall spread into a large, lofty room. It was filled with stuffed chaises and chairs, and the walls were lined with books, statuary, paintings, porcelain, and bronzes. They were clustered haphazardly, without any sense of taste, more like a storage warehouse than anything else. Something else caught her eye. She sucked in a startled breath. The floor was layered with white bearskin rugs from Ayvreshar, each dyed in the rich colors of the tribes. They were impossible to buy and even one was almost priceless. There were at least fifty of them.

In fact—

She ducked away. It was a pyrate's treasure trove in there. There were pieces there from Relsea and Tapisriya—countries that the Jutras had rolled over and squashed. Margaret rubbed the back of her hand over her trembling lips. If those things were here, then it meant the regent was involved with the Jutras. Though Avreshar remained free, rumors had it that the Jutras had begun raiding within its borders. It was only a matter of time until it fell.

Her stomach churned and she fought the urge to throw up. Ryland and Vaughn needed to know this. Again a burst of laughter. She shifted and peeked around again. Now she saw that there was a salon through an arched opening on the left. On the right were a series of closed doors. Each was barred from the outside with a small slot window at eye level. Prison cells.

She frowned. The entire arrangement was strange. Such luxurious accommodations side by side with a dungeon. She chewed the inside of her cheek. She should get out of Molford and back to Sylmont as quickly as possible. Ryland needed to know the regent was consorting with the Jutras. Her gaze slid to the cells. Inside one of those, Carston was trapped, terrified. She was sure of it. Her attention went back to the archway. She couldn't make out any of the conversation, but she'd give her teeth to hear it. So would Ryland. A tight smile tightened her mouth. If she got caught, she very well might be giving her teeth, and maybe the rest of her too. She was creeping across the opening even before she finished the thought.

The thick jungle of treasure lent her concealment even as it provided a field of danger where she risked revealing herself by knocking things over. It took half a glass to cross through the gauntlet. By the time she was done, sweat was trickling between her breasts.

She stopped beside a wide-bellied cabinet that was carved to resemble an open-weave basket. The wood was fragrant—sweet and spicy at the same time. A set of squat frog statues carved from a gray-green stone were set in a semicircle in front of it, and several bolts of cloth were stacked to the side. She wriggled in behind and settled in to listen.

She could hear the speakers clear enough now.

". . . have done remarkably well," said a deep, raspy voice. "The Dhucala is pleased."

Margaret went cold. The Dhucala was the Jutras king. If she needed any confirmation that the regent was colluding with the Jutras, she had it.

"However, you have promised to open Blackwater Bay to our ships, and compasses and Pilots to keep us safe on the sea. When can I tell the Dhucala to expect them? He is most eager. He hopes the gifts he sends will encourage you to go more quickly with your plans."

"I have already taken steps," came the regent's smug voice. "Nicholas Weverton will soon be powerless to stop me. I will seize his property and put his family in chains. His allies will drop him like a handful of hot coals and switch allegiance to me. He has underestimated me and will pay the price for it. He has no idea what is about to happen to him."

"And what about the Ramplings?" A different voice, younger, more agile.

"Toothless."

"Are they? I have heard young Prince Ryland is stirring up resistance against you. It is said that many of your people disapprove of you."

"He is a green boy."

"Yet he eludes you."

"I have had my attention on more critical matters. What Ryland does is of little consequence."

Margaret's lip curled, but there was truth to what he said. Ryland was an excellent diplomat, but he knew nothing about war or the real politics of Crosspointe. He was just too damned inexperienced. He was collecting support and biding his time until Vaughn had built an army, but the longer he waited, the more entrenched the regent became. Soon it would be nearly impossible to pry him off the throne. And the bastard wanted to be king. She didn't doubt for a single moment. How he'd thought he'd ever keep it by letting the Jutras overrun Crosspointe, she couldn't imagine.

The Jutras didn't leave anything left of a country after they conquered it. They first murdered anyone who defied them, including any leaders. Next they killed off anybody too old or too weak. The rest they gave a choice: become Jutras or die. Those men and women with some fighting ability would join the warrior cast—called *picrit*. They would remain forever at the bottom of the cast, though their children would be able to rise. If they were permitted children. The rest would become slaves—the *neallonya* caste. Geoffrey Truehelm would be lucky if he was just killed.

"Perhaps it is time you turned your attention to the Ramplings. They are inventive and it would not do to underestimate them." The first voice again.

Margaret itched to see them for herself. She gripped the legs of the cabinet to keep herself anchored and wondered just where in the black depths Truehelm's bitch wife was in all this? It wasn't like Alanna Truehelm to let herself be excluded.

"Once I have Weverton in hand, I will send my troops to scour Crosspointe. I will have him and any other errant Ramplings in shackles before the end of the summer season. After that, it shall be simple enough to take control of the Pilots' Guild. Then the Dhucala will have his compasses and Pilots."

The irony was bitter. King William had been selling compasses to Glacerie to gain allies on the water against the Jutras, and here the regent was planning to hand them over to the Jutras. The man was a snake and he needed to have his head chopped off.

"And what about this unfortunate business in Sylmont?" came the second voice.

The question was met with a long silence. Margaret frowned. What unfortunate business?

"It appears that the fall of the Kalpestrine has had an unsettling effect on our majicars. They are not quite themselves. It is my hope that when trade opens between Jutras and Crosspointe, I may depend on your aid in this matter. In the meantime, I have issued an order to execute any majicar on sight, and have sent men to clear out Sylmont. It should be safe enough to return there soon."

Margaret breathed in a long, slow breath, feeling like she'd been kicked in the stomach by a mule. Executing majicars? She remembered Keros's battle in the Riddles and worry wormed through her stomach. What had happened? Was the city in ruins? What about Ryland?

"Let us not keep you any longer," the older Jutras voice said. "Your servants will wonder what you do down here so late in the night."

"They are paid not to wonder," came the regent's dismissive reply.

"But it is their nature, yes? And you must be circumspect until your hold on this country is complete."

Circumspect. That was how the man had managed to get this far. He'd always been so careful to manage his ambitions so that he didn't get caught. Though her father had suspected him of gray dealings, he'd always main-tained an untarnished public character. Margaret turned one of her poisoned rings around her finger. He'd had as much reason or more than Nicholas to assassinate her father. She'd dearly love to return the favor.

There were shuffling sounds as the men rose and began to exit the room. She hunched herself down, keeping well hidden.

"When will you return to the Dhucala?" the regent asked.

"He has asked us to remain here in your service," the younger Jutras replied. "We are at your disposal."

Margaret shook her head. Their language and accents were flawless and smooth, as if they'd been born in Crosspointe. That sent a creeping shiver down her spine. It said a lot about how long the Jutras had been after Crosspointe, and how deeply their plots were rooted. They were a brutal, terrifying people, but they were not stupid.

"Surely you do not plan to stay here at Molford Manor," Truehelm said in alarm.

"Of course not. We would not risk revealing our alliance, and we have other business to attend to. We will depart as soon as may be, Eved-cala."

The last word made Margaret gasp. *Eved-cala?* The word meant something like viceroy. She shook her head silently. The regent wanted more than the throne. Was he insane? Did he really believe they'd give him so much power? He was a fool!

"Other business?" Truehelm echoed. Much to Margaret's disgust, there wasn't even the slightest hint of concern in his voice about what the two Jutras might be up to.

"Yes. We may have further information for you soon," said the younger one.

There was a quiet smugness to his voice that sent a curl of fear through Margaret. What were they up to?

She chewed the inside of her lip. She was going to have to find out.

"One more thing," the elder one said. "Visitors arrived in Molford a day ago. They are staying at the inn. They were on horseback."

There was a sliver of silence. "Horses, you say? That is interesting. I will look into it," Truehelm said. "How will I find you should I need you?"

"Take this. Hold it in the palm of your hand and blow across it. We shall know to come to you."

Margaret couldn't see what *this* was. A cipher made from Jutras majick, no doubt. She tensed, then slowly eased up behind the frog statuary. And had to bite her tongue to keep from cursing.

They were both compact in stature and their fingernails were long and pointed. They each had long black hair down to their waists, with dark skin and yellow eyes, which were bordered above and below by black and red dots. The younger one's face was marked by black triangle tattoos on his left cheek, and a series of scars on his right jaw. The older Jutras had a flowing tattoo down the left side of his prominent nose and ritual scarring that ran from his right temple all the way down his neck. The facial scarring and tattoos along with the long, loose hair indicated they were *kiryat*—the priest caste, and that meant they were also majicars—wizards—and likely powerful ones. Margaret swallowed. The tattoos on their faces indicated that they were cultists—servants of one of the two Jutras gods and high up in the *kiryat* caste. Which meant that they truly were close to the Dhucala; and no matter what lies they may have told the regent, one thing was almost certainly true—they had the Dhucala's blessing on everything they did.

There was very little time to stop them. The regent had planned well in his conquest of Crosspointe. At this point, Margaret didn't know if there was anything that

Ryland and Vaughn could do to stop him. Except they had to. They had to find a way to cure the majicar insanity and prepare themselves for war.

She sank back down, her throat dry. This changed everything. She glanced at the doors of the cells. *Everything.*

Chapter 13

The regent and his companions left, returning back the way Margaret had come. She slumped down on the floor. What should she do?

She already knew the answer. She had to get word to Ryland. But what about the Jutras? She couldn't just let them leave. Which meant either killing them, or following them. They wouldn't die easily. The *kiryat* were trained as warriors as wells as wizards. If she could get them apart from one another . . .

But it still raised the question—what was their other business in Crosspointe? And did she dare leave before she found out? And what was she going to do about Carston?

She sat a moment before coming to a decision. She crawled out of the forest of statues and other treasures and hurried to the cells. She went to the first and opened the slotted window, standing on tiptoe. She couldn't quite see through. "Carston?" she whispered. No answer. She went to the next one and the next. At the fifth one he answered.

"Who . . . Who are you?"

"I'm friends with your father." Her mouth twisted at the irony of it. Right now, she and Nicholas *were* friends, if only because they shared the common enemy of the Jutras. "He's coming to get you."

The boy made a whimpering sound and there was a rustling and then scraping sounds inside the door as if he was trying to climb out. He was crying softly and desperately. "Want to go home." His voice rose.

"Shhh," Margaret whispered. She unlatched the clip that secured the bar and pushed it up. Wards flared blue and majick bit sharply down on her fingers. She pulled away, shaking them. The pain didn't leave. She looked down. The tips of her fingers were white as if there was no blood left them. She touched them to her cheeks. They were glacial. She flexed them and shook them out. Prickles ran down into each of the tips. Thank Chayos. She wasn't going to be able to free him. She needed Keros.

She stood on tiptoe at the window, her fingers working at the leather band on her wrist. She pulled it off and slid it through the slot. "Carston, look at my hand. Do you see it? Do you see the band?"

"Yes." The word was stuffy with tears and frightened.

"I'm going to drop it. I want you to put it on. It has a spell that will tell your father where you are. He'll bring a majicar to open the door. Do you understand?"

"Yes," he said again, sounding tremulous.

Margaret dropped the bracelet and heard him shuffling around. "Did you put it on?"

"Uh-huh."

"Good. I've got to go before someone comes. I promise you, we'll get you out. Don't tell anyone about your bracelet. They'll take it away." She hesitated. "Carston, it will be all right. I promise." He sniffed and whimpered as if he was trying to hold back his tears. Brave boy. Margaret's heart ached for him. "Carston, I'm going to give you something else. Stand back." She heard a shuffle of movement. "Ready?"

"Yes," he said hesitantly.

She pulled one of the knives from her hair and slid it through the slot. The blade was small, easy for a small boy to conceal. Plus it would be easier for him to use, and she didn't doubt that he had some training in that direction. The Weverton family was famous for making sure every member of the family could defend themselves, and they liked to start them early. Carston wouldn't have a lot of skills, but he'd know what to do with a blade. She dropped the knife and the clatter seemed to echo resoundingly. "Get the knife, Carston. Wait for your father. He's coming."

With that she closed the slot and retreated back into the cover of the treasure horde. She waited to see if anyone had heard the telltale noises. When no one appeared to investigate, she began her retreat out of the manor. The only way back was the way she'd come, past the accommodations for the Jutras. She went to the entrance to the hallway and peered down it. The door was shut now and the *sylveth* lights had dimmed. She chewed her lip. They'd brighten when she went through. It was too much to ask that their majick fail conveniently. She quietly blew out a breath. She'd have to run and hope she wasn't noticed. She didn't have time to wait until the Jutras left to attend to their so-called business, and even if she did, she'd have to deal with servants and staff in the kitchens.

Keros and Nicholas didn't expect her until night fell again. Should she wait? But just the fact of the Jutras being in Crosspointe and the regent's collaboration with them spurred her to get the news to Ryland. That and knowing Truehelm's plan to give Pilots and compasses to the Jutras. What he didn't know, what hardly anyone knew, was that Crosspointe had no majicars left capable of making compasses. Once he gave away the Pilots' Guild compasses, there would be no more until a new compass-majicar was found. It wasn't a skill that could be learned; the majicar had to be born with it. Fairlie—

Shaye Weverton's lover—had the power, but she despised the Ramplings and Crosspointe. She wouldn't be making them any time soon. Not just that. She had discovered that *sylveth* was sentient—that it didn't like to be worked into hard form; it was a kind of torture for it—them. Margaret wasn't entirely sure. Fairlie would not easily be convinced or coerced. The regent simply had to be stopped from giving compasses away. and every passing minute that she sat doing nothing was time he consolidated his power. No. She had to get out now.

All the same, she waited another glass to be sure that the two Jutras wizards had settled into sleep. She kept running over the conversation she'd overheard, her anger and worry growing. At last she crawled out from her hiding place and returned to the hallway. She tensed, pulling a knife out and holding it ready, then began to skim down the passage as silently as she could manage.

The light flared like the sun around her and Margaret ran faster. She was just a few feet away from the door of the Jutras priests' suite when she stepped in something sticky. It held her like tar. Her ankle twisted as she wrenched her foot up. Her boot started to slip off and she pitched forward. She reached out to catch herself, trying to rear backward, snatching her hands back as she saw the floor rising to meet her.

All around her a tracery of red majick pulsed. It was a spell and it had activated the moment she'd stepped on it. It clung to her foot and ankles.

She hit the floor with a thud, the breath exploding from her gut. She squirmed and rolled, trying to get up, but found herself trapped in the sticky strands of the spell. In grains she couldn't move. She was trussed, head to foot.

A moment later the door opened and the two Jutras wizard priests stepped out into the hallway, gazing down at her.

"Do you think the regent knows he has such big rats?" the younger one asked, kneeling down to look more closely at Margaret. Her mouth was smothered by the spell. She struggled to scream, to swear at them, but her lips were literally sealed.

"What should we do with you, rat?" the older one said.

He reached out and stroked a finger over the web spell. Instantly fire flared over it. Margaret bucked and her eyes bugged with the force of the scream she couldn't release. Tears ran down the sides of her face and she breathed hard through her nose, feeling like she was suffocating. Unable to stop herself, she thrashed again.

"Little rat, you cannot escape." Again he slid a finger over the spell.

The pain roared again. It sliced through her in rising knife-edged waves. She struggled and her throat swelled with the force of her trapped screams. Her vision went gray. The smothering sensation increased. She rolled from side to side, flopping and banging her heels and head. Then her stomach lurched and bile flooded her mouth. She swallowed and snorted the burning liquid into her nose. Overwhelming primal fear swept over her and she struggled harder. She twisted onto her stomach. Her chest hurt. It felt like someone had his hand around her heart. Again her stomach clenched and she vomited and choked, then tried to cough.

Suddenly it felt like her heart was ripped out of her. Her head spun and her body twitched with uncontrollable spasms. She slumped and everything went black.

Margaret woke slowly, her body throbbing. She ached liked she'd been beaten, and her throat and nose felt raw. She opened her eyes. She was laying on the floor. The spell still held her, though it no longer covered her lips. Her mouth was sticky and tasted like a chamber pot. She glanced about warily and found the younger of the two Jutras priests squatting beside her, watching her. He smiled. It was both gentle and menacing.

"Little rat, you will die for us, but not today, and not that way."

Margaret didn't answer. He ran a hard, calloused finger over her lips. She resisted the urge to bite it.

"You are strong. You would make an admirable *picrit arrai* for the empire."

Knowing that *picrit* were the warrior cast, Margaret guessed that the *arrai* must be the conquered people who served the empire as warriors.

"Crack yourself, you mother-dibbling bastard," she rasped.

He smiled and his eyes crinkled. He had dimples. Margaret found that extraordinarily disconcerting. The Jutras were a cold, brutal people. Their entire culture revolved around blood sacrifice and death. His grin was almost friendly and it didn't match anything she knew about his people. "Little rat, the gods will enjoy you."

He looked past her. She turned her head to follow his gaze. The older Jutras emerged from the bedchamber. He was carrying a pack and dressed in well-worn leather pants topped with a close-fitting canvas shirt and a black vest. His boots came up to his knees and laced down the front. He'd clipped his hair at the nape of his neck. Around his waist was a sword belt. Through it was stuck a short sword. Its blade was red and the end was hooked wickedly.

"Saradapul, we must leave quickly. Before light," he told the younger Jutras.

Margaret frowned. How did the two manage to travel through Crosspointe without being seen? Illusion, no doubt. Margaret wondered if Jutras majick was working any better than Crosspointe majick; and was it driving the Jutras wizards insane? She didn't know what to fear more—Jutras majicars who had gone mad or those who had not. Either way did not bode well for her.

Saradapul stood. "I am ready, Atreya."

Now she realized that Saradapul was dressed like Atreya, with a similar sword in his belt. He looked down at her.

"Little rat, it is time to go." He tipped his head, considering. "But not like that, I think." He bent down, splaying his hands over her stomach and chest. His yellow eyes unfocused and he began chanting. The words were first smooth-edged and sweet, then guttural and staccato. Back and forth they went, his voice rising and falling, then he began to drum a pattern with his fingers.

Margaret felt the spell changing. It unraveled and rewove itself. Every movement of every strand sent a pulse of pain through her. She clenched her jaw, holding herself rigid. She wasn't going to lose control like she had before; she wasn't going to give them the satisfaction of seeing her suffer.

At last it was over. She lay panting, her eyes hot and dry. Her body throbbed and her skin felt like it had been flayed. But she no longer was bound tightly. Her hands fell loosely to the floor and her legs were free.

"Good little rat," Saradapul said, patting her shoulder. "What's this?" He hooked a finger around her necklace and pulled it up. "Atreya, our little rat is a Rampling."

The older Jutras came to stand over Margaret. She felt like a freshly roasted side of pig.

"Very good. She will do well."

"Do we tell the Eved-cala?" He smirked as he said it, confirming Margaret's suspicions that the Jutras had no intention of giving Truehelm any power once they overran Crosspointe. "He might be interested to know he has Rampling rats in his house."

"He might wish to take her. We will put her to better

use than he will," was Atreya's dismissive response. "Let us go."

Saradapul dropped the necklace and hoisted Margaret to her feet. Every movement felt like hot needles were prodding through her skin. She gasped and he smiled in a kindly way. "Little rat, your pain tastes sweet to the gods. We must milk it from you as we would milk a goat, and when you can give no more, we will offer your blood and your flesh and Uniat and Cresset will feast. Come now."

Margaret was hardly aware of anything that happened after that. The pain was constant. Nothing didn't hurt. Inside and out, she was seared and shredded. Her feet felt bloody and raw and every rub of her clothing against her skin was torture. It was everything she could do not to fall down. But the spell encasing her was like a vine trellis—it held her firmly. There was no escaping.

She wasn't sure how they left Molford Manor. They went on foot through another storm, lightning flashing and the wind driving the rain sideways. Margaret allowed herself to weep, the storm washing away her tears. It would be hours before Keros and Nicholas suspected anything was the matter. She thought of Nicholas's words to her: *I'll come for you. I promise you that. Don't do anything stupid. I* will *come.* It was a nice sentiment, but nobody was going to find her and no one was going to keep the two Jutras men from sacrificing her to their gods. All she had was herself.

Stubborn, fierce determination hardened in her stomach. She was not helpless. They would not kill her easily—and if it took everything she had, she'd see them dead first.

Chapter 14

Nicholas paced. It had been nineteen turns of the glass since Margaret had departed and he was chewing nails. He couldn't understand himself. His worry for her was nothing he'd expected or wanted. But he couldn't help himself. Tied to it was his concern for Carston. He hardly dared think of his son. Every time he did, his entire body seized and he felt paralyzed. It made him useless. Helpless. He wanted nothing more than to tear Geoffrey Truehelm limb from limb with his bare hands. Once he got Carston back, he would take thorough, bloody re- venge. And not just for his son. He'd promised Margaret he would make an end to the slavery and he intended to do that. He'd ignored the regent's antics for far too long. He'd been lazy and negligent, or perhaps it had simply been arrogance. He'd thought he held Truehelm's leash and he'd been wrong. Terribly wrong.

It was a crime. And he was paying for it. But he was going to rectify it and soon.

He clenched his hands, starting when Keros emerged from the bedchamber. "Well?" he asked.

"She's coming around."

Keros went to the table and poured a cup of tea. The pot was nearly empty and tepid. Nicholas didn't have to be asked to ring for more. When Cora came, he ordered a full meal. She was subdued and a fresh bruise blossomed on the corner of her mouth. Nicholas's jaw hardened. Another soul on his conscience. Unforgivable.

Keros took the tea back to the bedchamber and Nicholas followed, watching from the doorway. Ellyn reclined against a pile of pillows, her white eyes half shut. Her face was slack and her body quivered. Keros sat beside her, holding the cup to her mouth. She sipped obediently then pulled weakly away, her mouth twisting in repugnance.

Nicholas fetched a glass of water. This time Ellyn swallowed, reaching up to grip the glass in both hands and drinking it down loudly. Nicholas went to get another. Ellyn drank it as well. Her countenance became more animated and she sat up without help, pushing her legs over the side.

"How are you?" Keros asked.

"I don't know," she said. She frowned at him. "I see—"

"I know. I see the lights too."

She blinked her uncanny eyes, her gaze shifting to Nicholas and then past. "What happened?" she asked.

"I don't know. I was . . . My majick went wild and . . . You tried to heal me. I . . . I don't know what happened to us," Keros repeated lamely.

"Where is Margaret?"

"She went to the manor," Nicholas said, still leaning in the doorway.

Ellyn stiffened, twisting her head and frowning at him. "Alone?"

"We were distinctly not invited."

"And you agreed to that? Did she also cut your balls off?"

Nicholas winced. It felt like it. He ought to have gone with her, no matter what she said. His mouth tightened and he gave a little nod, then backed out of the doorway. The others soon followed.

"So what happens now?" Ellyn asked as she tottered out of the bedchamber. Every step lent her strength and steadiness as her vitality returned.

"She'll return late, escaping once the manor settles down for the night."

"No, she won't," Keros said suddenly. He was staring down at his *illidre*. It was pulsing with a soft orange light.

"What do you mean? What's that?" Nicholas demanded.

Keros scowled. "She's leaving the manor. Going . . . northeast. And she's left the bracelet I made to track Carston in the manor."

"How do you know?"

"I put a tracking spell on her when I created the spell for Carston. I was afraid she might get caught and we might not find her."

"Good thinking," Nicholas said, keeping his voice steady with effort. "But where is she going?"

"The question isn't where is she going, but where is the regent taking her?" was Ellyn's tart response.

"You think she's been taken." It wasn't quite a question.

"Don't you?"

He did. He couldn't imagine another reason for her to leave without a word at least to Keros. And there was nothing he could do to help her. Not now, not yet. He had to get Carston out first.

A knock sounded at the door and he went to open it. Keros tucked his *illidre* out of sight. Cora wheeled in a cart. She set the food out on the table and Nicholas tucked a couple of coins into her apron pocket. She curtseyed and turned to go, then hesitated. She glanced at the door and then at Nicholas, and then at the floor.

"Some of the regent's men came asking about you," she whispered. "They wanted to know about the horses and who owns them. They left guards. They said the regent himself is coming to pay you a visit."

Nicholas looked at Keros. They had to leave and now. "Thank you, Cora," he said and slid another coin into her pocket. She gave a little bob of her head and scurried away.

"Eat," Nicholas ordered. "Be quick. We have to go." He paused, glancing at both of them. "Will you still help me rescue Carston? Or are you going after Margaret?"

Keros folded his arms, looking down at the floor. Nicholas waited, his stomach twisting. He'd need to find more help if these two quit on him. He couldn't do it alone. Ellyn had gone to the table and was eating. She watched the two men from beneath her brows, as if her decision was dependent on what Keros decided. She looked almost demonic with those eyes.

"Margaret asked me to do this. I'll finish it," he said at last. He smiled, a thin, malevolent expression. "Then I'll burn the Meris-damned place down."

"Please do," Nicholas said, relief making him sag. He pulled himself together. "Thank you."

Keros shrugged. "You'll owe me." His expression said he had every intention of collecting.

"Whatever you want." Nicholas meant it. There wasn't anything he wouldn't give for Carston's safe return. Even put the Ramplings back on the throne. The majicar's brows rose, but he said nothing. Nicholas looked at Ellyn. "And you?"

She shrugged. "It is good for Azaire if I help you. The Gerent would enjoy having you owe him."

"Afterward we'll get Margaret," Keros declared firmly.

"We'll need the horses," Nicholas said. "We'll overtake her much faster that way." He'd promised her he would come for her. She hadn't believed him; she wouldn't expect him. But he would keep his promise.

"She may not need rescuing," Ellyn said. "I have seen what she can do to an entire squad of Crown Shields. She will not be easy to hold."

"I hope you are right, but we will not depend on it," Nicholas said.

"What is your plan?" Keros asked.

"Can the two of you do majick?"

They looked at each other, expressions tight as if they feared learning the answer to that question.

"Only one way to find out," Keros said. He held out his hand and majick flickered to life on his palm. It spun in a ball, akin to the one he'd used on Nicholas on their journey. He flicked his fingers and the majick flew at Nicholas, who flinched back. The swirling majick caught him, unraveling over his skin until he was cocooned. This time there was no pain. Instead, he felt a heaviness settle over him. It pressed hard against his chest and his movements felt thick and ungainly.

"Looks like it works," Ellyn said, looking Nicholas over from head to toe.

"What have you done?" he rasped.

"A disguise," Keros said smugly. "Have a look." He jerked his chin toward a mirror on the far wall.

Nicholas did as bid, staring at himself in stunned surprise. He looked like Geoffrey Truehelm. He had grown four inches and his face had become sharp, with a hawk nose and thin, unpleasant mouth. He was dressed fashionably, with a frothy cravat fastened with a gaudy brooch. His maroon jacket was heavily embroidered with purple thread and his trousers were tight fitting, revealing scrawny legs. His shoes had three-inch heels with *sylveth* buckles. Around his neck he wore the newly minted chain of office for the regency, and on his hands he wore a half-dozen rings. His cheeks were brushed with rouge and his eyes were outlined in kohl.

Nicholas's lip curled at his reflection and he turned to glance at Keros. "What's this about?"

"We have to go now. The quickest way to successfully obtain your son and retrieve the horses is if the regent says we can."

A bold plan, and Nicholas liked it for its audacity. "And if the real regent objects?"

"Cora thinks he's on his way here. He'll be desperately curious about you and will want to know everything there is to know about who you are and where you came from and where your allegiance lies. When he gets here, you will change places with him, then return to the manor, having invited us for the evening. We will ride our horses, of course, wishing to make our entrance. In the meantime, you will retrieve Carston. We will then escape."

Keros made it sound so simple. "He will come with guards—he never meets with anyone alone. He may very well have a majicar with him. How will we effect the exchange without them knowing?"

"A stun spell should do it," Ellyn said around a mouthful of cheese.

"What's that?"

She swallowed and drank some tea. "It's a minor spell. Causes someone's mind to go to sleep for about a minute or two. I've used it frequently. It should be enough." She glanced at Keros. "I can stun the regent, if you can do his guards."

He nodded. "You'll have to show me the spell."

Soon the two were sharing majickal knowledge as they ate. Nicholas forced himself to eat something, though he tasted nothing. His heart pounded. He knew Geoffrey well enough to imitate him, but Alanna would surely see through the ruse. His jaw hardened. He'd not give her the chance.

By the time the regent arrived, Cora had cleared the dishes away and Nicholas had retreated into the bed-chamber to wait. Keros and Ellyn had adopted their own disguises.

A knock sounded and Nicholas moved instantly to the bedchamber door, pulling it open a crack so he might see. In his hands he held a gag and bindings for Geoffrey. Once the two majicars stunned their guests, they had to get the regent tied up and out of the room quickly and Keros would have to adjust Nicholas's illusion to match what the regent was wearing.

Keros answered and stood nervously out of the way as the regent strutted inside followed by four body-guards. They were Blackwatch, wearing tall brown boots that rose over their knees, black breeches, red shirts, and short black coats with a top cape that hung down just be-low the shoulder. Two were women and two were men.

"By Chayos! My esteemed Regent Truehelm! You honor us, sir. Please come in," Keros said effusively. He retained enough of the look of Nicholas so that if the regent had a description of Avery Dedlok of Shevring, Keros would match well enough. Likewise Ellyn's dis-guise matched Margaret.

"Please sit, sir. I must apologize. We are hardly pre-pared to receive visitors. Dear sir, you do us such a great honor! I am utterly flabbergasted. Sit, sir, sit!" Keros flapped his hands and stuttered, smiling like an excited imbecile. "Ring for a maid, Sophia. Have the innkeeper send his best wine and cakes and tea and— Send every-thing! The regent is visiting! We must have the best of everything! Quickly, dearest wife! Quickly!" His voice rose as he went and yanked the bellpull with furious energy so that Nicholas thought he might pull it loose entirely.

Ellyn was looking frozen with fear, her mouth slack and her hands clutching the front of her skirts as she

stared at the regent with glassy eyes. She made a gur-
gling sound and slapped a hand over her mouth. Then
she swept a deep curtsy.

"Your highness . . . regency . . . s-sir," she stammered
in a high, wheezing voice. "I must beg your pardon, for
we are ill-equipped to meet you. We lost everything, you
see, and we are waiting for help to come from Shevring
with all my things, and I must be a sight!" she wailed.
"Here we are with the regent and I look like a scullery
maid!" She put her hand dramatically over her heart
and sank onto the chaise, fanning herself with her other
hand.

"My dear lady, do not put yourself out of countenance. I assure you, you are lovely and I am delighted to
make your acquaintance," Geoffrey said with oily defer-
ence. "May I sit with you?"

"Oh my— Chayos forgive me!" she shrieked. "Avery, you didn't ask the man to sit down! Where are your
manners? Dear regent, please forgive my husband. It
was the accident and I've been so ill since. I haven't been
able to keep a thought in my head and I haven't even
been to see my horses. They were all we were able to
save that terrible night. My poor babies—so alone and
without blankets or proper grooms. They must be frightened out of their wits. They won't eat a bite unless I go
sing to them, but Avery hasn't let me stir a step out of
this room. He almost lost me, he says, and he won't risk
me. But I told him I'm feeling very well now and my
beauties need to stretch their legs, and it was all just nervous exhaustion. My nerves are quite steady now and,
my dear regent! Why are you still standing? Please, you
must sit."

Nicholas bit his lips to keep from laughing out loud at
Ellyn's chatter. Geoffrey looked as dazed as if his ears
had been boxed. He sank down into a chair.

"Oh, very good!" Ellyn said, clapping her hands.

Just then there was a knock at the door. She leaped to
her feet and swept to answer. "Avery, sit down now. You
are making me nervous with all your fussing. You, too,
you behemoths," she said, shooing the Blackwatch away.
They fell back as she herded them, her hands brushing the air as if to sweep them before her. She forced
them into the dining room and then went to the door.
She opened it and stepped outside. Her voice rose and
fell, though Nicholas could not hear the words. She returned, her cheeks spotted red as she wrung her hands
together.

"Avery, we must move from here as soon as possible.
The staff is impossible and the inn is filthy. The girl had
dirt under her fingernails, can you believe it?" She shuddered and then sniffed. "There are bugs everywhere.
They don't even use a decent ward against crawling
creatures. And the food—it is mediocre fare, at best. Fine
enough for peasants, but not for people of our quality.
Surely there must be a better inn in Molford. My dear
regent, you must have a recommendation for us. Please,
we suffer so much here."

"Oh, my dear Mistress Dedlok, I am sorry to hear of
your travails. Of course you must come stay at Molford
Manor. I insist."

Ellyn gasped. "My dear regent! Such generosity! Such
kindness bestowed on two poor bereaved strangers?
How can we ever repay you?" She shook her head vig-
orously. "I've said it once if I've said a hundred times—
Crosspointe surely was blessed when you became regent.
You are worth a thousand Ramplings." She looked at
Keros. "Haven't I said so? Haven't I told everyone so?
My dear, Avery, did you hear? The regent has been sent
by Chayos in our time of need. It's truly a miracle."

"I am pleased to be of service," Geoffrey said. "But
please, let us not be strangers. Tell me about yourselves.
You are from Shevring, I understand."

Ellyn launched into an animated story of their journey. It wasn't long before the regent was glazing over, as were his guards. She was just getting to the terrible imaginary mudslide when she nodded to Keros. It was but an instant later that the guards went preternaturally still. They neither blinked nor breathed. Instantly Ellyn cast her spell at the regent. It was quietly done. Her hands had been dancing wildly throughout her tale and even Nicholas could hardly tell when she flicked the spell at him. But suddenly the regent slid stiffly sideways.

Nicholas thrust through the door. He and Keros carried Geoffrey into the bedchamber and set about binding him.

"Hold still a moment," Keros said, staring down at the prone man. A few grains later he sent a ball of majick at Nicholas.

He felt the spell adjusting, like a lock snicking into place. He looked down at himself. He was dressed identically to the regent. He glanced at Keros. "Well done. Now let's finish this charade."

They returned to the sitting room, taking their former places. Ellyn launched into her story again. Within a few grains the guards woke, none the wiser.

The next glass was spent dining on roast beef, potatoes with butter, cream and onions, tender greens, crusty bread, and a berry tart. The innkeeper's daughter was brought in to taste each dish before Nicholas would deign to touch anything. Ellyn complained nonstop, never allowing anyone else a word. It was well done. She did not give Nicholas a single chance to betray himself to the regent's guards.

When it was over, he stood and excused himself. "Perhaps you might wish to come with me now. You may send for your things later. We can collect your horses and bring them with us. They will have good care in my home."

"I have no doubt of it. You are more generous than I can say. Certainly we shall accompany you."

"But my dear," Keros said with a worried look at the bedchamber door, "we must make preparations."

Nicholas nodded. "But of course. I will wait in the taproom. Will a quarter of a glass be sufficient?"

"Make the regent wait? Oh, no! It is not done! Avery, we mustn't. And my darling horses need me. We must go at once, do you hear? At once."

Nicholas exchanged a frowning glance with Keros. They could not just leave Geoffrey behind. He would be found all too soon.

"My dearest heart, are you certain?" Keros asked, his trepidation evident in his voice.

"Of course. I shall just fetch my coat. If you'll pardon me for a moment," she said to Nicholas. "I won't be long at all."

She retreated into the bedchamber, shutting the door firmly behind her. Minutes passed and she did not return. Keros shifted uneasily in his seat, tapping his fingers together. At last he stood.

"I should go check on her. Please excuse me. I will not be long."

He disappeared inside the bedchamber as well. What were they doing? There was a small window leading to the outside, but they could not dispose of the regent that way, not without being seen. Perhaps they were using majick. But for what? To kill him? Nicholas hoped not. He wanted to do those honors himself, after he asked a lot of questions, beginning with where he'd sent Margaret.

He tapped his fingers impatiently, letting his expression turn forbidding as Geoffrey's was wont to do when he was forced to wait. The four Blackwatch eyed him uneasily. More minutes trickled away. At last the bedchamber door opened and Keros entered.

"My apologies, regent. Sophia will join us in just a moment. I humbly beg just a few more moments of your patience."

Nicholas smiled stiffly and gave a slight bow. "Of course, Mister Dedlok. Your wife has been through a great trauma and I wish only to make her time in Molford easier."

"You are too kind. She is certainly far more delicate than she appears. Indeed, I wonder, sir—perhaps we might retrieve the horses and tie them to your carriage before exposing Sophia to the weather?"

It had begun to storm again during the night and continued to bluster and rain.

"Certainly." Nicholas glanced about himself. "Where are your servants?"

Keros frowned. "The girl is in with Sophia. My man will be along shortly."

"Then she will not be alone. Very well. Shall I send for your horses?"

"I'm afraid it is unwise. They must be handled by those with some experience. They are far too valuable to take chances with. I should be there."

"As you wish. Let us go, then."

The Blackwatch preceded them out into the passage and into the taproom, where one of the Blackwatch went to fetch the regent's carriage. Though the room was half full, the diners were subdued and quiet. Many were soldiers in the regent's army. When Nicholas entered, they stiffened and came to quiet attention. Nicholas scanned them with a cool eye, and then gave a slight smile and nodded his approval. No one was drunk, no one was boisterous and unruly. There was a visible wave of relief at his nod. Geoffrey kept his men on a tight leash. It was an impressive feat, and spoke to their discipline and readiness to fight. But against whom?

"May I offer refreshment, lord regent, sir?"

It was the innkeeper. He kept his gaze fixed firmly on Nicholas's chest as he knotted his hands together. He'd put on a clean apron and shirt and his bald head gleamed.

"No. We are on our way, Bleeg. We shall return shortly to retrieve Mistress Dedlok."

"Perhaps a dram of mulled wine to warm you?" Bleeg didn't wait for an answer, but trotted off, returning in a moment with two pewter chalices of hot spiced wine. "Compliments of the house, sir."

Nicholas stared disdainfully at the proffered wine, then at Bleeg. The fat innkeeper flushed. "I think not," he said at last, waving the man away. It was exactly what Geoffrey would have done.

"Sir, the carriage."

Nicholas nodded to the Blackwatch who stood waiting at the door. "Let us go, Mister Dedlok."

He didn't wait for Keros, but walked out. A footman was waiting outside with an umbrella. The carriage was pulled by a pair of bay horses, both covered with blankets. Soon both Keros and Nicholas were inside, on their way to the nearby stable. It was used primarily for mules—horses being so much more rare and expensive.

"What about Geoffrey?" Nicholas murmured as the carriage pulled away. "What are you and Ellyn up to?"

"We thought it better if we brought him with us. Ellyn is arranging it."

"How?"

"You'll see."

After that they said nothing until they arrived at the stable. Nicholas waited while Keros fetched the horses and tied them to the rear of the carriage. The animals were skittish, prancing and rearing. Suddenly they settled as if spelled, which Nicholas had no doubt they were. Whatever had happened to Keros to turn his eyes white and make him see lights, it had also stabilized his majick. He no longer struggled against its effects.

He returned to the carriage, his clothes and hair dripping. He took a lap blanket and wiped away the worst of the damp. The carriage began rolling again and soon they returned to the inn. Keros disappeared inside, returning just a few minutes later. He had his arm around Ellyn, who was bundled against the weather. Behind trailed two servants—a man and a woman. Keros pushed Ellyn inside and motioned for the other two to ride up on top with the driver. He clambered back inside and shut the door and they set off again.

"Who are those two?" Nicholas asked, jabbing his fingers in the air, pointing at the roof.

"Ellyn and Cora," Keros said. "And this worm here is your friend the regent." He pulled away the regent's hood. He was wearing the same illusion Ellyn had been. His eyes glittered with fury, but he was preternaturally still. Bound by majick.

"Not my friend," Nicholas said. "He never was. A tool only, and that was a mistake."

Keros's brows rose. "A mistake? More like a catastrophe."

Nicholas thought of Carston. "I cannot disagree."

"The question is, can you fix it? Put Crosspointe back together?"

There was no good answer for that, so Nicholas switched subjects. "And Cora?"

"Four of us arrived, four of us have to leave. Cora was not unwilling to lose her collar."

"Those spells aren't easily broken."

Keros sobered. "It was easier than it should have been, like tearing apart a rotten rope." He hesitated as if considering saying more. Then he glanced at the regent and his lips clamped shut as he sat back against the seat, his jaw hardening.

What had he intended to say? Nicholas felt his stomach tighten and the hairs on the back of his neck prickled with foreboding. He'd imagined he knew all that was happening in Crosspointe, but now he knew better. What worried him was just how much he didn't know and how much it would cost him. He caught himself. No, he wasn't just worried about himself. He was worried about his family and all of Crosspointe.

He thought of Margaret and twisted his head away from his companions to hide his expression. What was being done to her? He frowned. Something did not sit right. If Geoffrey had caught her, he wouldn't have sent her away. He would have spent time questioning her and gloating. But if Geoffrey didn't have her—who did?

His hand slowly clenched as fear curled tightly inside his gut. Geoffrey would leave her alive, wanting to watch her suffer as he took control of Crosspointe. Nicholas had counted on it; he'd counted on Margaret being safe until he was able to rescue her. But now—

Somebody else had her. There was no telling who or what they wanted.

He looked back at Keros. "That parcel that went northeast—he didn't send it." Nicholas gestured at the regent.

The majicar's mouth twitched and he nodded. "I think you're right. We'd better hurry." He paused. "Your disguise should hold up well enough, but you should be warned. If you remove any of your clothing, it will lose its covering illusion and give you away."

Nicholas looked down at himself. He would be expected to change out of his wet things and into evening attire. Both Alanna and Geoffrey were sticklers for the niceties and always kept a formal table, which meant dressing for dinner.

"How long will it take you to find Carston?" How much time did he have to keep Alanna in the dark? If only he had something to drug her with. He didn't doubt that Geoffrey had just what he needed, but locating it would be like finding a needle in a strawstack.

"I'll take Mistress Dedlok to our quarters," Keros said, nodding toward the disguised regent. "Cora will watch over him while Ellyn and I find Carston. With luck, it should not take long—perhaps two or three glasses."

It was a long time. Nicholas nodded. He'd find a way to keep Alanna distracted, whatever it took. He might even be able to delicately pump her for information about what she and Geoffrey were up to. If it came down to it, he'd kill her and enjoy doing it.

"When we have succeeded in finding your son, we will start a fire in the manor. Hopefully as everyone evacuates and fights the fire, it will allow us to retrieve Cora and the regent and get to the stables unnoticed."

Nicholas nodded. "I'll meet you there." He held out a hand. "Good luck. And thank you."

Keros looked at his hand, then gripped it firmly. "Be careful."

Nicholas's mouth quirked in a grim smile. "Did you ever imagine in your wildest dreams that you'd be cautioning me to be careful?"

The majicar's smile was equally grim. "Don't get used to it. I still might have to kill you."

Chapter 15

They entered the gates of the manor and pulled up beneath the portico at the front. Fluted columns held up the broad roof and a flowering vine grew up over it in a pink mass. The rain pelted in fat, stinging drops and the wind gusted.

A footman opened the carriage door and Nicholas regally stepped down. Keros followed, half carrying the regent.

"Sophia, my dear, you must hold on! Do not leave me, my sweetest love! We'll have you by the fire in a moment," Keros said in a panicking voice.

They hurried inside.

"Be sure the animals are well cared for," Nicholas said to the stable hand who'd come out to seize the bridles of the horses, then followed Keros inside. The butler was waiting. Porskip was a tall, spare woman with broad shoulders, a blade nose and weak chin. She was dressed in dark green with orange piping, her skirts severely cut, her lace collar high around her neck.

"These are the Dedloks of Shevring," Nicholas told her. "Take them immediately to our finest guest quarters. Send tea and brandy and anything else they require."

Porskip responded quickly and soon Keros and his "wife" were on their way to their quarters, leaving Nicholas alone in the foyer. He stood a moment, then wandered away toward what he supposed would be the sitting room. He'd not gone more than five steps when Alanna Truehelm's voice stopped him in his tracks.

"Geoffrey, you're home. Come upstairs and change out of those wet clothes. You can tell me about the Dedloks."

She swept out of a salon on his right. She was dressed in a burgundy dosken dress layered over with Tirsol lace. It sparkled with glittering *sylveth* beads. It was worth fifteen dralions if it was worth a single copper crescent. She wore several rings on every finger and her neck and wrists were heavy with jewelry. She was a fine figure of woman—tall and slender with hair the color of tarnished sunshine, which was piled high in an elaborate coif. He schooled his expression into one of fond welcome. Whatever could be said about Geoffrey and Alanna, they were a love match and well paired. If Geoffrey was a cold-blooded snake, Alanna was a rabid dog who'd eat her own children to get what she wanted. Which might not be too off the mark. Her youngest son was dead. He'd been murdered by Edgar Thorpe in his plot against the king. Nicholas had never been certain that Geoffrey and Alanna had not been part of that plot.

Their eldest son had disappeared years before. It wasn't generally known what had happened to him. Nicholas knew. The nine-seasons-old boy had run away and spent time on the docks before finding a post aboard ship as a bosun. Then by some crook of fate, he'd become a Pilot. He'd disappeared half a season ago, presumably lost at sea. Nicholas had been unable to discover for certain. Why the boy had run away from his family was the question he'd never been able to answer, though he would have paid dearly to know.

"Of course, my dear," he said. "If you'll allow, a glass of something to warm me first?" He gestured vaguely in the opposite direction where certainly there was a study or sitting room.

"Nonsense. You come up right now. Porskip will bring up a bowl of Bully Dawson. That will do nicely. I had Cook prepare it this morning. Come now, before you ruin the floor. You're a sight."

He gave an ironic bow and gestured toward the staircase. "After you."

She sniffed and gave him a frowning look down her patrician nose, then mounted the steps regally. Nicholas let go a silent sigh and followed. At least he wouldn't be roaming the halls blindly looking for his chambers. But Alanna was as suspicious as a rich man in a crowd of pickpockets, and even the countenance of her husband wasn't going to quell her distrustful nature.

Their apartments were on the third floor of the west wing. Inside was large and extravagantly decorated. Every surface was crowded with ornaments and there was so much furniture it was impossible to walk without knocking into something. The heavy curtains were flounced and gathered in billowing folds and the floors were swathed in dozens of rugs, each with a different pattern and color. There wasn't a singled square inch of the walls that wasn't covered with a painting or tapestry. It resembled nothing more than a high-end pawnshop. Nicholas chewed the inside of his lip and carefully schooled his expression to keep his repugnance from showing.

Alanna preceded him, tugging the bellpull as she entered. She maneuvered her skirts through the jumbled maze of teetering bric-a-brac without toppling even one tiny vase, glass figurine, or carved box, and went into his dressing room. He followed more slowly. As with the exterior room, this one was equally garish and ostentatious. Except the rugs swathing this floor were the colorfully dyed white bearskins from Avreyshar. Nicholas paused before entering. Where had they come from? Avreyshar did not trade these. The tribes would go to war to prevent it. These had to have been smuggled out and just one cost as much as ten horses. Where had Geoffrey obtained them? And how?

"Geoffrey! Your shoes," Alanna chided sharply.

He looked down at his muddy footwear. He was wearing boots up to his knee, but his illusion said he wore a heeled shoe. If he removed them, Alanna would instantly know something was wrong. Instead he rubbed his forehead with exaggerated exhaustion. "I apologize, my dear. I do not know where my head is." He stepped back and returned to the sitting room, flinging himself down and putting his feet up on the broad footstool.

"Geoffrey!" she admonished.

He waved a desultory hand. "We'll purchase new furniture, my dear. Unlike those skins in there, this is utterly replaceable. We can certainly afford it and I am damned tired."

She came forward, taking his hand in hers and bending to brush her lips against his. It was all he could do not to recoil. Instead he brought her hand to his mouth and kissed her knuckles.

"Tell me about these Dedloks," she said, settling primly down on the chair opposite him. "Who are they?"

"They claim they are from Shevring and that they were on their way to Tixora for the wedding of Mistress Dedlok's brother."

"Going overland?" she said with raised brows.

Nicholas nodded, then glanced at the door. "Where in the depths are the servants?"

She rose and went to yank the bell again. "If we are to stay here as planned, then we will have to encourage a higher standard of work," she said. Only a moment later, someone knocked tentatively on the door. She returned to her seat. "Come in," she called and a footman entered. He bowed low.

"How may I help you, madam?"

"Bring some Bully Dawson at once," she ordered. "Make sure it's hot. Get going." She clapped her hands together sharply and the footman leaped as if stung and he fled.

Once he was gone, she turned back to Nicholas. "Overland?" she prompted.

"It seems she wished to demonstrate her wealth by arriving in some state," he said. "They were caught in a mudslide and ended up here. They have been waiting for assistance from Shevring."

"Do you believe them?"

He shrugged. "I've invited them to stay here at Molford until their people arrive. We can get the answers soon enough."

That earned him a considering look. "You were very certain their arrival was too coincidental. What changed?"

Nicholas shook his head. "They are foolish people. Hardly a threat."

"I have never heard of them."

He gave an impatient, dismissive gesture. "As I said, my dear, we will have ample time to ascertain their purpose here. If anyone can get to the truth of their story, you can."

Her lips turned in a tight smile; then she frowned thoughtfully. "I could start with dinner. . . ." She rose and disappeared down the hallway, returning with a heavy wooden case made of carved jasaic wood. She set the case down on the low table and stroked her fingers over the four wards that locked it. Alanna was nothing if not careful with her secrets—some might say fanatical.

She opened the lid and a set of split trays unfolded

from it as she did. They contained vials of every shape and size. She studied them, running her fingers through the air above them.

"I suppose I should not poison them," she said with a glance at Nicholas.

"Preferably not. They might prove useful."

She picked up a dark pink bottle shaped like a feather. The liquid inside was thick as syrup. "This might do the trick. It is sweet and difficult to taste. I shall give it to them in their wine and they will tell us all we want to know, though it will be a bit uncomfortable for them."

"I do not wish them to remember."

She selected a round green vial. "This will make them forget. They will wake feeling weak and feverish and no wiser."

"I trust you entirely, my dear," Nicholas said. "Where is that damned punch?"

A knock at the door answered his question. It swung open and two footmen came in carrying a covered silver urn and a tray with cups and an array of food. They set them down on the sideboard and ladled out a small cup. One tasted it and waited for several minutes before Alanna nodded and he served two more steaming cups. Nicholas sipped his gratefully, savoring the sweet-tart flavor of lemons, sugar, wine, stout, and brandy. Underlying it all was the spicy flavor of arrack imported from Beynto dal Corus.

He wiped the foam from his lip as the heat of the drink warmed him. An idea struck him and he eyed the drink thoughtfully. Alanna's case remained open on the side table. If he could give her a dose of her own medicine, he might learn a great deal about her and Geoffrey's plans.

The two footmen departed and Alanna went to the sideboard to serve some food.

"None for me," Nicholas said. "I ate that appalling swill they call food at the inn. I may not be able to eat again for a sennight."

"I wish you hadn't. You never know about poisons."

"I had the innkeeper's daughter sample everything. There was no harm."

She frowned. "You should get out of those clothes and into a warm bath before you catch your death."

"What would I do without you, my dear?" he asked and held out his hand to her.

She rose and came to kiss him again, then stepped behind him and began rubbing his shoulders. Her grip was hard and sharp, like the claws of an eagle. He forced himself to relax beneath her ministrations, considering what to do. His glance fell on the tempting case again.

"Has the post come?"

"It is on your desk in your study."

"My darling, would you be so kind as to fetch it?"

She gave a final squeeze. "Of course. I should have thought of it sooner. You will want to hear the latest news. I shall return directly."

She hurried out and Nicholas leaped to his feet. She'd hardly touched her Bully Dawson. Would she pour it out and get a fresh hot cup when she returned? He couldn't take the chance. He carried the cups down the hall to the garderobe and emptied them. He poured a measure of the drug from the feather-shaped vial into each and rubbed it about so that it coated the inside of each cup. He then set them near his hand and put his feet back up. He slumped as if dozing.

He heard the door open and flinched awake as Alanna called his name.

"Here you are, Geoffrey dear," she said and came to set the pouch of mail on the table beside him.

"Thank you. Oh, would you mind? I'm afraid I was lazy and drank your punch as well as mine. They warmed me quite nicely, but I would like another." He gestured at the cups and she went to refill them. He fished in the inside pocket of his coat for the ring of keys he'd taken from the regent in the carriage. He fingered through them, looking for the postal packet key. Any other time, the packet would have been warded by majick, but with it acting so erratically, ordinary locks had to do.

He found the proper key and opened the pouch as Alanna set his steaming cup beside him and sipped her own. He had no idea what sort of dose of the drug was required to be effective. He might very well have given her too little or too much. But hopefully, while Keros and Ellyn were rescuing Carston, he'd discover some useful information about the regent's business.

He unfastened the pouch and withdrew the correspondence. He flipped through it.

"Any word from Sylmont?"

He glanced at Alanna. She perched on the edge of her chair, her color high as she sipped her drink. There was something in the question that suggested she was looking for specific news. For the first time he wondered what had brought the two of them to Molford. He'd assumed it was something to do with Carston, but if the boy was safely locked up, there would be no need to visit. So either something had driven them from Sylmont, or they'd come for business other than Carston.

He slid his fingers under the seal on the first letter and popped it free. It was from Geoffrey's steward in the castle. He expected it to be full of the ordinary business of the castle. Instead it read more like a battle report.

> *The clash between the majicars has destroyed much of the docks and the ships sitting in the harbor. Many majicars have died, others have gone into hiding. The people have risen up against them. Food is becoming even more scarce than before.*

*The riots in the city have caused fires and looting.
Many people have come to the castle for refuge. We
have kept the gates locked against them, but I fear
they will soon overrun us. Majick is very irregular
and I must tell you, sir, that I fear the city is on the
verge of collapse. The people are <u>begging</u> for you.*

*Additionally, it appears that the lights of the Pale
have begun to dim. It is quite worrisome.*

I await your instructions.

Nicholas reread the report twice, unable to cover his
astonishment and horror.

"My dear, what news? You look alarmed."

He glanced at her. She'd nearly finished her Bully
Dawson. Her face was flushed and her mouth was tense
as if she felt pain. She pressed a hand to her stomach.

"The news from Sylmont is distressing," he said. "It
appears the city may be in ruins."

She *tsk*ed. "I had hoped it would not go so far. But we
will rebuild. The Dhucala will give us all the funds and
slaves we need."

That rocked Nicholas back in his chair. "The Dhucala? You're in this with the cracking *Jutras*?"

"Me, my love? We are in this together." She frowned
as if beginning to sense something was off. "I am feeling
rather . . . unwell." She slid off the arm of the chair and
landed heavily on the floor.

Nicholas leaped to his feet and came to stand over
her. He gripped her shoulder and shook it. "Tell me
what you've planned with the Dhucala. Tell me now!"

She stared up at him, her eyes glassy, the ring of
brown around her pupils a thin scrap of color. Her body
clenched tight and pain rippled across her countenance.
She let out a long, raw moan. She began to shake and
the tremors shook her like an aspen leaf. Suddenly she
went boneless and still. Nicholas swore and gripped her

hair, pulling back her head. She looked sightlessly up at him, her mouth gaping.

He let go of her and staggered back to the scattered mail. His throat felt like someone was crushing it in their fist. He read through everything and then began a search of the apartment. He found little, but now the Avresharian bearskins held a more sinister significance. They had to be gifts from the Dhucala. Or bribes. How long had Geoffrey been an agent for the Jutras? How could he? It was insane. The Jutras would have killed him and Alanna once they overran Crosspointe. How could Geoffrey believe otherwise?

But the man had an extraordinarily healthy sense of his own abilities. Of course he would think he was the exception to what everyone knew to be the truth, especially with Jutras agents plying him with unimaginable wealth and no doubt making extravagant promises.

Nicholas slammed the flat of his hand against a door. His mind was a cauldron of fury and fear and it bubbled with unanswerable questions. What had Geoffrey given the Jutras? When were they coming? Were they already here? He dragged his fingers through his hair. Damn Geoffrey to the depths! With the majicars going insane, riots in Sylmont, no king or regent to lead, Crosspointe was a plum ripe for the picking.

Suddenly he strode back to the sitting room and stepped over Alanna's body. He picked up the vial of the truth drug and slipped it into his pocket. One way or another, Geoffrey was going to answer his questions.

He stepped out into the hallway and pulled the door firmly shut behind him. He found the key on the ring and twisted it in the lock before striding down the corridor. He needed to find Geoffrey's study and search it.

This was his fault. If not for him, Geoffrey never would have been regent; he'd never have been in a position to so thoroughly tear apart Crosspointe. Nicholas pushed the guilt aside. It wasn't productive. Now he had to think how to fix this mess.

He stopped, putting a hand against the wall to steady himself as fear seized him. It couldn't be too late. There had to be time yet to prepare for the Jutras invasion. *Additionally, it appears that the lights of the Pale have begun to dim. It is quite worrisome.* Nicholas pushed himself away from the wall. Even if he could stop the Jutras, he could do nothing to save the Pale. Without it, the Jutras didn't matter. Crosspointe would be a land of spawn.

He pushed the thought aside. He'd do what he could— what he knew how to do—and pray to the gods that the Ramplings still had Lucy Trenton in their pocket and that she could fix the Pale a second time.

Chapter 16

Keros dumped the regent onto the floor inside the bed-chamber and just barely restrained himself from kicking the bastard. He returned to Ellyn and Cora in the main salon. The girl was peeling off her borrowed cloak and shivering. Ellyn had released the illusions disguising them and now Keros did the same for himself. His majick responded better than it had before whatever had happened to him at the inn, but it still no longer felt like it welled from a rich and dense sea as it had done before the fall of the Kalpestrine. Now it felt shallow and thin, like the difference between a hearty stew and a watery soup.

The footmen had stirred the fire and warmth was slowly creeping through the room. Ellyn went to look out the windows. She opened one and peered up and then down before pulling her head back in. Keros gave her a curious look. They both wore glamours that hid their white eyes, but nothing seemed to change the constant flow of lights. He was beginning to get used to it and was no longer quite so distracted by them.

"Do you see anything interesting out there?" he asked.

She shrugged. "I like to know where the exits are."

He stared at her a long moment. He could hardly see the girl he'd known and loved so many seasons ago.

She'd changed in almost every way. She'd always been strong, but then it had been the strength of a green sapling, deeply rooted and wild in the wind. Now she was a weapon—a flashing sword honed to a bright edge. She was dangerous. He was, too, he thought. That was what this life had made of them.

He was shocked to find that for once he did not regret it. Because now he was a man who could curse the local brothels to make men pay for abusing Margaret's enslaved family; he could help rescue a kidnapped young boy; he could burn this despicable place to the ground when he was done and then he could go help Margaret. He could kill and he could heal—he was a man to be feared, a friend to be depended on, and a majicar with the power to do what he needed to do. Today he was glad to be who he was instead of who he might have been had the Gerent not thrown his entire village into a *sylveth* tide.

"Where is the boy?" she asked.

He concentrated on the link to the bracelet spell. Carston was downstairs somewhere, likely in the cellar. He told Ellyn so, then turned to Cora, who hung back by the door, watching her two companions uncertainly. She wasn't cowering into herself, he was pleased to see. Her neck was raw and red from the collar, as if it had grated against her skin. It had been roughly made.

"You'll need to stay here and wait for us," he told her.

Her gaze fixed on him, her eyes sunken and large. "Who are you?" she asked.

"I'd rather save that until we are on our way," he said. "Suffice it to say we are the people who took the iron collar off your neck. You're free."

She blinked, dazed, then shook her head. "Doesn't matter. The regent will only sweep me up again. I've nowhere to go and no way to live. Besides, we're in his house." The last was angry and accusing.

"You don't have to worry about the regent anymore, and we'll make sure you get out of here safely."

She wrapped her arms around herself, her mouth pinching together. He wasn't sure what she was thinking or feeling. She didn't look particularly grateful or happy. But, then, she'd not had an easy time of it and she was entitled to feel however she wanted.

"What do you want?" she said, staring down at the floor.

"Me?"

She nodded shortly. "It's got to cost something, doesn't it?"

She had learned the rules of survival fast.

"You already paid us. You warned us the regent was coming. If not for you, we might have been in some trouble. But the regent's kidnapped a young boy and is keeping him prisoner here. Ellyn and I have to go find him. We need you to wait here for us. Don't let anyone come in."

She frowned. "What about Mistress Dedlok?"

Ellyn snorted, covering her laughter with her hand. Keros smiled. "*Mistress Dedlok* is . . . indisposed. You need only to divert anyone from entering. Can you do that?"

She nodded, chewing her upper lip. "You'll come back?"

"We will."

She nodded and moved farther into the room, giving Keros a wide berth as she went to stand near the fireplace. He went to the door and Ellyn slipped out into the corridor with him.

She led the way, moving swiftly and surely. She'd been here once before for a few days, while serving as Alanna

Truehelm's lady's maid. It was enough to give her the lay of the land.

She quickly wound a path down to the main level, into the kitchens and through to the wine cellars. They used a glamour to keep from being noticed. She went directly to a rack of whiskey casks and reached between them, touching a spot beneath the third cask. There was a slight click and Ellyn pushed against the rack. It swiveled, revealing a door behind it. She fished some metal tools from her boot and picked it. A moment later they were in the lavishly appointed corridor on the other side.

"I never got any farther than the door before," she murmured. "Lady Alanna is very demanding and suspicious."

Keros hardly heard her. He tipped his head, his eyes drifting nearly closed. The lights down the left side were different somehow. They moved strangely. More oily and undulant, slowly billowing. He followed them like a trail. The farther he went, the more they pulsed and bulged. Their colors changed as well—growing red-tinged. Almost bloody. The bright jewel tones muddied and turned flat and dull. A sort of a scent accompanied it—more psychic than real. It was meaty and slightly sweet, and altogether stomach turning.

He glanced at Ellyn, who paced along beside him.

"I see it." She wrinkled her nose. "Smell it, too, though it isn't *quite* smell . . ."

Carston wasn't far. He felt the closeness of the ciphered bracelet. They turned a corner and both stopped dead.

"What happened here?" Ellyn asked, sliding a knife from its sheath on her thigh.

"I have no idea," he said.

They looked down a wide passage. On the right was a single door. It was closed. Ahead the corridor opened into what appeared to be a lofty room full of expensive flotsam and jetsam. But what stopped them both were the lights in the middle between them and that room—the room where they had to go to get Carston.

It looked like someone had plunged a careless hand into their careful pattern and snatched a clump. Strands hung broken or twisted together in knots and tangles. The color was so dark that it looked black, but even as Keros stared, he realized he was wrong. They were red.

"What is it?" Ellyn whispered.

He started. He'd almost forgotten her. He didn't answer and instead took another few steps forward. He reached out and touched one of the strands. It sent a flash of heat through him and he felt instantly nauseous. He jerked away, but not before he felt a taste of something he'd experienced once before. The thing inside him pulsed hot as the flavor of it burned through him.

His cods shriveled and his bowels clenched tight. Instinctively he reached out and grabbed Ellyn's hand.

"Come on."

He ran forward through the lights, pulling himself in tight to avoid touching them where he could. He fled to the other side, dragging Ellyn like a sack of turnips. When he stopped, he was panting and his skin twitched. It felt like he was being smothered under a hill of ants.

He shook himself and Ellyn did the same.

"What was that?" she whispered. Her face was pale and she still held his hand.

"Jutras majick," he said around the boulder in his throat. "The remnants of a spell."

"What? Here?"

"The cracking bastard is working with the Jutras," he said and spat to clear the taste from his mouth.

"How do you know?"

"I've tasted Jutras majick before," he said. He'd been there in the throne room when they invaded and killed

Queen Naren. He'd witnessed the horrors of their blood majick as they tortured and killed two people. If not for Lucy, he'd have been the next under the knife. If the truth be told, that was the reason he'd signed on to help the Ramplings. The Jutras scared him nearly witless and the idea of them overrunning Crosspointe still gave him horrendous nightmares.

"When?"

He hardly heard the question. Pieces of a puzzle were falling into place. He looked at her, horror nearly stealing his voice. "That's who took Margaret. The Jutras have her."

She looked sick, but she didn't really know. She had no idea. If she had, she wouldn't look merely sick— she'd be digging a hole in the floor to hide in. He stared broodingly back at the spell. "I assume you know the Jutras use blood magic. It's not just blood, but pain too. They make sacrifices to their gods to fuel their spells. I've seen them. I've seen them carve the flesh from a living person and then crush every drop of blood from their bodies. They'll do it to Margaret, or something like it. They'll sacrifice her to make their magic and she won't be the only one.

"You asked me before me why I serve Crosspointe. This is why. I've seen for myself how brutal they are, how evil. This is my home now. What family I claim lives here. So when King William asked me to help protect Crosspointe against the Jutras, I said yes. You and I may have different masters, but we have the same goals. Do you understand?"

She nodded jerkily.

"Good. Here's what you have to do. I'm going to start tracking Margaret and the Jutras. Right now. I want you to get Carston and warn Weverton of what's going on. Tell him to warn Prince Ryland and tell him he damned well better figure out that he's got to work with the

Ramplings if Crosspointe is going to survive. Have you got that?"

"I've got it."

"Once he's on his way to Sylmont, you follow me. I'm going to need your help. Come as fast as you can. The regent has horses. Take one." He dropped her hands and ran his fingers through his hair. "Before you go, burn this place. Start the fire down here. Burn it hot. Hopefully it will destroy any spells they might have left behind. This will guide you."

He spun a thread of majick from his *illidre*. He twisted it around the thread that connected him to Margaret and then slipped the end around Ellyn's wrist. "Can you follow that?"

She narrowed her eyes, concentrating, her opposite hand closing over where he'd attached the spell. Finally she nodded. "I can." Her voice had firmed and she looked resolute.

"Good. I'll see you when I see you," he said and hesitated. He felt like he should say some other farewell. If he overtook Margaret and the Jutras and had to fight, he might not survive. But what lay between them was both as vast as the sky and as thin as his own breath. "Fair winds and following seas," he said finally. It was the traditional farewell of sailors and all that he could scrape together.

With that, he fled back through the tatters of the Jutras spell and back through the cellars. He stopped into the kitchen to steal a sack full of food—cheese, hard sausage, two loaves of bread, and a half-dozen apples. He returned to the foyer, dodging footmen and maids, and found his coat hanging in a closet. He shrugged it on, then was forced to wait an eternity while the butler and housekeeper argued over keys and the cleaning of the silver. It was nearly half a glass before both stormed off, leaving Keros free to escape his hiding place. He suffered the delay with ill grace, silently cursing the two and barely resisting the urge to storm out. It wasn't until after they'd gone that he recalled Ellyn's stun spell. He was too distracted by the memories of Jutras wizards carving the flesh from their sacrificial victims. He kept imagining Margaret's face beneath their knives.

It took him a few minutes to find the stables. The barn was warm and teeming with people. Weverton's three horses had been groomed and blanketed and now were eating hot mash while nearly a dozen men, women, boys, and girls goggled over them. Across the corridor were the regent's four carriage horses, all equally pampered. With such a spectacle, the crowd would not soon disperse. He'd have to encourage them. The stun spell would not give him enough time.

He stepped inside a supply stall that was full of grain and straw. He leaned back against the wall, holding his *illidre* in his hand. It took him a moment to focus himself. His mind spun with fear of the Jutras and what they might be doing to Margaret. But worrying about it wasn't going to help her. Forcibly he narrowed his attention to the task at hand.

The half-formed spells that a majicar stored in his *illidre* allowed him to quickly improvise a variety of spells. Keros considered what he could do to clear the people out of the stables. Better still, he could put them to sleep. That would give him time enough to saddle up and depart without being seen. Hopefully it would leave time for his companions as well.

He started with the web he'd created to catch the men frequenting the brothels in town. He'd build sleep into it. He used *Water* and *Stone* for the body, *Blossom* for peace, *Stillness* for undisturbed calm, *Vine* to bind them so they could not easily wake. He threaded the weaving into the web, targeting the spell for the people rather than the animals. It took longer than he liked, nearly a half a glass—when it was done, he was exhausted. A chill sweat trickled down his neck and into the small of his back. The majick was thick and heavy like cold molasses. It was a struggle to draw on it.

He carefully edged into the stall doorway. The spell was wrapped around his fingers. He lifted it to his mouth and gently blew. It drifted into the air, spreading wide. It swept over the small crowd, catching each person in its strands. One after the other they fell to the ground. The horses snorted and shied, prancing and pawing the ground uneasily. One kicked the wall of the stall with a shuddering thud.

"Easy now," Keros said softly, approaching the first stall and reaching out to stroke the chestnut mare. She nickered and came to him, thrusting her nose against his hand. He rubbed her forehead and behind her ears.

He checked the sleepers. Some were snoring. He pulled some apart to be sure that they wouldn't suffocate and went to fetch his tack.

A quarter of a glass later, he was leading the mare out into the rain. She balked at the door, pushing her nose into his shoulder in protest.

"We've got to hurry," he told her, tugging on the bridle. "Margaret's in trouble."

With a shake of her head, she complied, and a moment later he vaulted into the saddle, his body remembering the skills of his boyhood. Then he'd spent most of every day on horseback.

He honed in on the link to Margaret and kneed the mare into a swinging walk. He went out the main drive because the barracks were in the rear of the house, and he'd have a harder time getting away unnoticed. He rode through the open gates unchallenged. His mouth tightened in a grim smile—thieves didn't brazenly ride out the front gate, and the rain no doubt encouraged the guards to stay under cover.

Outside the gates he urged the mare into a canter until they rounded a corner out of sight from the house,
then he slowed to a trot and turned off the road, heading
northeast around Molford. His prey had maybe a day's
start on him and were likely on foot. Margaret would
be doing everything she could to slow them down. On
horseback, he should overtake them quickly.

He'd only ridden for a little over a glass when a brilliant orange light flared in the night behind him. He
twisted around in the saddle to watch Molford Manor
burn. It flamed like a beacon despite the rain. He hoped
there had been time to get people out, but was glad to
see the spent Jutras spell burned. He nodded and silently
urged Ellyn to hurry and catch up. Then he turned and
urged his mare faster.

Chapter 17

Nicholas found Geoffrey's study on the first floor. It was warded, but they weren't meant to stand up to a couple of solid kicks. The jamb splintered and the door crashed inward. He pushed it shut behind him, not caring whether any servants overheard. He pried open the drawers of the desk, dumping the contents onto the desktop. He shuffled through the papers, but there was nothing about the Jutras. He pulled books from the shelves, digging through ledgers and other documents, then ransacked the cabinets. Nothing.

"Sir? May I assist you?"

Nicholas spun about. A short gray-haired man stood in the doorway, his expression carefully neutral as he surveyed the mess.

"If I may be so bold—if you are looking for something in particular, I may be able to find it for you."

"If I had wanted help, I'd have cracking well asked for it," he replied through gritted teeth. "Now get out before I put you in an iron collar."

The man blanched and stumbled back out of the doorway. Nicholas swore, rubbing a hand across his mouth. It was time to get out of the manor. It wouldn't be long before someone discovered Alanna's body. Where were Ellyn and Keros? Had they found Carston yet?

He strode out of the study and up to the third floor,

thrusting open doors and trusting that the illusion disguising him would be enough to stave off curiosity and interference. Geoffrey was entirely capable of throwing quite a nasty tantrum and so it was not a surprise that the servants seemed to have vanished, lest they be unfortunate enough to face him in his wrath.

At last he came to a locked door. He hammered on it. No one answered. Once again he kicked it in. The splintering wood gave him no little satisfaction. He found a mound of clothes on the floor inside. They appeared to be Geoffrey's livery. Nicholas crossed the bedchamber and swung the door open. Inside a naked man lay beneath the sheets, tied to the bedstead. He stared wide-eyed, struggling with his bonds, flushing red wherever skin was showing.

"My lord regent, sir! I can explain—"

"It's an explanation *I'd* truly love to hear," Ellyn murmured by Nicholas's right shoulder. She peered past him at the bound man.

He started at the sound of her voice. "My son?"

"With Cora."

Relief flooded him and his knees sagged. He collected himself with a sharp movement and frowned. "Where is Keros?"

"He went after Margaret. We should go. If you want him to live, you should cut him loose or he's going to get roasted," she said, gesturing at the tied man.

"What? Keros left without us?"

She didn't answer. She was already moving across the room to the door. Nicholas cut the man free with a swift swipe of his rapier.

"Sir, thank you, thank you. I beg you—"

Nicholas heard no more. He was hurrying after Ellyn. He overtook her in the corridor. "Tell me what has happened."

She glanced warily over her shoulder and then up

at him. Her face was pale, her lips bracketed with tight lines of worry. "The Jutras took Margaret. Your regent has been working for the Dhucala."

Nicholas felt the blood drain out of his face and his throat seized closed. The Jutras had Margaret?

"Consider yourself lucky," Ellyn said. "They didn't take your son."

Her words struck him like a fist in his gut. He followed her quickly through the corridors. His search had taken him in the opposite direction of their rooms. The few servants they saw dodged away with expressions of fear. Geoffrey was not a patient or kind master and, at the moment, Nicholas gave him the appearance of being brutal.

He shouldered Ellyn aside as they arrived and flung open the door. Carston was huddled on a chair with Cora kneeling in front of him. He was thin and there were bruises and scrapes on his face. He blanched as he saw Nicholas and scrabbled to get away over the chair, even as Cora straightened and backed away. Nicholas pulled up sharply and held out his hand.

"Carston—it's me. I'm your father."

The dark-haired boy braced himself back against the chair, his expression fierce. He had a slender blade in his hand and he held it before him like he knew how to use it. He did. "You're the bastard regent," he said defiantly.

Nicholas shook his head. "It's a glamour. So we could come find you. I'm your father." He struggled for some proof. "Your colt's name is Snipper. I gave him to you last Ember Day. He is black with one white rear sock and a white snip on his nose. For the first two sennights you had him, you sneaked out to the barn to sleep with him. Carston, it's me. I swear. This—" He patted the front of himself. "This is just an illusion. I promise."

His son had relaxed fractionally but didn't look convinced. Nicholas ran his hands through his hair. "Take it off," he told Ellyn. He was tired of wearing Geoffrey's traitorous face and having Carston look at him like he was spawn was killing him.

"Is that wise? We still have to get out of here alive."

"Just do it, damn you."

Ellyn settled a hand on his shoulder. At first he felt nothing. He looked at her. Her face was screwed tight. Her hand clamped tighter, her fingers curling into claws. At last he felt a faint *give* and then the feeling of unraveling, like a thread pulled from a sock. Slowly the glamour unstitched itself and slid away in cold, sticky strands. Nicholas shook himself with a grimace, feeling lighter.

"Daddy?" Carston's voice was uncertain and desperate.

Nicholas strode forward and pulled his son into his arms, clutching him tight. Carston's arms and legs wrapped him, and the boy's chest shook as he began to cry.

"It's all right. I'm here now," Nicholas said, stroking a hand over Carston's back. "You're going to be safe. No one is going to hurt you." He pressed his face against the boy's shoulder, tears sliding down his cheeks. "No one is going to hurt you."

"We should go," Ellyn said.

He lifted his head and looked at her. Her face was strained and the illusion covering her white eyes was gone. "Are you all right?" he asked.

"Breaking Keros's illusion was harder than I expected," she said. "He's far more powerful than I am."

"Can you hide your eyes?"

She blinked and a moment later she was looking at him from ordinary brown eyes. "I've set the spell to burn this place. I only have to trigger it. We should leave before we are discovered." She hesitated. "What about the regent? Do you want to take him or leave him?"

Nicholas dearly wanted to let him to be burned, but there were questions only Geoffrey could answer about his activities with the Jutras, questions that had to be answered if Crosspointe was going to survive. "Bring him."

Ellyn motioned for Cora to help her and the two marched Geoffrey out between them. He still wore the guise of Sophia Dedlok. He tottered and obeyed Cora's commands, unable to resist. It was all Nicholas could do not to set Carston down and put his hands around Geoffrey's neck. Instead he went to the door and opened it, peering out. There was no one in the passage.

He tightened his arm around Carston and then lifted him down to the ground. He knelt. "Hold hands with Cora, son. We'll be out of here soon."

Carson sniffed and swiped his nose on the arm of his shirt. He held himself straight and nodded, his chin trembling.

Nicholas stroked a hand over Carston's head, his throat tightening in pride. "Brave boy. Let's go now." He waited until Carston had slipped his hand into Cora's. The girl nodded firmly at Nicholas, her mouth set. She would protect the boy. Nicholas turned away, biting the inside of his cheek. Did she know how much he'd contributed to her suffering? To her slavery? He had a lot to pay for—a lot to set right.

He slid his dagger from his belt and drew his rapier before stepping into the corridor. Ellyn joined him and took the lead, clearly knowing where she was going better than he. She motioned for the others to fall back and prowled ahead. She dropped down a stairway and made a low whistle for them to follow.

They reached the first floor without incident, but their luck could not last. Ellyn led them toward the front door. They could not leave without their coats, not in this weather.

"You! What are you doing there?"

Nicholas spun around. A liveried footman stood behind them carrying a tray. For a moment, everyone froze in place, then the footman dropped the tray with a thunderous crash. He leaped inside the nearest room and yanked the bellpull furiously.

"Move it!" Nicholas urged.

They broke into a run, the unarmed footman following at a safe distance, shouting at the top of his lungs. Nicholas broke away and ran back to quiet him. The man danced out of the way, snatching up a vase and throwing it. Nicholas dodged it and lunged forward as the footman shoved a table down between them. Nicholas jumped over it. The man shouted again and rammed up against the wall as he tried to flee. He waved his hands to fend off the rapier. Nicholas slapped his hands aside with his blade and closed on him, smashing the side of his head with the hilt of the sword. The footman dropped to the ground and Nicholas whirled away.

Footsteps pounded ahead and behind and Nicholas ran to join his companions. He entered the foyer and found a half-dozen footmen and the butler, each armed with a sword and shouting questions at one another. Ellyn, Cora, Carston, and Geoffrey had managed to duck inside the coatroom closet. The majicar peered out, unseen for the moment. Nicholas didn't wait for his opponents to collect themselves. He leaped at them.

He was a much better swordsmen than they were, but there were seven of them and more on the way. Nicholas ducked beneath the swing of one of the footmen and shoved him into the others while parrying another chopping cut. He retreated, sweeping his rapier before him. His sword had greater reach than the shorter cutlasses, but it lacked a cutting edge. He had to stab to kill.

One drove too close and he twitched the blade away, lunging and driving the point of his sword into the man's heart. He yanked back as the footmen thudded to the floor and parried aside another cut just in time to save his head. He drew back. The wall was behind him now and he had little room to maneuver. A semicircle of blades closed on him. He readied himself to drive to the side and flank them. Before he could move, something struck the half circle of adversaries—majick. It butted hard against them, sending them staggering toward Nicholas with yelps of surprise and pain.

He leaped aside and whipped his blade across wrists and forearms, breaking bones and disarming them. Ellyn and Cora rushed out of hiding, each carrying walking sticks. They clubbed the footmen and butler until no one was moving.

"There will be more soon," Nicholas panted. He grabbed his coat and snatched one from a hook for Carston.

They ran out the doors and into the pelting rain. It was past sundown, which lent them some cover. Nicholas paused in the shadow of one of the towers to get his bearings and put on his coat. He wrapped Carston in the too-large garment and picked him up.

"Over there," Ellyn said, pointing across a broad expanse of lawn.

They ran. The ground was muddy and more than once Nicholas skidded and slipped. Carston clutched his arms tightly around Nicholas's neck, his little body tight with fear.

"It will be all right," Nicholas murmured, as much for himself as for Carston and hoped to the depths that it was true.

They slipped inside the horse barn, crouching in the shadows of the flickering *sylveth* lights. Nicholas heard the soft, snuffling sounds of horses, but no people. He frowned. Ellyn motioned for them to wait and edged forward, disappearing around the corner. A few minutes later Nicholas heard quick footsteps and she came jogging back.

"Keros put them all asleep," she reported. "They could wake at any moment. We must hurry."

Within five minutes they'd saddled Nicholas's two geldings. He found riding tack for the carriage horses and in another five minutes had two of them saddled—one for Cora and one for Geoffrey, who was sitting on an overturned bucket. He was as still as a puppet.

Cora eyed her mount with wide-eyed fear. "I've never ridden even a mule," she said.

"Just hold on to the saddle. I'll lead him," Nicholas said. The rattle of the wind and rain on the roof tiles made it impossible to hear any sounds of pursuit. Certainly the bodies in the foyer must have been discovered and an alarm given. "We can't wait. Let's go."

He hoisted a stiff Cora into the saddle and tossed Carston up on his own bay gelding while Ellyn mounted the gray. He ordered Geoffrey to mount, then tied his hands to the saddle horn and gave the lead rein to Ellyn.

Nicholas led them down to the far end of the barn and slid open the door a fraction. A crushed gravel drive circled away through a stand of trees, no doubt leading back to the main drive, allowing the carriage to drive in a circle without having to turn around.

He squinted through the rain. He thought he heard shouts and the clang of a bell. Off to the left was another expanse of lawn and beyond, open fields. That path would take them closer to the barracks than he liked, but with the alarm ringing at the house, hopefully the soldiers were converging there.

He started to push the door wider and Ellyn held up a hand. "Wait."

She put her hand around her *illidre*, her eyes closing as her face set in furious concentration. Her gelding tossed his head and sidled in a circle as she stiffened. Nicholas put a hand on the bridle, holding him still. Grains trickled past. Nicholas wasn't ready for what came next. A boom sounded and the walls of the barn shuddered. Tiles rattled down from the roof. The horses neighed. Cora's horse backed away and gave a half-rear, then settled spraddle-legged. Geoffrey's horse spun wildly and pranced away as Ellyn dropped the lead rein. The two geldings crow-hopped and slewed about, jouncing against each other.

Ellyn dropped her hands to the reins and patted her mount's shoulder. She was shaking and her jaw was clenched tight. Cora clenched her saddle with white-knuckled fingers, her mouth open in a silent gasp of fear. Nicholas soothed the horses, proud of Carston, who sat the anxious gelding with loose ease. Nicholas retrieved Geoffrey's horse and handed the lead rein to Ellyn again.

He shoved the door wide enough to let them out one at a time, then swung up in the saddle behind his son. He led the way, turning across the lawn toward the fields, leading Cora right behind. The night glowed orange and red.

Nicholas twisted around to look. The house was engulfed in flames and the rain did nothing to diminish the violent surge of the fire. Nicholas nodded satisfaction. That should put paid to any pursuit. Everyone would be too busy trying to get people out and save the house to worry about anything else. He turned back to the night, kneeing his gelding into a trot. Keros should have seen the fire too. He'd know they were coming.

They rode for a glass without speaking or slowing. Once he was certain they were not being pursued, Nicholas pulled up. "Tell me what you discovered," he told Ellyn.

She glanced once at Cora. "We encountered a Jutras

spell. Keros is certain that the regent has been working with the Jutras and that they have taken Margaret."

"How many?"

She shrugged. "One is too many. Keros told me to get you and Carston free and send you back to Sylmont. He said to tell you that you should warn Prelate Ryland about what the regent has been up to and that you should work with him if you want Crosspointe to survive. I am to join him as soon as I can to help Margaret."

Nicholas looked away, his jaw tightening as he considered. Keros was right. Except he didn't know that there had been a majicar battle in the city and riots. It was possible Ryland hadn't survived or that he had fled. He grimaced with acid humor. He knew better. The prince would not abandon Sylmont. He might be dead, but he hadn't run away.

Nicolas had promised Margaret he'd come for her, no matter what. He didn't care that she didn't believe him. He kept his promises. He wasn't a Rampling— Crosspointe didn't run in his blood taking priority above all else. He glanced down at Carston, who had fallen asleep. Did he take his son and risk putting him into Jutras hands? But Sylmont was no safer.

"The trail leads toward Sylmont," Ellyn said as if sensing his indecision. "At least for now."

He glanced sharply at her. "Then for now we follow it."

The groups set off again. Their progress was faster than had they gone on foot, but slower because of the two carriage horses on lead reins. Glass after glass passed and still they did not overtake Keros. Day broke and with it the rain. The trail led around the western edge of Lake Ferradon and then turned northeast up into the Cat's Paw Mountains, following a charcoal-wagon track. The trail gave out at the kiln camp, where smoke billowed from the tall clay chimneys and the sounds of axes echoed in the forest. Mules brayed, men shouted, and dogs barked.

They found the tracks of Keros's mare running wide of the camp and followed them higher into the mountains. He seemed no more inclined to stop than they were. Carston woke and asked for food and something to drink. They'd filled flasks at a mountain spring, but Nicholas had nothing to feed the boy.

From inside her coat, Ellyn produced an apple. "Here."

Nicholas took it and gave it to Carston. "Thank you."

"We'll need to find something else soon. Need to rest the horses too."

"How far away is Keros?"

"Farther than when we started. We are going slower than he is."

He eyed her, wondering just how far he could trust her. She was an agent of Azaire. That much he knew. Which meant she had no loyalty to him, Crosspointe, Keros, or Margaret. She seemed intent on helping Margaret—she wanted something from the Ramplings and aiding Margaret might mean a reward for her cause. But was any of that enough of a reason to risk herself against the Jutras?

She caught his doubting glance and tipped her head slightly. "I despise the Jutras," she said. "It would not serve Azaire to lose Crosspointe to the Empire."

That much was true. He nodded. He didn't have any choice but to accept her word. She'd helped him rescue Carston. That said something in her favor. Still, he didn't intend to turn his back on her.

They found a meadow a little more than a glass later. Nicholas called a halt, removing the bits from the horses' mouths so they could graze. Cora huddled with Carston beneath a traveler pine, both exhausted and sore. They tossed Geoffrey beneath another tree and Nicholas and Ellyn held the horses while they fed. They rested for a glass and then began again. Carston whimpered quietly as he straddled the saddle again, then bit back his pain and exhaustion. Nicholas bent and kissed his head.

"You're a brave, strong boy, Carston. We'll rest as soon as we can."

He pushed harder, trying to gain more speed, but Cora turned white, bouncing from side to side as her horse jogged along, and soon he slowed the pace back to a swinging walk.

They crested a ridge at dusk to discover a narrow valley, at the end of which Nicholas could see the flicker of lights. He smelled woodsmoke and heard the bleat of goats.

"Let's see if we can get some food here," he said, his voice thick with exhaustion.

They zigzagged down the steep-sided valley and followed it up to where a cottage nestled above a frothing creek. A pen held a couple dozen goats; and from inside the small barn, Nicholas could hear the low of cattle.

They drew up outside the house and were instantly surrounded by barking dogs. The door of the cottage opened and a wedge of light fell out.

"What's your business here?" a deep voice asked. The owner of the place carried a crossbow leveled at Nicholas's heart, even as his glance took in the horses.

"We're in need of food and a place to sleep," Nicholas said. "We can pay you."

"Who are you?"

He stepped forward so that the light illuminated his face. "My name is Nicholas Weverton."

The man stared, his broad face ruddy and round. He glanced again at the horses. Nicholas Weverton was well-known to be one of the few men who could afford horses. He was also well known for traveling in high style and with a retinue of guards.

"You're a fair distance from home," he said finally, his crossbow still leveled on Nicholas's chest.

"Aye. Will you give us food and a place to sleep? We'll need fodder for the horses as well. No harm will come to you or your family."

Another hesitation and then the crossbow dipped. "Name is Durmon—Peers Durmon. You're welcome to bed down in the barn and put the horses in with the goats."

Nicholas lifted Carston down and settled the boy on tottery feet. "Thank you."

Durmon frowned at Carston, then turned. "Aggie. Bring some bread and cheese. Gotta a young'un out here."

A slender woman pushed out from behind Durmon. She had a strong face with a definite nose and a stubborn chin. Her brown hair was braided in a crown around her head and she held a child against her shoulder. She looked at the visitors and then her gaze settled on Carston. She turned and handed the child on her shoulder to Durmon and came and swept Carston up in her arms.

"Poor little thing. You must be cold and hungry. Come on in and sit by the fire. Do you want some milk? That's a good boy . . ." She swept back into the house.

Durmon smiled at Nicholas. "That's Aggie. No child is a stranger."

"I thank you." He held out his hand to the goat farmer, who set the crossbow down and shook it, still cradling his little girl against his shoulder. She peered out at Nicholas, her thumb tucked firmly in her mouth as she nestled against Durmon's chest.

"Come this way," he said and soon they had rubbed

the horses down, fed them a mash of grain and warm water, and then put them in the corral with the goats.

Durmon kept an eye on them, his gaze falling frequently on Geoffrey, who sat stiffly against the wall, still wearing the guise of Sophia Dedlok. "What's wrong with her?" he asked at last, his expression drawing down with sharp suspicion.

"She is ill," Ellyn answered. "She is the boy's nursemaid and they were kidnapped. They gave her a drug or majicked her—we are not certain. But we are taking her to Sylmont to get help."

It was her turn to suffer Durmon's scrutiny. "And who are you?" he asked at last.

"I find things," she said. "This time I found the boy."

"And her?" he jerked his chin at Cora. The red rawness of from her collar was visible around her neck.

"She helped us," Nicholas said. "So we are helping her. Is that a problem?"

"I don't have much truck with slavery," the goat farmer said, scowling at Cora.

"Neither do we."

Durmon nodded slowly. "Come inside then. Aggie will have some supper for you."

The cottage was larger than Nicholas expected. Carston was sitting in a small chair before the fire. He had a slice of bread covered in toasted cheese in one hand and a cup of milk in the other. His cheeks were stuffed full as he chewed. There was a loft above with beds covered in brightly colored quilts; a lean-to for making cheese on the back, fully as large at the house; and a small kitchen and a roughly hewn table large enough to seat ten people. Pegs on the wall held several crossbows, long bows, and snares as well as quivers of arrows and crossbow bolts. As he sat at the table, Nicholas's gaze snagged on the sword hanging above the door. It was standard Crown Shield issue. The scabbard was plain leather and the hilt was wrapped in a black and red cord. Durmon caught him looking.

"Was a Crown Shield, once upon a time. Left three seasons ago to marry Aggie and take over the goat farm when my da died. Honorably discharged," he added pointedly as he lifted his daughter and settled with her on his lap. He held her gently. "Don't care much for what's happened to the Ramplings lately," he said with a long look at Nicholas.

"Now, Peers, no politics at the table," Aggie admonished as she bustled about, setting cups and a pitcher of milk on the table. She returned with a wheel of cheese, knives, several warm, crusty loaves of bread, butter, and berry preserves. "It isn't much, but it's filling," she said.

"It's a bounty, thank you," Nicholas said and they fell to eating. Peers continued to watch Nicholas with a heavy eye.

They each ate until they could eat no more. Carston sagged asleep in his chair and Aggie made a bed for him in front of the fire. Soon Cora joined him. Aggie covered her with a quilt, casting an angry glance at Nicholas as she, too, noticed the red ring around Cora's neck. Aggie set about clearing the table with quick violence, her disapproval evident in every motion.

Peers caught one of her hands and pulled it to his cheek. "He says he took the collar off her."

She leaned her hip into her husband and glared at Nicholas. "Is that so?"

He nodded.

"Good, then. That slavery business is wrong and the Ramplings deserve better. The regent—" She broke off, shaking her head meaningfully. "That one is going to tear the heart out of Crosspointe if he hasn't already. Making slaves of the Ramplings when they've given this country their blood, sweat, and tears—their very lives! And to be repaid this way. It's depraved, that's what it is;

and Chayos willing, he'll get his comeuppance. It can't ever be as bad as what he's done to the Ramplings."

Nicholas looked at Geoffrey, who had begun eating, mechanically, once Ellyn had ordered him to do so. "I think he'll pay for what he's done."

Aggie brought a pot of tea and poured it out. Soon Ellyn yawned and pulled the regent to his feet. "We'll go get situated in the barn." A short time later, Aggie followed suit, taking her sleeping daughter from Peers and carrying her up to the loft.

Nicholas stepped outside to relieve himself and to pull a hidden dralion from his belt. He returned to the cottage and set the coin on the table. "For your kindness," he said.

"That's a lot for a meal and a bed in the barn."

"I thought I might ask a little more of you."

Peers sat back in his chair, his blunt fingers tapping slowly on the tabletop. "Oh?"

"I would venture to say you're a Crown man. Is that fair?"

"I am and I don't apologize for it."

Nicholas nodded. "Then I have something I would ask of you—you and your wife." He leaned forward, propping his elbows on the table. "The regent kidnapped my son."

Peers blinked. "You don't have a son."

"I do. Carston." He pointed. "And the woman we told you was his nursemaid isn't. That's the regent. He's been disguised and bound with majick."

The other man's mouth had fallen open. Slowly he closed it and gave a sharp shake of his head as if to clear his mind of a fog. "That's quite a story."

"There's more."

"I have a feeling I need a drink for this." Peers rose and took a clay bottle from a tall shelf. He returned and uncorked it, pouring each of them a measure of clear liquid. "Meris's Tears," he explained.

Nicholas took a drink and felt a jolt go through him, then his entire body went numb for a few moments, followed by a feeling of rejuvenation. He took another sip. The powerful liquor was generally reserved for sailors at sea. It gave men clarity, numbing emotions and the pains of the body rather than getting them drunk. He glanced up at the loft space overhead and then back at Peers. "Maybe we should take this outside."

The other man shrugged. "I have no secrets from Aggie. She'd cut off my balls if I tried."

A smile flickered over Nicholas's lips and then faded. "Very well." He hesitated. Could he trust Peers? His instincts said yes and he had little choice.

He leaned forward. "I need you to take a message to Prince Ryland for me. And I want to leave Carston here with Aggie for a little while."

Peers was taken aback. "Why don't you take your message yourself? Why leave your son here with strangers?"

"I've got business to attend to that can't wait. And Carston is safer here." Nicholas reached inside his vest pocket and withdrew the letter he'd intercepted to Geoffrey. He laid it on the table. "Finding Prince Ryland may be quite dangerous."

Peers unfolded the page and read it, his face turning bleak. He scanned it again, then looked at Nicholas. "Is this true?"

"There's no reason for it to be a lie."

"This is no time for a man to leave his home and family."

"It isn't," Nicholas agreed. "But it is important. I must get news to Ryland."

"So take it yourself."

Nicholas hesitated. "I would. But there is more." He licked his lips. "The Jutras are involved. The regent has been working with them."

That rocked Peers. The other man's face went blank and then hardened. His meaty hands clenched. "Working with them? What do you mean?"

"He's in the Dhucala's pocket. There's no doubt. The only question is how far has it gone?" He paused, then said slowly, "There are Jutras here on Crosspointe. That's where I must go. To hunt them down. I need you to take the news to Ryland and take the regent with you. Ryland will get answers from him. I'm afraid the Jutras have spelled him so that if he's questioned, he'll die before we can get the answers we need." Nicholas itched to demand answers now, but the Jutras wouldn't have trusted Geoffrey to not get caught. They would have made it impossible for him to spill his secrets if he was questioned. If Ryland still had sane majicars at his disposal, they might be able to dismantle the Jutras spell. Ellyn couldn't. She wasn't powerful enough. It had taken all she had just to remove Nicholas's disguise. Maybe Keros— But that wasn't an option either.

Peers thrust abruptly to his feet and strode to the door, yanking it open. He drew several heavy breaths as he stared out into the night. Finally he turned. His expression was bleak. "I'll take your message. And the goat-cracking regent. I'll head out at first light."

"And Carston?"

"Aggie won't let any harm come to him. Leave the girl too. She'll look after them both until you get back."

"Thank you. Do you have parchment and ink? I'll write a letter to Ryland."

It was nearly half a glass later before Nicholas finished. He sealed the missive, enclosing the letter to the regent describing the state of affairs in Sylmont. Not that Prince Ryland wouldn't already be well aware of what was happening. He stood. "I had better turn in now." He stretched out a hand. "Thank you."

Peers's hand was hard and calloused. "These Jutras you're hunting—can you stop them by yourself?"

"I won't be alone. We'll stop them. One way or another." Nicholas hoped his words weren't mere bravado.

Chapter 18

The pain of the march was unceasing. Margaret had wept so many tears she was dry. The Jutras fed her and she fought to keep the food down, despite her constant nausea. Even when her captors allowed her to rest, there was little relief. Lying still quieted the pain, but did not end it. She burned with fever. Her flesh felt parched and her joints were knots of fire. But despite the agony, her mind remained clear.

She was propped against the trunk of an aspen tree watching Saradapul and Atreya perform a ritual. It was a kind of dance, done silently. Their movements were at first jerky and crude, then switched to something fluid and smooth. They moved opposite one another in an invisible ring, each mirroring the other. Their bare feet slapped out a careful pattern in the leaf meal and mud. It was limned in a dull red glow. Each step brightened the light and revealed scrolling lines and jagged corners. Their pace sped up, sweat slicking their bare chests, their ribs heaving with the effort of the dance. Long black hair rippled with blue lights and yellow eyes flashed as if lit from within. Their faces were twisted with something like joy or pain—it was impossible to tell.

Their legs stamped harder and faster and Margaret felt a swelling in the air. It pressed against her, feeling oily and hot. She recoiled, but it surrounded her, filling her nose and mouth, sliding down into her belly. She jerked, pulling her knees up to her chest. Pain streaked along her skin and burrowed into her flesh. Margaret kicked and struggled to get away, but it was relentless. Her pain flared hotter. She whimpered, drool running down her chin, her legs kicking feebly.

It took all her control to hold herself still. She forced herself to breathe slowly and relax her clenched body. Suddenly she became aware that there was something near. She could hear a rough, heavy breath and the air rippled as if something was passing through it. Her skin prickled and she let go a sharp scream as something grabbed her—a *mouth*. Teeth gouged into her. Pain spiked but Margaret gritted her teeth against it and forced herself to remain limp. Pain only fed Jutras majick. The more she struggled, the worse it was and the more she helped them. She gasped as she was lifted into the air and the invisible creature shook her from side to side like a dog shakes a rabbit. Margaret whimpered in blinding agony and jerked into a ball. The creature shook her again, harder, and Margaret prayed to Chayos for oblivion. But the goddess did not answer and the Jutras spell refused her that kindness. Sleep she might have— but not unconsciousness.

She was shaken twice more, then the creature dropped her like a rag doll and its attention wandered away. Margaret stared up at the green leaf canopy above, her chest heaving. Sobs crowded her throat but she didn't let them go. She couldn't remember not hurting. She was beginning to feel the edges of herself rubbing away beneath the assault. It was harder and harder to swim above the pain, to remember who she was and what was happening to her.

She turned her head. The two Jutras wizards were finishing their ritual. Their dance had changed. They moved at one another now, like fighters in an elegant, deadly duel. They whipped around one another, faster and faster, kicking, chopping, flipping, and punching. Blood ran freely from the wounds they inflicted on each other. The spell rose up around them, the red lines of it winding and weaving through the air. Suddenly they stopped, both dropping to their knees and pressing their faces into the ground. The spell continued to twist above them, then slowly settled, sinking into the ground to disappear from sight.

The two Jutras rose slowly. They touched their palms together and bowed, spreading their arms wide, palms still pressed together. They straightened, and each backed away. Saradapul came to stand beside Margaret. He ignored the blood that ran over his skin, mixing with sweat. His long hair clung to the wounds. He stirred up the fire and put some wood on it.

"What did you do?" she whispered. Her throat was so tight and dry she could hardly get the words out.

He looked at her in surprise, then squatted down beside her.

"Some *thing* was here. What was it?" she pushed.

"It was Forcan, the hound of Uniat. He will guide the gods along the path."

Margaret didn't know she could feel more fear. She was wrong. Her stomach curled. "What path?"

He ran a finger over the bridge of her nose to her lips and chin, then up over her cheek, tracing the bones of her brow. The sharp point of his talonlike nail scraped lightly over her skin. The spell wrapping her turned the delicate touch into pain. "The path to Crosspointe. They come. They *return*. Once, long ago, this land belonged to them, before the dark times, before the birth of younger gods. Uniat and Cresset were All. They will be again."

She blinked. What was he saying? That his gods—that his people—had lived in Crosspointe and the Freelands long ago? It wasn't possible. She said so.

He smiled his dimpled smile and once again she was struck by how remarkably handsome and friendly he appeared. Margaret shivered. He was evil. She must not forget that. She turned her rings on her fingers. She hadn't tried to kill either of them yet. She wanted them both to be within reach so she could do it at once. It was the only way she'd be able to free herself. Atreya rarely came within arm's reach and he seemed to always be watching her. Tangled as she was in the spell, she had to be sure she could poison him before he could stop her. As quick as he was, she knew she had to do it when his attention was elsewhere.

Saradapul settled cross-legged beside her on the ground, pulling her upright to sit across from him. He pulled his hair back and tied it with a leather thong. Scars pebbled his chest and arms—each colored with skin inks. The tiny dotted knots formed a complex pattern of swirls and lines. Margaret was sure it meant something but had no idea what.

"Shall you hear the story?"

"I'd like to."

"Many seasons ago, long before the dark time when the sea filled with night and stars, my people roamed these lands." He gestured in a broad circle as if to indicate all the countries surrounding the Inland Sea. "We were few, then. Uniat and Cresset held the balance of light and dark, warm and cold, life and death. They walked among us and we were grateful for their love and protection.

"But then came the others. They rode astride great horned beasts with teeth like knives. They came in hordes and drove us from our lands and across the White Sea into the rising sun. But before they abandoned this place, Uniat and Cresset struck at their gods and cast them down. He of the winds and the storm, they cast into the sea and turned it black. They stole the light from she of the sky and stabbed her through the heart so that her blood fell into the sea. The green one they trapped on this island. This great battle destroyed the flesh of Uniat and Cresset so they could not walk among us anymore. Now we feed them with flesh and blood and pain to make them strong. Now we return to the lands of our ancestors so that we may destroy the usurper gods and Uniat and Cresset may walk among us again. Before we were weak; now we are strong. We will not fail."

Margaret could only stare. That Saradapul believed every word was evident. But—kill the gods? It wasn't possible. A shiver ran down her spine. But what if it was? Did it even matter? The Jutras believed it was possible and they were willing to slaughter everyone in their path to make it happen. They weren't just greedy, they were on a holy crusade, and that made them even more dangerous, as impossible as it was to imagine.

"Who is Forcan?"

He nodded as if appreciating her question. "He is Uniat's hound. He was once one of the great horned beasts. He was ridden by the king of the death riders. Uniat took him and remade him in blood and pain. Now he leads the gods back to the land of their birthing. Where he comes, Uniat soon follows." He stood suddenly, glancing at Atreya. The older Jutras was crouched a few feet away, listening.

They exchanged words in Jutras and then Saradapul lifted Margaret up to her feet. "We must go. It is not far now."

What wasn't far? Sylmont certainly. But they couldn't be going there—could they? The Jutras offered no clues, silently picking up their packs and marching away with Margaret sandwiched between them. Atreya went ahead, holding a rope that was fastened around her neck. Knots were spaced every few inches around the collar. Her neck was ringed with bruises from his sharp tugs whenever she slowed too much.

She marched, hardly aware of her surroundings. Surely Chayos and Braken and Meris must resist the attack of the Jutras gods? Surely they would rise up and fight? But their silence so far had been deafening. It was said Chayos was angry with her people—that was why the rains fell so heavily and crops wouldn't grow. But perhaps it was more than that—had the Jutras gods already found a way to strike at her? And at Meris? *Sylveth* was her blood and majick wasn't working properly . . . Margaret went cold as black fear clutched her in a bony grip. Was it already too late for Crosspointe?

They climbed up and down ridges, splashing through marshy meadows and swift running creeks. Her feet were blistered and raw and her clothes were muddy and torn. Blood ran from scratches and welts on her hands and she'd torn away two fingernails when climbing the steep rocky hillsides.

She wasn't sure how much time had passed since they'd taken her from Molford. She thought it might be just three days, but she couldn't be sure. They rarely halted to rest, and only for a glass or two. Oddly enough, the pain began helping her to hold on to herself. It didn't let her slide into hazy oblivion. Instead her mind slowly sharpened and now she kept her wits about her. They were nearly there, wherever it was they were going. When they got there, she was going to have to kill them.

She swallowed, her body throbbing with endless pain. If she had the strength.

It was past nightfall when they stopped again. Saradapul had given her some water and dried meat sometime in the afternoon, but it hardly sustained her. Even chewing and swallowing was excruciating.

They'd spent what seemed like hours climbing ever upward and now emerged onto a mountain summit. The ground was blessedly flat.

"Sit," Saradapul told her.

She slumped down onto a granite outcropping. She pulled the stillness around her like a balm. Slowly the pain abated to a more tolerable level. When it had, she glanced at her two companions. They stood fifty paces away where the slope fell away. Beyond them in the distance she could see the lights of the Pale. Which meant they weren't far from Sylmont. She frowned and stood, tottering forward. Abruptly she halted, the bottom falling out of her stomach.

They stood high in the Cat's Paw Mountains above the city. It was still another day's walk away at least. But from here it seemed like she could touch it. Except that swaths of it were eerily dark and the rest was sparsely lit. The harbor was usually swarming with firefly lanterns bobbing on the ships and now the broad expanse of Blackwater Bay was stygian. Acrid smoke drifted in the air above the city.

"What happened?" Margaret whispered. Everything seemed unnaturally still.

"The gods favor us," was Atreya's response.

She looked at him. Now was her chance. She flicked her rings open and began to ease toward him. She jumped when Saradapul gripped her upper arm and pushed her back to the rock. She sat down, her body quivering with reawakened pain. She closed her rings, furious at herself. She should have been quicker.

"Stay here." He took her neck rope and tied it around a low-growing bush.

The two Jutras strode away into the darkness. Margaret shivered and went to the bush to untie herself. The pain made her fingers clumsy and the knot was wet and tight. She couldn't budge it. She kept at it, stopping to rest for a few minutes when her shaking hands refused to hold the rope. Before long traitorous exhaustion caught her in its net and she slid down onto the ground and fell asleep with her head on the rock seat.

She wasn't sure how much later she woke. It was not yet dawn. She sat up slowly, wincing as the pain came rushing back. She looked around for the Jutras wizards. They were performing another spell. It was their chant that had woken her. It seemed very similar to the previous one, only this time the spell didn't rise up out of the ground. Their movements grew faster and more violent and their voices rose into shouts. Both were nearly naked, wearing loincloths and carrying their swords tucked in beaded strings around their waists. Their skins were oiled and their hair hung loose. The earlier wounds had healed, no doubt by majick, and now they inflicted new ones on each other.

Suddenly they halted, both caught in grotesque poses that looked like they might be about to kill one another, or else make love. Slowly they eased backward and stepped out of the spell pattern. With ritual pacing, each picked up a slender pole about eight feet tall. They were identical, both lacquered red and tapering to a point at each end. They looked to be about six inches in diameter in the middle before they widened out.

They didn't seem heavy. Atreya and Saradapul hefted them easily, holding them at a diagonal, and began tracing a complex path back to the center of the spell. They rotated around the outside, then started inside. They began another chant. This one was low and guttural. It scraped at Margaret's bones and made her shiver. The air filled with a waiting, like a lowering storm. Her heart thundered with primal fear. She should have tried harder to kill them. She shouldn't have let them do whatever it was they were doing.

Once again she felt the creature from before—Uniat's

hound, Forcan—as it shimmered into being. Margaret's stomach clenched. Heat flowed over her like hot breath and something bumped hard against her. She yelped as pain bloomed again. She tried to scramble away, but it followed her. Forcan's breath swept her again and she cringed against the ground, waiting for it to pick her up and shake her again. The grains dribbled past. Nothing happened. She sat up slowly and was knocked down again by what felt like a massive paw. She sprawled on her back, her head snapping against the rock.

Her brain spun and her vision whirled. She lay still as Forcan snuffled around her. The hound shoved against her ribs, and then she heard it pad away. She let out a weak sigh, then bit down on her trembling lips. She wouldn't let them see her fear. She eased upright again.

She saw a shimmer of motion at the edge of the spell pattern. Forcan circled—tall as a horse. As the creature paced around the circle, it grew more visible. She swallowed, her mouth dry. It had the loose bearing of a cat with a heavy head and no tail. It was the color of twilight. Its coat was purple, gray, and charcoal with brindles of dull orange, pink, and red. Its tongue was black and its eyes were tarnished gold. It watched as the priests erected the two poles in the center of the spell, leaving a pace between.

The wizards' chant swelled loudly and then dropped to a low musical murmur, then rose again, louder. The pattern repeated until they ended in a shouted crescendo that rang through the night air. By now the hound was fully visible. He panted, his black tongue lolling between his long, curved teeth. His gold gaze swept the mountaintop, and then he turned and disappeared. Margaret wasn't sure if he simply vanished, or if he went down the mountain. Her stomach churned to think of that beast loose and hunting in Crosspointe.

She didn't have much time to think about it. A moment later Saradapul approached her. Even as she watched, the wounds of the ritual healed. Sweat beaded on his oiled skin and his eyes glowed with an unnatural light.

He pulled her to her feet without a word and marched her to a nearby spring. It bubbled up in a shallow pool and ran down the mountain in a narrow rivulet. A copse of trees surrounded it.

He yanked off her coat and tossed it to the ground, then began on her clothing.

She shoved his hands away, gasping as claws of pain raked her skin. "What are you doing?"

"You will stand before the gods pure." Then he began again. When she fought him, he tied her neck rope to an overhanging limb, pulling it taut. When she could no longer move without strangling herself, he set about undressing her again. He was not gentle, tearing what gave him too much difficulty. Margaret flexed her fingers. He would take her rings and she'd be helpless.

Surreptitiously, she slid one down into her palm and lifted it to her mouth, tucking it in her cheek. He had pulled off her boots and was now tugging off her trousers. She forced herself not to flinch away. Lastly he removed her small clothes with a sharp tug. Cloth ripped and he dropped the tatters of cotton on the ground. He looked her up down.

"The gods will be pleased," he said, like he was evaluating a painting or a piece of jewelry.

He untied her and pushed her into the spring. The water was frigid and numbed her raw feet almost instantly. From a pouch on the bank Saradapul pulled a handful of red crystals. He dampened them, then began to wash her from head to toe. The crystals abraded her skin, rubbing her raw. Blood seeped through the wounds and turned her scarlet. Combined with the spell, she almost fainted, holding on to consciousness by sheer stub-

bornness. He reached for her hand and began sliding
off the poisoned rings. She clenched her other hand, her
body swaying from the deluge of pain. It was now or
never. She was out of time. She'd have to hope she could
surprise Atreya.

She clumsily pushed a catch and a needle sprang free.
She turned it to her palm. Slowly, quietly, with no fuss at
all, she put her hand on his shoulder and pressed, scratching the needle across his skin and raising a thin thread of
blood. He looked up at her. His mouth opened and then
he stiffened. His body spasmed and he splashed into the
pool at her feet. She eyed him blearily. Something inside
her prodded her to run. Where? She staggered up onto
the bank and turned in a confused circle. Fire burned
her skin where the red crystals had scraped her and her
head spun like she was drugged. Her teeth clamped on
the gold ring in her mouth.

She took a step and her leg turned to pudding. She
fell to the ground. All around her the earth moved in undulating waves. The crystals must have drugged her too.
Her stomach lurched and she vomited. There was little
in her stomach but bile. The ring fell to the ground as
she vomited again. She drew a breath and the air seared
her lungs. She coughed and knives stabbed through her
chest.

Blossoms of black agony bloomed around her throat
as she was hoisted to her feet. Atreya held her rope. His
yellow eyes gleamed at her from a face that softened
and ran like wax. She struggled against his hold, trying
to get away. But she found herself falling to the ground.
The world whirled in a storm of colors and shapes. The
earth swelled and diminished like it was breathing. Ants
boiled inside her body. Snakes wriggled through her
bones. She shuddered and convulsed. Pain exploded and
exploded again, swallowing her in a tornado of fire.

A hard claw clamped her arm and pulled her upright.

Atreya's voice rumbled through her like a stony avalanche. "Saradapul was one of Uniat's favorites. You will suffer long between his teeth before he swallows you."

He dragged her back to the pool and finished methodically bathing her with the red crystals. Margaret was lost in a melting world of sensation. Fear pulsed hard inside her, but she was helpless beneath Atreya's impersonal ministrations.

When Atreya had finished, he dragged her back to the middle of the summit meadow. Margaret had little sense of what was happening to her now. She was a ball of pain. All her senses slid away from her. She was the center of a writhing, melting world. Nothing made sense anymore.

Her last thought as her mind melted into the cauldron of pain and chaos was that she'd failed. She should have killed Atreya when she had the chance.

Chapter 19

Keros swore loudly in the mountain silence, then clamped his teeth shut as the sound echoed up the ravine. He was on foot. His mare had come up lame a day ago and he'd been forced to turn her loose. On foot, his progress was too slow. The Jutras hardly seemed to rest. Keros was muddy and exhausted. His legs ached and his feet were wet and blistered. Still he did not stop. He'd been within a few hours of his prey when he'd abandoned the mare and had been falling behind ever since. His link to Margaret told him that a few hours before the Jutras had halted, and he was determined to use the time to overtake them.

He hoped he was not too late.

He was panting by the time he reached the top of the ridge. The ground dropped away and rose again. Ahead was a collision of three peaks. The middle one was lower with a dull, flat top. He frowned. A dull red mist swathed the top of it. Gauzy crimson folds swirled as if on a patiently building storm. All around it, the light patterns darkened and slowed like dying embers in a fire. A stillness fell over the mountains and even the wind quieted. The air tasted of blood.

In that moment, a jolt shook Keros to the heels of his feet. He jabbed the walking stick he'd made into the ground for balance. Grasping his *illidre*, he searched for the link to Margaret. He found only Carston. His mouth went dry and without thinking, he began running down the slope in jagged leaps and bounds.

Near the bottom he fell and rolled into a grassy gully. A moment later he was up again. He fought his way out of his pack and dropped it, snatching up his walking stick and beginning the steep climb to the summit. He wound back and forth, skidding and slipping on the wet grass and mud, bracing himself with his stick. He found a vein of rock and followed its snaking path back upward. His ribs bellowed as he fought for breath. Dawn was breaking. The sun would rise in less than a half a glass.

At the top he slowed. The circling curtain of mist blocked his path. He could see through its billows and what he saw stopped his heart.

Two slender poles rose from a brilliantly lit spell pattern. They were narrow at the bottom, widening slightly midway up before tapering to sharp points at the top. Both were a dark red. Stretched between them was Margaret. Her hands had been impaled on the points and her body hung limp. She was naked, her skin coated in a film of blood. Faintly Keros could see the pattern of her lights—leaf green, velvet blue with specks of brilliant orange, pink, yellow, and scarlet. She was alive. But barely.

Movement caught his eye. A Jutras priest was dancing widdershins around the edge of the spell circle. He wore a breechclout. A red sword was clutched in his hand, the tip of it turned in a wicked hook. His steps were intricate as he stamped out the dance. His body swayed and shimmied up and down and side to side as he twisted and turned his arms in a brutal, beautiful cadence. His lights were brilliant gold. They swarmed like a horde of bees and were heartbreakingly beautiful. As the wizard priest danced, he chanted. Majick built in the air. Keros had to suppress the urge to duck down and hide. Something heavy and terrifyingly large swept searchingly through the night. The priest was calling it.

Inside himself, Keros felt the stir of the presence waking. Or rather, it no longer felt separate. In the last days it had melded with him somehow. It felt like an extra limb, or a new sense. It stretched and he felt *more* somehow. Everything was cast into sharper relief. It felt entirely natural—a gift of the gods rather than an invader. He drew a breath and let it out slowly. He hoped it was a gift. But there was nothing he could do about it now. He turned his attention back to the scene before him.

Cracks of light gleamed from the two poles. They traced the rivulets of Margaret's blood as it trickled from her hands. The Jutras sped his dance and now he began to spiral through the spell. The edges rose up as he passed. When he reached the middle, he'd complete the sacrifice. Keros was certain of it. He was out of time.

He reached for his majick. It was thick and syrupy and did not want to answer him. He hauled with all his might. There was no time for finesse. He needed to smash the Jutras and his spell with brute strength. Caught in the middle of the shattered spell, the priest would not be able to defend himself.

Taking a breath, Keros stepped into the red mist.

It closed around him like a swarm of stinging wasps. He shuddered from the sudden sweep of poison pain and pushed forward. The air was dense and fibrous, resisting him. He swung his arms and shoved into it like it was a hard wind. Step by step he closed the distance.

The sound of the Jutras priest's chanting grew louder. It vibrated through Keros's bones. He shook his head. The words felt familiar somehow. They glided over him like petting hands, trailing a biting mixture of venom and pleasure. The sensation spread, sinking down through his skin to his muscles and bones. He trembled, caught between ecstasy and anguish. He closed his eyes, swallowing hard.

When he opened them, he found himself inside a dancing ethereal world of shining stars. They spun around him, each pulsing and twinkling with rainbow colors. Entranced, he reached out a hand and caught one. It flared inside his fist and when he opened his hand, he found that it had sunk into his palm. His hand glowed red. A moment later yellow light veined through the red. It flowed over his hand like a net of roots, then spread up his arm. He felt it sinking inside him, digging deep into places he hadn't known existed. It didn't hurt. Quite the opposite. It burned with a pleasure so intense that it nearly dropped him to his knees. He felt a welcoming inside him as if two halves of a whole came together, even as something else inside him clawed back with painful fury. A fullness swelled inside him, then drew into a tight hard ball. He gasped and struggled for breath, unable to move, every part of himself pulling taut until he thought he would snap apart. Grains drifted past. His heart ached and blood thundered in his ears.

Then suddenly, there was a *give*. Slowly the hard knot released. No. It blossomed. He felt the spears of it unfurling like a thistle flower. He sobbed as majick flooded him. Except—it wasn't majick. Not like he knew it. This was different. It felt hot and raw. It *hurt*.

It gouged at him, demanding release. Tears rolled down his face and he clenched his arms around himself as agony shredded him. He groaned, the sound torn from him. Not knowing what else to do, he reached for the strange majick to thrust it from him.

It surged. He blindly flung it away. A dozen paces away it exploded. Fire roared upward into the night. The relief was temporary. Instantly he was filled again. Keros clenched his hands, holding it, his gaze fastening on the Jutras priest. Whatever this power was, he could use it.

He took a step. There was no more resistance. He strode forward through the firefly stars and red mist, stopping outside the spell circle. It floated, enclosing Margaret and the Jutras priest in a rising sphere, the top drawing closed like a mouth as it rose in the air. When he reached the center and Margaret, the Jutras would cut her open and close that mouth, completing the spell. Keros only had moments if he wanted to save her. Still, he hesitated. He'd kill her if he just blasted the priest and the spell. Even if he managed to keep his strike from hitting her, the backlash from the disrupted majick would roast her for certain.

An idea struck him. He grasped his *illidre* and reached for the web spell inside it. As soon as he did, he was caught up in maelstrom of power. It crashed against him like a churn of Chance-driven waves. He staggered beneath the battering pressure. Instantly the majick thistle inside him thrust thorny spines through him. Where the two powers touched, red lightning crackled and snapped. It sizzled through him. His body convulsed, his arms twitched, and his legs quaked.

Suddenly he understood. Somehow—he had no idea how—he had become the battleground between two powers: Jutras blood majick and Crosspointe's *sylveth* majick. He was trapped between horror that Jutras majick could take root in him and the gut-deep primitive urge to survive.

He drew back hard on the spines of the thistle, trying to pull it back inside himself. It didn't move. Blood majick. He bit down hard on his lip and blood spread across his tongue. Majick flared like the sun and, with it, a physical pleasure. He grappled with it, driving it back to the center thistle. He hammered at it until it gave and compressed down into the pulsing flower.

But the waves of *sylveth* majick continued to pummel him. He clenched his hand around his *illidre*, straining at the wild majick. As soon as he turned his attention from the thistle, it opened again. He pushed at it and from the corner of his eye he saw the Jutras priest make his final circuit around the spiral. He stood in front of Margaret, his legs splayed, his arms outstretched, his head thrown back to the sky.

Keros didn't think. He shoved to his feet and snatched at all the majick in reach—blood and *sylveth*. He forced them together, forging a long lance of power. It rippled and bubbled, resisting. He brutally smashed down on it with all his need, demanding obedience. To his shock, the majicks answered, bending to his will. He didn't wait. He whipped it through the Jutras priest's spell, aiming to hamstring the man.

The strands of the spell cut apart like a spiderweb. The sphere collapsed with a burst of sickly orange light. Wind roared. A cyclone spun up out of the broken spell. Pebbles, twigs, and dirt whirled on the spiraling wind. It shrieked with elemental fury. More than that, Keros realized, feeling a brush of fear and pain as the winds expanded and picked at his clothing. The spell was fed by Margaret's suffering as well as her blood. Suddenly she flung her head back, her spine arching. The tendons in her neck corded as she screamed. Orange majick played over her, winding around her in a tight funnel at the core of the cyclone.

Fury blazed in Keros. He drove the lance at the priest. The Jutras leaped aside, chopping his sword down. The lance shattered. Thunder exploded and the ground heaved. The broken majick lashed back on Keros. Pain spiked through his skull and he clutched his hands to head. The thistle of power opened and its spikes thrust outward. *Sylveth* majick seized him in a meaty fist and squeezed. He sucked in a raw breath as he fought to bring the two majicks under control again.

The Jutras priest had fallen to the ground. Blood trickled from his mouth as he turned onto his stomach and tried to push himself up. The backlash held him pinned. With a mighty thrust, the priest found his feet. He staggered, buffeted by the majick winds. Cuts and welts rose on his skin as debris slashed across him. He still clutched the hilt of his broken sword. Now he sliced the jagged end down his forearms. Blood ribboned down his skin. His yellow eyes glowed as he pulled in power.

Keros gritted his teeth. He couldn't let the Jutras gather back the power of the spell or he'd be unstoppable. Without thinking, he flung himself into the maelstrom.

Instantly he was assaulted by pain, horror, and terror—Margaret's. Tears ran down his cheeks and he sobbed for her, with her. But there was no time. A bolt of raw majick struck him in the chest. He staggered back as fire seared him. Instinctively he grabbed for *sylveth* majick and felt its cooling waves smother the heat. The priest struck him again, this time harder. Keros held his *sylveth* shield, but knew it couldn't last. He wasn't strong enough and *sylveth* majick didn't answer him the way it used to.

He didn't let himself think about what he was doing. He opened himself up to the whirling majick of the broken spell. For a moment he was lost. He felt Margaret's pain. It was unbearable. It roared through him and he screamed. His body went limp and he felt himself falling. No! She'd suffered, but he could still save her. If he was strong enough.

He pulled himself back up, but nothing could stop the shudders that quaked through his body. He pulled Margaret's pain close. The thistle inside opened wide and glowed brilliant white as it fed. Now Keros reached into the chaos of the winds, siphoning away the majick. Another bolt of majick hit him. His *sylveth* shields held.

He felt the balance between the two majicks as they settled into an uneasy peace inside him. All around him, the wind died into preternatural quiet.

Once again he fashioned a lance of the two powers, holding it firm in his hands. The priest saw the weapon and blanched, stepping back and bumping against Margaret. He turned, then turned the hilt of his broken sword in his hand. He raised his arm to slash open her throat. Keros didn't wait any longer. He swept the lance down, slamming it into the crease between the priest's neck and shoulder. It severed flesh, bone, and sinew and drove him to the ground. Blood fountained. The blood majick in the lance absorbed it and fed it down into Keros. The *sylveth* majick fluttered and recoiled, but Keros ruthlessly welded it back to the blood majick.

He lifted the lance and whipped it down again, chopping through the priest's neck, severing his head.

Silence fell, broken only by Keros's harsh breathing and Margaret's faint moans. He dismantled the lance and absorbed back the majick before stumbling to her side. Her head dangled limply backward. Her throat was circled with a solid ring of black bruises. Her entire body from head to toe was scraped bloody. His stomach lurched and bile flooded his mouth as he examined her impaled hands. Majick still lit the poles where her blood ran. He felt the pulse of it.

He put his arms around her and lifted, reaching up to remove her hand from the pole. She made a high whining sound. Her eyelids flickered and stilled. He tried again, but his strength was quickly draining away. He swore.

"Can we help?"

He started and jerked around. Ellyn and Weverton stood behind him. Both were white-faced and grim beneath a layer of grime. Weverton shoved passed him to Margaret's side, his expression turning cold and vicious.

"Hurry," he said.

He lifted her, and Ellyn and Keros released her hands. Weverton carried her away from the poles and the dead priest, laying her on the grass. He struggled out of his coat and wrapped her in it as Keros crumpled to the ground, unable to stand anymore. His head sagged to his chest and black shadows smothered the edges of his vision. His head spun.

"Can you heal her?" Weverton asked.

Groggily Keros looked up. But it was Ellyn who answered. "I will try."

He sat dazed as she began her work. He shut his eyes. The ground felt like it was rising and falling like the waves of the sea. Off to the side he could feel the steady pulse of the poles. What were they? Nothing good. He had to take them down—destroy them. He smiled mordantly at himself. He could barely sit up, much less stand. How was he going to tackle the poles? But Ellyn was here now. Together they would manage it.

He felt the surge of her majick and the thistle inside him twisted and opened. He pressed it closed again, feeling the prickle of it piercing him deep inside.

Time passed. He wasn't sure how long. He wanted to sleep, but didn't dare let himself. Finally he felt the press of Ellyn's majick letting up. He opened his eyes, blinking.

Margaret's skin was unblemished beneath the dried layer of blood. The skin of her hands was whole and tissue thin.

"Will she be all right?" Weverton asked, his voice gravelly. He held Margaret's head on his lap, his fingers stroking her head.

Keros cocked his head at the other man. His colors were moving rapidly as if stirred with a stick. The misty tendrils reached for Margaret, sliding over her and fastening onto her. Keros watched, fascinated. Slow realization seeped inside him. Weverton *cared* about her. Really cared about her. Perhaps even loved her.

"I think her hands will heal. She has lost a lot of blood. I've done what I can, but she needs rest."

Weverton rubbed a hand over his face and glanced around, then to Keros. "She's not the only one. We'll make a camp."

He gently settled Margaret back on the grass and then disappeared down the slope of the mountain. Keros looked blearily at Ellyn.

"Did you get the boy?"

She nodded, then stretched out a hand to brush the hair from his face. He flinched away from her touch. She frowned, her mouth tightening.

Keros grimaced. "I do not mean to insult you," he said.

She snorted and started to stand up. "Don't flatter yourself."

He reached for her, catching her arm. Power swirled around his fingers and inside him the thistle spread wide. He pulled away, his brow furrowing. He touched her again and this time didn't draw back when power twined around his fingers. Horrified realization settled heavy in his gut. He squeezed his eyes shut, spearing his fingers in his hair and knotting his fists. *By the gods!*

"What's wrong?" she asked. "You look awful, like that day—" She broke off.

He didn't need to ask which day she meant. There could only be one—the day Etelvayn had been sacrificed to the *sylveth* tide. Slowly he unfolded himself and stood, going to stand by the poles. Spiderweb veins of gold light continued to trace across them. Exactly the same light that had tangled him in the mist. He glanced about. It was gone now, and with it the dancing stars. Or was it? He squinted and saw a faint cloud of gossamer red undulating around the poles. Inside it flashed golden sparks. He scowled at them, his mind moving sluggishly. There was something here he needed to understand. Something terribly important.

"What is it?" Ellyn stood next to him, glancing at him and then at the poles. "What's going on?"

"What did you see? When did you get here?" he asked.

She made a growling sound of frustration. "We were just southwest of here when we saw the crimson mist. We nearly killed the horses and ourselves getting here. We left them in the valley below and climbed up, just in time to see you cut through the spell and battle the Jutras priest."

He turned to her. "What do you see when you look at me? My lights. What do they look like?"

She narrowed her concentration and scrutinized him. She jerked back. "What's that?"

"What?"

"There's something . . . *burning* . . . inside of you. And a kind of a net of gold majick woven through your lights. It's anchored to that *thing*." She blinked, her jaw setting as she looked at him. "Are you sick?'

How to explain it? He wasn't sick. He was changed again—a new kind of majicar spawn that was a melding of Jutras blood majick and *sylveth* majick. He wasn't the only one. He looked at her, sorting through the shift of green, scarlet, and white. He felt it more than he could see it—the slow pulse of blood majick. It was lodged deep inside her like a seed waiting for germination.

He didn't understand. How had this happened? He needed to think. He spun around and strode away. She called his name, but didn't follow.

For the first time in sennights, the sun shone with a radiant glow. The mountains glistened green and the waters of the sea sparkled. Keros hardly noticed. His thoughts were turned inward as he wrestled with what had happened—what was still happening.

The Jutras had found a way to infect majicars with Jutras majick. He'd thought the backlash from the fall of the Kalpestrine had caused the growing majicar insanity. But what if it hadn't? What if it was the blood majick? The two kinds of majick were incompatible—even hostile to each other. Trying to hold them inside at the same time could easily explain the why the majicars were going mad.

He sat on an outcropping and rubbed his forehead, trying to remember when he'd slid over the edge himself. He'd cast the spell for the last brothel. Using his majick had only made the presence in his mind stronger. That presence—was it blood majick?

A chill slid down his spine and he thrust himself violently to his feet. He wanted to run. But there was nowhere to go. No escape. Not if it was true. Not if the Jutras gods had touched him . . . blessed him.

Cursed him.

His mouth twisted. He felt hollow and sick, just as he had that day he'd become a majicar.

Somehow the Jutras gods had planted seeds of themselves in the majicars of Crosspointe and it was driving them mad trying to fight it. Their only way out was through—they had to surrender and become . . . whatever it was he had become.

He thought of the two poles. Even if he could, did he destroy them? The star he'd captured had fertilized the seed of blood majick inside him and allowed it to flower. Without that catalyst, would it have remained dormant? Should it have?

His head throbbed and exhaustion weighed on him like an anchor. But one thought remained clear: if *sylveth* majick was fading and majicars were killing each other, then how could Crosspointe hope to fend off the Jutras? Was blood majick the answer?

He sat there, the sun warm on his shoulders and back, unable to come to any answers. At last he heard a step and turned his head. Ellyn stood watching him.

"There is food, if you're hungry," she said. "Will you tell me what happened?"

He stood slowly. "As soon as Margaret is awake. She and Weverton need to hear this too."

Her lips pinched together. "We need to uproot the hoskarna as soon as possible," she said after a moment.

"Hoskarna?"

She waved in the general direction of the poles. "Don't you know what they are?"

He shook his head.

She blew out a harsh breath. "When the Jutras conquer a country, the gods must establish a connection to the land. The *kiryat*—priest caste—plant pairs of them. Usually they are white and red, one representing the god of peace, the other of war. The Jutras gods switch roles frequently, though now the hoskarna are all red. Both Uniat and Cresset have gone to war. The gods use the hoskarna as a conduit to penetrate the land and make it theirs. Already the Jutras gods are digging into Crosspointe. The longer the hoskarna stand, the stronger the foothold they gain here. We must take them down. On the mountain, it will be easy enough. We simply start a landslide and it will take them with it. We must do it right away before they take root."

Her fervor was edged with desperation. Her hatred of the Jutras was as deep as his. How would she react to find that she carried inside her the seed of their enemy's blood majick?

The knowledge might drive her insane. But no. She was strong. She faced adversity head on and did not run away. She would not crumple before this news. But he'd tell her later. Just as he'd tell her that the hoskarna might have to stay if the majicars were to fend off the Jutras. Because he was sure they were coming and soon.

Quietly he followed her back to where she and Weverton had built their small camp. It was in the lee of a pile of boulders. Margaret was wrapped in blankets with Weverton's coat on top of her, her head pillowed on a saddle. She slept fitfully, twitching and kicking and making choking noises in her throat.

There was a fire and Nicholas was heating water for tea. He sat beside Margaret, watching her with brooding eyes. If ever a man was ready to commit murder, he was one.

He looked up as Keros and Ellyn approached, his bloodshot gaze fastening on Keros. "What happened here?"

Keros sprawled on the ground. He shook his head. "I'd rather tell it just once when she wakes. Until then, I need rest."

With that he dropped to his back and rolled onto his side, pillowing his head on his arm. He was asleep within grains.

Chapter 20

Nicholas could not tear himself from Margaret's side. The vision of her hanging naked and brutalized was branded in his imagination and he could not make it disappear. He couldn't recall ever feeling such rage as he felt now—not even when he'd learned of Carston's kidnapping. Perhaps it was because he'd been reasonably certain that Geoffrey would not harm the boy. Carston was more useful alive as leverage against Nicholas.

But Margaret . . . she could have died. And given her employment, she still could. She risked herself regularly and, to his mind, recklessly—and he was beginning to find the notion intolerable.

He didn't understand his feelings for her—how could he feel so much? He hardly knew her. He'd spent less than a sennight in her rather prickly company. Her tongue was sharp enough to cut stone, so why should he feel like his guts had been torn out? Why should he feel like he wanted to kill anyone who came close to her—Ellyn and Keros included. Why should he feel like he failed her utterly?

He gulped some tea and burned his tongue. He set the cup aside and stared again at Margaret. He'd washed the blood from her face, but her hair was matted with it and the rest of her—

He scraped his fingers through his hair and glanced at

the sleeping Keros. He wanted to shake the other man awake and demand answers. But what would he do with them? His gaze slid inexorably back to Margaret. Answers would not change what had happened to her.

It was nearly night when she woke. All day she'd slept restlessly, at one time getting swept up in a nightmare. She screamed and fought invisible attackers until Nicholas shook her awake. She'd looked at him with glassy eyes, then collapsed back into unconsciousness. He'd held her head on his lap, stroking her shoulders. Wakened by the commotion, Keros had gone prowling. His face was haggard and he looked gaunt. His clothing hung loosely, as though he'd lost a lot of weight, and his eyes were sunken deep and swallowed by dark circles. Ellyn followed him.

He became aware that Margaret was no longer asleep when her breathing changed and her body went stiff and still.

"It's all right," he said. "You're safe. The Jutras are dead. Ellyn healed you." The words tumbled out.

She opened her eyes. They were full of horror and fear. She struggled to sit up. He helped her. She clutched the blankets around herself and scanned the small nook in the rocks, then looked beyond. The tops of the hoskarna gleamed in the setting sun. She recoiled from them and Nicholas put his arm around her, pulling her against his chest. She pushed away, but he didn't let her go.

"You're safe," he said again. "I promise."

She went still and then began to sob. They were deep, tearing cries. Her body convulsed and she pulled her knees up into a ball, clinging to Nicholas with all her strength. He held her tightly, rubbing her back and whispering soothing nonsense against her ear. The sun had gone down by the time she quieted. Keros and Ellyn had not yet returned, no doubt giving Margaret privacy to recover herself.

At last she sat up but didn't pull away. She sniffed and rubbed her face against the blanket. Then her face was swept by a stricken look. She lifted the blanket and looked at herself beneath it. Instantly she started to shudder and shake. Nicholas thrust himself to his feet and grabbed one of the packs and tossed it over his shoulder before picking her up in his arms. She clutched his neck. Her exposed skin was covered in a sheath of dried blood.

He carried her to the nearby spring. Earlier he'd discovered the body of the other Jutras priest there and he and Ellyn had carried it away. He'd been grimly satisfied by Ellyn's quiet, "Margaret poisoned the knobbing bastard. Good for her."

Now he stood her on the bank, holding her loosely in his arms as he pulled the blankets away. He picked her up and waded into the spring. It was shallow, coming only to his knees. He bent and set her down in the frigid water, then pulled the pack from his shoulder. He fished out one of his spare tunics and a bar of soap and tossed the pack back onto the bank. He knelt down beside her in the water. She hugged her knees, her teeth chattering as she shivered.

He rubbed soap on the tunic and then began to gently wash her back. She flinched from his initial touch, but then remained still as he worked. He washed her shoulders and legs, then tackled her hair, picking out twigs and leaves and loosening snarls as best he could. She let him push her head back, sitting still while he lathered her scalp and rinsed the soap away.

"Do you want to finish?" he asked, holding out the tunic.

She nodded jerkily and took the cloth. But when he made to leave the pool she grasped his hand. "Please don't go."

"I'm not. I won't," he said and then turned around to

give her privacy. He heard the slosh and drip of water as she straightened her legs and finished washing.

"I'm done," she said.

He turned back around. Her lips were blue and she was clenching her teeth to keep them from chattering. He stood and slid his arms under her, lifting her up. He carried her to the bank and stood her on her feet. He grabbed one of the blankets and wrapped it around her, then pulled her against him and rubbed her arms and back to help warm her. She pressed her head against his shoulder.

"You came for me," she said.

"I told you I would. But Keros saved you. I did nothing." All he had done was watch. The helplessness of that still burned in his gut.

"Your son? Is he all right?"

"He is."

"Good." Then, "They didn't . . . The Jutras didn't use him at all?" Her voice broke.

Nicholas's arms clenched around her. "No."

"Good," she said again.

After a moment she pushed away. He loosened his arms reluctantly.

"I'm sorry," he said hoarsely, the guilt that had been gnawing at him since her capture breaking free of its dam. "It's my fault. If I hadn't pushed to make Geoffrey regent— He killed your father. I'm certain of it. And then he was working with the Jutras. I didn't know. I should have. I will never forgive myself."

The words tumbled out with jagged violence and he let go of her, stepping back. He had no right. It was because of him she'd suffered so horrendously. He should walk away. He couldn't.

She stared at him. Like Keros, her face was gaunt. Her skin hugged the contours of her skull, her bones thrusting in sharp relief. Her eyes were sunken and haunted. His hands clenched at his sides.

"I think . . ." She began, then trailed away. She licked her lips. "I think we need to be friends now. Crosspointe needs us and"—a faint flush rose on her cheeks—"I would rather not be enemies."

His heart jerked in his chest. "You can forgive what I've done?"

Her mouth tightened. Not quite a smile. "What have I to forgive? Why didn't we know what the regent was doing? Why didn't we know he was working with the Jutras? We had spies on him constantly and still we didn't figure it out." She shrugged. "There is plenty of room for blame. But now we have to go forward. We have to save Crosspointe."

He nodded. Of course. Crosspointe. That was her primary concern—she was a Rampling after all. "Let me fetch your clothing so you can dress."

He returned to the campfire. Keros and Ellyn were waiting there. Ellyn was holding two rabbits. Keros wore an expression of uneasy pain.

"How is she?" he asked.

"Sane," Nicholas said, reaching for the pack containing Margaret's things. "She'll be all right, I think." He looked at the rabbits. "Better skin those out of sight." Margaret didn't need a reminder of blood and cutting.

He didn't wait for an answer. He returned to Margaret and handed her the pack before starting to retreat.

"Please stay." She didn't look at him. Her jaw quivered.

"Of course," he said, not wanting to leave anymore than she wanted him to. He turned around. He heard her unlatch the buckles of the pack and dig out her clothing. "We found your boots," he said. "You won't have to go barefoot."

Silence. Then, "Good."

He clamped the inside of his cheek in his teeth, tasting blood. He was a Pale-blasted fool. She didn't need to be reminded of her ordeal.

"All right," she said a few minutes later.

He turned. She was dressed much as she had been when she was prowling his house. She wore a pair of close-fitting trousers and a shirt tucked into them. She laced up the neck and held her arm out. "Will you do the sleeves?"

He obeyed. When he was done, she dug in the bag for a comb. At a loss for what to do or say, he collected the blankets and folded them, then picked up his pack.

Her hair hung to her waist and it took a while longer for her to pull the tangles out of it. He watched her, wondering what it would feel like to run it through his fingers. He pulled back from the hunger in that thought, not daring to examine it more closely.

She clipped her hair at the nape of her neck and put away her comb, then turned back to Nicholas. She glanced down at her fingers. "My rings." She glanced back toward the spring and a shudder ran through her. Her jaw knotted.

He frowned. He'd found the rags of her torn clothing with her boots and the body of the Jutras priest. He'd found no rings. He said so.

She gave a short jerk of her head, her expression contorting as her hands clenched on the leather of the pack. "He took them off in the water. They are in the spring. They are gone." She swallowed. "It doesn't matter."

But clearly it did. And he could do nothing to make it better.

"Come," he said. "Ellyn and Keros are roasting two coneys. You need to eat."

She hesitated, then nodded and started to follow him. Then suddenly she stopped, her face going gray.

"What is it?" He swung around, looking for enemies, then turned back to her.

Margaret's mouth worked, but no sound came out. Her body began to shake. She looked like she was about to collapse. Nicholas dropped the blankets and his pack and put a steadying arm around her. She drew a breath, then finally squeezed the words out: "Forcan—Uniat's hound. He's loose in Crosspointe!"

Nicholas frowned. "Uniat's hound? What is that?"

Margaret sagged against him, breathing like she'd been running uphill. He pulled her close, rubbing her back and shoulders to calm her. Keros and Ellyn appeared and halted when they saw the two embracing.

"She says Uniat's hound—something called Forcan—is loose in Crosspointe," Nicholas told them.

Both exchanged a frown, looking perplexed. Nicholas shook his head to indicate he had no better sense of it than they did. But Margaret's reaction told him whatever it was, this Forcan was not to be taken lightly.

He picked her up and carried her back to their camp and settled her beside the fire. Ellyn handed him the blankets and Nicholas wrapped them around her. She clung to him still and he held her as she slowly gained control of herself. At last she sat up straight. She groped for his hand and held it tightly.

Without any prompting, she began telling her story, starting with her capture. None of them interrupted, and when she stumbled and her breathing turned ragged, Nicholas pulled her tight against his chest.

When she was done, the silence lay thick and heavy. The fire crackled and an owl hooted and swept low over them. The smell of the roasting rabbits turned Nicholas's tense stomach. Margaret snuggled against him and he didn't know if he could have let her go if she chose to pull away. Not after hearing the fullness of what had happened.

Suddenly Keros stood and stalked away. A few minutes later he returned.

"Sylmont is—" He waved his hand, his mouth twisting. "The lights of it are chaotic and there's Jutras majick tied up in it. I can *feel* it." His gaze flicked to Ellyn and away. "We have to get down there. We have to go stop the majicars from destroying themselves and Crosspointe. If there are any majicars left."

"How?" Margaret asked, sounding stronger now.

With a heroic effort, Nicholas forced his arms to relax as she sat up.

Keros hesitated. "I need to speak with you alone," he told her. He didn't look at Nicholas or Ellyn.

Margaret drew back, frowning. "I don't think—"

"This is a Crown matter," he said, interrupting. "You're the closest thing I've got to a king right now. If you think this is information for Azaire and Weverton, then that's up to you."

She nodded and stood, walking out of the light of the fire. Keros followed close behind. Nicholas had climbed to his feet with her and watched them go. A hollow space opened in his chest. Whatever Keros was going to say, it could only mean danger to her. Danger she might not share with him because he was a Weverton and she was a Rampling and there were lines that could never be crossed.

Nicholas looked at Ellyn. Her expression simmered with fury and perhaps a dash of hurt.

"They need us," she said.

He nodded, turned away from the darkness and sat back down. "They do. But they may not want us."

Chapter 21

Margaret followed Keros into the darkness. She wrapped her arms around her stomach, finding herself missing Nicholas's warm strength. Her eyes narrowed. His care of her had seemed ... personal. More than just the common kindness of a man looking after an ailing woman. He'd seemed to be truly worried for her, and she had felt safe with him.

She grimaced. If she was truthful with herself, she'd been attracted to him for some while—even before this journey—but he was Nicholas Weverton, her family's enemy, and she'd never dared even think of it. Her father had taught her to uproot such feelings ruthlessly from their first birth. She knew she should crush them now. She couldn't afford to have any deep attachment to anyone. That's what being a Rampling meant—putting Crosspointe ahead of everything and everyone else. Caring for people interfered with that, or meant eventually betraying them in horrible, ugly ways. As her father's weapon, she had even less choice in such matters than the rest of her family.

But the idea of killing those tender green shoots was more than she could bear. She huddled around them, taking warmth and strength from them.

Keros led her a good distance from camp. Finally he

swung around to face her. "I know what's driving maji-cars insane."

Whatever she'd been expecting, it wasn't this. "What?"

His mouth pulled down and he looked away. His hands knotted and he began to pace as if he couldn't stand still. "Somehow, I don't know how, the Jutras have infected them—us—with their majick, in a similar manner to the way that *sylveth* infects us."

Margaret could only stare, despite the roar of questions that spun through her mind.

He grinned at her astonishment—a violent, bitter expression. "*Sylveth* majick resists the blood majick infection. That's what's driving majicars mad. That's the feeling I had of something inside my head." He rubbed his hand over his beard. "I don't think it's any more curable than taking away the transformation by *sylveth*."

"You said you thought it was the backlash from the Kalpestrine falling," she said, her stomach plummeting as she thought of the ramifications of his news.

"It was a reasonable thought and it may be having some effect on the situation. But it is not the cause. I am sure of it."

"Why? How do you know?"

He looked away again. "In breaking the spell to rescue you, it was necessary for me to use blood majick." And then he told her what had happened, from breaking through the crimson mist and capturing the firefly star, to melding the two majicks into a weapon and using Margaret's pain and terror to do it.

When he was finished, he stood in front of her, his shoulder slumped, his arms hanging loose at his sides, his face a wash of horror and despair at himself and what he'd become. He dared not look at her.

"You think all majicars are . . . infected?" she asked, knowing the answer already.

"Yes."

"And there's nothing anyone can do about it?"

He shook his head.

"And if the majicars don't accept this transformation, then they will go insane?" She didn't wait for his answer. "Ellyn is infected?"

He nodded, then slowly, like the words were pulled out of him, "But she is not fully transformed. Not yet. Not like me."

"The star—she needs that to finish the transformation?"

He shrugged. "Perhaps. I think it likely, though it could be that she simply needs to try the majick."

"So the Jutras don't fully have a hold on her?" Not like Keros. He flinched and stepped back.

"No. I don't know. Maybe."

Margaret was silent a moment. It was only long training that kept the froth of her emotions from spilling out in a terrified wail. If what Keros said was true and the Jutras had managed to infect all of Crosspointe's majicars with blood majick, then it was a disaster beyond all imagining. The majicars would be driven to madness. She shook her head. They already were, if the destruction in Sylmont was anything to go by. Which meant they would spread destruction like a disease, and what was left of Crosspointe would have no defenses when the Jutras armada arrived. It was coming. Margaret couldn't doubt it. She didn't know how they would navigate the Inland Sea, but they would. They already had at least twice.

She swallowed hard, reining in the panic that flashed through her. "We have to get this news to Ryland and Vaughn."

Keros shook his head. "There's no time"

She frowned. "What do you mean?"

He drew a breath. "Ellyn says that those poles are hoskarna and they allow the Jutras gods to establish themselves in the land. They are pushing down into the land even as we speak. She wants to knock them down."

Suddenly she remembered the story Saradapul had told her about the Jutras gods and how they wanted to return to these lands. "Do it."

"What if they are fueling my new blood majick powers? Meris's tits, don't you see? *Sylveth* majick is failing. Even if all our majicars were sane, we might not have the power to stop the Jutras wizards. Using their own blood majick against them could be our only chance. I defeated that Jutras priest because he couldn't fight the combined majick. If we knock out the hoskarna, we might kill our chance to defend ourselves."

She stared. She couldn't see any flaws in his logic. Except . . . infected with blood majick, was he still loyal to Crosspointe? Was any majicar?

He saw her doubts and his face twisted. "I don't know either," he gritted from between clenched teeth. "I hate the Jutras with every part of me. But have I become their tool? I wish to the gods that I knew."

His anguish was real. He looked sick.

"No. You saved me. You are my friend and until you do something that screams Jutras spy, I trust you," Margaret said, knowing her father and brothers would have slit his throat just to be sure. But that was why she was entirely unfit to rule. She didn't have the necessary ruthlessness.

His eyes closed and then he opened them slowly. "You are certain?"

She nodded. "Ryland and Vaughn may have other ideas," she warned him.

"Perhaps you should take your cue from them."

She smiled tightly. "I can't. That's not—" She drew a

breath and blew it out, her throat thick with emotion. Her chest ached. "I don't want to. Now, we have to remove the hoskarna. We can't chance leaving them." She explained what Saradapul had told her. "We'll stand a better chance of defeating the Jutras if their gods aren't here helping them."

He nodded, but there was something reluctant in his expression. Margaret frowned. "What is it?"

"What about Ellyn? Do I tell her? Do I help her make the full change to blood majicar?"

Whether she liked it or not. He didn't say it, but Margaret knew that's what he meant. Sympathy made her reach out and take his hand. He'd been made a majicar against his will, and now a blood majicar. Forcing Ellyn would hurt him deeply. But he'd do it—for Crosspointe. If she needed confirmation that he did not belong to the Jutras, she had it. *Unless it is a ploy to create another Jutras majicar.* Her father's voice niggled up from the grave. She quashed it. No. She had to trust him. She couldn't stop the Jutras alone. Without him, without Nicholas and Ellyn, too, she had little chance, especially with Forcan wandering about. She shuddered, remembering the enormous beast. Her hand clenched on Keros's.

"We'll talk to her," she said, prevaricating. And if she said no . . . Margaret didn't know what she would do.

"And Weverton? What do we tell him?"

"Everything," she said and knew in this her brothers would disagree as well. Perhaps even put a dagger through her throat for treason. But Nicholas had resources, and right now the Crown was in shambles. Crosspointe needed him whether anyone liked it or not.

Keros nodded. "I agree, for what it's worth. He seems to have learned some things on this journey. He will make a good ally."

"And Ellyn? She belongs to Azaire. How much can I rely on her?"

"She has done more for us than is justified by her service to Azaire. But I don't know. She hates the Jutras. That much is true. She would not like to see them overrun Crosspointe."

"Then let's go get this over with."

Margaret started to turn away, but Keros caught her arm. She turned back.

"There's something else. I didn't have time to tell your brother and now— I don't know how it fits into any of this, but you should know."

Something in his voice sent a chill racing across Margaret's skin. She folded her arms and clutched them tight, bracing herself. "What is it?

"What do you know of Lucy Trenton?"

"My cousin? As far as I know, my father confided everything to me about her." As far as she knew, but her father kept a lot of secrets. Keros's wince told her that he was equally of aware of her father's penchant.

"She is a majicar of the magnitude of Errol Cipher," he said.

Margaret nodded. Errol Cipher was one of the founders of Crosspointe and had built the Pale. No majicar since had even come close to matching his power and abilities until Lucy had been transformed last season. Except Shaye Weverton. Her stomach twisted with guilt. Nicholas had been searching everywhere for his nephew. As much as family in general and Shaye in particular meant to him, she couldn't imagine he'd forgive her when he found out. She'd known what her father was doing and she'd kept his secret.

"She came to see me that night before I came to meet you at the safe house," Keros continued, pulling Margaret back to the present. "She warned me that majick isn't working the way it's supposed to and she said the Pale could fail."

Margaret stepped back, her stomach twisting. "What?"

"She was worried. She was going to the Bramble to look through Errol Cipher's library. She told me we should feed the Wall tree as a precaution—to try to strengthen it. I didn't have the chance before we left Sylmont. And another thing, Marten was with her. He went in to explore the remains of the Kalpestrine. He said there was an enormous *sylveth* ball the size of a ship deep down in the depths of it. He didn't know what it was or what it meant. They said they would send word when they knew more."

Margaret chewed the inside of her cheek, trying to sort through this new information. There was a tremble deep inside her that wouldn't go away, and she felt like she might shatter to pieces at any moment. She felt overwhelmed and wanted nothing more than to lie down and sleep and let someone else deal with this entire mess. She held herself in a hard grasp. No. There was no time to fall apart and no one else who had this information. She had to figure out a way to deal with it all.

She dismissed the business about the *sylveth* ball. There was nothing she could do about it, even if she wanted to. Nor was the tree her first priority. She drew a breath and blew it out, squaring her shoulders. "So, we need to uproot the hoskarna, find Forcan and kill him, find a way to stop the majicars, and then at some point, feed the tree. That's all?"

"That's all." He grinned tiredly. "Plus get word to your brothers. Weverton sent a man to find Ryland and warn him about the regent working with the Jutras."

"I guess we should stop wasting time," she said. "Let's go give the others the news."

She linked her arm through his. He stiffened and then pressed her close.

*   *   *

The smell of roasting meat wafted on the air and Margaret was surprised when her mouth watered. How long had it been since she'd eaten last? Her mind shied from the question, from remembering the last few days.

"Are you all right? You've gone white." Keros covered her hand with his.

"Fine," she rasped, forcing her legs to firm. "Just hungry."

He didn't push and for that Margaret was grateful. She'd told the story once and that had been enough. She didn't want to think about it anymore. Never again.

Ellyn was turning the coneys on the spit when they returned. Her face was pinched tight with fury. Nicholas was nowhere to be seen. Margaret felt a twinge of something like disappointment.

"Where's Weverton?" Keros asked before she could.

"Checking the horses," was the frigid reply.

Margaret sat down near the fire and pulled a blanket around herself.

"Did you two have a nice walk?" Ellyn asked caustically.

"No," Keros said.

She drew back at that, her brows winging downward. Just then Margaret heard the sound of footsteps and Nicholas returned. He paused, his gaze riveted on her, and then came to sit. He chose a place on the opposite side of the fire. He said nothing. Margaret felt a chill that had nothing to do with the Jutras or the danger they were in. She hadn't realized how much she had wanted to be near him.

Silence fell, broken only by the sounds of the spit turning, the flitter and chirp of night birds, and the sneeze of one of the horses. Margaret was searching for the words to begin what must be said when her stomach growled loudly. She flushed.

"The rabbits will be done soon," Ellyn said, not quite as coldly.

Nicholas stood and went to rummage in one of the packs. He brought out a hunk of cheese and two loaves of bread. He cut slices off both and passed them around. He never said a word, his fingers brushing Margaret's impersonally. He set a flask of water down beside her and returned to his seat.

Margaret ate slowly. The bread was dry and the cheese hard, but the flavors were delicious. She sipped the water and ate more. She finished quickly. Ellyn pulled the rabbits from the fire and cut them up. She served them on a slice of bread. Margaret ate more slowly, careful not to burn herself.

When she was through, she looked at Ellyn and Nicholas. "I need your help," she said.

"We've been helping you," Ellyn said sharply.

"Yes, but the point has always been to help Azaire, has it not? Now I need you to help me—help Crosspointe. The things I'm about to tell you may make you want to scurry home and tell your Gerent, but there's no time. Not if we are going to save Crosspointe."

She looked at Nicholas. "And you—I know you hate the Crown rule. But there's no room for division now. We have to fight together."

"And you'll trust me?" he said, the words sharp as hammerblows.

"Yes." She looked down at her hands, trying to decide where to begin. But Keros spoke first.

"The reason the majicars of Crosspointe are going insane is because we have been infected by Jutras blood majick. It is taking root in all of us. The *sylveth* majick is fighting it and it's driving us mad." He looked at Ellyn. "We can't change it or stop it. It's done. We've been thrown into the tide and we are changed. There's no going back."

She stared, her face slack. "No. No, you're wrong." She thrust to her feet, her fists clenching. "I am no Jutras majicar. What is this? A joke? You talk about trust and then tell me this? You're a lying bastard!"

She strode over to him and slapped him hard. Once, then twice. Her mouth was a snarl. She cocked her arm to hit him again and he caught her wrist. "It's true. I can see it in you and if you look, you'll see it in me. I can't hide it."

She held still as she scrutinized him. Suddenly she wrenched away and staggered back. The illusion fell from her eyes, turning them white. "No." It was a broken sound, one that Margaret had never imagined hearing from Ellyn. The woman was too certain, too controlled. "No. I *can't* be Jutras."

"That's right," Margaret said briskly. "You can't be. You hate them. So does Keros. You've been changed, but you get to choose how you will use that change. And right now, with *sylveth* majick weakening, the blood majick may just save us all."

Ellyn looked dazed. "You can't possibly trust us now."

"I can."

"Your brothers would disagree," Nicholas said, looking shaken.

"Undoubtedly." Margaret lifted her chin, staring at him. "Do you?"

A thin smile turned his lips. "I've always put my faith in my family and friends. I see no reason to stop now."

She was surprised at the relief she felt. She wanted his backing more than she knew. "We're friends, then? And allies?"

He nodded. "For now."

Her brows went up, but he said no more. Her throat knotted. *For now.* What did that mean? As long as the crisis lasted? And then what? She didn't want to know the answer to that question. "I'll take that," she said.

"You've got no choice," Keros murmured. She glanced at him sharply and he shrugged. "No point in pretending otherwise," he said.

"None at all," she said. And then she told them the rest, leaving nothing out, laying out secrets that her family had killed to protect. Keros chimed in with an explanation of what had happened when he fought the Jutras. By the time she was done, she was shaking and wishing for a stiff drink. How could she do this? Uprooting the hoskarna—Keros was confident he and Ellyn could manage to do that. But what if there were more of them hidden somewhere on Crosspointe? And how were the four of them going to stop Forcan and who knew how many mad majicars?

"What do you plan to do?" Ellyn asked.

"Take out the hoskarna first," Margaret said. "Before the Jutras gods dig too deeply into Crosspointe."

"How do you propose to do that?" Nicholas asked.

She looked at Keros. "By mixing blood and *sylveth* majicks," he said. "The same way I broke the Jutras spell and killed the priest."

Ellyn suddenly thrust to her feet and stormed out of the camp.

Keros stood. "I'll talk to her." He looked down at Margaret. "You should get some sleep. We'll tackle the hoskarna at first light." With that, he went after Ellyn.

Margaret felt like a wrung-out rag. She took a sip from her water flask. She started when Nicholas stood and set more wood on the fire. He hesitated, then sat down beside her.

"He's right. You should rest."

She shrugged. She was exhausted, but sleeping meant dreaming and she was certain she'd have nightmares.

She wasn't in a hurry to experience those. "Where's Carston? Was he all right?"

"Scared, but unharmed. I left him with Cora at a goat farmer's cottage. They'll be safe there."

"Cora?" she asked in surprise.

He nodded. "From the inn."

"That was kind of you."

"It would have been kinder if Geoffrey had never been in a position to put her in chains," he said heavily.

There was nothing to say to that.

"I want you to know you can rely on me. My resources are at your disposal. I won't let you down."

She glanced at him. His gaze was steady, his expression stern. "I know," she said. And was surprised to find that it was true. "For as long as we're friends," she added with a wry quirk of her mouth.

He reached out and took her hand. He opened his mouth to say something, then closed it with a little grimace. "Come on. Sleep. I'll keep the nightmares away."

He sat back against the boulder and pulled her against his chest. She stiffened, then relaxed and closed her eyes, trusting he would be as good as his word.

Chapter 22

Ellyn didn't go far. She stopped on the edge of the Jutras spell circle. It was ash now, but Keros no more wanted to tramp on it again than she did. A flicker of gold light gleamed here and there on the hoskarna, reminding anyone who looked that the Jutras gods had arrived. Or perhaps it was only he and Ellyn with their changed perceptions that could see the gleams and the glimmers of gold dancing like fireflies.

Her arms were crossed over her stomach and her face was drawn. It was the first real emotion aside from anger that he'd seen from her since meeting in the carriage a sennight ago. A glisten of tears tracked down her cheek.

"I'm a monster."

"No. They have only changed you. The same way the *sylveth* did."

She whirled. "It is not the same!"

"Isn't it?"

"No. The Gerent did this to save Azaire—to have a weapon against the Jutras. Now I'm one of *them*."

He shook his head. "And the Jutras gods remade you to make you a weapon for their side. What did they do that was worse than what the Gerent did? Neither gave us a choice; neither cares what we think or what will become of us. Don't try to argue that the Gerent is better.

He's just as bad, or worse. At least the Jutras inflicted this on their enemies and they make no bones about the way they conquer—they force the people they overrun to help them or they kill them. The Gerent used his own people and gave us no choice in the matter. He used us like cattle."

His mouth pinched shut on his fury. They were old wounds and they didn't matter. Ellyn stared at him, her expression mulish. She wasn't going to change her mind. She couldn't without loathing everything she'd become.

He drew a breath and let it out, trying to speak calmly. "But here is the thing you are forgetting—just because they made you, doesn't mean that they own you. You can choose what you will be and who you will serve. I did the first time and I'm sure as the black depths not going to start serving the Jutras now."

Her chin trembled and she firmed it. "The Gerent will never accept me. Not tainted like this."

"Margaret will. Crosspointe will."

She snorted. "This is not my land. *I* want to go home."

"So go. Explain what has happened. You don't think that the Jutras gods will stop here? They'll infect Azaire and everywhere else. Azaire will need you. The Gerent will see that."

"But he'll never trust me again."

Keros shrugged. It wasn't much of a loss as far as he could tell, but it clearly pained her deeply. "You'll prove yourself."

She nodded without any conviction and turned back to look at the hoskarna. She wiped at her cheeks with one hand. "Can we really resist the call of the Jutras gods?" she whispered.

"I'm damned well going to try," he said. "Starting with uprooting these cracking sticks."

She gave a bark of laughter that was instantly smothered. Grains dribbled by. Finally, "This blood majick. How do I use it?"

The question shocked him. "Use it?" he repeated stupidly.

"You said it yourself—*sylveth* majick is weakening. I'll do whatever I have to do to stop the Jutras. Even use their cracking majick." Her lip curled as if she wanted to spit. But she looked entirely resolved.

He looked at the whirling glimmer of stars. They had been the catalyst. He licked his lips, looking down at his hands. The gold veining pulsed lightly through his lights. Could he pass the power to her? It would make sense. The Jutras wanted their majick to spread. Having to send every majicar to the hoskarna to capture a star was not particularly practical or efficient and the Jutras made a habit of both when it came to conquering.

He held up his hand. "I may be able to help. But are you certain?"

She eyed his hand with a scowl. She clenched her fists. "Yes. I'll do whatever I have to do."

He nodded, then reached out and touched her cheek. At the same time, he called on the power of the thistle. Nothing happened. He grimaced. Blood. Withdrawing his hand, he pulled out his dagger and cut across the pad of his middle finger. Instantly he felt the thistle inside him flex and expand. With it came a rush of pleasure that made his entire body tingle. His cods tightened. He ignored it and this time when he drew on the majick, it flowed through him easily. He wondered what he could do with it really. He was no more than a base apprentice again, not knowing the chants or the patterns that blood majick seemed to require. But at the moment, he didn't need any of that. He pulled power into his hand, forming it into a little ball. He put his fingers on her cheek again and gave a *push*. The droplet of power slid from him into her.

Instantly gold veins started to grow, spreading like cracks over her face. She went rigid and swayed like she was going to fall. Keros didn't steady her—he didn't dare touch her.

He only vaguely remembered the moments of his own transformation. There was the pleasure—intense almost to the point of pain. There had been a sense of something inside him melding into a whole with the majick of the firefly star, followed by the clawing reaction of the *sylveth* majick. He wondered whether he'd have survived the confrontation if *sylveth* majick weren't so weakened.

He rocked back on his heels as realization hit him, and wondered how he had not seen it sooner—it was so obvious. The Jutras had poisoned *sylveth* majick somehow. He swallowed. *Sylveth* in the seas was all that really kept the Jutras from overwhelming Crosspointe. The chaotic currents, the Koreions, the bores—the various hazards of sea were treacherous indeed and a Jutras armada would lose plenty of ships in the crossing, but if there were no *sylveth* tides, some would surely make it, even without Pilots or compasses. Without *sylveth*, perhaps the sea would even lose the churning chaos and the Jutras would sail across without losing a single ship.

Without an army or majicars to put up a defense, Crosspointe was nearly defenseless. It would take only a handful of Jutras warriors to smother any resistance. And though Prince Vaughn was assembling an army to challenge the regent, Keros didn't know what sort of progress he'd made or whether it would be enough to counter the experienced Jutras warriors.

He speared his fingers through his hair, staring impatiently at Ellyn as he waited for her transformation to be done. She was breathing harshly and sweat beaded on her forehead and upper lip. Then suddenly she jerked hard and dropped to the ground like a broken marionette. Keros knelt beside her. Her chest moved shallowly and relief slid through him. A jolt quaked through her body. She moaned. Heat rolled off her in palpable waves. Another jolt and her mouth opened, but no sound emerged. Her faced twisted.

Keros hesitated a moment more. She convulsed and yellow liquid bubbled from her lips. She needed help. He grabbed her outflung hands. Her fingers clenched on his, though he doubted she was even aware of him.

He didn't know what to do. He felt majick roiling through her, felt the skim of pleasure seeping into him through their touch and, with it, the snarling fury of *sylveth* majick fighting the invasion of the blood majick. He scraped a nail over the cut on his finger and blood flowed again. He gathered himself, pulling together a melding of his *sylveth* and blood majicks. They went together more willingly than previously, though he could still feel the friction between them.

He pushed his awareness into Ellyn. Instantly he was assailed by sensation—an overwhelming tide of pleasure and pain. The gold net of blood majick was still growing, encasing her inside a cocoon of power. Her lights flashed and fought against it, attacking ferociously. They converged on a portion of the net like a pack of wolves, biting and tearing. The blood majick responded with a hot flash of pure energy, sending the lights fleeing, only to converge together and attack again. Each time sent a tremor of pain through Ellyn's body. It was weakening her terribly.

Suddenly they changed direction. Instead of going for the net of light, they were swarming the thistle inside her. It was closed tight. It needed to open and she needed to find a way to balance the two majicks inside her. No, she needed to want to. That was the heart of the problem. She didn't want the blood majick to succeed inside her. On some level, she wanted her lights to kill it, except that the blood majick was already part of her. Killing it would kill her. She didn't want to die. That much he knew for certain. And at least part of her was willing to embrace the blood majick.

And then suddenly he knew what to do. He pulled a hand away and snatched his dagger. He dragged the point along her forearm. Blood welled and ran.

Instantly the gold veins of the net flared brilliantly. Inside her he felt the thistle open.

"Tame the majicks," he said, bending close to her ear. "Find your balance. They are both yours to command."

He wanted to hold on longer, but this battle was hers alone now. He withdrew and released her hands. He watched intently. He could see her lights shifting and coalescing in bulges and knots, but he no longer could see inside the net of majick.

Minutes dribbled past, measured in Ellyn's short, gasping breaths and his own thundering heartbeat.

Then without warning, she opened her eyes. The illusion that gave her ordinary brown eyes was gone and the vacant whites fixed on him. "Thank you," she said, then struggled to sit up.

Keros slid an arm around her shoulders and lifted her.

She looked down at her arm and put her hand over it to staunch the bleeding. She grimaced. "That shouldn't feel so good," she said with a little groan. "No wonder those bastards are so bloodthirsty."

"Torturing and sacrificing others must give a great deal of enjoyment as well," Keros said.

She shivered and shook her head. "I can't do that."

He nodded, but said nothing. Because in the end, they both knew that it didn't matter what they could stomach—if it would keep the Jutras from invading, they'd do it. He swallowed the bile that rose in his throat. Please the gods that it didn't come to that.

Ellyn made no effort to stand up. She settled her elbows on her bent knees. "How are we going help the majicars?" she asked. "You know they won't like this business of becoming a blood majicar. But on top of that, how do we help them make the transformation?"

Keros sat on the ground beside her, raising his brows at her. "You're going to stay and help?"

She shrugged. "I'm here on Crosspointe and so are the Jutras. I'm not running away until I kill some of the bastards. After that—" She shook her head.

He grinned and stood up, holding out his hand. She took it and let him pull her up beside him.

"We have a lot of work to do tomorrow," he said, motioning to the hoskarna. "We'd better get some sleep."

She nodded and they began to return to the camp. "Will they solve it, do you think?" she asked.

"Who? Solve what?"

"Margaret and Nicholas. He's ass over teakettle for her. She's harder to read, but even if she feels the same—she's a Rampling and he's ..." She waved a hand. "Rumor is that he had King William murdered."

Keros nodded soberly. "I know." He remembered the way the odd gauzy tendrils of Weverton's lights had caressed her and fastened themselves to her. The man was besotted. And Margaret—he had no idea how she felt. But what a choice for either of them. How could she ever trust him? And the rest of Crosspointe—it would be a scandal. More than that. It would be treason for her and insanity for him.

"But then again," Ellyn said slowly, looking down at the cut on her arm. "Other stranger things have mixed. Perhaps there is hope for them."

They rounded a boulder and found Margaret curled up on Nicholas's chest, asleep. He had one arm around her, the other pressed gently to her cheek. He nodded at them and closed his eyes.

Ellyn exchanged a raised-brow glance with Keros. He lifted a shoulder. Maybe there was hope for them; maybe there was hope for all of them.

Keros was stiff when he woke the next morning. His neck and shoulder ached from lying on the hard ground and he had a bruise on his hip from a sharp rock. He sat up slowly, muttering a litany of curses colorful enough to make a sailor blush.

Weverton coughed and Keros cut off abruptly.

"Impressive," Ellyn said, sitting up on the opposite side of the fire. She stretched and yawned. She'd restored the illusion to her eyes.

"You might have to teach me a few of those," Margaret said. "They sound quite useful." She pushed up from Weverton's chest. She glanced down at him, her cheeks reddening, then clambered to her feet. "Excuse me a moment." She hurried away and disappeared behind the boulders, no doubt going to relieve herself. Weverton watched her go, looking like a whipped puppy. Keros shook his head, reluctantly pitying the man.

He stirred up the fire and laid more wood on it while Ellyn fetched water from the spring for tea. Nicholas stood and stretched, then went to check the horses. A half a glass later, the four companions had eaten the last of the bread and cheese and were drinking their tea in tense silence.

"You and Weverton should head for Sylmont," Keros told Margaret. "You can't do any good here; if this Forcan shows up, you won't be able to defend yourselves. You'll just be in the way."

Weverton looked at Margaret measuringly, but she looked only worried, not unwilling.

"We won't do much good in Sylmont without you," she said to Keros. "We'll need your majick."

"Fine. Wait for us behind the Maida of Chayos. You

should be safe enough there until we arrive." *If* they arrived. He didn't say it. But he could see from the expression on her face that she was thinking the same thing.

Margaret and Weverton left soon after. They took
all three horses. They'd spook from the majick, and if
Forcan did show up, the animals would be lost.

"Be careful," Margaret told Keros as she hugged him.
"As careful as you can."

She felt bone-thin in his arms. He held her carefully.
"Same to you." He shook Weverton's hand. "Keep her
safe."

The other man's lips pulled into a humorless smile.
"Swords aren't designed for safety and neither is she.
But I'll do my best."

Keros nodded understanding and then watched the
two mount and ride out of sight before joining Ellyn by
the hoskarna.

She was pacing around the burnt-out spell circle,
frowning at it. She looked up as he approached. "How
do you want to start?" she asked without preamble.

He glanced up as a gust of wind picked at his hair
and drove a splatter of raindrops against his cheeks and
forehead. "The ground is soft from the rain. I think we
can push it into a slide and the hoskarna will go with
it."

"We're on a flat. It will be like lifting up a mountain."

"There's a slight slope. It will be enough." He sounded
more confident than he felt.

"Perhaps if *sylveth* majick weren't so sluggish," she
said with a frown. "But I don't know if I can't call up
enough power to do anything that big."

"Together we can. And we have the blood majick."

"Do we dare use it on the hoskarna?'

He made a face. "I'd rather we tried to get away without it. But if we have to use it, then we will. We can't

let the Jutras gods keep this foothold." Providing they could figure out how to use it with enough skill to accomplish anything.

"It may not uproot them," she said. "They've had time to dig into the land. If they've rooted too deep, we won't be able to budge them."

"We have to try."

"I know. How do you want to start?"

Keros walked uphill from the spell circle. He found where the flat of the summit started to shift into a barely noticeable downward grade. He picked up a stick and scraped a wide arc on the ground, about a hundred feet wide and twenty feet from the burned-out Jutras spell at the closest point. He considered it with a frown, then glanced at Ellyn.

"That should do it. If we push down here, we can get the whole cap of the slope to move. We'll have to pull water into it and saturate the dirt and then shove it downward. With luck, the roots of the hoskarna won't be able to hold on."

She glanced at the two poles with a scowl. Gleams of yellow light continued to pulse along the lacquered red wood. She folded her arms as she thought about it, then nodded. "We could do it. We could build on the web spell you made. If we layer in a call for water, the web could hold it until the ground turns into a marsh."

"Then we shove against it and slide it down the mountain."

She looked doubtful. "Do you think that just above it will do the trick? We really need the whole slope to slide and I don't know that we have the strength to push hard enough to move everything we have to."

He frowned. She was right. They needed to soak the ground below the hoskarna as well. But it was going to take time and plenty of energy. "We can divert the spring and channel it into the web. If we add another one downslope, we may loosen things enough. See there where it grows steep again? If we can push it that far, then its weight and speed should do the rest."

They began with the web. It was a more difficult task than Keros had anticipated. *Sylveth* majick was not just slow to answer his call, but it was also stiff as cold taffy. Stretching the spell to cover the broad swath of ground was nearly impossible. Both Keros and Ellyn dug hard for their *sylveth* majick, but it was elusive, like grasping at misty vapors. Soon Keros was panting and sweating. He peeled off his shirt and swiped his forehead with his forearm.

He glanced at Ellyn. Her face was strained and pale. She chewed her lips, her eyes closed, her hands clenching around her *illidre*. Slowly the two of them stretched the web across the long scalloped line Keros had dug in the dirt. They pushed the web down into the earth and then both stopped to rest, panting. They exchanged a look, neither voicing their worry. If it took that much effort simply to plant the first web in place, how would they manage to implant the second web, call up the water, and lever away the slope?

Ellyn took a drink from her water flask and offered it to Keros. He swallowed gratefully, his mouth parched. He glanced up at the sky. The air was still and heavy and pewter clouds hung low and pregnant. The earlier splatter of rain had not yet fulfilled its promise of a downpour.

He drew a deep breath and let it out. "Ready?"

Ellyn nodded wordlessly and they walked down below the hoskarna and began again. Keros felt her exhaustion. She tugged and pulled unevenly at the web, shaking with effort. He was the master majicar; he should carry the heaviest part of this burden. He gritted his teeth and reached for more majick. He stretched, but it was as if it had drained away from the land and even the sea. It was terrifying. His stomach tightened. He pushed himself farther, finding a few puddles and rivulets hidden far away. He drew in the power and poured it into the web. It stretched into a broad net across the downhill slope. He pushed it down into the dirt as far as he could, hoping it would be enough.

When he was through, he staggered over to Ellyn. She had fallen to her knees. Her face was white and her hands were shaking.

"I'm sorry," she said. "I just couldn't hold it any longer."

He wanted to sag down to the ground beside her, but kept himself upright by sheer will. There was no time to rest. "We'll have to try blood majick," he said quietly. "It's our only hope."

Her lip curled, but she did not object. "How?"

"The web makes a pattern to hold the water. We just need to make another to draw it in and meld it to the *sylveth* majick." It sounded so easy. But he knew well enough how difficult it was to bind the two together.

"I have an idea," Ellyn said. She clambered to her feet and went to her pack. She retrieved her water flask, a tin cup, and several thin strips of cloth cut from a spare tunic. She sat cross-legged on the ground above the hoskarna, laying her materials on the ground before her. "It's about intent, isn't it? From what I can tell, the chanting just reinforces the intent in the pattern."

Keros squatted down beside her. "Seems logical." Though truly he had no idea. All he really knew was that he could invoke the blood majick. But how powerful it would be and how he could make real use of it was a mystery.

"Since we don't know any Jutras chants, we'll have to make up something of our own. Something simple that we can repeat. And they use a kind of dance to re-

inforce what they want. We could do that too. Keeping
it simple."

Keros raised his brows skeptically, but nodded. It was
a good idea. "What do you plan to use those for?" he
asked, gesturing at the things she'd gathered together.

She dug a hole in the ground and pushed the cup
down into it so that it was below the level of the ground.
She put the ends of four strips of cloth into it, spreading them across the ground in the cardinal directions.
Next she filled the cup loosely with dirt, then poured
water from her flask into it. Drawing her dagger out of
the sheath on her belt, she cut down the side of her left
forearm. Blood ran in a thin stream. She held it over a
strip of cloth and let it drip until the entire strip of cloth
was soaked, then did it again with a second one.

"Your turn," she said to Keros.

When he was done, she took the point of her dagger
and prodded the ends of the cloth down into the dirt.
"What I hope will happen is that the cup will echo our
web spell. The water and dirt is what we want to happen
inside the web, and our blood will help us channel the
blood majick into the web."

Keros grinned at her admiringly. "That just might
work."

She shrugged. "It's a lot like the hedge-magery of the
Huantarians. They travel through Azaire selling potions
and charms. They do not have the power of real majicars, but what they can do, they do well. I spent some
time with a caravan and learned some things about their
majick."

"Lucky for us," Keros said. He was more than a little
impressed at her ingenuity and prayed that it would
work. "Now what do you suggest?"

She rose to her feet. "We walk the circuit around
the two webs that we made. We should walk a winding
pattern—like waves. Something like this." She suited her

actions to words, sashaying from side to side in a graceful dance. She looked over her shoulder at him. "Can you do that?"

He nodded. "But it might be better if we held hands." He held up one hand and pantomimed slicing his palm. "Mixing our blood might increase our power."

"Good idea. Now, for our chant. What do you think?" she asked.

"Something simple and to the point—water rise and come to our call."

She made a face. "That's good enough, but maybe we should say something about filling the web or making mud. Otherwise it might rise up and we'll get a river and that's not going to do a lot of good. How about, water rise and fill this bowl."

"Bowl?"

"It's close enough. It's about intent. Visualize it filling the web."

He drew a breath and let it out. "It seems too simple to work."

"How do we know their chants aren't just simple demands repeated over and over? Besides, do you have a better idea?"

He shook his head. "Let's get going."

He took his dagger and cut across his palm deeply. Blood ran freely from the wound. Ellyn grimaced and did the same, her jaw clenching. He clasped her hand in his, weaving his fingers through hers, palms pressed tightly together. Blood dripped to the ground.

He reached for the power of the thistle inside him and felt it unfurl, the spikes of it biting and stabbing as it swelled with power. His body clenched and his hand tightened on Ellyn's, first with extraordinary pain, followed by a wash of bone-melting pleasure. He gasped and his cods hardened and he almost fell to the ground in mindless bliss. Ellyn clutched his hand equally hard.

"Ready?" she rasped and her chin shook.

"On three," he said. His own voice shook. "One. Two. Three." They both stepped in the pattern. He let Ellyn lead, staying a half step behind. Together they began to chant the simple mantra, "Water rise and fill this bowl." He repeated the words, driving his awareness deep into the dirt. He felt the web pulsing. It grated against him, making him feel raw. He pushed past it, hauling in on the flare of hostile blood majick that sought to tear the web to shreds. Ellyn's presence intertwined with his. Together they pushed out into the mountains, summoning water.

The spring was closest and it rose up from the depths of the island, following a sprawling trail of cracks and fissures. Keros bent his attention to it, pulling on it. He felt Ellyn doing the same. The power of the blood majick connected to their pounding steps and the simple, staccato words of their chant. They were both breathless, but neither stopped.

The ground turned damp and then marshy. It squelched and then splashed. Their feet sank into the mud as it deepened and turned into a mire. It was all Keros could do to keep going. His feet pulled out of his boots and he staggered on. Ellyn dragged in deep breaths between words. She leaned hard on him as she kept going. The blood in their hands had ceased to drip and Keros wondered if they could afford to stop and open the wounds again.

Or he could make another. He fumbled for his dagger and slashed at the top of his wrist. The blade scraped the bone and blood ran over his and Ellyn's linked hands. Instantly he felt the pain and pleasure of the majick and a surge of power. It gave him strength to push on. He wasn't aware when Ellyn followed suit, but suddenly there was a second surge of power from her. They renewed the energy of their chant and walk, calling even more water.

Was it enough? Keros couldn't be sure. He kept going until he fell to his knees. He could do no more.

Ellyn pulled him up. He was knee deep in a ring of mud surrounding the hoskarna. Water burbled up through the enormous bog and ran in a tangle of streams down the mountain. The webs they'd created below the ground were swollen.

They climbed out of the morass and onto the sodden grassy ground. Each foot sank ankle deep into the soil. They went to stand at the top of the circle. Keros shook with loss of blood and the tremendous burst of power he'd sustained for so long. He looked at Ellyn. She was pale, her mouth set in a flat line. Sweat made her hair cling to her forehead and cheeks.

"Ready?" he grated. His throat was dry and raw from the chanting—how long had it been since they'd started? He glanced blearily at the sky. It had been at least two glasses.

"Now or never," she said, her hand firming on his.

"*Sylveth* majick now," he reminded her, though he doubted she needed the reminder any more than he did. Both of them had figured that any power that was in the hoskarna would be less able to resist *sylveth* majick than blood majick.

He licked his lips, sending a silent prayer to Meris for strength and power. "Now," he said, squeezing Ellyn's hand.

He reached into the web. Water pressed tight against it like a bladder. He could feel the slippery uncertainty of the slope. It needed only a slight *push* . . . But he meant to give it far more than that.

He bore down into the web, unraveling the bottom of it slowly until only the upper half was still intact. Ellyn was a quiet, steady presence, feeding him her power. Compared to the volcanic burst of the blood majick, it was a bare flicker on a dying fire. Still, it *was* enough.

He hardened the upper remnants of the web until it was a stiff wedge. Then with all his might, he twisted it, shoving the top of it down and levering the muddy slope away.

The ground made a slurping sound and it lurched, and then began a low grumble as it moved. Suddenly the top of the slope rippled and the hoskarna wobbled and teetered. Then an enormous scallop of mountain slid away. The hoskarna tipped and disappeared. Keros felt an odd wrenching in his chest as they fell, but he was too busy dragging Ellyn to higher ground to notice more than that.

The two majicars reached the sturdy safety of the boulders that marked their campsite and turned, both staring in openmouthed awe at the devastation they'd created. The mountain shook and the air was filled with the thundering growl of the slide and the sounds of splintering trees and crashing rocks.

The sound went on and on—seemingly forever. But it could only have been a few minutes. At last silence fell again. Keros sank down on a rock, still shaking. Not just with exhaustion, but also with exhilaration and even fear at the enormity of what they'd done. This was the work of gods, not men.

He glanced up at her. She was staring at the brown scar in the verdant mountainside. A frown furrowed her brow. Slowly she raised a hand and covered her mouth and slowly shook her head.

"What is it?" Keros asked, following her gaze. But he didn't need her answer. His stomach dropped and fear turned his chest to stone. Where the hoskarna had stood, gold lights sent spidery veins over the ground, spreading like the roots of a weed.

Chapter 23

Nicholas watched Margaret covertly as they rode down through the mountains toward Sylmont. She sat straight, her face pale and set. Every so often she turned and looked over her shoulder as if expecting that she would see something of Keros and Ellyn, though the trees and ridges hid any view of the mountain summit.

His mind tumbled with all that he'd learned in the last day. He couldn't believe the trust she'd placed in him. The burden of it weighed heavily. He was determined to be worthy of it, but the cost would be high—higher than he might be able to pay. She was a Rampling and her loyalties were completely contrary to everything he'd spent his life working for.

Over the years he'd made many promises to many people—promises that he could never break and yet would fly in the face of almost anything Margaret asked of him. He'd told her they were friends for now. The reality of his own feelings was that he wanted far more from her. He wanted her bound to him in every way that the law and the gods provided. But he could see no way to make it happen; he was destined to break her trust. At some point he'd have to choose between her and his family or an oath he'd made, and sooner or later, she'd be the loser. The hard truth was that they were friends for now . . . until he betrayed her and became her enemy again.

Yet even so, he wanted to reach out and touch her. He wanted to brush her cheek with his fingers and hold her hard in his arms the way he had last night as she slept.

The clouds threatened rain and every so often, a few drops spattered them. The horses were eager and rested and made good time. Neither Margaret or Nicholas spoke to each other. She rode slightly ahead and he led Ellyn's horse behind him.

They'd been riding near two turns of the glass when suddenly the horses spooked. Margaret's horse reared and lunged forward, galloping away through the thin trees as if a pack of wolves was after him. Nicholas's horse tried the same, but he held the animal with iron control. The carriage horse squealed and reared back, snapping the lead rein. He whirled, hurtling away down the valley, his tail raised high like a flag.

Nicholas let him go, vaguely hearing an echoing rumble in the distance. He urged his bay into a gallop, following Margaret. His heart was in his throat as he hunched down close against his bay's mane. There were too many low-hanging limbs and he expected to see Margaret lying in a heap beneath one at every moment.

He came out of the copse into a clearing and found her. She was on her feet beside the panting gray. Sweat turned his hide to pewter and his eyes were ringed white. As Nicholas pulled up sharply, the gray leaped back to the end of his reins, his haunches bunching. Margaret held him tightly and talked soothingly to him. She followed him, stroking his neck and shoulder. He settled slowly, finally dropping his head and pushing his face against her chest. He gave shuddering sigh, his skin still twitching like he was being stung by flies.

Nicholas slowly dismounted and came closer. "Are you all right?" he asked.

"My legs are pudding," Margaret said, scratching behind her horse's ears. "And I didn't duck fast enough." She turned to look at him and he saw a bloody scratch ran across her cheek and along her neck. "But that's about the worst of it." She drew a shaky breath. "Do you think they succeeded?"

He didn't need to ask what she was talking about it. It could only be Keros and Ellyn. He remembered the growling rumble he'd heard when the horses had panicked. He nodded. "They made the slide. I heard it."

"Good." Then she frowned. "That could have brought Forcan down on them."

Nicholas was digging in his pack. He had no reassurances to offer her. Anything he could say would be hollow at best, downright lies at worst. He found a wadded shirt and pulled it out. He dampened the sleeve with water from his flask and dabbed at the scrape on Margaret's face. She winced, but didn't pull away.

When he was through he returned the shirt to his pack. "We should get going. They'll be hungry and tired when they get to the Maida. We should have things ready for them."

She looked at him, then gave him a bare smile of gratitude that he presumed their friends were safe and on their way. "Let's go."

He stood beside her to help her into her saddle. She gave him a startled look, but bent her leg obediently. He levered her up. Her gelding snorted and sidled, but she gathered the reins firmly and patted his shoulders. Nicholas mounted and this time they rode beside each other as they headed to Sylmont.

They found a wagon track that took them back to the city. Rain started in a slow drizzle, then turned quickly

into a downpour. Nicholas had long since lost his hat—
he had no idea where. He pulled his coat close, but the
wet ran down beneath his collar. Margaret was no better off. She hunched, her head bent dogged and low.
She was wrapped in a blanket, since her cloak had been
left behind in Molford and she'd refused to take either
Nicholas's or Keros's. But even the heavy rain couldn't
suppress the rising smell of smoke. The hair on the back
of Nicholas's neck prickled. He'd seen from where they
had camped that things in Sylmont were bad, but he
was about to find out just how bad. There was *a lot* of
smoke.

The two of them came over the final hill at the edge of
the city, just north of the Mystery of Hurn. They pulled
up as one and stared.

"By the gods," Nicholas murmured in shock.

Smoke and rain hid a great deal, but fires burned all
over the city, some in unnatural colors that indicated
majick. Their spotted glimmers extended far out, all the
way to the headlands. In places, entire blocks of buildings were razed. Nicholas couldn't see the Riddles. It
was hidden in a pall of smoke. His gaze slid out to the
harbor. It was full of the detritus of sunken and broken
ships. All the wet docks and piers were gone. It looked
like someone had taken a spoon and madly stirred the
entire harbor to bits.

"Look," Margaret said. Her voice was thick and Nicholas was certain that the rain hid her tears. She pointed
north toward the Maida of Chayos.

A pale green glow rose like a bubble over the broad
domed hill of the Maida. Inside was a strange, wondrous
place where night and day and every season existed all
together at the same moment. The exterior was ever-
green and ever fruiting. The poor lined up every day
for fresh fruits, vegetables, grain, eggs, milk, butter and
cheese, which the delats—servants of Chayos—handed

out freely. Nicholas wiped a hand over his mouth as nearly unbearable relief swept over him. If Chayos was protecting her Maida, then Sylmont still had hope. His gaze flicked to the Mystery of Hurn. The windowless, black stone tower of the stranger god was as unrelentingly quiet as ever. Nicholas could not see the Ysod of Meris or the Font of Braken.

"Come on," Margaret said and turned her horse to follow the ridge toward the Maida.

She made no effort to ride down into the city. Whether because she feared that someone might attack them again to steal the horses or for some other reason, Nicholas didn't know, nor did he ask. He thought of his family. Most of them were outside of the city. But everyone else—his servants, his employees . . . He glanced again at the devastation, then up toward his manor. Smoke hid it as well as the royal castle and all of Salford Terrace. A chill ran down to his toes. What horrors would be seen when the smoke cleared?

He urged his bay into a trot and quickly pulled up even with Margaret. Her lips were pulled into a fierce snarl and her eyes blazed. Her chiseled features—sharpened by the loss of weight during her ordeal with the Jutras—were harsh. Her entire expression was one of ruthless fury. Her hands flexed on her rain-slicked reins. She looked at him as if feeling the weight of his gaze. He wanted to say something, though he didn't know how to reassure her, or even what to reassure her about—that her brothers had survived? That the Jutras would not suddenly arrive and take the city? That the people of Sylmont had escaped the devastation? That the majicars who must have done this had killed each other and now were no threat? And then there was the question of Forcan—did the unnatural animal even now prowl the city, slaughtering everyone in its path?

Something in her eyes made him go cold. Then as he

watched, her face changed. Her jaw relaxed, her mouth softened, the grooves running from her nose to her mouth disappeared. In a moment, a bland mask of kindness and confidence settled over her countenance. Only her eyes continued to burn, and that fire was slowly banking.

"What did you do?" he asked, his mouth dropping. She looked more like the princess he'd known before—the one made of porcelain, whose conversations were always about fashion and the gossip of court, who didn't know how to wield a knife and who shrieked in fright when a mouse ran across the floor.

She straightened, pulling in on herself so that she looked positively regal. Even in the travel-stained clothing she wore, everyone would recognize her, which no doubt was the point. "Ryland may be dead. Vaughn is in Brampton. The rest of my family is dead or enslaved. There is no one else for the people to look to and someone has to lead or we will have chaos." She scanned the wreck of Sylmont. "More chaos. I must take command until one of my brothers can."

The words were cool and deliberate, but Nicholas heard the bitter tang to them. "Do you *want* this?" he asked.

For a moment the fires flared in her eyes. "I have *never* wanted to rule," she said. "But I am a Rampling, and this is my duty. I am the only one here and the only one who can do it. I have no choice."

"And if your damned duty gets you killed?" It was a stupid question. He knew it even as it left his lips. Her life had been in constant danger since she was a child. She didn't need to say the words; her shrug and the sharp quirk of her mouth was eloquent.

He reached out and grabbed the right rein, pulling both of their horses to a halt. He put his hand over hers.

They were cold as ice. "You aren't in this alone. We'll do this together."

Her brows rose. "You'll help me out of the kindness of your heart?" She shook her head, and a fleeting expression of something that looked like hurt or possibly sadness was replaced by prickly suspicion. "And when this is done—if Crosspointe survives—then what? Business as usual? You'll have me poisoned or knifed in the dark? Murdered like my father was? We're friends just for now, remember?"

Fury rolled through Nicholas with searing heat. She was right—she had no reason to really trust him. And he could offer no guarantees. Except—

The feelings that clenched his heart in a killing grip drove him. He legged his gelding close into hers. He put his hand around the back of her neck and jerked her close. His lips pressed against hers. They were cold and wet from the rain.

His mouth ground harder. Whether in surprise or desire, her lips parted. His mouth slanted over hers in triumphant eagerness. His tongue licked hungrily inside her mouth. She tasted faintly of the tea they'd drunk that morning and something else—something purely Margaret. It send a scorching shaft of need through his gut. He pulled her closer, wrapping his arms around her and lifting her off her horse. He settled her onto the saddle in front of him, her legs dangling over the left side. He held her tight, one arm across her back, the other hand sliding up to hold her head as he deepened the kiss.

Her tongue slipped inside his mouth, tracing his lips. It was unbearably exquisite. He gentled his touch as she grew more bold. Her touch was deft and sure. She slid her arms around his neck and he found she was clinging as tightly to him as he was to her.

The kiss went on far longer than he dreamed she

would allow it. But at last he felt her start to draw away. His arms tightened; then he loosened them slowly. She leaned away from him, but she did not release him. The expression on her face was anything but controlled or indifferent. Fires burned in her eyes again, but this time not with fury or hatred. This time the fire was for him and it was breathtaking.

"This is—"

Impossible. He didn't need to hear her say the word. He shook his head, refusing it. "This *is*," he said, giving her a gentle shake. "It *is* and by the black depths I won't let it go. I won't. I *can't*. I don't give a damn if you're a Rampling and I'm a Weverton or what's happened between our families or anything else. We'll find a way."

The words were as much a question as a declaration. It didn't matter what he wanted if she didn't want it too—if she didn't want it more than her damned Rampling duty. His body filled with ice. Everyone knew that Ramplings put Crosspointe above all personal concerns. It was in their blood, it was inscribed on their bones. It was why Geoffrey had enslaved them rather than let them run loose. He'd known he could never make them betray that innate sense of duty to their land and people.

She licked her lips and rain ran down her cheeks like tears. Nicholas wanted to crush her back against him and steal back that moment that was now forever lost.

Suddenly she leaned forward and kissed him again. Her mouth was urgent against his and demanding. He responded with all his frustration, need, and desire. This time when she pulled away, they were both breathless. She said nothing, but pushed out of his arms. She slid down to the ground and went to catch up the reins of her gray gelding who was cropping grass a few feet away. She swung up into her saddle and nudged her horse into a trot, never saying a word.

Nicholas followed, feeling as if he'd been clubbed in the head. He ached with a pain that drove down into the depths of his soul and it hurt like nothing he'd ever imagined.

She wanted him, he told himself, trying to find some comfort to ease that bloody wound. But it didn't matter. She had the strength and will to walk away, no matter what she might feel for him. His jaw clenched. He didn't make a habit of giving up on what he wanted. Somehow he'd sap the walls of her defenses. He didn't let himself think about what would happen after that.

The Maida of Chayos was a broad, tall hill standing alone on the edge of the city. It was more than a quarter of a league across and was just west of Cheapside and south of Blackstone. A pale green nimbus surrounded it now, extending out forty or fifty paces from the base of the hill. Knots of people huddled within its glow, clustering at its foot and hiding among the bushes and trees along its top.

Delats wearing their green and brown robes stood around the perimeter just inside the protection of the light. They were armed with swords and spears, alternating every other one. But the weapons were nothing like Nicholas had ever seen before. The swords were a clear green—like sharp emeralds. They twisted slightly in a hint of a spiral and tapered to a deadly point. Each was four feet long. The two-handed hilts were made of what looked like a dark wood.

The spears—no, they were lances—had the same twisting green blades, except that they were about six feet long and attached to a shaft that was five feet long and made of the same dark wood of the sword hilts. The delats held them with one hand near the butt, the other near the base of the blade.

Every single one looked like he or she knew how to

use them. Nicholas found himself smiling grimly. He had always prided himself on the extent of his information-gathering network. But in the last sennight he'd discovered just how very much he didn't know, and it was humbling. He would never have believed that Chayos's delats were anything but meek acolytes whose entire lives revolved around the peaceful worship of Chayos and giving aid to the poor. He would never have imagined that they could wield anything more than a pitchfork or a hoe, and then only in agrarian purposes. But looking at their ready stances and the deadly set of their faces, he could see that they knew very well what to do with the weapons that they held.

"Did you have any idea?" Margaret asked him.

There was no inflection in her voice—no accusation that he'd been withholding information. But he felt it all the same. "No," he said. "Did you?"

She shook her head. "My entire life has been devoted to searching out secrets for my father. I was a dog digging for bones and I was very good at it. Or so I thought. But it appears I was mistaken."

"Aye," he agreed. "What else did we miss?"

The delats closest to them had called a warning to the others around the circle and many now turned the points of their weapons toward Margaret and Nicholas. The rest continued to vigilantly keep watch for trouble around the rest of the perimeter. The two riders rode closer and suddenly Nicholas became aware of green-robed archers on the crown of the hill. Like their brethren below, they held themselves ready, arrows nocked and fingers on the strings, ready to pull back and loose a rain of death. He didn't ask Margaret if she'd seen them. She was too good not to.

She had once again assumed the mask of her court self, though there was nothing pliant or docile about her. She radiated authority and competence. When she spoke, her voice rang with confidence. It was, in a word, majestic, and it demanded obedience.

"I am Margaret Rampling. Can you tell me what happened here?"

The three delats closest to them looked at one another, clearly nonplussed. The middle one looked back at Margaret and Nicholas. He was tall with close-cut gray hair. His face was long and his eyes were hard.

"The majicars attacked all over the city."

He shook his head, his expression turning childishly bewildered and Nicholas understood his feelings. Majicars were Crosspointe's special guardians and benefactors. For them to turn suddenly on their own people was beyond comprehension if one didn't know the truth of their insanity.

"They was fighting each other and they didn't care what or whoever got in the way."

"Regent did nothing," the stout man with the sword beside him said. "Ran off with his tail between his legs."

"That was before it began," the first delat admonished.

The other man spit on the ground, his mouth twisting in disgust. "Hasn't come back, though, has he?"

"The regent has been removed from office," Margaret declared. "I am here to assume his duties until such a time as my brother, Prelate Ryland, can take over and an election can be held."

An audible gasp rose sharply from everyone gathered. For a moment no one spoke. Then a woman's voice rose sharp and spiteful.

"You talk just fine, Princess. But I seen you. Yer hands be white and soft as roses and ain't never touched real work in yer whole life. Yer a pretty thing, but I don't see as how you can help us."

There were loud sounds of agreement. Nicholas clenched his teeth. If only they knew what Margaret

really was made of—stone and iron. The rest was all illusion of her own making.

Margaret raised her chin, waiting for the din to die
down, as the woman's sentiments were echoed across
the crowd. A swell of murmurs rose as Margaret's news
spread around the broad mound as if carried by a hot
wind. Men and women came striding around to crowd
in behind the line of delats. There were hundreds of
them. They were frightened and angry and clearly Margaret was not the hero they'd been looking for. Nicholas
wasn't sure anything but an army would have satisfied
them, but certainly a Rampling princess whose only
claim to fame was her prim beauty and elegant parties
was no prize.

She made no move to quiet them, sitting impervi-
ously astride her gelding as the rain continued to fall
in a steady curtain, letting the waves of their ire wash
around her. At last the din began to subside and a tense
silence settled over the mob.

"I understand your doubts," she said, her voice ringing loudly so that everyone could hear. Margaret spoke
calmly and with the same inexorable authority that had
always infused every word her father spoke. It was regal
and compelling; it made everyone bend to listen. Nicholas had always suspected it was a trick of majick, but it
appeared to be a family trait. "I, too, would prefer that
one of my brothers was here to lead you. They are, *perhaps*, better suited for battle."

As she spoke, her hand dropped slowly to the dagger
in her belt. Ellyn had given it to her to replace those
the Jutras priests had taken. Margaret flipped away the
leather loop that kept it from accidentally sliding from
its sheath and drew the blade. She held it close against
her thigh. Nicholas doubted anyone had paid attention
to the quiet, deft movement.

"But Crosspointe is threatened and my brothers are

not here. I am." She smiled, a cool, dangerous expression. "And like all Ramplings, I may be more than I seem."

She lifted the dagger so that everyone could see it. Then she spun it in her hand so fast it looked like a shining wheel. In one quick movement, she caught the blade in her fingers and threw it. It lodged in the trunk of a tree and quivered there.

There were surprised sounds from those who were close enough to see and a murmuring wave rippled back through the rest of the throng. Nicholas suppressed a grin. Let them chew on that. Margaret turned her head and nodded to him. Time to get down to business and give them something else to worry about besides her worthiness to lead.

He legged his horse closer so that he was beside her. "I am Nicholas Weverton," he said loudly. "What Princess Margaret has told you is true. We discovered the regent is a traitor."

The stocky man delat broke in. "Thought you hated each other—the Ramplings and the Wevertons."

Before Nicholas could answer, Margaret turned an icy stare on the man. He wilted, his eyes dropping and his shoulders slumping. Nicholas watched in wonder. Had her father even known what she was capable of? Had anybody?

When she answered the delat's question, Margaret's words rang out for all to hear. "Whatever may have been said in past disagreements, Nicholas and I stand shoulder to shoulder in complete unity now. Crosspointe is in danger and we must defend it. All of us together. There is no more room for petty squabbling and personal feuds. If we do not unite as one, if we do not fight together, then we will be scooped up by the Jutras to become their slaves."

It was as much a command and a call to arms as a declaration. It seemed to have the intended effect. In the silence, bodies straightened and shoulders firmed, even as expressions set with fear.

Margaret continued. "You cannot hide here within the arms of the Mother goddess. You must prepare for war. You must pick up your knives, your swords, your boat hooks, your rolling pins, hoes, forks, and bricks—whatever weapons you can put to hand." She paused, her jaw knotting. "The Jutras have come and they are among us."

That was met with an explosive gabble of voices. Nicholas held up his hand and let out a piercing whistle. It did little to cut through the noise, but those before him grabbed the arms of their fellows and slowly a jittery silence fell again, every eye fixed on Margaret and Nicholas.

"The regent has been collaborating with the Jutras." He said it baldly, and even as he did, he wondered if Margaret had meant to keep it a secret. It was the sort of thing that could stir the country into a panic. But then so could the majicar attacks. It was far too late to pretend. Secrecy would undermine Margaret's fragile beginnings of control and people needed to understand the danger was immediate. They needed to be frightened into uniting into an army, as ragtag as that army might be.

"The Jutras have poisoned our majicars and it has driven them mad," Margaret said, picking up the story without pause. "It *is* possible to cure them, but *they are not responsible* for what they have done. It was the regent and the Jutras."

The aura of authority that she'd pull around herself made it hard to doubt her. She looked down at the delats before them. "We would speak to the Naladei and the Kalimei. They must hear the news that we bring."

They were the light and dark priestesses of Chayos and wielded a power entirely unlike that of majicars. Nicholas felt a sudden surge of hope. Perhaps the priestesses could help against the Jutras wizards. But the gray-haired delat who'd first spoken to them shook his head, his long face grave. "They have set us to stand guard and retreated to the heart of the Maida. No one may enter."

Just then an eerie cry wailed across the city. It raised gooseflesh all over Nicholas's body and sent a jolt of fear through to the core of him. He clamped his legs tight as his bay reared and neighed. The sound continued almost unbearably, worming down deep and stirring up a whirl-wind of terror inside him. Nicholas wanted to cover his ears. He held his gelding under a tight rein as the animal spun and fought to bolt. Margaret's gray threw up its head and bucked. Margaret went flying and Nicholas's heart leaped into his throat. But somehow she flipped herself and landed on her feet. Her horse galloped away.

The sound faded into a screech like the sound of tearing metal.

"What in the black depths was that?" someone asked. Some people were on their knees, others huddled against each other. A few lay on the ground.

Margaret's face was white. She exchanged a look with Nicholas. Forcan—the hound of Uniat. It could be nothing else.

She pushed the hair from her face and her hands shook. She dropped them quickly to her sides, firming her shoulders. She looked at the gray-haired delat.

"Is it safe inside the barrier?" she asked, pointing at the green shield.

His cheek twitched. "From majicar attacks." His lips pressed tight for a moment and he swallowed hard. "That's something else, isn't it?"

Margaret nodded, then looked at Nicholas. "It will come here. The majick of the Maida will draw it like a meaty bone."

He grimaced agreement, his heart still thundering with terror. He didn't trust himself to speak without his voice breaking. He breathed slowly. He'd never in his life let fear get the best of him. He gathered it and pushed it off like a wet cloak. It fell away and he pulled himself together with cold resolve.

By the time he had, Margaret had turned back to the delat. "Is one of you in charge?"

The gray-haired delat's twist of the lips might have been a smile. "At your service, Princess."

"What do I call you?"

"Red will do."

"Red?"

He touched his fingers to his gray hair. "Once it was quite appropriate, I assure you."

"Very well, Red. Several days ago, two Jutras wizard priests conducted a spell. It involved summoning a creature called Forcan, the hound of Uniat—the pet of one of the Jutras gods."

She spoke rapidly and low. His expression went first slack, then he gathered himself, his hand gripping his spear with white knuckles.

"I believe that sound was this beast and I believe it is coming here. You need to get these people away from here quickly and prepare to fight."

Before he could answer, the howl came again. It was impossibly closer, as if the beast had crossed half the city in the space of a few grains. The sound coiled and curled through the gray afternoon. Nicholas's horse reared and nearly toppled over backward. Nicholas threw himself forward against the animal's neck and the gelding dropped to the ground and bolted. Nicholas yanked back hard, but the bay had the bit in his teeth. Bracing himself against the stirrups, he dropped the right rein and pulled on the left with both hands. He hauled the horse's nose around until it nearly touched his shoulder. The bay turned, his speed dropping to a canter and then a trot as Nicholas heaved harder.

At last the animal came to a standstill. His ribs bellowed and foam gathered around his mouth. His eyes were ringed white with fear and he shuffled and pranced, every muscle twitching with fright. The sound of the howl was fading, but as soon as Nicholas started to loosen the rein, the gelding started to leap away.

Nicholas glanced back over his shoulder at the Maida. The horse wasn't going back there. Still holding the animal tightly, Nicholas swung to the ground. Instantly the bay pulled back to the end of the rein, snorting. He gave a hard yank and pulled the rain-slicked strap from Nicholas's hand. A moment later he was galloping away into the hills.

Nicholas turned and broke into a run.

Back at the Maida, he found everyone cowering against the ground. Some were puking and there was a strong smell of piss and shit. A few were clawing their way over their companions, trying to flee. Even some of the delats had fallen. Margaret still stood, her feet braced, a look of fury on her face. She glanced at Nicholas as he rejoined her. A flicker of surprise swept over her expression as if she hadn't thought he would return.

"They aren't going to be able to run. That thing is using fear against them. Every time he howls, they fall apart."

Red was leaning heavily against his spear, his face gray, his lips compressed in a white line. His eyes were squeezed shut and he was panting like he'd been running.

"Why aren't you scared?" Nicholas asked. The fear had rolled up on him, but his battle with the gelding had distracted him enough to keep it from disabling him. All the same, his knees still trembled and a feral part of his mind was screaming at him to run.

"What could it do to me that they didn't already do?"

"It could kill you," Nicholas said, the thought chopping through his fear like a sword. He couldn't lose her. *She's not yours to lose*, a niggling voice in his head pointed out. His hands tightened into fists and his jaw knotted. But she was. He'd convince her somehow.

She shrugged. "I can live with death," she said and the corner of her mouth quirked up at the irony. "Besides, I have no intention of letting that cracking dog chew me up again. What about you? You don't seem quite as affected as they are." She waved at the people inside the Maida's green barrier.

"They tell me I'm a coldhearted bastard," he said. "It looks like they might be right."

She grinned and he saw in her eyes both fear—not inspired by the hound's howl, but by what he might do if he wasn't stopped. And he saw a wild recklessness. That, above anything else, scared him.

"Keros and Ellyn aren't going to get here in time to help," she said softly, turning her back on the Maida and scanning the nearby buildings, searching for signs of the hound. "If they even survived."

Her words sent a shiver down his spine and he knew exactly what she planned to do. She was going to face down the hound alone. But from her description, that was suicide, even for someone with her skills. Her next actions confirmed his thoughts.

"Got an extra one of those?" Margaret asked, turning back to Red. She pointed to his lance.

The delat had gained some color back in his face and no longer clung desperately to his weapon to hold him up. He looked at Margaret narrowly. "These are sacred weapons of Chayos and only for her delats."

"That's all very nice, but right now, that beast is driving you all to your knees and I don't think this barrier is going to protect you when he gets here. I'm going to be the one standing between you and that thing and I'm fairly certain that you'd rather I wasn't just waving my hands at him."

Just then another howl came. It was close. Too close. Nicholas's heart spasmed and he felt his bladder and bowels starting to loosen. He held himself on a tight rein. Still the fear drove him to his knees. He clamped his hands over his ears, but the sound seemed to burrow through his flesh and bones to the deepest part of him. He fought it with all his strength, hardly aware of anything else.

Once again it faded slowly. He found himself curled up on the ground, his heart beating like a woodpecker's pounding beak. Margaret squatted down beside him, but she wasn't looking at him. Red had dropped to the ground, his face twisted in a mask of horror and fear.

"So can I borrow that?" Margaret asked. There was a slight shake to her voice. "I'll give it back when I'm done. If Chayos doesn't like it, I'm sure she'll be the first to let me know."

With a jerky movement, Red pushed to his feet and thrust his lance toward her. "Careful," he rasped. "The blade is of the goddess herself. Do not touch it."

Margaret took it and stood up. Nicholas rolled onto his stomach and clambered to his feet. His stomach lurched and he turned and splattered its contents on the ground. He faced back to her, wiping his mouth with the back of his hand.

"Better get me one of those too," he said, his voice scratchy and thin. "I'm not letting you do this alone."

Her brows rose in silent question, but she said nothing. She turned back to Red. "What about another?"

He looked at his other delats. Many had fallen to their knees. But whether from deeply ingrained habit or something else, each had kept their blades pointed upright, even the sword-bearers. Red went and took the lance from a young woman who remained on her feet, her face gray, her eyes squeezed shut. As soon as he took it, she crumpled to the ground. He looked at her a moment, then handed the weapon to Nicholas.

"Chayos bless you both," he said. "What we can do to help, we will."

"Thank you," Margaret said.

Then they all heard the harsh rasp of hot panting and the crunch of stone and wood as if something large padded across a pile of rubble. The sound was loud, despite the rain.

"It's here," Margaret said in a brittle voice.

They both swiveled around to watch the monster approach. With him came a wave of fear that was almost tangible.

The beast was larger than Nicholas's bay gelding by three feet and it was four times as heavy at least. It padded along with heavy steps. Its coat was smooth and short and colored in a mix of grays and purples. Margaret had described him as being the color of twilight and she was right. Sunset-colored brindles ran down his bull-like shoulders over his back and haunches. His head was massive—broad and heavy with short ears and heavy jaws. His mouth hung open as he panted. His muzzle was long and bony, with long curving teeth. Between them lolled a long black tongue. His eyes were disks of old gold in his black face. They shone through the gray drizzle.

He emerged from between two half-demolished buildings. He stopped and raised his head, sweeping it from side to side as he sniffed the air. Margaret nudged Nicholas's arm, and jogged across the open plaza beside the Maida. It gave them both more room to swing their lances and fight the beast.

Her touch broke the spell of fear that had rolled ahead of the god hound and buried Nicholas beneath a smothering tide of terror. He shuddered and then took a hard hold of himself, tightening his grip on the spear as if it were his lifeline in a turbulent sea. Behind him he heard moans and whimpers, but kept his attention fixed on Forcan.

New fear ripped through him when he saw the creature's gaze hone in on Margaret as if he'd been searching for her. The hound's head dropped and his eyes narrowed to slits. Its black tongue swiped around its muzzle as if in hungry anticipation and it began to stalk forward. Suddenly Nicholas realized that the mother-dibbling bastard hadn't come to attack the Maida at all.

It had come for Margaret.

Chapter 24

Margaret held the lance steady in front of her as she trotted across the plaza. She felt it the moment the hound's gaze locked on her. She'd expected to freeze when she saw it again, but instead fury roared up inside her like a forest fire. As it turned to follow her, her lips peeled back in a vicious grin and violent energy streamed through her muscles. The beast wanted her, did it? Good. Let the bastard come.

She turned to face it, holding the lance out before her. It was well balanced and weighed less than she expected. She swung it from side to side, getting a feel for its heft. It was no heavier than a quarterstaff, though it was a good eleven feet in length. She raised it, holding it ready.

The hound advanced on her with slow, deliberate steps. She watched it, rolling forward on the balls of her feet, waiting for it to charge.

"Nicholas?" she asked in a low voice, not daring to look away. She half expected him not to answer. The waves of fear radiating from the beast were tangible. They buffeted against her, though she did not succumb. But then, after what Atreya and Saradapul had done to her, she didn't think she would fear anything ever again.

Except her nightmares.

"Twenty feet on your left," Nicholas answered, his voice rock steady.

Margaret felt a rush of something akin to relief, except that it was far more rich and wonderful than that. She'd never in her life had a partner of any kind. She'd always worked alone. Her father had meant for her to never need to depend on anyone else. If she got into trouble, she'd always known that no one was going to come to her rescue. But twice Nicholas had come when she needed someone most. To hear him answer, to know that she was not alone in this fight—it gave her strength.

"It's come for *you*," he said. "It's not paying any attention to me. I'll come at it from the side."

Margaret sidestepped to the right, pulling Forcan's attention farther from Nicholas. But she wondered if it could be killed.

It drew closer. It was now no more than fifty paces away. Its claws clicked on the cobblestones. Each one was as long as her forearm and wickedly hooked. It was the only sound the beast made. It no longer even panted; its muzzle was closed as it honed in on Margaret.

She firmed her grip on the lance, her muscles tightening as she prepared for its pounce.

It was fast. Faster than she imagined it could be. It bounded forward. Margaret leaped aside, swiping at its front leg. She missed. The long blade swiped through the air, wrenching her off balance. She heard the snap of teeth and Forcan's shoulder slammed against her. She hit the ground and rolled, never letting go of her weapon.

She came to her feet and spun to face the hound again, and stared in shock. A stripe of brilliant gold creased its front left leg. She'd cut it. Her blade had passed right through it and she'd not felt a thing. Another crease of gold ran down its right ribs where Nicholas had struck it with his spear. Forcan lifted its head and let out a long keening sound. It knifed through the bones of Margaret's head, sending streaks of fire down every nerve of her body. Her hands spasmed and her grip on the lance loosened as her legs trembled and sagged.

Fiercely she clamped her hands tighter and firmed her legs. The pain she pushed aside easily—she'd borne worse. A mad idea struck her. It could work. Forcan was distracted and not paying attention to her. She didn't take time to consider. She began running, holding her lance at an upward angle. She thought she heard Nicholas shout her name but Forcan's keening made it impossible to tell.

She felt like she was moving terribly slowly. The hound did not notice her. She could see now that Nicholas had not merely cut Forcan, but he'd driven his lance deep into the beast's side. The wood shaft protruded at an angle. There was no blood, but the wound gaped, the gold light of the hound's insides swirling and bubbling like molten glass.

Did she drive her spear into the same spot? But no. She had no idea if the creature had a heart. And its pained howling had given her a better target—and a far more dangerous one.

She slid her forward hand back along the shaft so she held only the last foot of it in her hands. If Forcan snapped at her, she'd be in no position to defend herself. She lifted the point of the lance, aiming for the beast's unprotected throat. If she was lucky—if she was tall enough and had enough strength—she could drive the point all the way up into its skull.

Chayos help me, she whispered, then vaulted up onto Forcan's heavy paw, thrusting the lance up through its throat and shoving it as hard as she could.

For a single grain there was still silence. Then came a sound that shattered the world. The paw she stood on flung itself upward. She felt herself flying through the air. Grains later she smashed against the ground and she knew nothing more.

It surprised her when she woke. She blinked her eyes. Above her she saw a beamed ceiling, the knotty wood interspersed with strips of whitewashed plaster. The grooved white was streaked with gray from woodsmoke. Somewhere close she heard the unintelligible murmur of voices and other noises. She tried to turn her head to look, but she couldn't. Then she became aware that she couldn't feel anything below her neck.

Horror swept her. She squeezed her eyes shut, fighting the clawing panic that rose up inside her. She could be healed. Keros could do it. Or Ellyn. *If they were alive.* She swallowed hard and opened her eyes. Her head throbbed like someone was pounding on it. Her mouth was dry as sawdust. "Is there anyone there?"

She heard sudden movement. "Margaret?"

It was Nicholas. His fingers brushed her brow and he leaned over into her line of sight. Both of his eyes were black and swollen nearly shut. His nose was pulpy and crooked. It was broken in at least two spots.

"You look like your horse kicked you in the face. What happened to you?"

His mouth twitched in a poor effort at a smile. "I stabbed the hound and the lance shaft caught me in the face."

"Improved your looks by far. Makes you almost handsome." She paused. She didn't want to ask what had happened to her. "Where are we?"

"The Gold Anchor Inn. Half of it was destroyed, but there are a few rooms left and the kitchen and dining room still stand." He pushed his hand along the side of her head. She winced and he pulled away. "Sorry."

"No. It just feels like the horse that kicked you is now stomping around in my head." She started to cough and panic swept her again when she couldn't feel anything below her throat. She started to breathe fast and tears leaked down the sides of her face as she struggled to move, to twitch even her little toe.

"Shh . . . shhh," Nicholas said, bending close and pressing her face between his hands. "It's going to be all right. The delats sent some of their own to watch for Ellyn and Keros. As soon as they get here, they'll help you. You'll be all right. *You'll be all right.* Just calm down now. Breathe slow. Easy now. It's going to be all right."

He bent close so that their breath mingled. For a moment Margaret remembered their kiss in the rain. It had felt so—

She squeezed her eyes shut again, pushing the memory away. It wouldn't go. She remembered his arms wrapping hard around her, his mouth hungry on hers. The feeling was so real that her eyes popped open. She stared up at him, just inches away.

She couldn't help herself. "Why? What do you want?"

He knew instantly what she was asking. "You. I want you."

She couldn't look away. "Weverton and Rampling? That's fire and oil."

"So we'll burn up. We'll do it together." He gently pressed his thumbs over her lips. "Don't say no."

She bit the tip of her tongue, wanting nothing more than to jump up and run away. Or pull his mouth down to hers and wrap herself around him. She could do neither. Even if her body would let her, there were secrets between them, and too much history. "Forcan?" she asked, switching the subject to safer waters.

"Gone. You drove your lance clear up into its brainpan. It made a godsawful noise and tossed you aside like an empty flour sack. When you landed—"

He broke off, his jaw clenching, his mouth rimmed with white. "There was a bright flash—like the sun—

then the hound vanished. I don't know if it's dead or if it just ran back to where it came from. But it's gone for now."

"The wizard priests had to summon it. If it's gone back to its own realm, then it will probably take another summoning to bring it back." Something itched at the back of her mind. Something about . . . She tried to focus on it and it slipped away. She reached after it and . . . nothing. She frowned.

"What is it?"

"I don't know." If she could have, she would have tossed her hands in frustration. She licked her lips, remembering how dry her mouth was. "Can I have something to drink?"

Nicholas hesitated. "You'd better not. Not until you've been healed."

Or else she might choke herself to death. He didn't say it, but it echoed in the silence all the same.

"Here, try this." He disappeared from sight and then reappeared a moment later. He pressed a damp handkerchief to her lips, moistening them. She licked the cloth. He repeated the action several times more until her mouth was no longer so parched.

"Thank you."

"Forcan wanted you. Just you. Why?"

"I don't know." Her response was instantaneous and without thought. But she considered it. Why her? Perhaps because it had already tasted her and knew she shouldn't still be alive? Maybe it was revenge for the deaths of Atreya and Saradapul. But neither of those answers felt quite right. She was missing something, something crucial.

She closed her eyes. Instantly Nicholas bent over her, his breath warm on her face. "Margaret! Don't sleep! You mustn't go to sleep!" His hand gripped her chin hard.

She opened her eyes again. His misshapen nose was nearly touching hers. His brow was deeply furrowed and he looked like he wanted to shake her hard. *Not that I'd feel it.* She pushed the thought away purposefully. Whether she walked again wasn't important right now. She had to figure out why Forcan had chosen her.

She started to speak but his grip held her jaw immobile.

Realizing her predicament, he yanked his hand away and flushed. "Sorry."

"If my brothers were here, they would be gleeful to find it so easy to quiet me. I'm sure that there were several times in the last two sennights that you would have done just about anything to shut up me up," she said lightly. "If I were in your position, I'd be making the most of the opportunity as long as it lasts."

Her humor fell flat. His gaze went flat with fury. "Do you think me such a vile worm that I would take advantage of you in this situation? I—" His lips snapped shut.

Margaret wondered what he would have said. She didn't ask. This thing between them—it was real. She felt something for him and she didn't dare think about it. When she even skimmed the surface of those feelings, she discovered a want so deep and so vast that she didn't know how she held it all inside herself. The want was for him, for his touch, for his single-minded loyalty to the people he loved and for his gentleness. But most of all, it was for this man who seemed to understand better than anyone else what she was, and still he wanted her.

Perhaps even loved her.

She fled from the thought. It wasn't possible. And even if it was, it didn't matter. They had bigger things to deal with.

"I need to think," she said and was startled to find that her tongue felt too large in her mouth and her words were thick and slurred. "That's why I closed my eyes. I'm not going to sleep."

"What is it?"

She scowled. "I can't think if you don't stop bothering me," she said, making an effort to articulate the words better. But she still sounded like she was deep in her cups. And now there was a buzzing in her ears. She swallowed and the throbbing in her head turned into a sharp pain, like someone driving an ice pick through the center of her forehead.

She made a whimpering sound and her vision clouded with pearly mist. The world spun and though she heard Nicholas speaking, she didn't understand the words. Blackness swirled like ribbons through her mind, tangling her reason. Thoughts snapped apart and the pieces floated away untethered. Tenaciously she fought to hold her ground, to keep the tatters of her mind from whirling away. But the mist ate away the edges of her being.

Her last single moment of clarity, before her eyes rolled up into her head and she sank down into the quicksand of nothingness, was that she knew why Forcan had come for her. But her epiphany came far too late. The hound had won the day after all, for she was dying and she could warn no one.

Chapter 25

Keros and Ellyn made their way down the mountains to Sylmont on legs that trembled. Each step was a victory over exhaustion. They slipped and slid over the rain-soaked ground, cursing with every misstep and fall.

At one point Keros eyed Ellyn and felt himself smile despite himself.

She caught his look. "What?" she snapped. Her draggled hair clung to her face and mud plastered her legs and the hem of her cloak. She'd wrapped the cut on her hand and the one on her forearm with a relatively clean strip of cloth torn from the bottom of her tunic.

"Would you ever have imagined that we'd both be majicars fighting the Jutras? I always thought I'd grow up and marry you and the Gerent would give us a holding."

The flat line of her lips softened. "I thought so too." Silence fell. A few minutes later, "I hate what he did—the Gerent. I forgave him because I had to, or I'd have gone mad."

He looked at her sharply, but her gaze was pinned to the ground in front her. "Why didn't you leave?"

"And go where? I still have family in Azaire. And I've seen for myself what the Jutras do—in Relsea. I went there after it fell." She shook her head. "After that

I didn't hate him anymore. Who knows? In his place, I might have done the same."

Keros's lip curled and he spat. But before he could argue, she stopped and looked at him, her arms crossed tightly over her chest.

"Crosspointe has never shared the secrets of its majick. If Azaire had more master majicars—if we knew more of what we could do—maybe he wouldn't have done it. Maybe if the Jutras weren't nibbling at our borders, it could have been different. But the Gerent was willing to sacrifice a few for the many, and he chose the people of his favorite and most powerful thane first to demonstrate that he was willing to forfeit those he cared about most—that he, too, was giving up a great deal."

Keros laughed harshly. "What did he give up? He had nothing in Etelvayn. And my father still serves at his right hand."

"But he risked losing your father, whom he loves and needs more than you know. Your father was—is— enormously powerful and could easily have stirred up a rebellion and overthrown the Gerent. He risked losing his entire people."

"A quick knife in my father's back or a bit of poison in his morning tea would have ended any possibility of that."

"But the Gerent didn't kill him; he didn't even try. Don't you see? He gave your father the opportunity to create that rebellion. But in the end, your father agreed that Azaire needed majicars, and not just any made from prisoners or gutter scum. Azaire needed men and women who were upright and dutiful. They needed us."

Keros shook his head and turned away, his jaw clenching tight. "It's a pretty campfire tale, but it means nothing. None of it's true."

"It is."

He whirled. A moment ago he'd felt entirely depleted. Now rage lent him energy. "How can you possibly believe that?"

She shrugged. "It is just as easy to spy on Azaire as
anybody else."

That took the air from his sails. He stared for a long
moment. "Perhaps you only discovered what they meant
you to discover," he said hoarsely.

"Do I look stupid to you, then? Naive perhaps? An
idiot?" Her lip curled. "What do you think I've been
doing the last fourteen seasons? I have studied majick
all that I can—that is true. But I have also learned to
fight, to kill, to mix with nobles, to disguise myself anywhere, to get into hidden places, open locks that can't be
opened, hunt whatever I'm sent after—in short, I am a
spy, and I am very good. I did not take the easy explana-
tions that perhaps were intended for me. I searched far
deeper than that and I am satisfied. I know your father
has continued to serve, and I know he has never forgiven the loss of his family. If he knew you were alive it
would give him joy beyond anything, and it would also
stab him through the heart."

"I don't believe you." Except that he did. Or maybe it
was only that he wanted to. "He married again."

"He had to have sons to inherit. And he was lonely."

Keros swung away again. Lonely. His father didn't
know the meaning of the word. He couldn't. The bastard had replaced his lost family and continued to serve
the man who destroyed them. The pain of the memories made the thistle inside him twitch and open. Pleasure blended with pain and an involuntary shudder ran
through his body as his prick hardened. Majick crackled
through the tracery of golden veins that ran across his
skin and bound his flesh. Ellyn's hand on his arm made
him flinch.

"We are what we are. You may believe me as you will

or not. I have chosen to set aside my anger and hatred because I love Azaire, and because I understand why the Gerent did it, even if I don't like his methods. In many ways, I am useful in a way I could never have been as that stupid young girl from Etelvayn. I am proud of what I've done for Azaire and there is a great deal I would not give up, even if I could."

"You were never stupid."

"I lay with you, didn't I?" she said with a sharp grin. "That was surely the act of an unhinged mind."

He found his lips turning in an answering smile. "I don't remember any complaints." And for a moment, the piercing pain of thinking about that day was nearly too much for him to bear. He put the memory away deliberately, as if packing away a piece of blown glass. It was a souvenir of another life that didn't belong to him anymore. He couldn't forget, but he could choose not to think about it.

Then something she'd said finally wriggled inside his brain: *There is a great deal I would not give up, even if I could*. The notion shook him and he started to walk again, his mind spinning. What of his life now would he give up to have the life he'd been intended to have? But no, the gods had intended him to have this life or the Gerent could never have succeeded in his efforts.

What would he give up?

Keros thought about all that had happened in those fourteen seasons since he'd swum away from Azaire. There'd been pain and horror. There'd been fear and dread and an army of things he'd prefer not to remember. But he'd faced them all—he'd conquered them all. Even Jutras blood majick. He'd come out of each challenge stronger than before.

What would he give up? *Nothing*. He was the man he needed to be to stand here in Crosspointe and fight the Jutras. He was the *majicar* he needed to be. So what sort

of fool would continue to hate the man who'd made him
into the very thing he needed to be to save Margaret,
tear out the hoskarna, and face whatever was coming
next?

He stopped and closed his eyes, drawing a slow
breath. Could he let it go? It, too, was a piece of him that
made him the man he was. But did he need it any longer? For a long time it had made him strong and made
the loneliness not matter. But now he had friends and a
land he'd come to think of as home. The hate was merely
a reminder of where he'd come from. It had no other
purpose now.

He let the breath out with a deep sigh. Hate made
people stupid. It made them refuse to see possibilities,
even ridiculous ones like a Weverton falling in love with
a Rampling, or a *sylveth* majicar embracing the power
of blood majick. It made them make mistakes and he
couldn't afford them. Not now with the Jutras on the
doorstep.

But letting go was not so easy. His hatred was woven into the fabric of his being. He was going to have to
pick it apart and pull each strand out. For now, he simply
made the decision not to hold on to it anymore. It wasn't
forgiveness, it was more like cutting a last tie.

Slowly he began walking again. Somehow he felt
lighter—inside and out. He was still marveling at himself, when the world exploded.

A wall of majick crashed into him, flinging him into
the air. The breath burst from his lungs as his head
snapped against the ground. His vision swam and he
fought to stay conscious. Majick continued to rush past
him and then almost imperceptibly it began to slow. Relief flooded Keros, but turned quickly to fear as he felt
the current reverse.

The majick sucked back the way it had come, its
speed increasing until it was pulling at Keros's clothes

and dragging him along the ground. He scrabbled for handholds in the dirt and grass. The majick was relentless and the current was too strong. It swept him along the ground like an autumn leaf caught in a gale. He bashed against rocks and trees, clutching at them wildly to try to stop himself. Fingernails tore away and he felt the thistle inside him responding to his blood and pain.

Finally the sweep of majick slowed again and he found himself slumping to the ground. He lay on his side, his body aching with cuts and bruises. The right side of his ribs hurt almost unbearably and his left knee throbbed. His thistle blossomed and he welcomed the rush of pleasure as it combated the searing pain of his wounds.

He struggled to his feet, staggering from side to side. Blood trickled down his forehead and dribbled into his eyes. He rubbed it away with one hand, clutching his side with the other. He stumbled around in a drunken circle looking for Ellyn. He called her name, but it was little more than a whisper.

He tottered up a slope, then realized he had no idea where he was or where he'd been. *Downhill*, he thought. They'd been walking downhill. But how far had the majick storm carried him? He braced himself against a tree and reached for his majick.

Closing his eyes, he pressed his senses outward, chanting in his mind—*Let me see Ellyn. . . . Let me see Ellyn*. It shouldn't have worked. But he quickly honed in on the bright fire of her majick. He didn't think it was a good sign. It likely meant she was hurt worse than he was and her thistle was drinking up her pain and blood. He opened his eyes and staggered off toward her.

He'd hardly gone twenty feet when he heard her calling him. Her voice was strong and carrying.

"Here!" he cried out and it was a mere scrape of sound. Even so, the effort cost him. He coughed and agony exploded in his side. His head reeled and he dropped heavily to the ground.

Suddenly Ellyn squatted beside him, rubbing his back soothingly as he continued to cough. Blood spattered his trousers and its coppery taste filled his mouth. Not good. He needed healing.

She seemed to think so too. She settled her hands on his shoulders and he felt her reaching inside him. It was a hot, sticky feeling and by no means comfortable. If he'd had the strength, he'd have wriggled out of her grip. But he didn't have the strength.

He clenched his teeth against his agonized moans as tentacles of power slithered through him. They brushed his ribs and the bones felt spongy, even to Keros. He flinched and sucked in a sharp breath, then coughed again, pain wrapping his chest in bands of molten steel. Ellyn's hands tightened and the tentacles prodded and wriggled into his flesh and bones and began to pull them right, smoothing out bruised muscles and piecing back together the shattered bone.

When that was done, she went further, searching out every little hurt. When she was done, the tentacles pulled out reluctantly. They groped and grabbed, trying to remain. Keros couldn't help himself. He had sat rigidly through the rest of the healing, his entire body drenched in sweat. He clutched handfuls of his cloak to keep from trying to strike out at Ellyn, and his jaw clenched so tight he thought his teeth might crack. But he could take no more.

Without thinking, he reached for the thistle. It throbbed with power. He grabbed the raw majick and slapped at the tentacles. He felt them and Ellyn recoil. Her grip loosened and fell away.

Instantly he turned, horrified. What had he done? But she just rubbed her head ruefully, looking tired. There was blood on her face along with a few scrapes and bruises, but otherwise she seemed none the worse for wear.

"That's going to give me a headache," she said and then yawned widely. She narrowed her gaze at him. "Just what in the four realms *was* that?"

Keros shook his head. "I have no idea. But it came from the direction of Sylmont. I think we should get there as soon as we can."

She nodded and stood slowly, reaching out a hand to help him up. He took it, though he felt almost spry. His exhaustion was gone with his wounds. He rolled his head on his shoulders and stretched his arms high above his head. He felt good, though he was so filthy he doubted he'd ever be clean again. *If* he ever got another blessed opportunity for a bath again before he died, which he thought might be very unlikely at the rate things were going.

"Thank you," he said to Ellyn. "How did you know what to do?" He wiggled his fingers in a semblance of the tentacles.

She shrugged. "Healing has always been a strength for me. Using blood majick is different, but my mind is very focused. When the Decardi—the school of majick that was established for training the new majicars—discovered my ability for healing, they made me learn anatomy thoroughly. So with you, I could see what was wrong and saw how it should be. Keeping the images sharp in my mind worked a little like chanting." She paused. "I've never been so strong." Both repugnance and wonder colored her voice. "I could feel your pain and it fed the majick— Is there any limit to the power of Jutras majick if there is enough blood and suffering to fuel it?"

The question struck Keros like a hammer to the gut. Was this the reason behind the violence and brutality of the Jutras invasions? The idea sent a chill sliding down his spine. Now he and Ellyn could draw on that same majick. Not only that, but the pleasure of it would be ... He didn't want to think about it.

He spat on the ground and bit his lower lip hard, tasting blood. The thistle inside him twitched and sweet delight swirled through him. He swallowed the bile that rose in his throat. "I don't know," he said hoarsely. "But there's no point to worrying about it now. First we have to get to Sylmont and find Margaret and Weverton."

"If they survived that blast," Ellyn said.

"Don't borrow trouble."

"What's another spoonful in the cauldron?" she asked with a sardonic grin.

"I'd rather not find out," Keros said. "We'd better get going. That blast was enough to knock down buildings."

No longer fettered by exhaustion, he found himself driven by the urgency of what the majick storm might have done to Margaret and Weverton. Keros snorted at himself. Who would have ever thought he'd give a damn what happened to Nicholas Weverton? He trotted up the hills and ran down the slopes. Ellyn kept up, despite the fact that she had not benefited from any healing—in fact, she ought to be more worn out than before.

Her expression was dogged and he had a feeling she'd stop only when she dropped dead. Her body was graceful and loose despite her fatigue, and her hands hovered near her weapons.

It wasn't until that moment that he really understood what she was—that he really *saw* her, not through the lens of the past, but as she was now. In every way possible, the girl he'd known as a boy was gone. This woman was cunning and strong; she was lethal and relentless. What she set her mind to, she went after with every part of her being—nothing held back in reserve and no concern for her own safety. She was hard—like tempered steel. She didn't give up and she didn't run away. She watched more than she spoke and she saw a great deal. Her mind was as quick as her wit, and she had the ability to fade into her surroundings like a chameleon. He had no doubt her lessons in anatomy had taught her to kill as efficiently as she healed. He was glad to have her at his side as they headed into whatever dangers were waiting in Sylmont. He was glad she was Ellyn and not Sperray.

At midnight they paused to sleep and at dawn they began again. As dusk fell, they crested a ridge above Sylmont and Keros dug to a halt. They were north of the Maida of Chayos and just west of the city center. A pall of dust and smoke hung over the city and it was difficult to see anything at all. Many of the fires had burned out or been smothered by the majick wave. He could see a gauzy green glow where he thought the Maida ought to be.

He pointed to it. "Over there."

They walked along. An unsettling quiet surrounded them, made more eerie by the fact that it wasn't a true silence. Keros could hear cries, moans, shouts, and whimpers, but nothing of the normal bustling city noises. He hurried his steps.

As they drew closer to the Maida, they began to hear more voices and frequent ragged coughing. The dust was so thick that it clogged their eyes and noses and made it hard to breathe. Ellyn tied a strip of cloth over her nose and mouth and Keros tore a strip from his tunic and followed suit.

Keros narrowly missed stumbling over the first body they came to. It was a man with graying hair and weathered skin. He lay on his back, his eyes wide and staring. Blood stained his upper lip where it had trickled from his nose. Likely he'd been thrown in the air by the blast and the fall had killed him.

More bodies littered the ground. Men, women, children. The majickal explosion had been indiscriminate in its choice of victims. They were scattered in and under a maze of wreckage—huge chunks of masonry, parts of roofs, doors, a stove, furniture of all sorts, cobblestones and bricks, a wood wagon, dead animals, and so much more.

"This one's alive," Ellyn said, leaning over an unconscious woman.

Keros didn't hesitate. "Leave her. You're already tired and we may need your healing abilities for Margaret or Weverton."

She straightened. "Or Weverton?" she repeated, her brows rising.

"We may need him. He's got power and resources to help fight the Jutras."

They continued on, approaching the Maida. Now people milled in the dusty mist.

"How're we s'posed to find 'em in this soup?" a male voice called out ahead.

"They're supposed to be coming here," a woman answered, her voice rough with the dust. "Names are Keros and Ellyn. They're majicars, but they're supposed to be all right. Not like the others." Fear laced her words tightly.

"Aye. The cracking bastards. I'd as soon cut 'em down where they stand."

"But the princess and Mister Weverton said it wasn't the majicars' fault—the Jutras poisoned them. Anyway, they said these two have been healed and can be trusted. After what those two did for us, I'm not going to argue. Comes to the Crown vote, Princess Margaret has mine."

Keros stopped cold. Margaret was alive. Relief made him nearly giddy. But then the next words shredded that relief to bits.

"Still can't hardly believe it. Never saw nothing like

it. We was all on the ground pissing in our pants and those two was facing down that beast alone. Thought she was nothin' but a bit of fluff and then she stood up on its foot and drove the lance through that cracking beast's head like it was made of cheese. That's a queen I could follow into the black depths," the man said.

"Might have to if what she said was true and the Jutras are already here. That is, *if* she survives. Those majicars better hurry if they're coming. I saw her after. She needs a healer but quick."

The words goaded Keros. He started to step forward and then caught himself as an idea stirred to life. It wasn't a new idea, by any means, but one he'd never entertained seriously. But now ... everything was different and there might be no better time. Besides, he was tired of living a lie.

Ellyn nudged him hard. "What's wrong? Didn't you hear? We have to hurry."

He looked at her. Then deliberately he let the illusion fall from his eyes. "Yes. It's time they found us."

He waited, his head tipped to the side. Her eyes narrowed and then with a quirk of her lips, she let her illusion dissolve. Like him, her eyes were white. A slight veining of gold ran through them.

"Let's go," she said.

He turned back toward the voices. "Hello? Is there someone there?"

The dust stirred and two delats emerged from the gloom. The woman was tall with broad shoulders and black hair pulled back in a severe braid. The man was shorter and stocky with a shock of short blond hair. They both carried lowered lances, the blades made of a translucent green material that shimmered in Keros's modified sight. He could feel the power of the majick radiating off them like a cold winter wind. He held very still. He would not like to get cut by one of them. Both of the brown-robed delats were braced for attack, eyeing Keros and Ellyn suspiciously.

"Who are you?" the woman demanded through tight lips, her gaze running over first him and then Ellyn, and then returning to stare him in the eyes. The lance in her hand shook.

"I am called Keros and she is Ellyn. We are majicars. We need to see Princess Margaret."

"What's wrong with your eyes?" the stocky delat asked.

"Nothing," Keros said. "I see quite well."

Beside him Ellyn snorted. The delat tossed her a fierce look and his spear lifted so it was aimed at the center of Keros's chest.

"Why are they white like that?"

He smiled slightly, his head tipping to the side. "Because they are. Why are yours blue?"

"Ain't natural." His lance twitched forward.

But before he could drive the weapon forward as his trembling hand suggested he wanted to, Ellyn interrupted. "Did we hear you say that the princess needed healing? Take us to her."

They exchanged a look and then lifted their lances out of the way. "This way," the woman said and started off. Keros fell in beside her with Ellyn behind. The other delat brought up the rear.

"What happened?" Keros asked, waving his hand through the dusty air.

The delat gave him a sidelong look, then switched her weapon to her other hand, away from Keros. "Majicars went crazy in the city and started attacking each other, none of them minding who or what might get hurt in the crossfire. Chayos raised a barrier to protect the Maida and people came running to take shelter. A lot of the fighting had died down when Princess Margaret and

Nicholas Weverton showed up. They said the regent was a traitor and the Jutras have invaded."

"That's true," Keros said, hearing the doubt in her voice. "And the Jutras have found a way to poison the majicars and drive them insane. That's why they were attacking each other."

"So how come you're all right?"

"It wasn't easy," he said softly. "And that's why our eyes are white. But that's a story for another time. I'd like to hear the rest of yours."

"After they arrived, there came a howling down in the city. It sounded like it came from all the way down by the harbor south of the Riddles."

"Howling? Like a dog?"

She shook her head. "Like something from the other side of Chayos's altar," she said and he could see goose pimples that spread over her skin at the memory. "It scared everybody. It wasn't until it howled a second time—a lot closer—that I realized the fear was majickal. It was sending it out. I wanted to run . . ." She trailed off, swallowing hard.

"Forcan," Keros said.

She looked at him sharply. "That's what they called it. But she wasn't scared—Princess Margaret. She asked for a lance and so did Weverton. Then that *thing* came. It was big—bigger than the horses they were riding. Its teeth were longer than my arm and its claws were bigger than my legs. By then the fear had us all on the ground. It was hard to breathe even. Then the princess started across the plaza to have room to fight. It followed her, like it had come just to find her. Then it pounced. Weverton cut it—stabbed a lance into its side." The delat shook her head. "You should have seen her. She ran right up to it and drove her lance up under its jaw into its head. Then it made a noise like the world was ripping in half. It tossed her aside and then there was a light—as bright as the sun—and then the majick exploded. It leveled buildings. If we hadn't been inside Chayos's barrier, I don't know that we'd have survived.

"When it was over, we found her and Weverton lying in the plaza. They were both unconscious, but he woke up soon enough. But her—when she woke up, she couldn't move. We found a place to take her to wait for you. It's just up there."

She hurried a little quicker and called out, "It's me, Des. I've got the majicars."

Suddenly a dozen delats materialized out of the dust and darkness. The middle one was tall with gray hair and he carried one of the lances. He looked at Keros and Ellyn, his attention fixing almost instantly on their eyes. "What's wrong with their eyes?"

"Says what the Jutras did to 'em turned 'em white." Des paused and when he made no move to get out of the way, she spoke again. "Red—the princess and Weverton said we could trust them. She needs a healer. There's no choice."

He hesitated another long moment and then sucked his teeth and stepped back. "I hope to the black depths you can save her," he said to Keros and Ellyn, and motioned with his head for them to follow.

They went into the courtyard of what appeared to be an inn. Or it had been. Lights illuminated the inside of what was left of it, revealing that half the building had crumbled into rubble. The other half still stood, though the exterior was dented and scarred and the second-story roof had been mostly torn away. The doors had been ripped from their hinges and then rehung drunkenly from the splintered jamb. More delats guarded the entrance, these carrying swords made of the same green material.

Keros eyed them narrowly. He'd never seen a delat carrying a belt knife before, much less weapons for battle. But these men and women held their weapons like they knew very well what to do with them. He smiled inwardly. Majicars and Pilots weren't the only ones hiding what they truly were. But why were they guarding the tavern? Why weren't they protecting the Maida?

Red handed his lance off to another delat and led them inside. Food was cooking in the kitchen and Keros's mouth watered. A pile of plaster and rubble had been swept into a corner and tables had been squeezed into every leftover bit of space. Each one was crowded with people. Most were filthy and all bore cuts and other, more serious wounds. As one person finished, he was replaced by another from the line that began in a gap in the far wall. Unarmed delats circulated, serving the hungry people and tending to their wounds.

A hush fell as Ellyn and Keros entered. All around was a scrape of chairs as people lurched to their feet; some stumbled back fearfully toward the gap in the wall. Palpable tension filled the room. Majicars were no longer trusted. Keros's jaw hardened and followed after Red.

He stopped at a door just beyond the dining room. He knocked softly and then pushed it open without waiting for an answer. He stepped aside to allow the two majicars to enter ahead of him.

Nicholas was sitting beside a heavy trestle table where Margaret lay beneath a quilt. He held one of her hands, his lips bent close against her ear. His head jerked up as Keros and Ellyn entered. His face was a bruised mess, his eyes nearly swollen shut.

"Thank the gods," he rasped. "Hurry. I don't think she's got much time."

Keros could see that. Margaret's lights had faded to dull sparks and they barely moved. The tendrils from Nicholas had anchored firmly on her and seemed to be feeding her, which Keros hadn't thought even possible.

But even as he watched, he saw her lights near the tendrils brighten and speed up. Then he noticed something else. He cocked his head, squinting. It looked like a thin layer of golden gauze lay over her—like a shroud. "Do you see it?" he asked Ellyn.

"Yes."

"What is it?"

"Majick, but what kind and what it does—I don't know."

"What are you talking about?" Nicholas demanded. He was covered in the same gauzy gold layer. "You've got to hurry. She's paralyzed and she fainted glasses ago. I haven't been able to wake her. Help her—please!"

Keros looked at Ellyn. "You're a better healer than I am, I think."

She nodded, chin firm as she raised it. "I'd like some food. And something to drink," she said to Red, and then moved forward, not waiting for the delat's response. "Quick as you can." He hesitated, then obeyed.

She stepped to Margaret's side and put her hand on the prone woman's forehead and another on her stomach. Her brow furrowed and her head sank down until her chin rested against her chest. The hand on Margaret's chest balled into a fist. Ellyn gasped low and she pushed herself away, breathing hard like she'd been running.

Keros caught her and she leaned against him for only a moment, then straightened. She wiped the back of her arm over her forehead. "Nicholas is right. We can't wait. She's barely hanging on. But it's going to require blood. And pain. And a lot of both."

"What?" Nicholas demanded. "What are you babbling on about?"

Keros looked at Nicholas. "It's Jutras majick. She can heal with it—I've experienced it myself. But it feeds on blood and pain." He turned back to Ellyn. "I'll give whatever you need to save her."

"No," Nicholas said. "Crosspointe needs majicars more than they need me. I'll do it. Besides, you can heal me later."

"If you survive," Ellyn said. "You may not."

"Then use me. And there are others as well," said Red from the doorway.

Keros swung around. Red was holding a trencher with a thick slab of bread covered in a bean stew and three tankards of ale in the other. Behind him came another delat with two more trenchers. "You heard what we need and why? That the Jutras have infected us with their majick?" he asked, frowning at the ease of their offer of help.

"And you can save her life with it," Red said, his gaze unflinching, his expression taut. "So we'll do what we have to."

"Chayos might frown on that," Keros said.

"If she objects, she will strike us down and refuse us a place on her altar. We do not believe she will oppose us."

"Why? Why is the princess so important to you that you'd participate in a blood majick ritual? Why aren't you trying to kill us right now, knowing we've become blood majicars?"

Red's mouth tightened into something that might have been a smile. "We believe she will be the next queen of Crosspointe. That would be enough, but we watched her stand between us and slavering, soul-destroying death with nothing but a lance. He did too." Red pointed at Weverton. "If they're willing to die for us, we're willing to bleed for them. And *she* said we could trust you."

The last was both a challenge and declaration of loyalty. *Prove yourself*, he was telling Keros. *Heal her and show us that blood majick hasn't turned you Jutras.*

Keros finally understood the guards around the tavern. They believed the future of Crosspointe was in this room and it was worth dying for; it was worth *hurting* for. He nodded, his mouth setting in a hard line. "Come in. We don't have much time."

"We could use the power from the city," Ellyn murmured to him. "With so much death and destruction, there's plenty there to be harvested."

He was shaking his head before she finished. "No. That's tainted with fear and suffering and betrayal. Margaret deserves better. Besides, if we must make use of Jutras majick, then let's do it our way whenever we can. This will be clean and unpolluted. There's also a chance that voluntary sacrifice will make a more powerful majick than forced. It is the better choice and we have willing volunteers. Now," he said, turning to Red and the delats crowding in behind him, "who wants to be first?"

Chapter 26

Margaret dreams.

A lustrous silver pearl in a bezel of ice-water black.

A winding coil of gold light twisting tighter and tighter.

A dimpled smile and yellow eyes. Saradapul. The name throbs hot with screams. They return. Once, long ago, this land belonged to them, before the dark times, before the birth of the younger gods.

Bobbin-lace weaving of pain and blood.

Bite. Agony like swords driving through flesh.

Gold light prods, digs.

Invasion.

Silver pearl flinches and contracts. Slides deeper down in a ruined mansion of ice-water silence. Waits.

Waits.

Shattered mirror. Shattered glass. Shattered stone. Drifting leaves. Falling snow.

Puzzle

Fragments seethe like moths around a lamp, settling like heaped bones in darkness.

Light.

Mirror. Glass. Stone. Tree. Snow.

Waits.

Blood pools.

Sifting grains in a crystal hour glass and no time left.
No time left.

Margaret dreams.

In silver dark, sunlight blooms and petals fall in a swirl of still wind. A storm.
The storm.
Beneath it boils a sea of gold, silver, green, and black in a glittering cauldron made of white ice. Shapes rise and fall—amorphous, hard-edged, sinuous. Mist and fire, flesh and root, smoke and spirit. Snow.
The cauldron cracks.

Margaret dreams.

Chapter 27

Nicholas watched Keros and Ellyn make their preparations, all the while clinging to Margaret's hand. Her breathing was slow and uneven. Every time she let out a breath, he tensed and held himself still until she took another, sagging in momentary relief until she let it go again—then he began the terrible wait all over again.

"How long has she been unconscious?"

It took Nicholas several grains to surface from the mire of his fear to realize Keros was speaking to him. He looked up. "What? I don't know. She woke up for a quarter of a glass after we brought her here, maybe a little longer. We talked. Then she fainted." He dragged his fingers through his hair. "I don't know how long it's been exactly. Maybe three glasses."

"It was twenty-two," Red corrected.

Nicholas stared, disbelieving. Twenty-two glasses? How was that possible?

"Why did you bring her here instead of the Maida?" Keros asked Red as he stripped off his cloak. "Where are the Naladei and Kalimei? Surely they could have healed her." He reached for a tankard of ale and drained it before forking stew and bread into his mouth. He looked gaunt. As much as Margaret was. And his eyes—they were white. He wasn't disguising them. Neither of the majicars were.

Nicholas squinted at Keros. For a moment he could have sworn he saw a gossamer spiderweb of gold light spreading across the other man's skin. He blinked and shook his head. He hadn't slept since—

He didn't even know how long it had been. His head was muzzy and he could feel Margaret slipping deeper into the shadows of endless night. Not for the first time did he wonder how he could possibly feel so much for her in so short a time. Losing her would be a mortal wound.

"The priestesses of Chayos have sealed the Maida. No one may enter until—"

"*Until . . . ?*" prompted the lean majicar.

The delat's lined face was pained. "Until Chayos sees fit to open it up to us again."

Keros stared.

"What does it matter?" Ellyn said impatiently. She'd drunk most of her ale and had gulped down half the bean stew and bread. "Right now we have Margaret to worry about and we have precious little time."

She went to stand over the unconscious princess again, studying her.

"What do you want me to do?" Nicholas asked.

"Keep her from dying until I can heal her," she said shortly. "Exactly what you've been doing."

What he'd been doing? Nothing. Less than nothing. It was her own stubborn strength and determination that had kept her clinging to life. It had nothing to do with him. Still his hand tightened on hers and he went back to listening to her breathe.

Vaguely he heard the shuffle of feet and the rustle of clothing as Keros directed people where he wanted them. The smell of so many unwashed bodies in the small room was smothering. Nicholas felt someone brush up behind him and he looked up.

Ellyn stood across from him with her hands hovering over Margaret. Red had a hand on her shoulder and the delat next to him had a hand on his. And so it went around the room, the last delat gripping Ellyn's left shoulder. Each of the volunteers had a set, determined expression. The men had removed their shirts and the women had rolled up their sleeves as far as they could; several had unlaced their collars to expose their shoulders and the swell of their breasts.

Keros stood behind Red. He held a dagger in his hand. "Whenever you're ready," he said to Ellyn.

She nodded, drew a deep breath, and let it out. She took another and closed her eyes. Her hands dropped, splaying across Margaret's forehead and stomach. Nicholas's fingers tightened and he prayed with all his soul.

"Remember," Keros murmured to Red, "this is *supposed* to hurt. And bleed." And with that, he began to cut.

The delat's jaw knotted and his lips clamped tight. His fingers curled tight on Ellyn's shoulder. She didn't seem to notice. A gossamer tracery of gold light rose on her skin. Nicholas stared. He *had* seen it on Keros also. Then he could hardly think of anything because Margaret convulsed, her body jerking and flailing.

"Keep her still," Ellyn said in a calm, detached voice. "I need her still or I might kill her."

How? But he didn't waste time asking. It didn't matter. She was *moving*. It was a sign that she would heal and he had to do all he could to help that happen. He leaned in between Ellyn's hands and lay across Margaret. He held her head between the palms of his hands and whispered in her ear. Words spilled out and he hardly knew what he said. He told her to be still, he told her what they were trying to do, he told her she had to fight. . . . Slowly she settled, but the tension didn't leave her body.

Ellyn was muttering beneath her breath. He couldn't

hear the words. He vaguely heard Keros repeating that
the cuts were supposed to hurt and bleed again and
again. Time slowed. The coppery smell of blood mixed
with the stench of fear, sweat, and grimy bodies.

Margaret bucked and hard shudders rolled through
her body. Nicholas pressed harder against her. From
where he lay, he could see Ellyn's grubby hand, the fingernails torn and broken. Her skin was scratched and
scabbed beneath the gold net of majick that slid over
her fingers like a glove and rose up to disappear inside
her sleeve. It was brighter now and pulsed softly.

Power swelled in the room and pressed heavily
against Nicholas. He breathed raggedly and the sound
was echoed by the bleeding men and women circling the
table.

"More. I need more," Ellyn said aloud before returning to her muttered chant.

Soon Nicholas began to hear wimpers as Keros re-
sumed cutting. The power in the room grew thick and
dense, like it was filling with molasses. He felt Margaret's chest jerk beneath him as she struggled for air. He
tried to lever himself up and off her. He moved barely
an inch.

"Fight," he whispered. "You have to fight. Don't let
the Jutras win. Don't let the Jutras beat you. You can do
this. Fight."

He lost track of time. He felt something moving inside
her, lumping under her skin. Majick. Ellyn had begun to
pant and her hand on Margaret's forehead was shaking. Then suddenly it firmed and the net of light flared
brilliantly and Nicholas shut his eyes against it. Blots
of yellow floated across the black of his closed eyelids.
The majick in the room impossibly seemed to double or
triple, and it felt like he was caught inside a crucible of
molten lead. Moments later the feeling faded and he felt
Ellyn step back.

"I've done all that I can," she said, her voice thready and weak.

For a single grain there was no sound. Then, "Catch her!" followed by a surge of movement. Nicholas pushed himself up, his gaze fixed on Margaret. She might have been carved from marble. Her eyes were wide open and she stared unblinkingly up at the ceiling.

"Margaret?" he said, stroking a hand over her hair. "Can you hear me?"

No response, not even a flicker of an eyelash. "Margaret!" he said louder. *"Margaret!"* The last was a ringing shout. Recklessly, he yanked her upright. Her head lolled back over his arm and her hands flopped loosely at her sides. He slid his arm around her and held her head up, turning her to face him. "Margaret. *Please.*"

Still nothing. The silence in the room was broken only by the rustle of clothing. Everyone seemed to be holding their breath. Then suddenly Margaret went rigid in his arms. Her mouth dropped open and she sucked in a sobbing breath and began to cough. She swung her legs over the table and leaned down over her knees, one hand clutching Nicholas for balance. At last she was able to sit up. She brushed the back of her hand across her lips and then her glance took in the room.

"What in the black depths happened here?" she asked, her voice cracking like winter-killed leaves as she turned her head to look at the bloody delats.

Each looked like they'd been through a hail of knives. Cuts spangled their arms, shoulders, and chests and blood drenched their skin and clothing. Each wavered on their feet and watched Margaret like she was the answer to a divine question. Keros held Ellyn on the floor. She'd fainted. If he'd looked gaunt before, now he looked emaciated. Ellyn was worse. Her skin was patched with purple and black bruises and the net of light had vanished like it had never been.

"What's going on?" Margaret demanded, looking commandingly at Nicholas. Her voice was stronger and she had straightened, her hand dropping from his arm.

"Ellyn healed you."

When he didn't explain further, she gestured impatiently toward the delats. "And them? What in the black depths happened to them?"

"Keros cut them to give Ellyn the majick she needed to heal you."

"What?" Margaret drew back, a look of revulsion and horror washing over her face. She slid to her feet. She staggered and when Nicholas went to steady her, she shoved his hand aside with angry violence.

She examined the delats, her attention hooking on Red. She marched stiff-legged around the table to stop in front of him, her chin jutting. She folded her arms tight across her chest and Nicholas was pretty certain it was to stop herself from hitting him. His lips pulled into a tight smile. She was going to live.

"This is . . . you cracking . . . of all the . . ."

Each time she began her diatribe, she broke off, unable to find words for her anger. She swung around, skewering Keros with a look. "How could you let them do this?"

"It was the only way to save you. Weverton wanted to do it, but they wouldn't let him," Keros replied, exhaustion making his voice thick and slow.

"But why?" she asked and her bewilderment sparked an irrational anger in Nicholas that she could not see her own value.

"Why? Because, my dear, they are determined that you will be the next queen of Crosspointe and as such, you are far too valuable to lose. You are the hero of the day. For you they were willing to bleed and to hurt."

His words mocked her modesty and he saw them

strike like blows. Her eyes widened and a flash of hurt crossed her expression before she took herself in hand. Her chin rose and she turned away. Nicholas's hand clenched. *Dammit!* What in the name of the gods was he saying? Everything inside him was bubbling with elation. She was alive! She was well. He wanted to dance on the rooftops. Why had he said that? Why had he sounded like he didn't care?

"Is that true?" she asked Red in a hollow whisper.

The delat nodded. "More or less."

"But that's ludicrous. Ryland or Vaughn will rule next. They are far more capable than I am."

"Begging your forgiveness, Princess, but it is not your place to choose," he said with a slight bow. He winced as he did.

Her lip curled. "I'm not a damned diplomat. I was raised to fight and kill," she said harshly as she realized her predicament. She could not refuse to be on the ballot. Each and every eligible Rampling had to put their name in the hat. It was their duty.

"It seems your skills have come in handy in recent days," Nicholas said. "You may be more qualified to rule Crosspointe than you think."

"No," she said quietly and started to push her way out of the room. She stopped and looked at Keros and Ellyn. "Are you all right? Is everyone all right?" She glanced at the delats, her gaze skipping past Nicholas as if he wasn't there.

"Ellyn and I need rest and food," Keros said. "The delats—"

"We will take care of ourselves. Our wounds appear worse than they are," Red said, interrupting.

Margaret opened her mouth as if to say something, then closed it and nodded. Almost before Nicholas realized what she planned to do, she was out the door and halfway across the dining room. He caught her as she stepped out of the inn into the dawn light. For a moment all both of them could do was stop and stare.

The city was broken. There didn't seem to be a single building within sight that hadn't suffered terrible damage. Too many were nothing more than heaps of rubble. Dust and smoke hazed the air and Nicholas wondered how far the damage extended. But he remembered the view from the mountains—the harbor had been decimated by the majicars and so had much of the city. The majickal explosion caused by the defeat of Forcan had only added to the destruction.

Margaret made an animal sound and started to step away. Nicholas snatched her arm. "Where are you going?"

She pulled away and kept walking. She wobbled, stumbling over the loose bricks and masonry littering the inn's courtyard. "To find Ryland."

He grabbed her again, pulling her around to face him. He held her firmly. "You fought Forcan and nearly died. You can barely walk. You need food and rest as much or more than Keros and Ellyn."

"There's no time." She stared past him, her eyes wide.

He could feel her muscles tensing. He was still holding her because she was letting him. If she chose to, he was fairly certain she could put him on the ground without a lot of effort, even in her current condition.

"You haven't heard what Keros and Ellyn have to say about the hoskarna or the Jutras majick," he argued. "Ryland will want to know all that, won't he? So come back inside and we'll find your brother as soon as you've heard their report."

For a moment she didn't answer. "What if he didn't survive?" she asked flatly, as if she didn't care. Except that her body was shaking.

"You mourn him and you keep going," Nicholas said.

Her gaze rose to his eyes from his throat, where she'd been staring. "My father never meant for me to be queen. The crown was for Vaughn or Ryland. I can't do it."

"You can," he said, his hands moving up to her shoulders, rubbing them softly. Her bones were sharp beneath her shirt. "You can do anything you need to. Your father didn't know the half of what you are capable of. He couldn't see the forest for the trees. In many ways he was no doubt brilliant, but in this, he was blind. Believe me, you will do well."

Her brows rose. "Are you suggesting that a Rampling should sit on the throne again?" she asked. "Haven't you plotted to be rid of the throne for most of your life?"

"Now is not the time for any of that. Crosspointe is in shambles; Sylmont is destroyed. The Jutras are invading. We are already at war, whether anyone else knows it or not. Crosspointe needs someone on the throne to lead them. They need you—the woman who took a lance and walked out alone to face Forcan."

"I wasn't alone," she protested.

"You didn't know I would follow and it didn't matter. You were going whether I came or not, because you are a Rampling, and that's what Ramplings do—that's what *you* do. You protect your people no matter the cost or how insanely large the odds might be stacked against you. You won't be alone. I'll do whatever you ask, whatever you need. I won't make that promise to Ryland or Vaughn. Now come back inside. You need to eat and rest. Just for a few hours," he added when she started to protest.

"Very well," she said in an aggrieved voice.

He turned, one hand sliding down to take hers. Miraculously, she didn't shake him off, following him reluctantly as she turned to look again at the carnage that was all that was left of Sylmont. Back inside, solemn eyes watched her from every table. Suddenly someone stepped in front of her. Margaret stopped.

"Your pardon, ma'am," the burly man said. He touched his forehead and bowed awkwardly. "Your pardon, but I wanted t' say thank ye for killin' that thing. It surely would've torn us all limb from limb. But ye stood it down, cool as can be. I never seen nothin' like it. Was a miracle, is what it was." He bobbed another bow and a slow gabble rose to echo him as he moved away.

Margaret slowly scanned the gathered people, the color running from her cheeks. A hush fell. They were waiting for her to speak. She swallowed and let go of Nicholas's hand. He curled his fingers into his palms to keep from snatching it back. He could see her weighing her words. Like him, she knew this was a pivotal moment. Did she speak as their queen and start girding them for war? Or did she speak as a princess and promise them help to come? Or did she break and retreat?

The latter choice was more than dangerous and not just because help might never arrive, but because these people were swimming in a sea of fear. She could rally them, unite them, or she could send them scurrying into hiding, each one looking out only after himself and his family. In which case, she would have done as much harm to Crosspointe as if she'd led the Jutras army herself. The people of Crosspointe needed someone to follow *now*—someone they could respect and who they knew would die for them if she had to.

He had no idea which she would choose when she began to speak.

Chapter 28

Margaret's gaze picked across the room. People crammed the tables. Families, grandfathers, and grandmothers, a mother with a child nursing at her breast, a hard-bitten sailor with hands made hard by years of hauling lines, and so many more. Outside, those who stood in line for their turn at a meal crowded inside. Soon the population of the room had quadrupled and more people were pushing at the doors. Just to see and hear her, she realized.

The enormity of their trust and their hope made her want to dig a hole and hide. Nicholas was wrong. She couldn't do this; she couldn't sit on the throne and tie the twisty knots of politics. She worked in the shadows where she didn't have to be responsible for other people's lives.

But there was no one else.

Vaughn was clear across Crosspointe and Ryland— she had no idea if he was still alive. But Nicholas was right: Crosspointe needed someone now and she was the only choice. She cleared her throat and the silence was instant.

"I know you have suffered," she said. "Many of you have lost too much already—your families, your homes, and your businesses. Believe me when I say that I understand that very well. The regent played us all for fools.

He has been conspiring with the Jutras, and, my friends, you must know, the Jutras are here in Crosspointe. Their ships have not yet landed, but there is no doubt—we are at war." She said the last words slowly.

An audible gasp met her words and her audience shrank in on themselves, huddling together as if to stave off a sudden chill.

"But the majicars have turned against us!" wailed a voice from the back. "How can we defend ourselves?"

A clamor rose in response. Margaret swallowed. This was going well. Just wait until they heard the rest. They'd tie a rope to her leg and sink her in Blackwater Bay.

She raised a hand, but the noise continued. A loud thudding broke it apart. She glanced behind her. Red stood to the left, his lance in his hand. He was shirtless and still covered in blood. That, along with the thump of his lance striking the floor, captured the silence again.

Margaret nodded to him and turned back to her audience. Resolve hardened inside her. There was no time for coddling or for painting the truth with pretty colors to make it more tolerable.

"I want you to listen very carefully," she said in a clear, carrying voice. "We have very little time left. The Jutras infected our majicars with their majick. It has driven them insane. They can be cured—in a way. But many have no doubt died." Or been killed. She remembered what she'd overheard the regent tell Atreya and Saradapul: *I have issued an order to execute any majicar on sight, and have sent men to clear out Sylmont.* Maybe more were dead than she expected. She swallowed her dismay, letting none of it show on her face.

"We may have only a few majicars left. The ones who survive are capable of using Jutras blood majick." She gestured at Red. "That is the result." It was a bald statement, and she knew it would shock them. But she also needed them to know the truth without any sugarcoating, because this was the least of the worst, and it was time they knew exactly what Crosspointe was.

When a shiver ran through the crowd and they drew back, muttering, Red stepped forward, and behind him came the other delats—twelve in all. Each was a bloody mess, but their faces were stoic and they carried themselves proudly. They lined up in front of the gathered crowd.

"You all know what Princess Margaret did for us," Red said loudly. "Some of you were there and saw what she did for yourselves, and the rest of you have heard the stories. As far as I'm concerned, if it comes to a vote for the throne, she'll be the one sitting on it. After she fought that beast, she was hurt. She was going to die. And then the majicars said they could heal her."

As if on cue, Keros and Ellyn pushed out to stand beside the delats. He had his arm around her and she slumped like a sack of bones. She looked like she'd been beaten with a club. Neither disguised their eyes as they faced the crowd.

"In order to heal her, they needed to use the blood majick of the Jutras. Nicholas Weverton was set on giving his blood, but he might have died and we figured Crosspointe couldn't afford to lose him either. So we *volunteered*." Red stressed the word. He paused a moment to let that sink in, then said, "And we would all do it again."

Another delat, tall with a severe black braid, stepped forward. Her shirt was in bloody shreds and cuts crisscrossed her skin. "And if it becomes necessary to feed every drop of our blood to our majicars to defeat the Jutras, then we will."

At her words, a knot rose in Margaret's throat. It felt like it would choke her. How could they be willing to give so much just for her? It was too much responsibility. Too much for just her. She felt Nicholas watching her and she refused to look at him. She knew what he would say—what her father would say. It wasn't just for her. It was for Crosspointe, and a headless dog could no more save itself than a headless country.

She squared her shoulders and looked at her subjects. *Her subjects.* Her stomach flip-flopped, but she kept her expression cool and regal. Masks. She'd worn them as long as she could remember. She hoped she could make this her real face in time, or at least until Ryland or Vaughn could don the crown.

"We are not the Jutras. We don't revel in the torture of innocent people. But we must use the tools we have to fight or they will take us the same way they took Relsea and Tapisriya. So there is something else I want you to tell you and I want you to spread the word. It's time you understood what we really are." She drew a steadying breath, feeling her legs shake, though whether from hunger, exhaustion, the aftermath of her healing, or what she was about to say, she didn't know.

"You have always hated and feared spawn. But they have walked among us since the founding of Crosspointe." She expected another gasp, but there was only silence. She continued. "When someone is cursed by *sylveth*, they turn into one of three kinds of spawn: majicars, Pilots, or the creatures you have been taught to fear from birth. But my father learned recently that many of those spawn who seem so horrifying and monstrous are neither. Except for their appearance, they are much like us. No," she corrected, "they *are* us. They are our brothers and sisters and fathers and mothers—every soul who has been touched by *sylveth*. Many of those who escaped our knacker gangs live on the Root where my father established another Pale. I am going to call them home. I am going to ask them to help us against the Jutras."

This time voices rose loudly. But Margaret wasn't

done and she felt her strength draining at an alarming rate. She held up a hand and Red banged his lance on the floor again. Instantly she had their attention again.

"One last thing. A short time ago, my father had the opportunity to befriend a ship of rebel Jutras. He foresaw that we would be invaded and did all he could to prepare for that eventuality. I will ask these rebels to fight beside us as well. I ask only this of you—welcome them. Crosspointe is at war and we are readying our armies. It will be a ragtag group, for certain, but together we *will* drive away the Jutras. This I promise you, but only if we *all* work together."

For a moment there was a pause, and then a ragged cheer rose and spread outside to those who hadn't yet heard what she'd said. Margaret turned and quickly pushed through the delats.

"Here, Your Highness," a young delat said and motioned toward a different room than the one she'd been healed in. It took a moment for her to realize what he'd called her. *Your Highness.*

She followed him into the room where a table laden with steaming food waited. Her stomach growled. Nicholas, Ellyn, and Keros followed her inside. Before the delat could close the door, she stopped him. "Send Red in as soon as he's able," she said. The delat nodded and departed.

Margaret turned to face her friends. No, more than that. These were her counselors and her generals. Red, too. She'd gather more in time. For now, these were the people who were going to help her save Crosspointe.

Keros helped Ellyn to a chair and sat beside her. Nicholas went to the other side of the table but remained standing, watching Margaret. She went to the head of the table and looked at each of them.

"We have a lot of work to do. I know you're tired and I thank you for all you've done for me. But before I can let you sleep, we have to begin. Can I count on all of you to see this through to the end?" Keros nodded and so did Nicholas. Her gaze settled on Ellyn.

"I'm not going home until the Jutras do," the majicar said. Her chin was braced on her hands as she leaned tiredly against the table.

"Thank you." She sat and Nicholas did as well.

Just then Red entered. He wore a loose tunic. He stopped inside the door. "You sent for me, Your Highness?"

"No. Absolutely none of that nonsense from you," she said. "Not from any of you," she said fiercely to the other three. "I am Margaret. Now, sit down. You decided you want me to be queen, well I've decided I don't care if you are a delat, you belong to me now. You're on my new Council of War."

He made no objection, but nodded and came around the table to sit beside Nicholas.

Margaret reached for bread and spooned the bean stew into her bowl. She ignored the others, devouring her food with single-minded purpose. She hadn't known how hungry she was. As she ate, something niggled at her. Something important. She reached for it, but it skittered away. *Dammit.* She waited for it to come back, focusing her attention on eating. Again the thought returned. She let it drift closer. Finally she pounced on it. A grain later she slammed her spoon down on the table and stared straight ahead, seeing nothing.

"What is it?" Nicholas demanded.

"I know how they did it. I know what they are doing," she said. She covered her mouth with her palm and began shaking her head. "By the gods," she whispered as the pieces fell together in her mind like a puzzle. It all made sense now. All of it.

"What are you talking about?" Nicholas prodded.

She licked her lips and sat back in her chair, her

finger curling over the arms. She looked first at Keros. "Remember what you told me about the *sylveth*? What Marten found in the depths of the Kalpestrine?"

He nodded, frowning. "That there was a huge ball of *sylveth* deep down inside of it. He didn't know what it was or why it was there."

"I think I do," she said. "I told you how the Jutras stopped and conducted a ceremony in the mountains— before the one where you rescued me. I told you that they made a ball of majick and it sank into the ground. Do you remember?" She glanced at the others.

Keros nodded, as did Ellyn and Nicholas. Red only listened intently.

"What if that's how they are attacking the *sylveth*? Or attacking the land and, through it, Chayos? What if they made a lot of those balls and sent them into the Inland Sea? *Sylveth* is sentient. My bet is that it—they— are hiding in the bottom of the Kalpestrine and hoping we defeat it before the Jutras kill them all."

"*Sylveth* is what?" Nicholas said slowly.

Equally dumbfounded, Ellyn and Red stared at Margaret.

"A majicar made the discovery by accident just before the Kalpestrine fell," Keros explained with a questioning glance at Margaret. How much did she want him to reveal?

She looked at Nicholas and then back at Keros, nodding slowly. Nicholas thought he wanted her, but that would change when he learned what her father had done to Shaye, Nicholas's favorite nephew, and that Margaret had known all along. He would not forgive her.

"Just before the king's murder, he discovered a means to accurately predict who, when exposed to *sylveth*, would be transformed into a majicar or a Pilot. At that time, he was involved with selling ships compasses to Glacerie. He had only a few to sell—those scrounged from sunken vessels by Marten Thorpe, who is spawn of a different variety than Pilots or majicars. He thought if Glacerie had compasses, we would have allies on the sea against the Jutras.

"He needed a compass majicar who was not bound to the guild, someone who would make the compasses he needed to cement his alliances. He learned that Fairlie Norwich, a talented master metalsmith, would make a compass majicar and so he had her cursed with *sylveth*."

That brought startled exclamations from Nicholas, Red, and Ellyn, the latter of whom was staring at Keros with a stricken expression; and it wasn't until that moment that Margaret remembered his childhood—that the Gerent had cast his entire family and village into a *sylveth* tide in an attempt to create majicars. Ellyn and Keros were two of only a handful who'd survived.

"You knew about it?" Ellyn asked him accusingly.

"I was told," Keros said after a moment.

"What did you do to stop it?"

He said nothing, only looking down at his hands folded in his lap. Margaret knew it hadn't been easy for him. He'd nearly left Crosspointe. She still wasn't sure what had made him stay.

"You're a cracking bastard," Ellyn said, shoving her trencher violently away. "You go on about the Gerent, but you're just as bad. You walk away from Azaire but not Crosspointe when the king does the same damned thing?"

He didn't reply. The silence stretched. At last he began the story again, leaving Ellyn's accusations hanging in the air like storm clouds. In the meantime, Nicholas was staring at Margaret, his eyes glittering like diamonds. She met his gaze, keeping her expression bland, though she wanted to squirm. He knew that Shaye had to be tied up in this somehow; his nephew had been in love with Fairlie.

"After Fairlie was transformed, she made it clear that she was not going to cooperate. She was very angry and too powerful for him to handle." The corner of Keros's mouth turned up in pleased malice. "She threatened to destroy Sylmont and free all the *sylveth* to turn everyone to spawn. Not wanting to waste her talents, King William turned her over to the Majicar Guild, knowing that they could bend her to their will. Eventually she *would* make the compasses." He rubbed a hand over the back of his neck and sighed. "When it was discovered she was taken, a close friend rallied others to rescue her."

"My nephew, Shaye," Nicholas said. It wasn't a question.

"Correct." Keros nodded at the other man. "He forced Prince Ryland to assist him, as well as enlisting the aid of the two Root majicars who had predicted what she would turn into."

"Root majicars?" echoed Nicholas, finally looking away from Margaret. The others were equally stunned.

"Yes. Do not be mistaken. They are very intelligent and very powerful majicars. The four of them raided the Kalpestrine and rescued Fairlie. Because of the majick they used to do so, the Kalpestrine fell."

Nicholas was shaking his head. "My nephew didn't have his master's badge and I can't believe that three majicars could be that strong. It isn't possible."

Keros smiled. "I don't have a master's badge either." He spun a ball of blue majick around his fingers.

Margaret shook her head at him and took over the story. It was her family's crime, after all. "After Fairlie was cursed, but before he turned her over to the guild, my father imprisoned Shaye in a smother room in the bowels of the castle. Your nephew destroyed it and escaped."

Now it was Ellyn's turn. "That's ridiculous. No majicar can escape a smother room."

"It turns out that Shaye was more powerful than any-one imagined. And he was very motivated. He was in love with Fairlie."

"How? How did he do it?" Ellyn demanded.

Margaret shook her head. "I cannot say."

"Why? Because you don't know? Or because you're keeping secrets?" Ellyn glared. "Do you know?"

"I do. Though I stole the information from my brother Ryland. Neither he nor Shaye know that I know."

"And?" This time it was Nicholas. He spoke wood-enly. "He's still alive?"

"He is. But to get back to the original purpose of this story—in the course of her imprisonment in the Kalpes-trine, Fairlie discovered that *sylveth* is sentient. It talks to her."

"Talks?" Ellyn asked in a strangled voice.

Margaret sympathized. She'd had much the same re-action upon having the revelation thrust upon her. "Ap-parently so. Which brings us back to the ball of *sylveth* hiding in the bowels of the Kalpestrine. If I am right about the Jutras using their majick to infect the sea and *sylveth* so that they can invade Crosspointe, then the *sylveth* chose a very stupid hiding place. It should have gone as far from the Jutras as it could—all the way to the Bay of Benacai or somewhere up inside the Gallows. But it didn't and I can't help but think there was a pur-pose to it. Perhaps to give us the benefit of its majick in this war we are about to wage."

"You're saying that the *sylveth* is trying to help us?"

Margaret nodded at Keros, ignoring his disbelief. "I think so. And why not? If it knows the Jutras have been poisoning the sea, then it knows that they have to be stopped. *Sylveth* has been Crosspointe's partner in its way for hundreds of seasons."

"This is . . ." Nicholas trailed away, shaking his head and looking up at the ceiling.

She wondered what he'd been about to say. Preposterous? Remarkable? Stupid? She could feel the tight hot flames of his fury despite the length of the table between them. She drew a shaking breath. She'd known that eventually something would wake him up to the impossibility of there being anything between them. Not that he would walk away from helping her defend Crosspointe against the Jutras. But anything more—anything like the kisses that still curled her toes—that was not going to happen.

Her mouth twisted in a self-mocking smile. She wasn't supposed to want any man. She was supposed to be satisfied with Crosspointe, or so her father had always said. But as much as she loved her country, it was a damned cold lover.

"So what do we do now?" Red asked, pulling Margaret away from her painful maunderings. "The delats are at your disposal."

"Good. First we need to start searching for any surviving majicars. Ellyn and Keros will try to help them with the blood majick poisoning. We'll have to find shelters and food so people don't starve. If the castle is still standing, we can bring them there. We also need to find Ryland and I'll send word to Vaughn about what's happened. We'll need to see if we can put together a newspaper or broadsides to inform people what's happening and where they can go for help."

She paused, then took a breath and looked at Keros. "It's time to bring everyone back from the Root. I want you to go as soon as we finish searching the city for majicars. If the Jutras poisoning is driving the Root majicars mad, you can help them through it. Go first to the Bramble for Marten and Lucy."

Keros frowned. "She won't come. She's protecting the grove to keep the Pale from failing."

Margaret noticed how carefully he didn't mention

that it was a blood oak grove. If anyone learned that there was an entire blood oak grove on the Bramble, they'd swarm the island, leaving not even a twig behind.

"It doesn't matter, now," she said. "The Pale isn't protecting us from anything anymore. There aren't going to be any *sylveth* tides. The Chance storms may be bitter, but there won't be any *sylveth* in the winds to protect us from. They are needed here. We need everyone here."

Keros nodded and Margaret could see both the fear and the doubt he tried to hide as he realized the full extent of what the Jutras had done.

"The last thing is this—all the slave collars come off. Every last one of them." Her voice was hard and suddenly she felt tired. Her body was trembling. She held herself still, refusing to give in to it. "Red, start sending your delats into the city. Ellyn and Keros—you need sleep. You're no good to anyone in this condition. Nicholas—"

She hesitated. It felt wrong to order him to do anything. It wasn't just that things felt strained between them, if not entirely broken. It was more that he was Nicholas Weverton and more qualified to take the reins of Crosspointe than she was. He was a pillar of Crosspointe with experience managing a business empire. She knew how to spy and to kill. What right had she to order him about?

"What would you have me do?" Nicholas asked coolly as the silence stretched thin.

"You don't look much better than Keros and Ellyn," Margaret said finally, her voice more curt than she intended. "You should sleep too."

She looked down at her trencher of stew and realized she'd hardly eaten a thing. A glance around the table told the same story for the others. "Eat now. Then go sleep," she said to her companions. "Then we'll get to work."

She suited actions to words, tasting nothing, chewing and swallowing mechanically, knowing she needed the nourishment.

Red was the first to finish. He stood and gave a bow. "If you will excuse me, I will start sending out delats."

Margaret nodded and he left. A moment later Ellyn pushed to her feet. She stalked out of the room with a glare at Keros. The other majicar soon followed, leaving Nicholas and Margaret alone.

She pushed her chair back and started for the door. She thought he might call her back or stop her, but he didn't move or speak. She swallowed the hard lump in her throat as she stepped out into the hall. He was angry with her about Shaye, as he had every right to be. She eyed the crowded dining room and then turned back to the kitchen. It was a hustle of activity as delats stirred pots, chopped vegetables, kneaded bread, and stoked the fire. She eased quietly around the edge of the chamber and out into the mudroom. She found several brown delat robes hanging on hooks and took one, pulling it on and drawing the hood up over her head.

A moment later she was outside and striding quickly away. It was midmorning. The wind gusted and she coughed as she sucked in a mouthful of dust. It stung her eyes and she squinted, ducking her head and watching her footing.

The streets were choked with rubble. Many were impassable. There was hardly a single building that wasn't leaning to one side or the other or had some part of it collapse. Rubble mounded in the streets. There were bodies everywhere, and despite the wind, flies and carrion birds swarmed in thick clouds. The damage and death were so overwhelming that Margaret nearly puked. She held her stomach down with iron will, but her chest was hollow and her throat ached with unshed tears.

Few people approached her, despite her disguise. She encountered a weeping woman who was carrying a baby. Two more children clung to her skirts. Dried blood smeared her forehead and cheek and the hair on the left side of her head was matted and crusty with dirt. The little girl tugged on her mother to move her this way and that as she guided the dazed woman through the rubble.

Margaret stopped in front of them. The little girl met her gaze with a frightened look, her hand on her mother's skirt clenching into a white-knuckled fist, while her brother burrowed into the cloth.

"Where are you going?" Margaret asked gently.

The little girl only gave a sharp shake of her head. Either she didn't know or she wouldn't tell.

"You must be hungry. And thirsty. Why don't you come with me? We'll find you someplace safe." Margaret held out her hand.

Again that sharp shake. The little girl's jaw jutted.

Margaret squatted and pushed back her hood. She fished in the collar of her shirt for her necklace. She held it up so the girl could see it. "Do you know what this is?" she asked.

The girl's eyes had widened and now her brother crowded closer to see.

"It says I'm a Rampling. My name is Margaret. I won't hurt you. I promise. My job is to make sure you get somewhere safe. That's what Ramplings do."

The girl scowled and finally nodded.

"Good. Then let's go." Margaret stood, letting her pendant fall so that anyone who looked at her would see it.

She helped guide the woman now. As they began to walk away, she heard the stir of stones and looked over her shoulder. A young man, perhaps fifteen seasons old, was following. Another man, balding with a pocked face, approached from the side, his arm around a limping woman. They were filthy and bleeding, but looked at Margaret with trusting eyes. She nodded at them, and walked on.

They soon attracted others as her followers whispered who she was and where they were going. Frequently they stopped to free someone from the rubble. It was done mostly in silence. No one seemed to have the strength to ask questions or talk. They were too full of grief and shock. Margaret was their lifeline in a seething sea. She felt the weight of their need and trust and squared her shoulders. She would not fail them.

By the time they passed the city center, she had at least two hundred people in her procession. At Harbottle Hill, she looked behind and couldn't see the end of the line. She was pleased to see that the damage here was less, the big houses looking battered, but still standing. Perhaps the castle was unharmed.

She reached the top of the hill. The gates to the castle were closed. She marched up to them and pounded on the inset door. Almost instantly, the small window was opened. A Crown Shield peered out at her and then behind to the silent mob.

"Open the gates," Margaret said.

"Against orders, ma'am," he said, his gaze fastening on the pendant.

"The regent is a traitor. The Jutras are invading. I am Margaret Rampling and I don't have time for arguments. Open the gates and make room for these people. The castle will shelter them until their homes can be repaired."

He stared and hope warred with uncertainty in his expression.

"*Now*," Margaret said and the command in her voice made him jump like someone had stuck him with the business end of a dagger.

"Yes, ma'am," he said, and then he stepped back and disappeared from sight. There was a clanking of chains as the portcullis was raised and then the bar slid back and the gates creaked open. Inside a silent group of a dozen Crown Shields waited. Margaret eyed them, wondering if any had been among those who pursued her as she fled the castle less than two sennights ago. They stood uneasily, shifting their feet, darting glances from Margaret to the silent crowd behind her and back.

"Thank you," she said and walked inside.

Just within the gates was the triangular tower known as the Wall. On it was inscribed the names of all the living Ramplings. Or had been. Paint had been splashed all over it. She smiled tightly. The Wall was protected by majick of the strongest variety. It would take more than hammers and picks to tear it down, though she didn't doubt the regent had tried. She remembered then that Lucy had told Keros to feed the tree to give it strength. She nodded to herself, adding it to her list of things to do.

She frowned as something flitted across her memory. It was an image—a pearl of silver on silken black. She rubbed the heel of her hand against her left eye, trying to remember. When had she seen it? Then she realized. She hadn't ever seen it. It had been a dream, one that had come to her while she was unconscious. There was more. Something important. Fragments danced at the edges of her mind, just out of reach.

"Ma'am?"

It was the Crown Shield who'd let her in. She looked at him. "Yes . . . ?"

"Kergins, ma'am. Thackeray Kergins. What . . . what's happening?"

"In short, Kergins, the regent is a traitor and has been conspiring with the Jutras. They infected our majicars with poisonous majick, which is why many have gone insane." She spoke loudly and deliberately, her voice carrying widely across the castle grounds and up to the battlements. "Even now, the Jutras are invading. We are now at war. I am assuming the regency until an election can be held.

"Now, find the seneschal and send him to me." She'd known the previous seneschal, but the regent had replaced most of the castle staff with his own chosen few, all but the Crown Shields. "I want to see your captain as well. Then find as many able bodies as you can and sort them into rescue parties. The delats are already searching. Go down into the city and see what you can do to help anyone who needs it. Survivors should be sent here for shelter."

Despite his obvious shock at her news, Kergins responded admirably, tossing her a sharp salute before spinning about and shouting orders, sending his people flying on errands. In moments they were gone. Margaret turned to the people behind her. She pointed toward the broad grassy terrace that had been designed as an outer bailey, though it had never had cause to be used as such. But soon it would be with the Jutras coming. "Rest there," Margaret told them. "As soon as possible, you will have a roof overhead and food to eat."

As she spoke, her gaze locked on a familiar face. Nicholas. He was leaning against the wall just inside the gates. He carried a delat's spear and his expression was forbidding, more so because his face was so bruised and swollen. Slowly he straightened and crossed to stand in front of her.

"You just walk away—alone and unarmed—knowing you will be the next to wear the crown of Crosspointe?" he asked, his voice so cold it made her shiver.

"I don't know anything of the sort," she retorted. "Besides, I don't know why you are angry about it. You don't even want crown rule. It would suit your politics just fine if someone did slit my throat."

It wasn't true and she knew it, but she was so full of anger and hatred and resentment about so many things, and she didn't need him treating her like a Pale-blasted idiot, which was exactly how Ryland treated her. On the other hand, maybe they were both right. She felt helpless and inadequate to lead Crosspointe. It wasn't what she was meant to do. *Please the gods, let Ryland get here soon! Let one of them take the crown!*

Nicholas's teeth bared in a snarl. He looked around and over his shoulder, then snatched her arm and dragged her toward a small copse of fruit trees surrounding a private courtyard. In the center was a miniature topiary surrounded by white marble benches.

He let her go as they stepped inside. She strode away, putting distance between them, clenching her arms across her chest. She felt fragile, like she was cracking apart and the merest breath of wind would blow her to dust. But she had to be strong. She had to find the strength and wisdom to lead her people and defeat the Jutras. She sucked in a steadying breath, grabbing onto the twisting maelstrom inside her for strength.

Finally, when he said nothing, she turned around to face him. He'd rested the lance against a tree and stood with his feet braced apart, his hands clenched at his sides, as if it was taking all his strength not to strangle her.

"I require an apology," he said through clenched teeth. "You know I do not want to see you hurt. You know it would kill me if anything happened to you."

Her eyes widened. She did? No. She shook her head and his expression went livid.

"So that's it? That's what you think of me? After all that we've been through? I'm a dishonorable bastard and always will be?"

"No," she said quickly. "I respect you. I trust you. You've been a friend. I do apologize. That was inexcusable of me."

"And yet you walked away from me. By the gods, you can hardly stand to look at me. Don't say it isn't true. You'd be lying. I want to know why."

Margaret blew out a breath and dragged frustrated fingers through her hair. "I don't know how to do this. I don't know how to tell you what to do. You've fought the Crown your whole life. How can I expect you to turn to me and say 'Yes, ma'am' when I know you despise everything my family is? Everything I am.

"And if that wasn't enough, now you know what my father did to Shaye, and the fact that I knew about it all along. Why would you want me to be—" She couldn't say queen. The word caught in her throat like a chicken bone. And because of that, the real question slipped out before she could stop it. "Why would you want anything to do with me?"

His jaw knotted and he scraped his teeth along his bottom lip. His eyes crackled with angry heat. "Even," he said slowly, enunciating every word carefully as if she were a child, "if the Jutras were not invading, and even if Sylmont wasn't in shambles, and even if there was someone else who could take charge and have the support of the people—even if none of that was happening and you were crowned queen—I would never do anything to undermine your rule."

"Not the way you rabidly went after my father, you mean? That's who you are. You believe in everything you've done to weaken the Crown and drive my family off the throne. I don't doubt you'd do it all again, given the chance. Now out of the blue you expect me to believe you've changed your mind? It's mule piss and you know it. Rivers don't run up hills and men like you don't suddenly reverse everything they've ever believed in. I don't know what your game is, but I am not playing."

"It's not a game," he said, taking a jerky step forward. "And I am not lying. You once told me not to make promises to you, but I promise you this—I mean every word that I've said. Whatever you want from me, you can have it. It's not just because of the way I feel about you. It's because I've seen how important the Ramplings have been and still are to Crosspointe. By the depths, those people followed you up here from the city only because you're a Rampling. They trust you to protect them even though Geoffrey and I have done all in our power to convince them that Ramplings are poison for Crosspointe.

"I've seen what you're willing to sacrifice—not just you, but your whole family. I've never known loyalty and duty to run true in a bloodline before, but it seems to in yours. I may disagree with your choices and I may want to chain you down to keep you from stupidly wandering into dangers that not even someone like you with your lifetime of training can handle, but I *have* had a change of mind and heart. You have to trust me. Crosspointe needs the Ramplings. I know that now. I also know that it needs you sitting on the throne and wearing the crown. Not Ryland, not Vaughn. You."

Margaret just shook her head silently and turned around. *It's not just because of the way I feel about you.* Of all the things he'd said, that one sentence kept ringing in her ears. How did he feel? Did she even want to know?

"Do you believe me?"

He was standing right behind her. She been too caught up in herself to hear him approach. She took a step away before facing him. She gave him a wordless shrug. Childish, but she could manage nothing better.

"What's it going to take? What do you need me to do to convince you?" He spoke gently, the anger leaching out of his voice. "I can't undo the past. But I think I've proven to you these last sennights that you can trust me.

I won't fail you. You know enough about me to know I don't make idle promises."

She nodded. "Yes, I know that."

"Then what more can I do?"

She looked down at her hands. They were knotted together. "Nothing." She faced him again.

"Nothing?"

"No. I believe you. I have to."

"Do you? Why?"

"I should get back. I'm sure they've found the seneschal. There's a great deal to be done."

She started to edge around him, but he caught her arm. His grip was firm, not tight, but he held her fast. "Why?"

Of course he *would* push. He wasn't the kind of man to let it go. She ran her tongue over the edge of her teeth. She was acting like a coward. "Because I need you."

That was true enough. People believed in him as much or more than they believed in the Crown, and he had resources she didn't. It was also another prevarication.

The muscles along his jaw rippled as he clenched his teeth, and then he gave a little nod and let her go. "Come on, then. Let's get to work." He started back toward the gate. Margaret watched him go, her eyes narrowed. She *was* a coward.

"Nicholas."

He stopped. His expression was carefully bland.

"I have to believe you because I want you so damned much it hurts," she told him baldly.

He stared. "Is that true?"

She grimaced. "Yes. Unfortunate, but true."

He started walking back to her, his gaze sharp and fixed. She suddenly had a feeling she knew exactly what it was like to be a chicken in a house of foxes.

"Unfortunate?"

She tossed a hand. "I was taught never to let anyone get close or I wouldn't be able to do my job, and with you—"

He stopped, just inches away. He reached out and brushed a strand of hair from her cheek, the backs of his fingers whispering over her skin. "With me . . . ?" he prompted.

She resisted the urge to back away. "I don't seem to think very clearly when it comes to you," she said, even as her cheeks flushed red. What was the point in keeping silent? She'd said too much already to bother trying to hide anything. In for a copper, in for a dralion, after all.

One side of his mouth turned up. "I don't think clearly when it comes to you either," he said.

She frowned suddenly, remembering something he'd said after he, Keros, and Ellyn had rescued her from the Jutras. "We're friends and allies *for now*," she said. "That's what you said."

He nodded. "Because I wanted . . . I *hoped* . . . for more. As impossible as it seemed."

"More?"

His expression turned fierce. "Everything. I want everything. Don't say no."

He'd said that, too, she remembered. In the inn after they'd defeated Forcan. It was stupid and impossible. Oil and fire. Ryland and Vaughn were going to have kittens. A slow grin spread over lips. It was the first time she'd felt happy since . . . never. She couldn't remember ever feeling this good.

Beyond the trees she could hear her name being called. She jerked her head toward the sound and then took a slow breath, her stomach wriggling with what felt like a dozen snakes. "Time to get back to work."

"Not yet," he said and pulled her back. He was kissing her before she knew what he was going to do. Her mouth opened beneath his and she clutched his shirt for balance.

"Oh! Your pardon, Your Highness."

Margaret slowly eased away from Nicholas and turned to look at the Crown Shield standing just under the trees. She wasn't one Margaret recognized. She had been running and clutched a parchment in her hand. Sweat trickled down her face and cut streaks of clean pink on her dusty skin. She was panting and her eyes were wide as she looked first at Margaret, then Nicholas, then back.

"What is it?" Margaret asked.

The Shield held out the parchment and Margaret took it. The seal had been cracked so that she couldn't recognize it and the outside of the missive was streaked with dried blood and dirt. Quickly she opened it.

She felt the blood drain from her face as she read the stark words. She read them again. It was addressed to the regent and the inside of the parchment was as bloody as the exterior. The writer had been wounded when he wrote it. Some of the words were unreadable:

Three Jutras . . . sitting at anchor . . . cove . . . east of Black Sea. Trying to stop them. Taking heavy wounded. Villagers . . . won't . . . soon. Need help as . . . possible.

Margaret handed the page to Nicholas and looked at the exhausted messenger. Several more had gathered silently behind her. "Where did you get this?"

"Runner brought it from Gale and I carried it the rest of the way."

"Do you know where he got it?"

"No, ma'am." The girl wilted under Margaret's stare.

"When did it come?"

"Early this morning. I've been running since just before dawn."

"Good work. Get some food and rest." Margaret turned to the other Shields. "Where's your captain?"

"Coming now, ma'am."

A handful of grains later, the lanky captain shouldered through and came to stand in front of Margaret. He eyed her compass pendant and then examined her face. "Princess Margaret, you have certainly changed," he said dryly.

She smiled despite the roaring fear surging through her. "Captain Strawler, I am very glad to see you. I thought the regent might have had you retired."

"No, Your Highness. But then I didn't give him much opportunity to notice me."

"You're a good man. But there's news and it's not good. Here." She took the message from Nicholas and handed it to the captain.

He read it, his long face hardening. He looked at her. "Them warships hold at least fifty warriors, more if they've packed them in."

"Expect them to be stuffed to the gills. And there are bound to be more ships coming. I want you to take three hundred Shields and find those Jutras. Stop them."

"Are you sure? That will take most everyone out of the castle. You won't have any defense."

"I'll call up my men. And there are the delats," Nicholas said.

Strawler tossed him a suspicious look and then turned back to Margaret. "Ma'am?"

"Get going, Captain. I want you out of the gates within a glass. Leave me Sergeant Digby and whatever people are left. I'll call on the Blackwatch, Howlers, Eyes, and Corbies as well. Dismissed."

He nodded and tossed her a salute before marching away with the other Shields in tow.

Margaret looked at Nicholas, her mouth taut. Warships. She'd hoped they'd have more time to prepare. "I need you to send someone on horseback to Vaughn," she said. "He's been building an army in Brampton."

"Of course."

"I also want you to bring the rest of your stable here. We'll have to commandeer every horse and mule we can find. We'll need them to stay ahead of the Jutras."

She turned and started for the castle to find parchment and ink, her mind reeling beneath the flood of all that needed to be done, anxiety chewing at her. She had no experience with war. The Jutras had a caste devoted to it. How could Crosspointe hope to defend itself, especially with most of the majicars dead or insane?

"I'm not going to let the mother-dibbling bastards have us," she said, hardly aware she was speaking aloud. "One way or another, no matter what it takes, Crosspointe isn't going to be swallowed up by the Jutras."

Nicholas took her hand, striding beside her. She glanced up at him. His expression was somber and she could fairly see his mind spinning. She wasn't alone in this. She had him, she had Keros and Ellyn and Red and many other smart, loyal people. She'd killed a Jutras priest and Forcan. Her father had made her to fight and to kill. He'd made her to be the queen Crosspointe needed now. Her shoulders squared. They would fight. She'd call back Lucy and Marten, Shaye and Fairlie, the Jutras rebels and all the spawn from the Root. She would forge an army that the Jutras invaders would never expect and she'd slaughter them all.

A sudden image rose up in her mind. She'd dreamed it.

In silver dark, sunlight blooms and petals fall in a swirl of still wind. A storm.

The storm.

Beneath it boils a sea of gold, silver, green, and black in a glittering cauldron made of white ice. Shapes rise and fall—amorphous, hard-edged, sinuous. Mist and fire, flesh and root, smoke and spirit. Snow.

The cauldron cracks.

The storm had arrived. Margaret lifted her chin, striding quickly across the castle grounds, her fingers tightening firmly on Nicholas's. When it passed, Crosspointe would still be standing, if she had to assassinate every single Jutras warrior herself. She would not let Crosspointe fall.

"You're smiling," Nicholas said, sliding a gentle knuckle down her cheek.

She looked at him. "Am I?" In fact she was. "That's because we're going to win," she said after a moment. "The Jutras think they've pulled all our teeth and now we'll roll over and let them take us. They are in for an ugly surprise. Before I'm done with them, they'll wish they'd never heard of Crosspointe."

"And what about us?" he asked quietly. "You never answered."

"Didn't I?" Her smiled widened. "Yes. I say yes."

About the Author

Diana Pharaoh Francis has been a storyteller for as long as she can remember. She tells broad, sprawling, epic stories, and loves magic and its possibilities. She also loves courage and honor and fear and looking at how one person's actions can impact an entire culture or world. She is interested in the way heroes and villains are created.

Diana is a lover of Victorian literature and nineteenth-century Britain, and consequently the Crosspointe books have a strong Victorian flavor. She also loves chocolate, spiced chai, sharp weapons, spicy food, and sparkly jewelry. Diana teaches English at the University of Montana Western. She was raised on a cattle ranch in northern California and spent most of her childhood on horseback or in a book. She spends much of each day writing, and everything becomes fodder for her books. For more about Diana, visit her Web site at www.dianapfrancis.com.

THE CIPHER

A Novel of Crosspointe
by
DIANA PHARAOH FRANCIS

A member of the royal Rampling family, Lucy Trenton's ability to detect magick has embroiled her in a dangerous intrigue that threatens her very life. Her only hope lies in her most persistent suitor, ship captain Marten Thorpe, but Lucy isn't sure she can trust him.

Also Available
The Black Ship
The Turning Tide

**Available wherever books are sold or at
penguin.com**